The First Faux Pas

Katy Leen

Dedication

For the girls upstairs.

ONE

NATURALLY, I HAD to get rear-ended when I had a case of stolen jewelry stashed in my trunk. Only me and one other guy on the road, and he decides to play bumper cars. Out in the middle of nowhere. I knew this shortcut was a bad idea. I hadn't so much as passed a cow in the last few miles. And now, as visions of impending crash and calamity clouded my view and I skidded off into the gutter trying to steer clear of the trees while I bumped along dirt and rocks, all I could think about was how much time would pass before someone came along and spotted me. Probably just long enough for me to lose consciousness or bleed to death. Or both. Then when my car got towed, the police would find the jewelry and think I was a common thief. That would be the worst bit. Even worse than being in an accident while I was wearing ratty underwear, which I probably was since I'd been too busy planning larceny to do laundry.

My car chugged a few times before stopping just three feet short of a massive tree trunk. I looked out through my windshield at the huge branch dangling above, its few diehard leaves quivering at me. Or maybe the quivering was coming from me. It was hard to tell. I was distracted by the long, slow hiss humming in my ears until I realized it was my lungs deflating, not my tires. I released my fingers from their death grip on the steering wheel, thanked the powers that be for sparing me, and did a quick inventory to make sure all my body parts were intact. Then I dug out my phone from my shoulder bag and got out to check on the guy who rammed me.

I spotted his car sitting up the road and headed over, speed dialing my boyfriend Adam on the way. As I got closer, I could make out a man's balding head resting on the steering wheel of a blue Spitfire. My chest stiffened and I went motionless, not sure what to do. Then automatic pilot took over and I hurried to get to him, slipping on a cluster of fallen leaves still damp from an early afternoon rain. My knee buckled and hit the ground, landing on something hard, and a jolt of pain sparked through me. I got up and hobbled on, swearing under my breath. When I reached the car, I yanked on the driver's door handle. Locked. I knocked on the window, pounding out the same tune on the glass as my heart now pounded on my ribcage. The man's head rocked to the side, then raised up and turned towards me.

"You all right?" I yelled through the glass.

A shaky hand reached up and brushed a wide strand of hair across his head, straightening the comb-over that nearly blended into the thickets of gray-flecked dark hair that bearded his face. He looked at me, and for a moment I thought he might faint as his skin went from sallow to white.

"Are you all right?" I asked again, wishing I'd paid more attention to the first aid class I'd taken back in college and trying to remember the signs of shock. Ten years with social services and six months with a PI firm had taught me plenty about emotional shock. Physical shock couldn't be that different. I pointed down at the door. "I can't get you out. You need to unlock the door."

He waved me back and motioned to get out of the car. When he was fully standing, the bulk of him dwarfed me, and I wondered how he'd managed to fit himself into the tiny Spitfire. His overcoat had a rip near the pocket, but I didn't see any visible signs of broken bones or major damage to his body. Only a trickle of blood from a cut on the side of his nose.

"How do you feel?" I asked him.

He scratched his beard and mumbled something I couldn't make out.

Instantly, I thought concussion, brain damage, blood clot. Or, maybe he'd had a stroke and lost control of his car before he hit me. I held up the cell phone still clutched in my hand, half expecting to hear Adam's voice yelling at me through the receiver, but no one was there. "Just hang on," I said. "I'm going to call for help."

Beardman shook his head.

I touched his arm and tried to steer him back to the car. "Maybe you should sit."

He pulled away from me, turned, and started running up the road.

"Hey," I called out to him. "Where are you going?"

He didn't answer, and he didn't stop.

"You could have a concussion," I said, wobbling after him, my knee still sore and likely developing a wicked bruise.

He kept running and disappeared around the bend in the road we'd just come along. It would be at least three miles before he reached the main highway. What was he thinking?

I watched a minute to see if Beardman would come back. When he didn't, I punched Adam's number into my phone again and limped back to my car. I pressed the phone to my ear and held it in place with my shoulder as I turned the key in the ignition. Silence— from both the car and the phone. I put the phone on the seat beside me and tried the car again. It sputtered on long enough for the front wheels to spin, sending blobs of mud up to cling to the white paint, then it died.

Grabbing my phone, I redialed Adam and got out to assess the mud damage. It didn't look good. But then nothing around me looked good. With daylight dimming, the near skeletal trees that lined the road were turning from breathtaking to ghostly. And the deserted street seemed less like a serene country lane and more like an isolated dumping ground for dead bodies.

I leaned in close to my Mini as I waited for the phone to connect. Nothing. I disconnected and tried again. Still nothing. I checked the settings. Low battery and no bars. Fabulous. I tottered around, holding my phone up now and again hoping to catch a stray ray, but even crossing the road didn't earn me any bars. There was no cell service anywhere. It figured. For most of my life, I'd rarely been off the island of Manhattan where anyone could get anything at anytime. When I moved to Montreal to be with Adam, things didn't change. Both islands, both bustling cities. But now, here I was in the wilds just outside Montreal, and I couldn't even get phone service. I should have known better than to cross a bridge. I was an island girl. So long as the island had more cement than grass and more buildings than trees. And cell service.

I tightened the belt around my coat and bent to get a closer look at the mud around my tires, careful to balance my weight as best I could on my good leg without letting my shoe sink into the sludge and bring the cuff of my jeans along with it. The wheels looked like doughnuts with their chocolate glaze oozing down the side and pooling into a sticky heap. Even if I could get the Mini's engine working, there was no way the car would budge. I stood and rubbed my hands together, wishing I'd brought gloves. A couple more drops in degrees, and I could send smoke signals with my breath. It wasn't enough to be stranded, I had to freeze to death too. Wherever Beardman was, at least his running was keeping him warm. Not as warm as he'd probably been snuggled in his cute little car, though.

My eyes scanned over to his Spitfire with its dented fender and broken headlight. And four tires sitting on dry dirt. And its open door. I went over and peered inside. With only two bucket seats up front and no backseat, my perusal didn't take long. I slid into the driver seat and got a closer look. The dash was small and made of wood. A radio sat dead center, a speaker took up the place of the glove compartment, and an S-shaped key ring dangled from the ignition. I tried the key and the engine revved. Bingo.

I sat back and weighed my options. One: sit in my car by the side of the road and wait for the police to happen by and stop. Or maybe some good Samaritan. Or a serial killer. Whoever came first. Or two: borrow the Spitfire and go home. Technically, some people would call borrowing without permission stealing. But those people weren't around. And they weren't stranded on a road with a forest of ghostly trees that was probably filled with less ghostly critters that came out to feed at night. And those people probably weren't carting around a case of jewelry that was better hidden from the police. More importantly, those people weren't me.

I went back to my car, collected my stuff, and locked up. And as I pulled the Spitfire onto the road, I told myself taking the car wasn't so bad. It was an emergency, and different rules applied in an emergency. Kind of like what happened with the case of jewels now sitting in the passenger seat beside me. Taking it was for a good cause. That had to count for something.

The Spitfire stalled almost immediately, and I struggled with the gear shift. Manual cars were not my thing. Operating the clutch with a weakened knee wasn't helping any either. I got a few more feet, the engine groaned, and it stalled again, this time with enough force to knock the jewelry box beside me to the floor and snap the seat belt tight against my body. I undid the belt, bent to retrieve the box, and instead touched on something cold and metal wedged near the underside of the seat. I gave it a good yank and my breath caught when it came into sight. A gun.

My fingers recoiled, the gun dropped back to the floor, and my heart rate picked up again as my sweat glands switched from sprinkler mode to soak. I glanced around and checked my rearview mirrors before looking back down at the gun and telling myself there was no reason to panic. After all, there were lots of reasons people had guns. Maybe Beardman needed it for his job. Or for protection. Or, for threatening women by the side of the road. I wanted to believe it was one of the first two, but it was hard given the game of bumper cars.

Suddenly, I didn't feel so bad for Beardman. Or for taking his car. But I still felt bad for not bringing gloves. Camille was going to kill me for getting prints on the gun.

ABOUT AN HOUR later, I pulled a giant tub of Baskin Robbins out of my freezer, ripped off the lid, and started hacking away at the ice cream with a spoon. By the time it had softened enough to scoop, my heart rate had returned to normal. And my pulse got downright slow the more progress I made. Got me seriously wondering if I could replace my yoga and meditation class with ice cream therapy.

I sat down at the kitchen table and propped up my leg on the chair next to me, positioning a bag of frozen peas around my knee to stave off swelling, then I turned my attention back to the ice cream. My dachshund, Pong, wandered over to sniff the peas before moving on to linger at the ice cream and shoot me her best imitation of a dog in the throes of starvation. From her curled-up position on the chair across from me, my cat Ping raised her head, peered in disgust, and went back to her nap. The phone rang just as I managed to pry a hunk of chocolate out of the minty smoothness, and I glanced over at the call display. The office. I'd called and left a message when I first got home reporting what happened with Beardman, so this was probably my call back. I reached out and pressed the speaker button.

"*Mais voyons,* Lora. What were you thinking?" Camille Caron said before switching to French and spewing out words that ran together so fast they made supercalifragilisticexpialidocious seem like an abbreviation. Camille was my closest friend and one of my bosses at C&C, the PI firm where I worked as an assistant. She was also French so she believed strongly in open expression, and that's what she was doing now. Expressing herself.

My ancestors, on the other hand, were English, and although the stiff upper lip had loosened through the generations, I could still hold my tongue when it suited me. I considered it one of my best assets. It nearly made up for the pale skin and dry, frizzy auburn hair that also came with my inheritance. I turned the speaker volume down a bit, readjusted the bag of frozen peas, spooned another chunk of ice cream, and waited.

The good thing about French people is that their rants are over fairly quickly. Like a fire, they often ignite suddenly and flame high, but once they die down, the few remaining embers contain mere mumblings to themselves. I'd learned to recognize Camille's embers about a year ago, probably three months into our friendship. I was so good at it now, I knew I could get in a couple more scoops before it would be my turn to weigh in on the subject at hand, which, in this case, had nothing to do with me getting fingerprints on the gun or being in an accident that could have ended with me injured or found dead in my car. It had everything to do with me getting out of said car.

When the room finally went quiet, I set down my spoon and picked up the extension. "What was I supposed to do?" I said in my defence. "I had to see if the other driver was all right. And for all I knew, there could have been someone else in the car. A kid even. We were in an accident. People could have been hurt."

"It wasn't an accident," Camille said. "It was a 'bump and rob.' Everyone knows about the 'bump and rob.' And you don't get out of your car during a 'bump and rob.' Especially when you're in the *Laurentides*. Alone. What you do is get the hell out of there."

"It may not have been a 'bump and rob.' And even if it was, I couldn't get out of there anyway. My car wouldn't move."

"*Voyons*, Lora. You should have called me. Or 911."

"There was no cell service," I reminded her. Not that I'd have wanted to make either of those calls anyway. Then I would have had to explain the jewelry. And I didn't think either the police or Camille would agree that taking the jewelry from Marie Roy was a good idea. Aiding and abetting clients hiding assets wouldn't be condoned in the PI handbook, if there was such a thing. But Marie had begged me to take the jewelry and a few personal items for safekeeping while she was trying to separate from her rat turd of a husband. One look in her bruised eye while her cut lip trembled, and I'd agreed. Helping seemed right in the big picture kind of way. And sometimes life was all about the big picture. Problem was, people didn't always see the same big picture, and it was best to keep your view to yourself. That's when the tongue-holding skill came in particularly handy.

Camille went quiet. Not a good sign. When Camille was quiet, she wasn't holding her tongue, she was loading it.

I decided maybe it was time to shift the focus from me to Beardman. He made a better target than me anyway. He was almost twice my size and well cushioned to withstand whatever got thrown his way. "Look, it's not like I knew the guy had a gun. This is Montreal, after all. Aren't you Canadians supposed to have gun control laws?"

"Criminals don't tend to worry themselves too much with those," she said.

"He didn't look like a criminal," I told her. At least not while his head was slumped over the steering wheel.

"Nobody looks like a bad guy to you, Lora. You social worker types are such do-gooders, you think everybody has a good side."

"Well, don't they?"

She paused before answering and took a deep breath. "No, Lora, they don't. This Beardman could have killed you."

"Maybe. But he didn't even try. He just ran away. So see there, he was probably thinking with his good side."

"He wasn't thinking with any side," Camille said. "The guy had a head injury."

She had me there.

Camille went on. "And what about your leg?"

"Beardman had nothing to do with that. I just fell."

"*Oui, oui*," she said, more to dismiss my explanation than to agree, and no doubt still blaming Beardman for my fall since he was the one who caused the accident in the first place. "But how is it feeling?"

I reached over, lifted the peas off my knee, and wrinkled my nose at the purple blotch forming to the side of my kneecap. "It's okay. More sore than swollen. Nothing serious."

Camille must have put me on speaker phone because I could hear the clicking of her heels as she paced. "*Bien*. And Adam's home to help?"

I made a face at the phone. Camille's protective instincts ran on permanent overdrive, which didn't always bode well with me because my independent streak was stuck in the same gear. "No, he's not home. But I'm good." I glanced over at the fridge door Adam and I used as a message board. "He had a business trip, and he's coming back late. I'm just ordering pizza and resting until bed. Maybe watching a movie. I'll be fine in the morning. When I get to the office, you'll see. It's really nothing. I have that intake meeting with the new client on that missing persons case, and then I'll be in."

I reached out and dabbed at the purple blotch as if to prove my point then stifled the quick inhale of breath that followed.

"Maybe I should tell Luc to cancel the guy who's coming to get the car and the gun so you won't be disturbed," Camille said. "I called him to set it up just before I called you." Luc was with the police. He and Camille had lived together a few years back, and they were still friendly. Sometimes, when they were each unattached and it suited them both, they were very friendly. "He ran the license plate number you gave us through the system already, but it's an old number that expired and it doesn't match the car make. They'll need to go over the car, but they won't get to it until tomorrow anyway. They could just do the pickup in the morning."

So Beardman wasn't a total loser. He'd had enough sense to make the plate switch. He'd left the car interior clean too. Aside from the gun. After I'd parked the car in my driveway, I'd given it a quick going over before locking up and found nothing.

"What about me? Will I get in trouble for taking the car?"

"*Non.* Luc is taking care of that."

That was a relief. At least I wouldn't be getting arrested for grand theft auto. That only left me with the aiding and abetting thing to worry about.

"What will the police do with the car once they're finished with it?" I asked Camille.

"Hold on to it as evidence for now."

"And then?"

"They're not going to give it back to you," she said, knowing where I was going. "That I can guarantee."

That was too bad. I'd come to like the little thing on my ride home. The curvy sapphire blue body, the cute fabric convertible top. Not to mention the vibration factor. The seat experience was something else. A girl could get used to those vibrations.

I got up and headed for the living room. The house I shared with Adam had been his mother's before she passed away, and it dated back to the early 1900s when houses were made to last with sturdy wood floors, plaster walls, and brick exteriors. The kitchen was in the back and connected to the dining room to the side, the hallway towards the front, and a tiny sun porch in the back. I took the shortest route to the living room via the dining room, went over to the side window, and peeled back the curtain to check out the car again. It looked pretty good sitting in my driveway. Almost like it belonged there. For about sixty seconds. Then the engine turned over and it sped away.

"I think it's too late to cancel the car guy," I said to Camille.

"What?"

"He just picked up the car."

"Really? Luc said he wouldn't be around to get it for a few hours. Who picked it up?"

"I don't know."

"Well, who picked up the keys and the gun?"

My eyes took in the keys still sitting on the hall table next to the gun and Marie Roy's jewelry box. "Nobody. Hang on a sec," I told her as I put down the phone and made my way to the front door and onto the porch to see if I could still see the car up the street, but it was already gone. Hearing the door open, Pong scurried out between my legs and made a dash for her favorite patch of grass surrounding the ancient maple tree planted not far from the sidewalk. I limped down the stairs and scooped her up, grateful it was evening and there weren't many squirrels around to chase. I turned to go back in and noticed a wad of paper sitting in the driveway where the Spitfire had been. I went over, picked it up, and hurried back inside. Pong wrestled to be put down and sat in wait for the treat she expected as a reward for going out. I pulled a bone from the box we kept on a shelf in the vestibule, dropped it for her, and then unfolded the paper.

It had my picture on it. And my name. And a C&C business card stapled to the top alongside a blotch of blood.

I couldn't be sure, of course, but I was thinking it all belonged to Beardman. Which creeped me out. But at least it meant I was probably right about the game of bumper cars. It was not random. And it wasn't a "bump and rob."

TWO

THE NEXT MORNING, I awoke to a barking dog. My barking dog. I removed a tangle of hair from my face, rubbed my eyes, and peered over at the alarm clock. Seven fifty-seven. Pong's canine Morse code started up again—four short barks, a pause, then four long ones—but this time I heard a faint knocking during the brief intermission she took between rounds. I freed myself from my boyfriend Adam's cocoon of lean arms and legs and stood up. Either he'd been really quiet when he got home, or I'd been in a deep sleep because I had no memory of him getting in beside me. Probably the latter since I'd been so exhausted from jumping at every house creak or wind howl most of the night that when I'd finally dropped off to sleep, I'd fallen into a near coma. I watched to see if Adam would wake up, but he just moaned softly, pulled the covers up around his shoulders, and turned over. So I wrapped my robe around me and went downstairs.

I put the chain on the front door and opened it a crack to find a tall man in a dark flak jacket, light blue shirt, and navy slacks accessorized with a gun holster standing on my porch.

"*Bonjour mademoiselle,*" he said and grinned. "*Luc ma demandé de venir chercher les clés de l'auto.*"

I closed the door to unhook the chain and opened it again. "Excuse me?"

"Oh, you speak de English," he said, letting his gaze wander from my face long enough to take in my robe and bare feet. "I come for the car keys." He pulled out a paper from his pocket and read something before throwing me another grin and adding, "for the Spitfire car. And also, a revolver."

"Right. Just a sec. I'll get them."

"What revolver?" Adam's voice said from behind me. "What car keys?"

I smiled. Typical. The man could sleep through barking dogs and blaring sirens. The house could catch on fire, and he wouldn't rouse himself to smell a whiff of smoke. But he could detect the testosterone of another man circling his woman with the precision of bees trained to sniff out explosives.

The two men nodded at each other over my head by way of a greeting.

"I'll explain in a minute," I said to Adam as I dipped into the house to get the keys and the gun, each now snugly nestled in individual Ziploc bags as per Camille's instructions. I passed them over to the police officer, got his name, and waved as he made his way back to his blue and white cruiser. He waved back and pulled out.

"It's no big deal," I said to Adam as I closed the door and headed for the kitchen.

He followed behind me. "What's no big deal?"

I pulled out a carton of orange juice from the fridge, poured us each a glassful, and passed him his cup. "They're just evidence, that's all." Then I told him about my run-in with Beardman and subsequent loss of the Spitfire, minus the note and blood blotch.

Adam sat down at the table, and when he bent to sit, the white t-shirt he wore rode up just as his jeans slipped down, and I noticed that in his haste to dress he had forgone his boxers. He circled his hand around his glass. "I'm not sure which job is worse. Your old one in New York counselling hotheads with anger-management issues and dealing with drug addicts squirming for a fix or the one you've got now mingling with low-lifes and thugs on roadsides."

I sat down across from him. "There's no mingling," I said. "And only the occasional thug." Which was true. Most PI work involved a desk, a telephone, a computer, and the ability to bend the truth for the greater good.

He sighed and shook his head. "You're avoiding the subject. What did Beardman want?"

My eyes drifted out to the hallway where I'd left the box of Marie Roy's jewelry the night before, too tired to lug it upstairs with my sore knee bogging me down. The box was gone.

I shot up and into the hall. "Did you see a box on this table when you got home?" I asked Adam, my finger pointing at the antique washstand that caught our mail, our keys, and anything else we wanted to unload when we came through the front door.

"You mean the Queen's jewels? They're upstairs under the hide-a-bed in my office. If they're real, they've got to be worth a fortune. Not the best idea to just leave them lying around. It's not like the jar of loose change we keep there to tip delivery guys." He came up behind me, his body so close I could feel his heat penetrating my robe. "Unless there's something you want to tell me about you and the pizza delivery guy. In which case, I hope you didn't go overboard. I finished off the last few pieces of that pizza in the fridge when I got home, and it was a little dry."

"Very funny," I said as I rushed upstairs and into Adam's home office. The box was under the couch just like he said. I pulled it out, opened it to make sure nothing was missing, and took it into my own office. I was wedging it into the back of the file cabinet when Adam's hand reached in and pulled out a framed photo from the drawer.

"Who's this?" he asked.

I grabbed the picture and placed it back. "Nobody."

"No, it's somebody, Lora. Who is it?" He reached in, brushing by another picture, and pulled out a small box made of popsicle sticks. "And what's this?" He opened the box and took out a ceramic magnet with "*Bonne fête maman!*" printed on it in big, square letters. He looked down at me, waiting for an answer.

"Careful with that," I said, taking it from him. "It's just some stuff I'm taking care of for a friend."

"You telling me this belongs to Camille?"

"No. Somebody else."

"You haven't made any other friends since we moved here."

I was about to object when I realized he was right. Plus, I'd lost touch with most of my old friends in New York when they'd moved away before I did. The few still around were more acquaintances. Camille wasn't just my best Montreal friend, she had become my best friend period. Which was fine with me. Except at times like this when it left me without a cover.

"Okay, fine. It belongs to a client," I told Adam.

He sat down on the loveseat under the window that faced the street. "This like the time you lost track of that mom in the custody case or when you tipped off that tenant that her landlord was planning an eviction? Or is it more like when you misplaced the evidence of that guy having an affair?" He wiped his fingers over the floral print fabric on the cushion beside him. "Oh, no, Lora. Please tell me that stuff's not evidence."

I pushed the file drawer closed. "Of course not."

"That's good." He exhaled and sat back. "Because last time you said you wouldn't pull any more stunts like that again."

My cheeks grew hot. "Those were not stunts. I was doing the right thing. That guy wasn't having an affair. His wife set him up for that one-night stand just to get pictures so she could sue him for more money in a divorce. *She* was the one who'd been cheating on him for years. He never even cheated either, he only went to the hotel with the floozy his wife hired to bait him and then left before anything happened. I had to delete those pictures; they were misleading. As for that landlord, he was really crummy and shouldn't have been evicting that old lady in the first place. She needed to know what he was planning to prepare herself. And, I did *not* lose the mom in the custody case. I just gave her a few extra days to pull together the evidence she needed to win sole custody and protect her kids from their derelict of a dad."

Adam ran a hand over his cropped, brown hair not disturbing it in the least. "Lora, you can't do that. You can't mess around with cases like that. PI work *isn't* social work."

"Yeah, it is." Or it can be if you do it right. Only with better pay and flexible hours. And, okay, maybe it was social work with guns sometimes, but I didn't think I should point that bit out to him at the moment. I sat down in my desk chair and whirled it around to face Adam. "It's not all cheating spouses and insurance fraud, you know. What about the man with Alzheimer's we found after he wandered away? Or that brother and sister we reconnected after they were put up for adoption as kids?" I said to prove my point.

"Those cases were different. Doesn't mean you can treat every case like you're fighting for the underdog. You can't manipulate things so the good guy wins. Do Camille and Laurent know what you've been doing?"

"I don't think so. Camille may suspect, but she's my friend. She won't rat me out to Laurent. He may not understand."

"You bet he wouldn't understand. Cops tend to frown on people fooling with procedure."

"Laurent's not a cop anymore," I reminded Adam.

"No. That's right. Now he owns his own PI agency. His name is on the line."

I glared at him. "It's not just his agency. Camille owns half."

Adam shook his head. "I'd be careful if I were you. You may think you're doing good deeds, but not everyone will see it that way. You could be out of a job. Scratch that. You could be out of the *only* job you've been able to get since we moved here." He brought his eyes up to meet mine. "And then you'll have to go back to your French lessons and get a real job."

Hmmm. Those would be the French lessons I quit over two months ago. The French lessons that caused my instructor to cringe every time I spoke. The French lessons I needed to apply to pretty much any job in my field here since bilingualism was required by law. Also, the French lessons I had been pretending to still be attending because I hated to admit to my suckiness at languages. Everyone told me there was a learning curve, and they kindly cut me a lot of slack. I didn't have the heart to tell them the curve had come to a dead end.

"Back?" I said, keeping my voice innocent.

"I create educational software, Lora. I know how to measure learning progress. You don't think I noticed you can barely say those touristy phrases they teach, let alone understand any real stuff like basic grammar or some rudimentary vocabulary. You couldn't even follow a conversation with the four-year-old down the street."

"Who? Phillipe? Hey, he talks really fast and slurs his words. Half the time his own mother doesn't understand him."

"How would you know? You can't talk to his mother."

I got up and locked the file drawer. "Anyway, I have a *real* job. I don't have to learn any more French. We get lots of English-speaking clients, and most of the research involves searches of English databases and social media sites. There's plenty I can do."

"The job at C&C was supposed to be temporary."

"I know," I said, dropping the file key in behind some books on the shelf by my desk. "But I've changed my mind about that. I love this job. I'm going to turn it into a full-time thing." I had to. There was no way I'd qualify for the local social worker's association membership, let alone get a job in my field. Without the French bit, this was as close to being a social worker in Montreal as I was going to get.

Adam sat back and crossed his arms over his chest. "And when were you planning on telling me?"

"Well, it's not official yet. My dual citizenship comes through in a couple months. Then I'll be eligible to have a permanent job, and this is the one I want."

"I thought Camille said they couldn't bring you on full time."

That was true. When she first hired me it was mostly out of friendship and convenience. They needed periodic help with overflow, and I needed a job. Turned out, my social work skills were an easy fit for PI work: all my years of perfecting interview techniques, delving into people's backgrounds, and bonding with clients were good training. And since most of our work was for lawyers, insurance companies, and the occasional disgruntled spouse, I got by pretty well. But there was a snag. I didn't have any police training, security experience, nada. And, the only knowledge I had of criminal behavior came from a couple of courses in criminology at university and two muggings I'd experienced firsthand back in New York. Convincing Camille and her brother that I could take on more than just admin stuff would be a challenge. But I had a plan. I was going to prove I could solve a case on my own, starting with the new missing persons case that just came in for a woman who wanted to find her daughter's deadbeat dad. The dad went by the name Puddles. How hard could it be to find him?

"I'm going to change Camille's mind," I told Adam. "You'll see."

Adam gestured at my file cabinet. "You mean by hiding expensive jewelry for your clients behind her back?"

I frowned. In hindsight, maybe not my best decision.

Adam reached out and pulled me down on his lap. "Look, I know coming here wasn't your idea. It was great the way you dropped everything to come home with me and help take care of my mom. Nothing about cancer is easy. I don't know what I would have done without you. And deciding to stay on afterwards was beyond great. You know I'll support you in whatever you want. But couldn't you want something else?"

I laughed. "It'll be good. Really."

"That's what you said the first day we met at the community center in the Upper East side right before that kid said my computer game sucked and nearly poked my eye out with the end of his pen."

"The eye poking was an accident. His pen slipped. Anyway, you're the one who decided to test out your new software with my at-risk group. They weren't going to make it easy for you. What did you expect?"

He shook his head. "Damned if I know. All I wanted was the credit so I could get my graduate degree."

"Well, then I was right. It *was* good. You got that."

He twined a length of my hair around his finger. "Yup. And the hot group leader with the smokin' blue eyes who made the kid apologize. I just wish you'd stop hanging out with the at-risk group. I'm not crazy about men running you off the road."

I wasn't crazy about that last bit either. And I was guessing it had something to do with Marie Roy and her jewelry. Like maybe her husband found out I had it and sent someone to get it back. It was the only thing that made sense. But I couldn't focus on that now, and I knew if I mentioned the blood-stained note I'd found,

Adam would go into full blown worry mode. I didn't have time for that. I was due at Francesca Bellinni's in an hour to talk about her missing husband, and if I was going to make this case my proving ground, I needed to give it my full attention.

I looped my arms around Adam's neck and kissed him. "Not to worry. I have no plans to ever see Beardman again. I'm starting a new case today, and the client is a socialite who lives in a good neighborhood right here in the city. Camille sent someone out to get my car last night, and I'm picking it up at her cousin's garage first thing. She even had a car alarm installed. I'll be nice and safe."

THREE

FRANCESCA BELLINNI LIVED in Outremont—one of Montreal's oldest neighborhoods. Close to the downtown core, it attracted urbanites of all cultures and was home to many of the French elite. Housing ran the gamut from grand historic buildings built by rich settlers to affordable rental units. Francesca's place clearly fell into the former category. From what Camille had told me, Francesca inherited the mansion from her mother when she passed away ten years earlier. In the decade since Francesca took over the house, she'd done some minor redecorating and replaced her mother's vegetable garden with an in-ground pool. With the money she saved on the seasoned seventy-year-old gardener, she hired a spicy twenty-four-year-old pool boy. Rumor had it that the exchange rate didn't quite take into account the change in tips.

I pulled my Mini into Francesca's driveway, parked in front of the three-car garage, and took a moment to review the Puddles file. Not much in it except the basic info Camille had been given when Francesca contacted C&C—Puddles' name, birth date, place of birth, last known work address. No next of kin besides Francesca and her daughter Lucia. Not much to go on. I tossed the file into my shoulder bag, locked up, and headed for the front door. I rang the bell, and a chime played a short tune inside.

Half a minute later, I heard static and then a voice. "Yes?"

I looked around and noticed a small intercom box tucked in beside a two-tiered gold mailbox fastened on the brick. I found the "talk" button and depressed it. "Hello," I said.

"Yes?" the voice repeated.

"I'm here to see Francesca Bellinni."

"And you are?" the voice asked.

"I'm Lora Weaver. I work with C&C inves..." A loud buzzing sound cut me off and implored me to open the door. I stepped inside and saw a fortysomething woman striding toward me with her finger pressed up perpendicular to her lips. The tap of her high heels on the marble floors faded when she stopped just short of me.

She smoothed her black skirt and tucked a strand of hair back into her dark bob of curls before speaking. "So nice to meet you," she said, greeting me with her outstretched hand. Several gold bangles slid together and tinkled at her wrist. "I've been looking forward to going over the seating with you," she continued with a quick wink. "Let's just step into the office, and I can show you the chart."

She led me across the hall to a square room, all wood paneling and leather seating, with a large oak desk positioned in front of French doors leading out to the backyard. She closed the main door, crossed the room, and seated herself behind the desk, gesturing for me to take one of the visitor armchairs.

"Thanks for playing along," she said. "My daughter's home, and I don't want her to know about the investigation."

"I understand," I assured her. "Is this a bad time then?"

Francesca glanced over at the door. "I think we'll be all right in here," she said.

I pulled the Puddles file out of my bag. "You have a lovely home."

She smiled. "Thanks. Most of the house has been updated, but I haven't been able to bring myself to redecorate this room." She skimmed her hand along the desktop, her eyes taking in the place. "It was my father's office. He died five years before my mother, but aside from storing a few personal things, she always kept the room the way he left it. I guess I've just done the same."

I nodded. I understood about that. My mother had kept my father's slippers under his side of the bed for almost a year after he'd passed away. And after she died, I wore her locket for longer than that. Still do most of the time. Letting go could be tough.

Francesca sat back, the large chair swaddling her with its billows of smooth, worn leather permeated with pipe tobacco. "So, what is it you need from me?" she said.

I slid a pen stand out of the way, placed the file on the desk, and got ready to take notes. I was big on notes. Notes and lists kept me sane. "Just a bit more information about your ex-husband," I told her.

"Well, he's not really my ex-husband," she said, keeping her voice low. "We were never formally divorced."

"Right," I said and made a note. "When's the last time you saw him?"

"It would be almost fifteen years ago now. He took off not long after my father died." Her eyes flicked to a photo of an older couple sitting among a bank of pictures on a nearby shelving unit. "He had heart problems," she said. "My father, not my husband."

"I'm sorry," I said and paused to see if she'd say more. When she didn't, I continued. "And since then have you heard anything from your husband?" Then remembering his given name from the file I added, "Piedro, isn't it?"

"It is, but most people called him by his nickname Puddles. And no. I haven't heard from him directly, but he sends birthday cards to our daughter."

"So they correspond?"

"No. Lucia never writes him back. There's never any return address. And I think she stopped opening the cards after the first few years. When they come now, she just tosses them out."

I couldn't really blame her. Probably the only way she has of showing her anger at him for abandoning her.

"And you never tried to find him before now?" I asked.

"I did. About six months after he left. When it seemed obvious he wasn't coming back, I hired someone to find him, but the guy had no luck. I gave up after a few months because my mother got ill, and between losing my father and caring for Lucia and my mother, I had about all I could handle. By the time my mother died, Puddles had been gone so long I didn't see the point anymore. And I guess, if I'm really honest about it, I wasn't so much hurt as angry by then and didn't really want to have anything to do with him. He'd gone off to live his life free and clear and left me with all the responsibilities. He never even sent any child support payments, and Lucia was only about ten when he left. I paid for her upbringing and university myself."

"What is it you do?" I asked her.

She sat forward and rested her arms on the desk. "My social position keeps me pretty busy. I sit on several charity boards. When my father died, my mother took sole ownership of Guido's Garments—that was their business—but then she sold it off to some of the employees before she passed away. I was left with a sizeable estate that's taken care of Lucia and me since."

"So you're not interested in getting any financial restitution from Puddles?"

She tried to stifle a laugh. "I doubt I could even if I wanted to," she said. "Puddles never had any money. When we met, he was just an Italian immigrant my father hired to work at his company—being an immigrant himself, my dad had a soft spot for them all but Italian ones in particular. Once we married, my father promoted Puddles to management, but he was only a salaried employee. He answered to my father."

"Any idea why he left?"

She toyed with the crucifix that hung in the cleavage of her ruffled blouse. "I must've asked myself that question a million times. No. No idea. One day he was here and the next he was gone."

"You think he could have been in some kind of trouble?"

Francesca shook her head. "Not likely. But he was quiet. Not big on talking, so he probably wouldn't have told me even if he was. It would surprise me, though. He was nice, well liked. And good to Lucia. A really good father."

I wanted to tell her that a good father doesn't just up and leave his kid. At least not unless there's reason for it, but I wasn't here to offer commentary. Instead I said, "and that's why you want to find him now? For Lucia?"

"Yes," she said. "Lucia's getting married in a few months, and I know she wants her father at her wedding. She tries to pretend he doesn't matter to her, but I overheard her talking on the phone to a girlfriend about how her dream would be to have her dad walk her down the aisle."

I could relate to that. I'd had a similar dream once myself. I could also feel the tugs at my heart at the thought of reuniting a father and daughter. While Francesca may think Lucia wanted her father at her wedding for the prance down the aisle, I knew there was more to it. That when someone's parent drops out of her life when she's young, it can feel like a part of her is missing, and the need to fill that hole can be consuming. Finding Puddles could change Lucia's life.

"And what about the business?" I asked Francesca. "Was there anything going on there that may have made Puddles take off?"

"Like what?"

"Like anything. Any kind of financial problems or behind the scenes drama?"

"It's the fashion business. It's something like a two-billion dollar industry for this city. There's always drama."

"Anything you remember specifically?" I said.

She sat back and slid her cross back and forth on its chain. "Let me think. Well, there were some fights over some designs. You know, like who owned them. But that kind of stuff was always happening. And some old guy retired, and there was talk that he'd taken some kind of confidential stuff with him. I really don't know the details. I had no interest in Guido's. All I ever heard was the odd talk over dinner."

The doorbell rang before she could go on, and Francesca tensed briefly then stepped over to the door. "Hang on," she said, pausing under a painting of the Madonna and child. "I'll just be a sec." She slipped out but was back only a minute later. "We'll have to cut this short. The real wedding planner just arrived, and she's insisting on talking to Lucia. You'll have to go," she told me, closing my file and replacing the pen stand to its original position.

I had a lot more questions. "Are you sure?" I asked her. "I don't mind waiting."

"No," she said, shoving the file at me. "We'll have to finish another time. Lucia can't know anything about this. If things don't work out, it would break her heart. I'll call the office and reschedule."

I gathered my things together and started for the door.

Francesca put her arm out. "Wait. You'll have to go out the back," she said, steering me towards the French doors and guiding me outside. "Just follow the path around the pool to the side gate and let yourself out."

I heard a lock click when she closed the doors behind me. I turned to say goodbye, but she was already gone. She'd even drawn the drapes.

I hiked my bag onto my shoulder, let out a breath, and tightened my jacket around me. I hated stopping things just when they were getting interesting. Almost as much as I hated being ejected out into the sudden cold. I looked around to orient myself and took in the tall, thick trees that dwarfed the neighborhood rooftops and the massive pool that took up the left side of the property. The pool was encircled by its own metal fence, and a dark tarp signaled it was closed for the season. The tarp had islands of water here and there and smatterings of burnished leaves adding to its deserted appearance. Still, the pool would be beautiful in the summer, and I could imagine myself swimming laps in it on warm evenings. A garden was more practical, certainly more eco-friendly, but I could understand how Francesca could have traded it for a pool. Pool boy not withstanding.

I turned to the path, made my way along the flagstones, and replayed our conversation. The only real lead I got involved Puddles' old job at Guido's, so I'd head over there later to follow up. Maybe I'd get lucky and someone would remember him. Nosing around about the possible business problems could be tough, though. People could be touchy about those. I'd have to be careful. I thought about the best approach as I rounded the pool, keeping my eyes glued to the ground while I continued along the twisty path. I had just about cleared the winding bit when I nearly bumped into Beardman scrambling out of the bushes. I froze, staring at him. His facial expression fell somewhere between astonished and petrified. Mine was likely the same. Only I didn't have the added accent of cedars sticking out of the back of my head.

A surge of energy spilled into my body, and I rammed my hand into my bag, digging for my cell phone. My sudden movement must have jolted him to life because he took off in the direction of the gate. I wavered a moment before chasing after him. I hadn't seen a gun this time, but that didn't mean he didn't have one. We ran full out, but my knee still wasn't a hundred percent, and I lagged behind. He reached the street first, jumped into a rusty green Volvo, and sped away. I stood in the driveway, waist bent, catching my breath, berating myself for not getting the license plate number. I felt my hand tingle and realized I still held tight to my cell phone. It rang again and I answered the call. It was Laurent—Camille's brother and the other half of C&C. He needed to speak with me and wanted me to come by the office as soon as possible. Sounded good to me. About now, being anywhere but here sounded good to me.

THE C&C OFFICE took up the first floor of the right side of a semi-detached old stone house in the Plateau that had been converted into four commercial suites, one up, one down on either side. Aside from subdividing the building, the conversion hadn't offered many updates to the original floor plans. The C&C unit featured a long hallway with doors running along the right side and ending with a kitchen. A small nook halfway down the hall now served as a reception area with a desk and chair as well as access to the basement. The first door off the hallway, the old living room, was Camille's office. The second door, the old dining room, was Laurent's office. And, tucked in next to the tiny kitchen at the back was a bathroom.

I arrived at the front door to find Laurent fending off a woman in a red suit. Her skirt length was short, her heels high, and her cleavage exposed. She teetered slightly as she passed me on her way down the stoop steps.

"Who was that?" I asked Laurent.

"Another saleslady," he said, bending down to kiss my cheeks hello, his scruff rough against my skin.

"What was she selling?"

"A long-distance calling bundle."

Yeah. Not likely. The only bundle that lady was interested in may be long, but she certainly didn't want it distant. As if the French accent wasn't enough, the Caron genetic bank had endowed Laurent with physical blessings that attracted more women to his door than spam to my inbox. The Carons were French Canadian with some Native heritage thrown in. Laurent owed his looks to the latter. His hair, almost shoulder-length, was thick, not quite black, and left wild. His eyes matched in both color and tone. And his build was a testament to the Native credo to leave nothing to waste—compact and solid. He dressed fashionably, tending more towards casual comfort. Today he wore dark jeans with a light shirt. His aura had a magnetic pull few women could resist, but despite the many volunteers, he had no intention of coupling permanently any time soon. The only courtship in his life was with hockey, which he played faithfully every Sunday.

"They don't sell phone services door-to-door," I said to him. "They call at dinnertime with harassing sales pitches that go on until your supper burns."

Laurent shrugged, but I caught the slight smile. He closed the door behind us, followed me into reception, and looked me up and down. "Glad to see everything is still in the proper place."

"Excuse me?" I said.

"From yesterday," he said. "The man with the gun. He didn't hurt you?"

"No, no. I'm fine," I said. Then I told him about my new run-in with Beardman at Francesca's.

He stepped closer to me, a look of concern darkening his face. "Camille told me about the paper you found. He must be following you. You sure you're all right?"

"Of course I'm sure. I can take care of myself."

He smiled now but said nothing.

My skin started to feel prickly. "I can," I said, as if he had questioned my capability. How was I ever going to convince him to take me seriously as a PI if he thought of me as some crumpet that crumbled under the slightest pressure? He was an ex-cop. It would take more to impress him than note-taking abilities.

He looked me up and down again. "I just had to be sure you were okay," he said. "For the insurance, of course. A boss can't be too careful."

Insurance nothing. He was toying with me now. He did that. He was French, after all. And everybody knows the French can't help but flirt. It's ingrained. Like hot tempers and a penchant for wine. It was nothing personal. He knew I had a boyfriend.

I rummaged in my bag and pulled out the Puddles file. As much as I didn't want to admit it, Adam's cautions about my job security echoed in my head, and I felt a sudden urge to prove my competency. "I added my notes from my meeting with Francesca Bellinni," I said and passed Laurent the file.

He took it and flipped it open, but his gaze remained on me a moment longer. I tried to focus on the file. Locking eyes with Laurent was like slipping into a warm bath—once you got in, you never wanted out, and I didn't need that kind of trouble. "The meeting was cut short, so I didn't get much," I told him. "But I figured I'd head over to Puddles' old workplace this afternoon to dig some more."

"Good," he said, scanning the file. "The client didn't give us much to go on by way of identifying information—no birth records, no SIN number, not even a driver's license. See if you can get anything from his employment records while you're there."

"Sure," I said. "I'll see about a picture too. Didn't see one in the file either."

"*Non.* Couldn't get one from Francesca. She said she'd packed them all up after he left and lost the box in the move."

"What about other family? Maybe we could get a picture from another relative."

He shook his head. "No other family. Francesca said he was orphaned back in Italy and raised by an aunt who died. That's why he decided to come to Canada."

I thought about that a minute. "After all these years and with such limited information, how does she expect us to find him?"

"That's why she needs us," he said. "If it was easy, she'd find him herself."

I eased around him and poked my head into Camille's office. "Camille not in yet?"

"*Non.*"

I took off my jacket and slipped it onto a wall hook in reception. "And what about Arielle? She not in either?" Arielle was the receptionist. She was also family. A cousin on their mother's side. Their aunt Claudette's daughter. She was barely twenty and younger than Camille and Laurent by more than a decade. I had found it odd when I first met Camille that her family had such a wide age spread, but I had come to understand that this was common in large families. And French Roman Catholic families were almost always large.

"She's not coming in today. That's what I wanted to talk to you about," he said and walked into his office. He removed a stack of papers from a chair to make room for me to sit, and I took my place at the round, glass-topped table that served as a desk. He considered the small navy sofa in the corner beside the filing cabinet before stuffing the papers on one of the built-in shelves that flanked the window overlooking the alleyway. Then he joined me at the table.

"My mother and tante Claudette had a disagreement, and they're not speaking," he said. "Well, tante Claudette isn't speaking to my mother, that is. And Arielle is taking a position of loyalty. She thinks if she comes to work, her mother will think she is taking my mother's side."

This all sounded very childish to me, but I knew enough about the Caron stubbornness, and even worse, the Caron pride, not to question it.

The front door lock tumbled, and we heard the door open and close. Laurent continued, talking faster this time. "So with Arielle gone, we have nobody answering phones and covering reception."

Camille appeared in the doorway. "What's going on here?" she said.

Laurent and I looked at each other. "Nothing," he told her.

She looked at me, waiting for my input.

"We were just talking about Arielle," I said.

Camille's eyes squinted, and the accompanying furrow of her brows made her short blond hair appear spiked. Laurent grumbled something to himself.

"That's what I thought," she said, bounding across the room, plucking me from my chair, and glaring at Laurent. "Oh, no you don't," she said to him. "You're not getting Lora on your side."

"Camille, be reasonable," he said.

She started to direct me out the door and into her own office. I noticed she towered over me by more than the usual seven inches or so. She owed the extra inches to stiletto boots—not her usual work footwear. "What's with the boots?" I asked her.

She adjusted the drape of her blouse and picked a clump of dog hair off her pants. "I didn't have time to go home and change. I came straight from Luc's."

That explained the dog hair. Camille didn't have a dog. It also explained the late start to her day.

Camille shuttled me into her office with Laurent not far behind. The phone rang before they could pick up their argument where they left off. Neither one made a move to answer. Eventually, the machine picked up, and Camille went to sit at her desk.

Laurent dropped a file in front of her. "Here," he said to her. "Call the agency."

"What agency?" I asked.

Camille shot me a look. "Laurent wants to hire a new receptionist."

"A *temporary* receptionist," Laurent clarified. "Just until Arielle comes back."

Sounded logical to me, but I wouldn't venture into a Caron sibling fight without a hose. And probably not even then.

Camille sat tapping a pencil against the plastic multicolored slinky she kept for what she called "stress relief." She claimed that balancing it back and forth focused her thoughts and calmed her. None of us had ever seen her do that. Mostly, she just threw it at people. The tapping wasn't a good sign. "Arielle won't like it," she said.

"Arielle's not here," Laurent pointed out.

Camille went quiet and fingered her slinky.

"You're the shrink," Laurent said to me. "Talk some sense into her."

"I'm *not* a shrink," I said. "I'm a social worker." I looked at the slinky and backed up some trying to calculate a safe zone should the slinky suddenly fly across the room between them. "And I'm staying out of it." I inched my way to the door, grateful that at least their disagreement had distracted Camille from asking about my knee, which although felt a lot better, didn't look it, and was better left hidden under my jeans. If my luck held, I'd be out the door before she even remembered about it. "I'm heading out anyway. I want to hit Guido's before everyone's on lunch break."

Laurent turned his attention to me. "I'm rethinking that. Not sure I want you out there on your own with that Beardman on the loose."

"What do you mean on the loose?" Camille said.

"She had another run-in with him this morning," Laurent said and filled her in.

"I don't like the sound of that," she said, getting up and heading over to the armoire she kept in the corner. "We'll settle the temp issue later. Just give me a minute to change, and I'm going with you. I want to get a look at this Beardman if he shows up again."

I felt torn. Given my second tousle with Beardman, the smart part of me knew having backup made good sense. Problem was, a bigger part of me was shouting "mine." Not out loud, of course. But in my head the sound was nearly deafening and there may have been a little foot stomping going on too.

Camille looked over at me. "Don't even think about it."

"Oh, come on," I said. "I'm fine. Honestly, you guys act like this is the first time I've dealt with some dodgy guy. Try talking someone off a window ledge sometime."

"Did the guy on the window ledge have a gun?" Laurent asked.

"Well, no."

"*Exactement*," Camille said and turned her attention back to trading in her stiletto boots for Doc Martens and selecting a new outfit. "You won't even know I'm there. You can do all the talking if you want. I'll just follow your lead."

Laurent and I exchanged a look. Camille couldn't even follow a trend.

"Fine," I said. "I'll meet you at the car."

I stepped out to reception to give her some privacy to change, and Laurent followed. I lifted my jacket off its hook, accidentally knocking Laurent's gun harness dangling from an adjacent peg. He steadied it, followed me to the front door, and reached around me to pull on the knob.

"Thanks," I said, "but men don't have to open doors for women anymore."

"Your anglophone does not open doors for you?" he said.

By my anglophone he meant my boyfriend Adam. "I guess sometimes he does."

"*Mais*, Lora. It is not enough for a man to take care of a woman only part of the time. A woman should be taken care of *every* time. When you get tired of your anglophone, you will see."

I wasn't sure if that remark fell into the teasing category or the flirting one. I checked his face for a clue and met his eyes briefly, just long enough to see that probably it was best not to stick around and find out.

FOUR

"IT'S THERE ON the left," Camille said as she directed me over to Guido's on Chabanel Street.

I pulled into a slot out front, cut the engine, looked up at the fat, boxy building we were about to enter, and sighed.

"What?" Camille said.

"I don't know. I just thought it would be more sleek or something."

She shrugged. "It's old. Most of these places used to bundle the showrooms and the manufacturing together. They needed space not pizzazz."

A glimpse up and down the street told me this building seemed to be in good company on that score. There were some obvious stabs at exterior facelifts here and there, but not much hinted at the creative genius that was housed inside this quarter of the garment district.

We got out, fed the meter, and headed over to the main entrance. I heaved open the door, and we stepped in. My nose crinkled when the crisp outdoor air was replaced by the overheated musty brew of the dimly lit lobby with its stone beige floor tiles and builders' beige walls. We took the elevators to the third floor and were greeted by more of the same when the doors slid open, only this floor had a half-moon-shaped chrome and melamine desk facing the elevators and two vinyl covered sofas lined up under huge windows overlooking the street. A pleasant-looking woman in her early twenties sat at the desk reading a paperback. Something from the Penguin classics collection. She looked up as we approached.

"*Bonjour*," she said. "May I help you?" Like many Montrealers, she blended the two languages fluidly. I was used to it by now having witnessed whole conversations like that.

We introduced ourselves and asked to speak with a manager.

The woman picked up a handset and poised her finger to punch in the extension. "Do you have an appointment?"

"No," I said. "We were just hoping to have a few minutes. We're family friends of the previous owners." Not exactly a lie, more an extended stretch of the truth. Since Francesca didn't want her daughter to get wind of the investigation, I wanted to keep things more on a need-to-know basis.

"Oh, the Mauris." She brought her hand back down to the desk. "Such a shame when they passed. We really miss them around here."

Given the receptionist's age, I had a hard time believing she'd have many memories of Francesca's parents, so I just smiled and nodded.

Camille drummed her fingers on the desk. I glanced at her, and she crooked an eyebrow at me before turning her attention back to the receptionist. "Were you very close with the Mauris?" she asked her.

Instantly, I realized I should have asked that follow-up. I'd have to be faster next time if I wanted to be the leader.

The receptionist smiled. "Actually, my mom was one of the first seamstresses Guido Mauri hired. My grandparents had just immigrated from Hungary and only spoke Hungarian, so they had a hard time finding work. Luckily, my mom knew how to sew and Guido hired her even though she was just a teenager then. My family has always been grateful to the Mauris for that. Without my mom's job, they would have had practically no income in that first year."

"Does your mother still work here?" I asked, pleased to get my question in before Camille resumed any finger drumming.

"Sure does," the receptionist said. "Guido's is a co-op company now, and my mom's one of the owners." She broadened her smile. "I'll just give her a quick call and see if she can see you." She punched in some numbers and after a brief interchange with her mother she said, "You can go on back. Her office is the first one on your left. You can't miss it."

"Thanks," I said, and we walked towards the double doors that separated the lobby from the office area. The door to the right buzzed, I opened it, and we stepped into a T-shaped hallway. It had the same décor as the lobby with an occasional rack of clothes lining the wall. We turned left and sure enough, there was an older version of the receptionist waiting in the first doorway.

She extended her hand. "Hello, I'm Miriam Tabor," she said.

We introduced ourselves and she invited us into her office. I followed her in while Camille lingered to give a clothes rack the once over with her eyes. Inside, Miriam led us over to a seating area of four upholstered chairs clustered around a round coffee table.

"If you could just have a seat, I'll be with you in a moment. I need to finish up a consultation," she said.

"That would be great. Thanks," I said and took my seat.

Camille sat in the chair next to mine, and as soon as we were alone, she leaned forward and started to pick through the heap of scarves that covered the coffee table.

"What are you doing?" I asked her.

"I'm looking at the samples."

She picked each up in turn and mumbled to herself as she discarded them. "*Non, non, non.*" Then she stopped at a colorful patterned red one. "*Ah, oui,*" she said. She held it up to the light and ran the material over the back of her hand before proceeding to shove the scarf into her handbag.

"Hey," I said. "You can't do that. That's stealing."

"No, it's not," she told me. "They're samples."

"How do you know they're samples?"

She stared at me, unblinking.

"Well, even if they are, you can't just take one," I said. "It's not like the little packet of shampoo that comes in the mail."

"When you go to a fine restaurant, do you not sample the wine before you agree to buy it?" she said. "This is the same thing."

"But you're not buying it."

"Ah, but if you like the designer, you buy more scarves."

I tugged the scarf out from her purse, and she grabbed hold of the tail as it escaped her bag. I tried to put the scarf back on the table, but Camille had a firm grip so it hung between us like a ribbon. The door opened, and we both turned to find Miriam watching us.

"We were just admiring your scarf," I said to her and let my end drop leaving Camille holding only her bit.

Miriam came over to sit with us. "You can each take one if you like," she said. "They're just samples."

Camille looked at me and cocked her chin ever so slightly. The Caron sign language equivalent of *so there*. "Thank you," she said to Miriam as she tucked the scarf back into her bag.

Miriam settled herself in her chair, crossed her legs, and let her wrists dangle over the edge of the armrests. When she spoke, her European accent, softened from nearly a lifetime of living in Canada, was barely noticeable. "So, my daughter said you're friends of the Mauri family. Would that be the present generation?"

"Not friends exactly," I said, getting down to business. "We're investigators helping Francesca locate Lucia's father. With Lucia getting married in a few months, Francesca was hoping to find him in time to attend the wedding."

"Oh. I see," she said, shifting in her chair. "I'm not sure I could be of much help with that. I haven't seen Puddles since he left. And I didn't know him very well, to tell you the truth. He didn't socialize much around the office. He wasn't here very long before he married Francesca and Guido moved him into management. After that he kept to himself."

"Is there anyone else working here now that may remember him?" I asked.

"No, not anyone I can think of. Besides myself, of course. It was quite some time ago. Most people have moved on, retired, or passed away."

"What about employment records?" I said.

Miriam paused before answering. "Legally, I couldn't share those with you. But even if I could, it wouldn't matter anyway. We don't have any file on Puddles."

"You mean there never was one or it disappeared?" Camille said.

"I wouldn't know. I only know that when Guido's went co-op and we went over things, there was nothing on Puddles."

I thought about what Francesca told me about company problems and missing files and wondered if there was a connection. Quite a coincidence to have both the man and all traces of him disappear at the same time. As a manager, he was likely privy to all sorts of company secrets. Not to mention whatever he'd learned when he'd first joined Guido's.

"What did he do before he went into management?" I asked her.

"He worked in the cutting room."

That was interesting. Probably he was one of the first to work on new designs.

Camille scanned a wall collection of employee group photos. "He in any of those pictures?" she asked Miriam.

Miriam glanced at the wall. "No," she said. "He never wanted to be in them. He was camera shy." She got up, went over to the photos, and tapped a picture hanging at the top. "You see, this whole row," she said drawing her finger downward. "They were taken while Puddles worked here, and he's not even in one." Then she pointed to another picture. "This one here was taken around the time Lucia was born. I know because my own daughter, Ingrid, is about the same age as Lucia." She removed the second picture from its nail and brought it back to show us up close. "See. If you look closely, you can see that I'm pregnant."

Camille and I both leaned in. If you weren't looking for it, it would be easy to miss the slight bulge in Miriam's apron.

She went on, pointing to the other people in the picture. "This is Guido and Antonia, Francesca's parents, of course, this one's Anita, a sewer like me, and this man, Vladimir, worked in the cutting room." She returned the picture then sat back down.

"Do you remember much about that time?" I said.

"I remember it vividly," she said. "I was very nervous during my pregnancy because I'd gone through years of infertility and miscarriages and wanted a child desperately. Antonia understood my anxiety because she had lost a child herself—her firstborn—a boy who died before his fourth birthday about a year before Francesca was born. Antonia was very good to me. A bit motherly at first maybe, even though she was only a dozen years older than me, but then we became close friends and shared our worries."

"And what was Antonia worried about?" Camille asked.

Miriam ran her fingers over her cheek. "Francesca. Always Francesca. When you lose one child, it's easy to become overprotective of any children you have left."

I got the sense that Miriam knew a lot about the Mauri family. "It must have been nice for her to have you to talk to," I said, hoping to gain her confidence and encourage her to share more.

Miriam looked at the early picture of Antonia. "We had each other. Things were not easy for Antonia. It was especially difficult for her when Guido passed on." She sat back in her chair and straightened the seam in her slacks.

That would also be around the time Puddles disappeared. "And for Francesca I imagine," I said.

"I expect so," Miriam agreed. "Antonia and Francesca had had a bit of a falling out by then and Francesca wasn't confiding in me. She saw me as her mother's friend, which, of course, I was, but Lucia was friends with my Ingrid and that brought Francesca and I together quite a bit, too."

The falling out was news to me. Francesca hadn't mentioned it. "Did the falling out have anything to do with Puddles?" I asked.

Miriam paused. "I really couldn't say."

That wasn't exactly an answer, so I tried another angle. "Do you have any idea why Puddles may have left or where he may have gone?"

"I'm afraid I don't. From what I understand, he didn't have family and he never spoke of any friends. Of course, given my relationship with the family, our paths crossed many times at family functions, but at those he devoted most of his attention to Lucia. He was a very doting father."

"And things here were going well for him?" Camille said. "There weren't any business problems?"

Miriam glanced from me to Camille. "Not that I remember," she said.

"Really?" I said. "I'd heard something about issues with some designs."

She gave it some thought. "If there were, I didn't know about them."

I caught sight of Camille's foot picking up the pace as it swung freely from her crossed leg. Either she was developing a nervous tick, or I was missing something again.

There was a brief knock at the door, and the receptionist poked her head in.

"What is it, Ingrid?" Miriam said.

"Sorry to interrupt, Mom, but you're kind of needed."

With the door open, we could hear raised voices not too far away. Miriam excused herself and went into the hall, signaling to her daughter to stay behind.

"Hi again," Ingrid said to us. She toyed with the short pleats in her skirt and they rustled, so she leaned against her mother's desk to quiet them.

"Nice top," I said, noticing its tailoring. Not every shirt goes well with a pleated skirt.

Ingrid blushed and folded her arms over her chest. "It's a Ribkoff," she said. "I'm not supposed to wear it at work. Don't say anything in front of my mom, okay? She'd kill me if she knew I told you. I'm only supposed to wear Guido's stuff."

I laughed. "Don't worry. I can't tell one designer from another. Although, for some reason the Ribkoff name does sound familiar."

"That's because he was in the news for dressing Miss America a while back," Camille said.

"Yeah, that was cool," Ingrid said. "The guy's been around, like, forever and he's still making good stuff. I can't really afford his clothes, but I got this through a friend who works over there."

The mention of a friend reminded me that Miriam had said Ingrid and Francesca's daughter Lucia were friends. "You must be really excited for Lucia," I said to her.

Ingrid gave me a quizzical look.

"Getting married, I mean."

"Oh yeah, right," she said. "It's going to be a big-deal wedding at the same place Céline Dion got married. You know, the Basilica Notre Dame."

Even Camille's eyes lit up on that one. Not so much because of the Céline Dion connection, but because the historic church was revered in the Catholic circles she grew up in.

"We were just talking about it with your mom," I told her. "As a surprise, Francesca's trying to find Lucia's dad before the wedding."

"That would be some surprise," Ingrid said, her hand springing up to partially cover her mouth. "Oh, sorry. I shouldn't have said that. I just don't think Lucia would really want her dad at her wedding."

Camille's foot went into motion again. "Really?" she said. "I thought they were close."

"When she was little, they were," Ingrid said. "Her dad was pretty cool then actually. They did lots of stuff together. He even used to let Lucia sit in his lap when he drove the convertible. And sometimes he'd let her steer. I used to think she was really lucky, having a dad like that. My dad would never let me do stuff like that. He would have had a fit if I'd so much as take off my seat belt before we came to a complete stop." After a second she added, "Of course, now I know my dad was just protecting me. Anyway, everything changed between them after what he did."

"You mean leaving?" I said.

Ingrid's eyes looked away before she answered. "Yeah, that."

"Must have been hard on her," Camille said. "Did he give her a reason?"

"Nope. It was pretty bad. But the guy probably went off to have a bunch of other kids. Some of my girlfriends used to say their mothers were sure he wouldn't be alone for long. They said he was too good looking."

"Was he?" I asked.

"I guess. I mean I was just a kid then. And he was, like, a dad." She went around to the other side of her mom's desk. "But you can see for yourself. She pulled open a drawer, dug around, took out a mini photo album, and came over to us. "This is from when Lucia's parents got married. Her grandmother gave it to my mom, and my mom's going to have a copy made as part of Lucia's wedding present."

She passed us the little book, and Camille and I held it between us as we went through it. The first page was a close-up of pink flowers. Had to be Francesca's bouquet. The next page had two pictures of a young Francesca in her wedding gown, no veil. On the left she was standing at the top of the staircase in her parents' home, and on the right she was sitting in front of their living room fireplace. Camille turned the page. More before-the-wedding pictures. After several pages, there was a picture of the bride and groom. I bent my head for a closer look at the latter. Piedro Bellinni, a.k.a Puddles, certainly had no reason to be camera shy. He was of medium build with a well-conditioned body. He had light brown hair smoothed back away from his face. His eyes were bright and captivating. He had a charming grin that suggested he was good-natured yet somewhat brooding. He was James Dean meets Brad Pitt.

Miriam came back into the room just as we closed the book. She looked from the book to Ingrid, and her face went from surprised to unreadable. "I had forgotten about the wedding album," she said when she finally spoke. "Good you thought of it, Ingrid. I don't know why I didn't think of it myself."

"Would you mind if we borrowed a few of the pictures?" Camille asked her.

"Not at all," Miriam said, although her tight smile suggested otherwise.

"Thanks, we won't keep them long," I assured her. "Ingrid mentioned you're having a copy of the photo album made for Lucia's gift. That's a lovely idea."

"Well, Puddles wasn't so happy about taking wedding pictures either," she told us. "But Guido insisted on it. Guido was traditional and wanted Francesca to have a large album as a remembrance, and it came with two mini versions. One for each set of parents.

Ordinarily, this album would have been for Puddles' parents, but since he didn't have any, Antonia gave it to me."

"Nice," Camille said as she extracted some photos from the book.

"It was. Antonia was like that," Miriam said. She looked at her watch. "Now I don't mean to rush you off, but I have a meeting."

"We understand," I told her while my brain sifted through our conversation for any loose threads I didn't follow up on. "I was wondering, though, about the man Puddles worked with in the cutting room. Do you have any contact information for him?"

Ingrid looked at her mother. "That's Mr. Dobervitch, right? The old guy who offed himself after Mr. Mauri died?"

Miriam flushed. Hard to tell if it was from the memory, her daughter's brusque language, or a breach of some company confidentiality policy. "That's right," she said.

Camille and I exchanged a look.

"He died?" I said.

"Yes. Poor man just couldn't face the idea of retirement," Miriam said, as she went to open the door for us.

I glanced back at the wall of photos, feeling pangs of sympathy for a man I didn't even know. Also pangs of curiosity. What were the chances of two men from the same small company dying and one disappearing all within weeks of each other. "That's really awful," I said.

Camille nudged me towards the door. "Yes," she said. "It is. But we've taken up enough of your time. Thanks so much for your help."

When we got into the elevator and had some privacy, I turned to her. "What was with the rush all of a sudden?"

She passed me a folded piece of paper like we were passing notes in school. I opened it, turning it upright so the faded blue lines were horizontal. It read: "My Dearest, No matter what the future holds, this day will make everything we have done all right and good. May God forgive us." It was signed with an initial too smudged to be legible.

"Where'd you get this?" I asked Camille.

"From the little book."

"What do you think it means?" I said.

"I think it means we may be dealing with a lot more here than a missing person."

FIVE

I SLOWED THE car for a stoplight up ahead, and Camille grabbed a handful of individually wrapped chocolates from her purse and poured them into her lap. She picked up a gold ball and peeled off the paper before popping the chocolate into her mouth.

She held one out to me. "Want one?"

"Sure."

She took the foil off for me and dropped the chocolate in my upturned palm. I put it in my mouth and let it melt. The light turned green, and we were moving again.

Camille chain-ate her chocolates, tossing the balled gold skins into an empty cup holder. "So, who do you think wrote the note?"

"No idea. But whoever received it had access to the photo album so that's got to narrow things down."

"Not just access," Camille said. "Someone thought it was a safe hiding place. Someone who wanted to keep the note instead of throwing it away."

"The obvious choice is Miriam," I said. "After all, she owned the album. I mean, there's no telling how long the note was in there. She may have tucked it in there recently. It may have nothing to do with the Mauris." I thought a bit more. "On the other hand, it could have been in there all along and she never knew. It was a gift, after all. She may have flipped through it when she first got it and tucked it away until she found out Lucia was getting married. But either way, she clearly knows more than she was telling. I bet she knew exactly what was troubling the business when Puddles disappeared."

"Probably," Camille agreed. "She's not the most trusting type either. You see how she had Ingrid stay to babysit us when she stepped out the second time?"

I let my eyes drift over to Camille's purse. "Maybe that's because you stole a scarf the first time she left."

Camille shook her head and let out a puff of air intended to dismiss my comment. "And Ingrid was covering something too," she said. "Although not as well as her mother. That bit about Lucia not wanting her dad at her wedding must mean something. Have you spoken to Lucia about her dad?"

"Nope. I've only met with Francesca. And she made it very clear that she didn't even want Lucia to know about the investigation."

"Hmmm," Camille said and went quiet for a beat before she continued. "After you drop me at the office, I'll look into that business with the Dobervitch guy, too. Awfully convenient time for him to die."

I agreed.

The pile of chocolates in Camille's lap now gone, she grabbed a Kleenex and wiped her hands. Then she pulled the visor down and finger-combed her hair and touched up her lipstick.

Her cell phone buzzed in her purse when she was done. She pulled it out, checked the caller I.D., and put it back.

I knew drivers weren't supposed to talk on cell phones, but I didn't think the law extended to passengers. "Aren't you going to get that?"

She shook her head. "It's Luc."

I thought about her earlier entrance at the office. "You guys seeing each other again?" I said.

"Just on and off."

I glanced at her. "You know, some people call that dating."

She shook her head again. "Lovers don't date. Dating is for couples who want committed relationships."

"So what do lovers want?" I asked her.

"Mostly uncommitted relations," she said. Then she lifted her sunglasses off her nose and leaned forward, her attention diverted from our conversation. "*Arrête*," she yelled at me. "*Arrête!*" When I didn't pull over fast enough she switched languages. "Stop!"

"Okay, okay," I said. "I'm trying to find a spot." Truth be told, not having driven much in New York, I'm not the most experienced driver, and I'm easily rattled. Plus, Montreal streets could be just as crammed with traffic in the core as New York streets, and drivers here seemed to rely more on telepathy to indicate lane changes than blinkers.

"Stop!" Camille yelled at me again. I gave up looking for a spot, jammed on the brakes, and was treated to several honks and significantly more dirty looks and hand gestures.

Camille bolted from the car. I tried to track her while I made my way over to the curb and idled in front of a fire hydrant. I couldn't see her anymore, so I cut the engine and stepped out. I caught sight of her blond head bouncing through the crowd along the sidewalk across the street. I locked the car and rushed over to catch up.

By the time I reached her a few blocks later, she was closing the distance between herself and some kid with too little eyebrow and too much hair gel who kept looking at her over his shoulder and losing his footing. The crowd, now thinned as people moved to the sides, watched with more confusion than interest as Camille's hand clamped onto the kid's hood, and he came to a choking halt. He swung his arm up and around to grab her hand and try to wrench himself free. When that didn't work, he brought his arm back down, reached into his pocket, and whipped out a switchblade. Camille saw the knife and let go of the hood. The boy grinned and spun around, swinging the knife at her.

Camille took in an audible breath, knocked the knife out of his hand with a blow to his wrist, then drop-kicked him. A second later, she had him pinned to the ground and was yanking a shopping bag from Best Buy out of his hand. She passed the bag to an older lady I hadn't noticed before who was sitting in a motorized wheelchair near the curb.

A couple of teenagers in the crowd whistled. Probably not so much because Camille had caught a thief, but because watching her in action was a thing of beauty. She had studied martial arts as a child the way other girls study ballet and had reached prima ballerina status a long time ago.

"*Merci mademoiselle,*" the elderly woman said to Camille before turning and rolling away down the street.

"*De rien,*" Camille said as she pulled the boy onto his feet and steered him back towards my car, gesturing at me to retrieve the knife from the sidewalk.

The Mini had a ticket on the windshield and a cop beside it when we got back. Camille and the cop exchanged a few words in French, and minutes later both the boy and the ticket were gone.

"Friend of yours?" I asked as we got into the car.

"Friend of Luc's," she said.

I pulled into traffic. "That was pretty impressive back there."

She shrugged. "It's only a practical skill like cooking or sewing."

I slid a glance at her before gluing my eyes back to the road. "You don't cook or sew."

"Those skills are for the Martha Stewarts of the world. I prefer to perfect more physical skills."

"You mean like subduing a man with nothing more than a few swift leg moves and deft hand strokes?"

She pulled the visor down again and retouched her lipstick before responding. "*Exactement.*"

AFTER A SOLID night's rest, I felt pretty good. Even better when I felt a tapping on my back as I languished in bed and rolled over to see if Adam was suggesting what I thought he was. Then I came face to snout with my dog Pong—head slung back across Adam's pillow, mouth ajar, tongue hanging out to the side, paws reaching for the sky, closed eyes twitching. Just the kind of thing that looks cute in a picture. In real life, doggy odor, not to mention hair, is a pain to get out of sheets. Ergo, Pong was not allowed on the bed. She knew this. I knew this. And Adam knew this.

"Pong, get down!" Adam said, coming into the room wearing nothing but a towel tied around his waist.

Pong's eyes snapped open and her body flipped right side up in one fluid motion. She sank her chin to the bed and looked up at Adam with innocent eyes.

"Don't give me that," Adam told her. "You get down."

I felt her body cleave to mine in protest before she relented and edged to the side of the bed to hop down. Not easy for a dachshund mutt.

"Good girl," Adam said and bent to stroke her side as she passed him. Pong's tail thwacked against the metal footboard in response until she spotted our cat, Ping, in the hallway and ran off to chase after her.

"What are you doing up so early?" I asked Adam, giving my body a good stretch as I watched him.

"It's not early," he said. "I just woke up before the alarm and thought I'd let you sleep while I had my shower." He went over to the bureau, pulled open the top drawer, and plucked out some white boxers. He dropped the towel and put on the underwear. His hair dripped onto the floor when he bent down to pick up the towel, and impure thoughts drifted back into my head while I admired his muscles in motion. He dabbed the floor with his towel then flung the towel over the post at the end of the bed and walked over to the closet.

"You in a hurry?" I said.

He returned the sweater he had been about to put on back to the shelf and came over to the bed. "Define hurry."

"You know," I said, sliding over to make room for him beside me. "Like expected elsewhere."

He got in the bed and moved close to me. I nuzzled up to his neck and soaked in the soapy smell.

"My meeting starts at ten-thirty," he said.

My eyes darted to the clock. It was nearly nine now. Just enough time for a quickie. I moved onto my back as he started kissing my shoulder.

"Then I've got that lunch with Tina at noon," he said between kisses.

"Mmmm," I said, only half listening as his lips made their way up my neck to my ear. "Wait. What?" I said when his words finally registered.

"I've got lunch with Tina after my meeting," he repeated.

I sprung up, nearly head-butting Adam. "What lunch with Tina?"

"I told you about it last week," he said.

"No. No, you didn't," I said pulling the blankets up around me. I knew that for certain because if he had told me, I wouldn't have been speaking with him all week. Tina was an old college friend of Adam's. She swallowed husbands the way other people ate chips and kept Adam in her life in case she ran out of salsa.

"Well, she's coming into the city and she wants to talk to me," he said.

I got out of bed, stomped over to the closet, and started getting dressed. "About what?"

He sighed, joined me at the closet, and pulled on his clothes. "She didn't say," he said as he took the blow dryer into the bathroom.

I pulled on some jeans and adjusted the sleeves on my black shirt. The blow dryer went off, and I met Adam in the doorway. "If Tina wants to talk to you, it can only be about one thing," I said. "Her latest marriage is breaking up."

He slipped by me and put the dryer away. "Could be," he said and went downstairs.

I went into the bathroom to wash up and brood some more. Tina was like the stubborn stain I couldn't get out of my favorite blouse—receded into the background but never completely gone. The problem was timing. Her friendship with Adam predated our relationship. She baited him with her damsel in distress routine and ever since he helped her survive university, he'd played her knight in shining armor. All the times he'd tutored her at the last minute so she could pass an exam for a class she'd rarely attended. Or picked her up when she found herself waking up in some guy's bed she couldn't remember. Even sitting in at dinners with her parents because she needed someone presentable to bring home. After a while, a guy gets to like donning the shiny steel suit. And with so few occasions calling for armor these days, what man could resist the noble call now and again?

By the time I got down to the kitchen, Adam was nearly ready to leave. "Oh, good, you're here," he said. "The phone's for you."

It must have rung when I was in the bathroom because I never heard it. I took the receiver from him. "Hello."

"Miss Weaver?" It took me a moment to place the owner of the voice. Francesca.

"Yes, Mrs. Bellinni, what can I do for you?" I wondered how she got the number for my private line. Clients usually called my business number or C&C.

"I was wondering if you could come by this morning?"

"To continue our meeting?" I asked her.

"Actually, something else came up I'd like your help with."

My curiosity was piqued. "Of course. I can be there in about an hour."

"Thanks. I'll be waiting," she said and hung up.

I started to speculate on what Francesca could want when Adam's voice called out from the hall. "I'm leaving now. I'll see you later, hon."

My mind wheeled back around to Tina, and I went over to Adam. "I've been thinking that maybe I should go along to lunch with Tina," I said. "If she's going through a tough time, she could use all the support she can get."

Adam grinned. "Liar. You just want to make sure she keeps her hands to herself."

"That too."

"After all these years, I think I know how to handle Tina."

Yeah, and she knows how to handle you. "Is there some reason I shouldn't go?" I asked, knowing there was no way he could answer that gracefully.

He waffled a bit then said, "Fine. Can you be at Le Pois Chic by noon?"

Le Pois Chic? Who was she kidding? She was no vegetarian. She'd eat her own cat if she had one. This must be big if she was willing to hang out in Adam's territory. "I'll be there."

He came over and gave me a long kiss goodbye. The kind that should have reinforced my rank in his life as the supreme one, the MATE. Instead, it reminded me of what other women were only too eager to have a crack at. And one woman in particular.

SIX

FRANCESCA WAS WAITING for me at the door when I pulled into her driveway.

"Thanks for coming so quickly," she called out as I made my way to where she stood on the veranda. Her hair was held off her face with a silk scarf fashioned into a headband, and she was wearing a jogging suit that bore the designer's insignia. There were thin vertical bands of dark smudges on the shirt. Her feet were snuggled into Rockports.

She ushered me into the house and led me through an archway into the living room—a large space clearly decorated to showcase the impressive marble fireplace standing dead center on the back wall. In front of it, a tapestry rug outlined the seating area that had two settees arranged facing each other and two wing chairs completing the square. Along the wall that looked onto the front of the house were three banks of leaded windows draped in taffeta. A grand piano took up most of the third wall space. Francesca sat in one of the wing chairs and motioned for me to be seated. I lowered myself gingerly onto a settee.

"I'm not sure what to make of this," Francesca said. "But, someone's been rummaging through my attic."

"You mean there's been a break-in?" I said, wondering why she'd call me for something like that. Most people call the police.

"I'm not sure. My parents' things are still stored up there, and I went up early this morning to look for an embroidered handkerchief that has been in our family for a few generations. I wanted it to be the 'something old' for Lucia. When I got upstairs, I could tell right away someone had been going through things."

"Maybe it was Lucia," I said.

"I asked her about it, and she said she hadn't been up there in ages."

"Does anyone else have access? Like a cleaning person?"

"No. The attic is off limits to staff. It's kept locked, and Lucia and I have the only keys."

A locked attic? Now that's interesting. "Was anything missing?"

"That would be hard to say. It's a big attic, and it's pretty full."

Hmmm. Moral dilemma here. I knew there wasn't a whole lot I could do to help with the situation. I also knew I could take advantage of it. Attics were notorious hideaways for long-forgotten things. Maybe I'd come across something that would help me find Puddles. "Could I see it?"

"Sure." She stood and led me up the curving staircase that went to the second floor. The stairs were lined with a runner and wide enough for four people. Most homes I knew would have to give up a room or two to make space for a staircase like this. At the top of the stairs to the right, the banister continued along the hall for about fifteen feet and overlooked the foyer below. Francesca turned left and walked the length of the hallway to a door at the end. She pulled a key from her pocket, unlocked the door, and pushed it open. Warm, stale air escaped as we entered and mounted a set of narrow plain wood stairs. The heat got heavier as we got to the top. Even in the dim light, I could tell the attic stretched the width of the house minus a few feet at either end. An industrious landlord could manage three or four decent-sized apartments in this space. The storage was well-organized with furniture in one section and boxes in another. I automatically calculated how many apartments I could furnish for the clients at a women's shelter with Francesca's family's castoffs. I figured at least six with the bare essentials.

She pointed to a cluster of boxes. "See all the tape on those has been cut open."

I walked over for a closer look. Sure enough, the seals of packing tape were broken. Some of the boxes were folded closed, others merely left with their flaps loose. "Do you know what's in those boxes?"

"Not without reading the notes on the side." She made her way along the path between the rows of stacked boxes and edged closer to the ones along the wall. "I can't make it out. I don't have my reading glasses."

"May I?" I asked. She retraced her steps, and I went in. The writing was scrawled on the side in faded thin black ink. I couldn't make out all the words. "Seems to be from someone's office," I called back.

"Must be my father's," I heard her say as I came out.

Francesca put her hands on her hips and surveyed the attic. Her eyes lingered on a trunk off to the side with a bit of fabric sticking out. "That's the trunk," she said walking towards it. "That's my mother's. That's where the handkerchief should be." She bent over and opened it. "Jesus, Mary, and Joseph," she said. She reached in, picked up some material, and lifted it out. It smelled of mildew with a hint of a musk thrown in. It was also shredded. She let it drop and withdrew another item. It looked like a formal wrap. The lining was sliced to pieces. Quite a hack job too. Like someone went at it with a dull nail file or something. The rest of the clothes looked the same. Probably before the slicing and dicing thing, these had been some mighty fine duds.

Francesca held some ivory-colored fabric to her cheek. "This was from my grandmother's wedding dress."

"I'm sorry," I said and stepped back to give her a moment of privacy. Well, that and to nose around the boxes from her father's office. I edged over and opened the tops. Four boxes held old LP records, and the other three were filled with sweaters. I slipped my hand into the ones with clothes and felt around, hoping something might be hidden in the folds of material. Nothing. I stood up and brushed my hands over my thighs to wipe away some errant dust. It didn't seem right that a man with a home office would have nothing worth saving besides clothes and record albums. Where were the files, the address books, the agendas? At the very least I needed something that would net me a writing sample I could compare to the note Camille found in the wedding album. I didn't want to come right out and ask Francesca for a sample. She'd wonder why, and I wasn't ready to share the existence of the note with her yet. Or how Camille and I came by it.

"Anything else disturbed?" I asked Francesca.

"Here and there," she said, her head still buried in the trunk.

In a storage area this size it could take all day to look "here and there." I tried to narrow things down a bit. "Anything that belonged to Puddles?"

She shook her head. "He was already gone when I moved into this house. There is a small box of things he left behind around here somewhere. I packed them up to save for Lucia in case she wanted them someday. Not much in it, though. Just odds and ends."

"No business files or date books or things like that?"

She stood and brushed some dust off her shirt. "Not that I remember. Hard to say for sure after all these years."

I looked over at the rows of boxes and debated whether or not I'd be able to manage the heavy lifting necessary to search for Puddles' box. The debate didn't take long. The place was much too tightly packed and I was less so. Plus, many of the stacks were taller than I was.

"So what do you think?" Francesca asked me, interrupting my thoughts. "Do you think I should call the police?"

Not an easy call. Hard to tell what this was about. Vandalism wasn't typical of a random break-in. The vandalism seemed personal. The timing had me wondering, too. "That's up to you," I said to her. "At the very least you've got a break and enter here. And damaged property. Are you sure nothing is missing?"

She bent to refold the stuff in the trunk so it would fit when she closed the lid. I wouldn't know what to look for," she said and stood up again when she was done, fanning herself with her hand. "It's getting hot up here, let's go back downstairs."

I followed her out and scanned the photos lining the walls while I waited for her to lock up. A wedding portrait of Francesca's parents caught my eye. Without the nuptial clothes, the couple could have been mistaken for siblings—same dark hair, olive skin, and angular features. Farther down the hall were more family pictures including a high school graduation photo of a young Francesca and another one of a rather serious-looking girl, presumably Lucia. She too had dark, full hair yet her skin seemed more fair than her mother's and her eyes lighter.

"Do you think there's any way to find out who broke into my attic without involving the police?" Francesca asked me as we made our way down to the foyer.

"C&C doesn't have to involve the police in investigations unless criminal charges need to be laid," I told her. "And we investigate thefts all the time even when the police are involved. Often, they're the ones who call us in."

She toyed with the scarf in her hair. "I'll think about it and let you know what I want to do."

"Sure," I said. "In the meantime, you may want to ask your alarm company to increase surveillance. And make sure you keep your security system on."

"We always put it on when we go out and when we go to bed."

"Does anyone else have the code?"

"No. Just family."

"What about Lucia's fiancé?"

"Jonas? I don't think so. I've never seen him disarm it."

"But, he's practically family, right?" I said. "Maybe Lucia gave him the code."

"You think Jonas Como went through my attic?"

Not necessarily. "I'm just trying to figure out how someone got into your attic without tripping the alarm. Is it possible one of you forgot to arm it?"

Francesca shrugged, "I guess that could have happened." She glanced at her watch. "Oh, I didn't realize how late it was," she said as we neared the front door. "Thanks so much for coming."

I had hoped to ask her a few more questions about Puddles before I left. And I wanted to learn more about the falling out with her mother that Miriam had mentioned. "As long as I'm here, maybe we could continue our conversation from the other day," I suggested.

"Sorry. I don't have time now. This attic incident ate up my morning, and I'm due at a function. I'll check my schedule and get back to you."

I didn't like the idea of putting it off again and thought about trying to persuade her to give me a few minutes, but when I checked the time I saw it was nearly eleven-thirty and I was torn. As much as I wanted to get moving on finding Puddles, I wanted to get to lunch with Tina before she put any moves on Adam. So when Francesca ushered me out, I said my goodbyes and left.

LE POIS CHIC was a vegetarian restaurant on the edge of The Plateau and tucked in between an alternative bookstore and a shop that specialized in Buddhist paraphernalia. Parking was minimal. I drove past just in case someone happened to be pulling out. No go. I would have to find a spot on a side street. I turned at the end of the block and started looking for a space. I found one two streets down, signaled, and was about to pull in when a red roadster on the opposite side of the street screeched to a stop and cut me off to make a three-point turn. I reversed a few yards, missing the car by mere inches, and idled while the driver completed the turn. I was about to lift my foot off the brake to inch forward when the driver pulled into my spot. I put the parking brake on, unlocked my door, and stepped out to give the driver a piece of my mind. I just reached the back fender when the driver door opened and Tina got out.

She did a double take and put a hand to her chest. "Lora. You scared the crap out of me."

"Sorry," I said, not knowing what to say next. I couldn't blast *her* for taking my spot. I tried to gauge how close I could stand to her without being swallowed up by her perfume fog. "How have you been?"

"Fine. Well, not really. Pretty shitty actually. I'm just meeting Adam for lunch to cry on his shoulder." She ran a hand through her long blond hair, momentarily exposing the dark roots underneath. She glanced around me. "Is that your car?"

I twisted my torso a little and looked at my Mini. "Yeah."

"You'd better move it. It's double parked. You'll get a ticket for sure."

"Yeah, I'll go do that," I said and started walking towards my car.

"It was nice running into you," she said as she found her way to the sidewalk.

Apparently, it hadn't dawned on her that I was joining them for lunch. I opened my mouth to correct her, but she was already gone. Eager to see Adam no doubt. I got back in my car and drove around until a parking spot opened up. When I finally got to the restaurant, I nearly elbowed the guy behind me in my rush to get inside. I turned to apologize and missed a breath when I saw the beard. The man's smile drew my attention away from his chin, and I realized this beard did not belong to Beardman. This guy was a tad shorter, much slimmer, and way more fashionable. And, unlike Beardman's dull, listless eyes, this guy's eyes crinkled with enough energy to power a small island.

I smiled back at him to be polite and make up for the elbowing and staring. In the process, I stumbled on the slightly raised step in the doorway. He took hold of my arm long enough to steady me. His touch was warm, even through my jacket, probably because his hands were protected from the outdoor chill by leather gloves. I thanked him, feeling even more foolish, and shifted my attention to the high-pitched voice giving specific food preparation instructions to a server. Tina.

I followed the voice to a four-seater in the back where Adam and Tina sat side by side. The waitress leaving their table let out an extended exhale by way of her upper lip as she passed me on her way to give in their order.

Adam saw me approach first. "Hey, hon, how was your meeting?"

Tina looked up, saw me, and withdrew her freshly manicured hand, French tips to be specific, from Adam's forearm. "Oh, Lora. Hello."

"Hi again." I took the seat across from Adam.

"They've got your favorite today, hon," Adam said. "You know, the fried rice thing. I already ordered it for you."

"Thanks." I slipped off my jacket. I was already feeling a bit warm.

"Adam never told me you were coming too," Tina said to me. "So that's why you were outside. Why didn't you say something?" she chided me.

I opened my mouth to answer, but Tina went right on talking. "Anyway, I've just been telling Adam what a shitty time I've had. You won't believe this, but Jeffrey wants a divorce!" She paused long enough for me to shake my head. "I know, it's unbelievable. And after all I've done for him. I can't tell you how I've helped his career. Well, let's just say, he wouldn't have a career if it wasn't for me." She reached for her purse, opened it, and pulled out a package of cigarettes. "And his family, he wasn't even speaking with them before I came along. I glued them back together myself."

Adam tapped Tina's hand to get her attention. "You're not allowed to smoke in here, eh."

"What? Oh, that just sucks. I hate these new laws. A girl's got to kill her appetite somehow if she wants to stay slim and trim. Right, Lora?" she said, quickly scanning my upper body to calculate which one of us had been more successful at keeping her shape. She dropped the package of cigarettes on the table. "Anyway, I've been busting my ass to keep this marriage together. I'm exhausted. I'm done, I tell you. Jeffrey has done absolutely nothing. I said to him, 'I can't save this marriage all by myself, Jeffrey' and he said he wasn't expecting me to, but he was. I could see it. Clear as the nose on your face."

The waitress came over and set down the food.

"What's this?" Tina asked, poking at the greens in her salad. "I asked for half romaine lettuce and half radicchio. This has spinach leaves in it."

"You could just pick them out," I suggested.

Tina smiled at me but lifted her plate and shoved it towards the waitress.

The waitress apologized and reached for Tina's plate, but Adam got there first. "It's fine," he assured the waitress, waving her off with a grin. "I'll fix it." Then he began pulling out the spinach leaves and setting them on the edge of his own plate.

Great. It was starting again. We weren't here five minutes and already he was taking care of her. I shot him a look that went unnoticed since his eyes were busy rummaging for the offending spinach.

Tina took a sip of her water. "So, how about you guys? What's going on with you? It's been ages since I've seen you."

"We've been good," Adam said to her as he passed back her plate. "We've been settling in to the house, fixing things up a bit. With my mom being sick those last few years, she wasn't able to keep up the maintenance."

Tina picked up her fork and poised it over her salad, seemingly oblivious to Adam's answer. "That's another thing. Jeffrey wants the house. He says since he paid for it, he should keep it. He says I can have the car and my choice of the furniture." She shook her head. "What am I supposed to do, I asked him, live in the bloody car? Who does he think he is? Like *he* gets to decide who gets what. If I had known Jeffrey was such a louse, I never would have married him. He's nothing like our Adam here," she said as she patted Adam's shoulder. "Why he's the perfect specimen of a man. You are so lucky, Lora. I should have snatched him up myself when I had the chance."

My eyebrows raised before I could issue the "down" command.

Tina looked at Adam. "Really, you're the only reason I hold out hope that men aren't a complete waste of time." She pierced a falafel on his plate with her fork and brought it to her mouth.

"Well, someone's got to carry the flag for us decent guys," Adam said.

Tina winked, "I don't know if I'd go so far as to call you decent."

Adam blushed a little. My eyebrows stretched upwards again. Hello, girlfriend here.

"I could tell you a few stories about this man here back in the college days." She was speaking to me, but her gaze remained on Adam.

"Like what?" I said.

"Ooh, like the time he turned down a date with Heather Pointer, a very sought after girl, if you know what I mean. She was so mad. She started a rumor that he had chlamydia to get back at him, and she was even madder when he said if he had it, he must have picked it up from her." She giggled. "He was so wicked."

"Were you now," I said, catching Adam's eye.

"It was only because he was so popular. All the single girls wanted to date him. And I personally know of several not-so-single girls who would have dropped their boyfriends in a shot for a chance at Adam. That's why most of the girls didn't like me. They were jealous because Adam and I were friends."

Is that how she explained her lack of girlfriends to herself?

She went on. "Then there was the time, remember Adam, that you helped me get rid of that clingy guy Pete somebody or other." She paused to laugh. "Remember what you did? You pretended to be my big brother and you got all dressed up like a mafia guy. And you made sure he overheard a conversation between us about how 'Dad' would kill anybody who got in the way of my planned marriage to Edouardo." She was still laughing. "I never heard from the guy again."

Adam tipped his head back slightly and let out a little laugh. "Yeah, I remember."

"Sounds like you guys had a lot of fun," I said.

"Those were good times," Tina agreed. "Mostly. Not like my life now. Now everything sucks." Her expression was serious again. "After our last fight over the house, I stormed out on Jeffrey. I'm gonna let him cool his heels for a while. See what it's like without me. I bet he'll be begging me to come home. So I packed up a suitcase and here I am. I thought, what better chance to spend time with my best friends Adam and Lora?" She looked at us each in turn. "You don't mind if I stay with you, do you?"

Stay with us! No way! Never, never, never! I searched my brain for an out. I knew it was up to me to head this off. Adam would cave in a millisecond. "Ordinarily we'd love to have you, but we're doing a little work on the house right now," I said, hoping the lie wouldn't bring me bad karma. "It's not really ready for visitors. And it's really a small house, we don't even have a guestroom."

"Oh, I don't mind. You know me, I'd be happy with a little cot somewhere," she smiled.

Yeah, right. "We also still have the dog and a cat now, too. Aren't you allergic?"

Her smile shrank a little. "Oh, yeah. Your pets. I'll just take an antihistamine."

I'd saved the big ammunition for last. "And, we only have one bathroom."

Her smile tightened more into a pucker. "That's sweet of you to be concerned, Lora, but really I can be happy anywhere." She placed one hand on Adam's hand and the other on mine. "It's having my best friends around for support that's important."

Adam finally spoke. "So, it's settled then. How long do you think you'll be with us, Tina?"

"It won't take long for Jeffrey to miss me," she said. "The first time he has to pull off a business dinner without me, he'll come crawling. A few days, maybe a week, a month at the most."

Adam refused to meet my eyes. Yeah. He handled her all right.

SEVEN

"**LORA, YOU'RE NUTS!**" Camille said. "You can't let that woman stay in your house."

"What am I supposed to do?" I had left Adam and Tina at Le Pois Chic about an hour earlier and headed directly over to C&C. I had already added my report about the break-in at Francesca's to the Puddles file, and now Camille and I were sitting cross-legged on the floor of her office in front of the marble-fronted electric fireplace having a little girl talk. I pulled two pillows down from the window seat overlooking the front lawn, passed one to Camille, and sat on the other one.

"*Merde*," Camille said, holding her linen dress aside while she tucked the pillow under her.

"Yeah," I agreed.

"So, when is she invading?"

"About now, I'd guess. I think her suitcase was in the trunk."

"And you left them alone?"

"I have work to do. Anyway, I can't be there all the time. I trust Adam. If something was going to happen with Tina, it would have happened long ago."

"Maybe it did," Camille said to me. "Maybe she's looking for a repeat performance."

"Adam said he was never interested in her that way."

"And you trust that?"

I was starting to feel defensive. "Yeah. This *is* Adam we're talking about."

"Okay, you're probably right about him, but she's still on the hunt. And, she's obnoxious."

Camille was right about that. "And she smells," I added. "But what can I do? She's his friend."

"I can't imagine what he sees in her," Camille said.

"You know how it is with old friends. They bonded back in college when all it took were a few classes together, a couple of parties, and the shared experience of being away from home for the first time." I stood up, stretched, and threw my pillow back on the window seat. "I'm lucky she didn't follow him to New York when he went for his Master's. Let's face it. Now that I'm living in Montreal, I'm stuck with her."

"Stuck with who?" Laurent said as he strolled into the room.

Camille stood up and went over to her desk. "An old girl friend of Adam's," she told him. "She's moving in with them."

Laurent stepped closer to me and smiled. "Maybe I underestimate your anglophone, eh Lora? Living with two girlfriends, *c'est pas mal ça.*"

"She's *not* a girlfriend," I said, trying to keep my voice even. "She's a friend who's a girl. And, she's married." Okay, maybe technically she was separated at the moment, but it still felt good to add it in there.

With Laurent so close, I could smell the lingering scent of coffee on his bomber jacket. It brought my attention to the sweatshirt he wore underneath and the worn blue jeans and work boots he was also wearing along with a head of greasy hair. Not his usual style. "New look?" I asked him.

He zipped the jacket. "I'm going to Stanley's," he said. Stanley's was a downtown bar near the hockey arena. Before the language laws came into effect requiring all signage be in French, it was called Stanley's Cup. The name was a play on the Stanley Cup, and the bar was a frequent post-game hangout for many hockey players. It was to hockey players what Sardi's was to theatre people in New York. Over the years, it had become a popular nightspot for locals and a must-see for tourists. Laurent sometimes stopped in there when he was looking for information on a case. "I'm meeting an informant who wants me to blend in."

I didn't want to kibosh his plan, but he would never blend in. Most women would have him on photographic redial for some time to come.

"The Mercier case?" Camille asked him.

Laurent nodded.

The Mercier case involved some behind the scenes scuffling among junior hockey team members. An easy fit for Laurent. He had played on a junior team in his youth, but decided not to go professional for reasons of his own. Instead, he studied criminology, went to the police academy, and eventually opened C&C. But he never lost his passion for the sport or the people.

He stepped out of the room and came back carrying a file. He handed it to Camille.

"*Ah, non. Pas encore*," she said.

"It's not about the temps. It's for the Puddles case. I ran Piedro Bellinni through every system and came up with nothing. Either the guy did one hell of a job erasing himself from existence, or he made it all up in the first place."

"What about the other dead guy from Guido's? The old one?" I asked Laurent. "Did you get anything on him?"

He leaned back against the door frame. "That checks out. Vladimir Dobervitch was found dead in his apartment after a neighbor called the police. Seems Dobervitch hadn't shown up for their weekly bridge game and that he hadn't been answering his door or his phone for days before that. The police found him in a recliner. Looked like he took a bunch of sleeping pills with a vodka chaser. No next of kin here, so his body was shipped back to a cousin in Europe."

Camille flipped through the pages of Laurent's notes. "No autopsy?"

Laurent shook his head. "Not that I saw. Police report didn't list any reason for it. Dobervitch left a suicide note."

"What kind of note?" I asked.

"Don't know. Why?"

I sat on the window seat. "Just curious. Maybe he gave a reason."

Camille shrugged and jotted something down. "We can check and see if it's on file." Then she turned to Laurent. "You turn up anything else?" she said. "Anything about Guido's having problems?"

"Haven't got to that yet. That'll take longer," he told her.

And it would probably take more time poking around Guido's. Instantly, my brain started working on a way to get past Miriam Tabor and her company ethics.

Camille met my eyes, clearly thinking the same thing. "We'll go back to Guido's tomorrow," she said to me. "I want to do a little background first."

"I can help with that," I said.

"*Non, non*," she said. "You go on home. I've got contacts at some fashion houses I can call, and they'll be less guarded with me. They don't deal well with, uh, new people."

What she meant was that they didn't deal well with English people who couldn't hold their own in a French conversation.

"Anyway," she went on as she fingered the slinky on her desk, "this case is shaping up to be more complicated than we first thought and will probably mean lots of overtime for you soon. You might want to get your houseguest settled first."

Laurent caught my eye and tipped his head towards Camille. "That's good advice. We should *all* get our house affairs in order to make life a little easier later."

I glared at him and shook my head, letting him know I still was not getting involved with the temp argument.

He shook his head back at me in mock disappointment before turning to leave.

Camille made a face at his back then dug out the temp agency file and drummed her fingers over it while she crushed the slinky in her other hand. And I decided calling it a day wasn't such a bad idea.

ONE OF THE advantages of working part time is that you get some daylight hours to yourself. Normally, I liked to spend some of those hours puttering around the house or maybe reading a book. There's something purely decadent about leisure time in a quiet house you have all to yourself. But when I hit Côte-de-Neiges Road, I remembered about Tina being at my house and realized I wasn't in such a hurry to get home this time. Instead, maybe I needed a little pick-me-up first. Something to fortify me for the evening ahead. I tossed a couple of options around in my head and settled on Starbucks for a soy latte and a brownie. I made a slight change in my direction, and ten minutes later I was at the counter placing my order with Rishi.

Rishi winked at me as he got my food together. "*Ah, bonjour mademoiselle. Vous êtes très jolie aujourd'hui. Nouveau manteau?*"

I smiled at him. Even with the Indian accent, his French sounded flawless. "*Merci,* Rishi," I said. "And no, it's not a new jacket."

He feigned a frown. "Come, come, *mademoiselle.* Don't use English. Practice your French with me."

Every time I came in when Rishi was working we went through a similar routine. Not only was he my friendly neighborhood barista, he was also my friendly neighborhood French tutor. Self appointed, that is. As a university student working on his second degree, he placed a high value on education.

"No time today," I told him.

He leaned over the glass counter and lowered his voice some. "Are you working on a big case?" He lowered his voice even more. "I heard the RCMP made a big drug bust, but that it is just the tip of the ice burg. Are you working on that?"

Rishi's image of PIs came largely from watching hours of TV and movies when he first came to Canada and immersed himself in the culture, so his view of my job could be a tad grander than PI work actually was.

"No," I told him. "I've just got to get home to a houseguest."

His face lit up. "Oh, guests," he said as he passed me my food. "That is very good. It is nice to have a house full of people."

People, maybe. A house full of Tina, not so much. But, I nodded, paid him for my food, and offered a small wave. "See you around."

He winked at me again. "*À bientôt, mademoiselle.* And next time we'll work on your verbs, eh?"

I smiled at him and turned to leave. No sense telling the man I had about as much chance of learning French as a snail had of learning how to fly. A man in a biker's helmet held the door for me on the way out. His face was turned away, but I recognized the gloves. They were the same ones the guy was wearing earlier at Le Pois Chic. The guy with the beard. Hmmm. I looked back after I got outside. It was him all right. I had a clear view of him as he stood in line to place his order. I turned away and hurried over to my car, beeping it open as I got near enough to grab the door handle and slip inside. I told myself this was just one of those small world things, just a simple coincidence. I mean, Montreal only had about four million people. It could happen.

As I drove away, I worked harder to convince myself that's what it was because otherwise I'd get to thinking I was under surveillance by some kind of bearded posse.

AS I DROVE back over to Côte-de-Neiges Road, I couldn't stop thinking about the bearded man. Between that, the third of the latte I'd already put away, and the brownie, I could have zipped along in the Flintstone car and collected a few speeding tickets along the way. Coming up on a turnoff for Beaver Lake, I pulled in to get out of the car and walk off some of my buzz.

Beaver Lake, or as Camille called it, *Lac aux Castors*, was part of Mount Royal. Mount Royal was to Montreal what Central Park was to New York. Originally designed by the same guy too. Probably why it felt like home to me, and why I found myself drawn to it so often. The entire thing was massive, but this was my favorite spot— the small, man-made lake with lots of footpaths and grass around it and plenty of space for picnickers, sunbathers, and naturalists alike. It was also nearby to the stables where the police kept their steed and if the conditions were just right it smelled of horse, but I told myself that was part of its charm.

I parked the car, bought a ticket from the machine, and went back to slip it on top of my dashboard. The brownie had only a couple of bites left, so I popped the remainder into my mouth, grabbed my latte, and locked up. Before walking away, I stooped to check for chocolate around my mouth in the side-view mirror. No chocolate, but I did catch sight of something else in the mirror. I turned around to confirm the image. Sure enough there it was, sitting only a few feet away in the row of cars behind me. The rusty green Volvo Beardman escaped in at Francesca's. Hmmm. Another coincidence or was Beardman a psychic stalker?

Scanning the parking lot as I went, I crept over for a closer look. Inside, the car seats had tiny tears in the leather here and there, and the floor carpets were dusted with food crumbs and dirt. A juice box lay discarded on the backseat, its straw twisted and chewed, beside a child's booster chair. And, on the dashboard sat a parking slip indicating that Beardman had almost an hour of parking left.

I stepped back over to my car and got in to call Camille but stopped mid-dial, an idea slowly pussyfooting into my brain. An idea that probably had no business in there. But there it was anyway, taking off its shoes and wriggling its toes and settling in for a good long stay. This was it. This was my big chance to prove that I could do more than interview people, conduct research, and lose cars. My heart quickening at what I was about to do, I ditched my latte and exchanged my flimsy sunglasses for an oversized dark pair. I grabbed an old baseball cap of Adam's from the door cubby, twisted up my hair, wrangled the amber lot as best I could, and shoved it into the hat. Then before I could change my mind, I locked up again and headed off to turn the tables on Beardman.

Given the size of Beaver Lake, I figured I'd start my search in the nearest quadrants: the area around the lake itself, the open green space to the right of it, the children's playground, and the Pavilion—a building that offered food, lockers, washrooms, and equipment rentals.

I went over to check the Pavilion first. No luck. Next, I scoped out the green space behind the Pavilion. Passersby strode along the pathways, friends chatted on benches, a few teenagers tossed a Frisbee, a group of kids played tag, and a couple canoodled under a blanket. Nothing unusual. And no sign of Beardman.

I turned right and walked over the incline to the kids' park. There, sitting on a bench off to the side, was Beardman finishing up a Happy Meal. With no backup, no plan, and nothing but chutzpah as a weapon, I took a deep breath and ambled over to him.

He jumped up when he noticed me approaching, and several French fries dropped down to his tatty black, slip-on dress shoes leaving behind a dotted path of ketchup along his cardigan and khakis.

I stopped about three feet from him, gave him a quick once-over for visible signs of a gun, and was relieved to find none. Then, not having formed an opening line yet, I glared at him.

"How did you find me?" he said.

Dumb luck didn't seem like a good thing to say, so I stuck with my glare bit until something better came to me. Besides, channeling my fear into anger did wonders for my nervous system; my heart was still racing but with more of a "who do you think you are?" vibe than a "fright and flight" one. I decided to just ignore his question and pose one of my own. "What makes you think you can stalk me and get away with it?"

"I wasn't stalking you," he said.

"Excuse me?" I said to him. "What do you call following me around and running me off the road?"

"I never ran you off the road."

"Hello. The other day in the Laurentiens. You know, with the car and the gun?"

His hands flew up to the whoa position. "What gun? There was no gun."

"So you admit you ran me off the road," I said.

He looked down at the ground, his cheeks growing pink. "Not intentionally. I just wasn't used to driving a stick," he paused before adding, "I borrowed the car from a friend." He looked up at me like that one point proved his case. "And I don't know anything about a gun. I never had a gun."

I shot him a disbelieving look. "Funny, because you left one in your car."

"It wasn't *my* car," he said. "If there was a gun in it, I have no idea how it got there."

I glared at him some more, but this time I wasn't biding time for something to say, I was trying to figure out if this guy was for real.

"Daddy?" a small voice said, and we both turned in its direction.

A young girl, maybe four or five years old, stood about two yards away. She was fair-haired, fair-skinned, and slight and wore overalls with a pink turtleneck and matching jacket. A white bonnet barely covered the top of her head. She held a plastic shovel in one hand and a pail half-filled with sand in the other. "Will Mommy be back soon?" she asked Beardman.

"Yes, sweetie," he said. "She just went to get you a snack."

"But, I'm not hungry," she said to him.

He glanced at me and then went over to her. "That's okay. You don't have to eat it right away, okay? Why don't you go back and play now. Daddy is talking to this nice lady."

She looked at me and chewed on her lower lip for a few seconds before offering me a shy smile, turning away, and trotting back to the sandbox.

Both calmed and intrigued by the interruption, I sat on the bench and waited for Beardman to join me. He sat at the other end, and with our height now more equalized, I noticed that his eyes were puffy and underscored with a darkness that appeared layered, like someone had played the old ink-stained kaleidoscope trick on him numerous times. Given that, his outfit, and the lack of gun, he didn't so much look like a crazed stalker as a worn out middle-aged man.

"That's my daughter," he said to me. "Sarah. She's the reason I've been following you."

"Okay," I said, wondering where this was going.

Beardman looked at his hands. "It took my wife and I over ten years to have her. The doctors said she was a miracle baby. She's certainly been a miracle to us. But now..." He let his eyes close briefly and sighed before continuing. "She's sick. She needs a bone marrow transplant, and my wife and I aren't the right match. We don't have other kids, and we've gone through all the candidates in our family. We need your help."

I empathized, but I was confused. What could I do to help? "I don't understand," I said.

"Aren't you looking for Puddles?" he said.

Puddles? Did he mean Francesca Bellinni's husband? In that case, I had to be careful what I said. I had client confidentiality to think about. "I might be looking for a guy named Puddles. Why?"

"Because he's our last hope."

"How's that?" I asked.

Beardman sighed again before answering. "He's my brother."

EIGHT

MY EARS PERKED up. "Your brother?"

"Yeah. Not the kind you see on birthdays and Christmas. But still family."

"When's the last time you saw him?" I asked.

"It must be over twenty years ago now. He'd stopped coming home long before he left his wife. We didn't even know about her until recently."

"What makes you think Puddles is your brother? The guy I'm looking for didn't have any family. And he's supposed to be from Italy."

Beardman shook his head. "Italy. Yeah. Try Lachute. It's the same guy. Puddles is a nickname he got when he was young, hanging out with the big boys, and trying to act tough. They laughed at him. Said he was so wet behind the ears a puddle formed at his feet. Even when Puddles smartened up and became a better con, the name stuck. Sort of became a badge of honor by then to show how far he'd come."

"So what's his real name?" I asked.

"Paul Bell."

So Paul becomes Piedro. Bell becomes Bellinni. That could work. Follows along the line that if you're going to tell a lie, it's easier to remember if you stick close to the truth. Probably Paulo would have been a little too close to the truth. Still, it wasn't enough to prove that the Puddles Francesca Bellinni was looking for was this guy's brother. I needed more.

"Aside from the nickname, anything else tie you to Puddles?"

"Yeah. A phone number. That's how we traced him. In the early years, Puddles would still call home every once and a while asking for money. He always called collect. Since my mother kept impeccable records for the farm, she has all her old bills. We tracked Puddles to a number at a place he worked called Guido's Garments."

Guido's Garments was the name of Francesca's father's business back then. That was a pretty tight connection.

"And I've got a picture if that helps," he said. He leaned forward, withdrew a wallet from his back pocket, slipped out a picture, and passed it to me. Really, it was two photos clipped off of a strip of pictures taken in a photo booth. They were black & white snapshots of a teenaged version of the same guy from Francesca's wedding album.

"You can hold on to those if you want," he said to me.

"No, that's fine," I said and passed the strip back to him.

He took it and put it away. "My name's Jim, by the way. Jim Bell."

"Good to meet you, Jim," I said shaking his hand as though we'd just met. Jim suited him. Definitely better than Beardman anyway. "I'm Lora." I paused while we released our hands. "So, I get why you want to find Puddles, but why stalk me?"

Jim shook his head as if he was trying to erase his actions like a child erases an etch-a-sketch. "I wasn't stalking you, just following you. When my wife and I found out that Puddles' wife was looking for him, it seemed like a golden opportunity. The plan was to follow you around until you found him."

"Ah, so that explains the paper with my picture and work info," I said.

"You saw that?"

"Yeah. Threw me for a bit of a loop. It had blood on it, too."

He rubbed the side of his head. "No wonder you thought I was stalking you," he said. "I don't know what I was thinking. This kind of stuff looks easy in the movies."

I let the movie comment slide, hoping the man was more distraught than delusional. "Why didn't you just hire a detective yourselves?"

"Can't afford it. We're still paying on fertility treatments we got in the U.S., and with Sarah's extra medical expenses, we're barely getting by."

"Why didn't you tell me about all this before? Why'd you keep running off?"

"I don't know. I felt foolish, I guess." He glanced at a woman now sitting near Sarah. "I should have listened to my wife in the first place. She wanted to tell you the truth straight off. She said you weren't just an investigator, but a social worker and that you'd understand."

His wife was right. I did understand. I watched his little girl sipping a juice box as she headed towards the slide. She was a little small, but I would never have guessed she was a sick child. She acted just like all the other kids. Lining up for her turn to climb the ladder so she could glide back down.

Jim seemed to read my mind. "She's having a good day today. This couple of hours of play will tucker her out, though. She'll have a good long nap when she gets home."

"So has everyone in your family been tested as a possible donor?" I asked.

"What there is of us. Besides Puddles, there's only my mother and my sister left. And my sister doesn't have any kids. My wife was an only child, and she was adopted at a time when all the files were closed, so she doesn't even know if she has any blood relatives. Even our friends have been tested. No luck."

"I've heard that hospitals keep records of potential donors. That even strangers can turn out to be good donors."

"That's right. And there's a long waiting list. We're on it, but it's a long shot."

I mulled things over for a minute then said, "and what about Puddles' daughter Lucia? Couldn't she be tested?"

Jim's face brightened. "Puddles had a daughter? Are you sure? We didn't hear anything about a daughter."

"Didn't you meet her when you met his wife?"

"We never got to meet his wife. When we first found out Puddles was going by the name Piedro Bellinni, I phoned the

Bellinni house a few times but got no answer, so eventually I left a message. No one called back for a couple of days. Then his wife's lawyer called saying Puddles was long gone and that his wife didn't want anything to do with us. I don't remember the exact wording the lawyer used, but it included things like emotional harassment and restraining orders."

"Well, Puddles does have a daughter," I said. "Lucia. She's in her early to mid twenties, I'd guess."

Before I had a chance to say anything else, Jim a.k.a. Beardman was up fast and dashing over to a blond woman with heavy bangs who I assumed to be his wife. "Joanne, Joanne," he called.

I followed behind him, and the woman turned.

"Joanne, he has a daughter," Jim cried. "Puddles has a daughter. She might match."

Joanne's face went from subdued to thoughtful. Almost cautious. Her eyes were nearly as tired as her husband's, but there was something else in them too. Skepticism maybe.

"Hi," I said to her. "I'm Lora. You must be Jim's wife."

She nodded. "Do you think she'd do it?" she asked me, her voice so sharp most people would have missed the hint of hope in it, and I realized it wasn't skepticism I'd seen in her eyes—it was battle fatigue. She was a warrior mom with one mission: to save her daughter.

"I don't know," I said. Which was true, I had no idea if Lucia would donate bone marrow or not. But I knew about going to battle for a good cause.

Sarah came over and held on to the back of her mother's leg. She peeked out at me from behind. I smiled and gave a little wave.

Joanne reached around and patted her daughter's shoulder. "I see," she said, catching her lower lip in her teeth and kneading it lightly.

"It's worth a try," Jim said.

"And how exactly are we supposed to get her to do that?" Joanne said. "Just knock on her door and say, 'Hi, you don't know us, but we're related to your father and we'd like to borrow a little bone marrow please.'"

Jim seemed a little embarrassed. "Joanne, please. Let's go sit and talk this over."

Joanne sighed and walked over to the bench with us. Sarah followed, still clutching at her mother. Joanne sat and swooped Sarah onto her lap in one automatic, seamless motion as only parents can. Sarah plugged her mouth up with her thumb and nestled against her mom. Jim sat down beside them, and I took the third spot.

After a few minutes of no one speaking, I ventured in. "I may be off base here, but wouldn't it be just as hard to convince your brother to donate as it would to ask Lucia?"

A lone tear eased down the side of Joanne's nose and dropped onto Sarah's sunhat. "It's all hard," she said.

Jim stretched his arm across Joanne's back and wrapped his fingers around her shoulder. "I think we should consider this." He turned his head towards me. "Lora, what do you think? *Do* you think she would do it?"

I really didn't know, but I didn't want to dash their hopes. "Her mother seems to be quite religious. A catholic. I haven't actually met Lucia, but I'd say family is important to her. After all, she wants Puddles at her wedding."

A hopeful look passed between them before Joanne spoke again. "But what about the talk about restraining orders? I don't think Puddles' wife wants to talk to us, let alone consider something like this."

She had a point. "Look," I said. "Why don't I see if I can set up a meeting? If you like, I can say that you guys turned up on the radar while we were searching for Puddles. I don't even have to mention the restraining order bit. Francesca doesn't have to know you told me about it."

"That sounds good. Let me give you a number where you can reach us." Jim took out his wallet again and extracted a business card. "Just call that number and leave a message."

I took the card and stood up.

Jim stood too. "Thanks. And about the Spitfire..."

"Yeah."

"Do you know what happened to it?" he said. "When I went back to get it, it was gone."

All this time, I figured he'd taken it back. If not, I didn't see the point of fessing up to my borrowing it. "You mean you don't have it?" I asked him.

He shook his head.

AS SOON AS I got back to my car, I called Camille on my cell to fill her in on what I'd learned. The words bubbled out of me, my pride and my excitement competing for airspace. I'd faced down my fear, gone after my man, and had real results to show for it. When I finally paused to catch my breath, it took nearly a minute to realize Camille wasn't responding. No "good job." No "way to go finding out the real identity of Puddles." No "what a relief Beardman won't be lurking around trying to hurt anyone." Not even a "what a shame about little Sarah." I knew we still had to find Puddles, but getting the Paul Bell name surely had to help.

"Are you still there?" I asked her.

I heard a slight rustling over the phone and then she spoke, her voice quiet. Too quiet. "So what happened to your phone this time?" she asked me.

"What?"

"Your cell phone. Since you called me now, I know it's not broken or out of service range. Why didn't you call me when you found the Volvo?"

"Oh, that," I said, sounding more flip than I intended—which I blamed entirely on the adrenaline feeding my excitement. I also blamed it for what came spilling out of me next. "I didn't call because I wanted to handle things myself. And I did. I got good information, too. I think I'm really suited to this PI stuff. I want to do this full time."

My words were greeted with silence again.

"Camille?" I said. "Did you hear me?"

"*Oui, oui,*" she said. "I'm here. I'm just waiting."

"Waiting for what?"

"To hear how you're going to convince Laurent to give you real field work. You're lucky he didn't fire you after the debacle in the Legault divorce case."

The Legault case was the one where the wife set up her husband to catch him cheating when it was really her who had been unfaithful throughout the marriage. I did the right thing deleting those phony pictures of him and the floozy. The husband was innocent and stood to lose a lot of money along with his dignity. Of course, I never told anyone I actually dumped the pictures, I just pretended to lose them, but the end result was the same; Mrs. Legault was none too pleased. And neither was Laurent. But, he never said anything about firing me.

"Would Laurent really do that?" I asked Camille.

"Fire an incompetent employee?" she said. "*Absolument.*"

Incompetent. I was *so* not incompetent.

"Fire you, little miss do-gooder, maybe not," she added. "For now. But he wouldn't give you a chance to pull another stunt like that again. It's not good for business."

Hmmm. So they did know about some of my rule bending.

"But that's not fair," I said. "That was just one mistake." Not that I thought it was a mistake, but I was trying to see it from their side.

She laughed. "Lora, *c'est une blague?*"

"*Blague?*"

"It means joke," she told me.

So I guess they knew about *all* of my rule bending. Except, hopefully, taking Marie Roy's jewelry. And now that I knew Beardman had nothing to do with that, I had no intention of telling them. I was glad I'd waited on that one and not run to them with my theory right away.

She went on. "Look, there's more to being a PI than good intentions. Laurent's not going to see your going after Beardman on your own as proof you've got what it takes. He's going to see it as you not following procedures. You didn't ask for backup. You didn't even phone in your location. Beardman was a known danger. A man who carried a gun. What you did was risky at the least and not just for you but for everyone around you."

I hadn't thought of that, but it made sense. "Well, yeah, but everything turned out fine. Nobody got hurt. And I helped the case."

"You got lucky," she said.

Now I went quiet, even my adrenaline rush deflated.

Camille seemed to sense my mood change over the phone. "Okay, if you're really serious about wanting to be a PI, I'll help you. But you'll need to forget your twisted Robin Hood act. And you'll need to work your way up. And you'll need proper training. And until you get it, no more acting on your own. Unless you're running errands, filling in paperwork or the other admin stuff, you'll need to be with me or Laurent."

That sounded fair. Except the Robin Hood bit. I didn't know if the label fit, but I couldn't help who I was. Being a social worker wasn't just a job I once had, it was ingrained in my DNA. My parents were activists. I was ten before I realized a peace rally was not a parade. And even longer before I knew that not all families spent Sunday afternoons visiting the animals at the pet shelter and dropping loose change into the ceramic dog in the lobby the way other people slipped coins into a church collection plate. I'd need to find a way to make it all work. "Okay," I said. "Where do I start?"

"You can start by weighing in about the temp. You think we should hire one?"

Uh oh, not this again. Now that I knew my job really might be in question, I definitely didn't want to get in the middle of the temp fight. But...if I had to pick a side, and it seems I did, it would be Laurent's. Mostly because I thought it seemed logical. Although the opportunity of scoring some points with him right about now didn't completely elude me either. The trick was not losing points with Camille in the process.

"It might be helpful," I said, all casual and noncommittal, not wanting her to take my answer as anything more than an impartial observation. "You know, just until Arielle comes back."

"I'm starting to think that too," she said. "The agency sent over résumés for three candidates. You think I should just pick one or have them in for interviews?"

"That depends. How long will the temp be needed?"

"I don't know," Camille said. "I guess until the feud between my mother and *ma tante* is over."

Since that was unpredictable, I figured worst case scenario ought to cover it. "Well, what's the longest time they ever went without speaking before?"

"Two years."

I shook my head at the phone. "In that case, if the agency allows it, I'd go for the interviews. It's a small office, so you might want to meet the candidates first and choose someone compatible." No small task, really. Finding someone who could duck a slinky with no more of a warning than the faintest shift in air velocity, or someone who would spend more time with her eyes in the file cabinet than on Laurent.

"*D'accord*," she said to me. "That's what I was thinking, too. I'll call and set it up. And after I'm done, I'll be over at your house. I should be there by seven."

"My house? What for?"

"You don't think I'm going to miss the first dinner with your new roomie, do you?"

NINE

I OPENED MY front door to a smell so vile my nostrils closed up shop. It didn't take long to pinpoint the source. Tina's animal print jacket hung from the iron coat rack, and her impossibly expensive Italian shoes lay discarded on the tile floor. Off to the side, a huge tote bag stuffed to the brim with more clothing fare sat half-blocking the inner door that separated the vestibule from the rest of the house. And the whole lot of it had been skunked by Tina's perfume.

I clamped a hand over my nose, rushed through, closed the door behind me, and made a beeline for my bedroom, taking the stairs two at a time. I could hear Adam's muffled voice as I passed his office door but didn't break my stride until I was safely inside my bedroom, where I let out my breath and sucked in some Tina-free air. Thankfully, Adam had had enough sense to close our door when Tina descended.

After my breathing normalized, I opened the window to keep the good stuff streaming in and stuffed one of Adam's t-shirts under the crack in the door to keep the bad stuff out. That done, I peeled off my clothes and went to the closet to change into home gear. I slipped into a pair of gray sweats and topped it off with a white tank top and matching hoodie. It felt soft and warm and comfy. It also made me look like a disheveled Q-tip with its bottom cut off and its tip crowned with a fur ball. What my body lacked in length, my hair made up for with volume. Balancing the two took effort. Ordinarily, I didn't worry about looking off-balanced around the house, but with Tina here, my equilibrium seemed crucial.

I went back to the closet and slid my hangers back and forth hoping some smashing new outfit had been born while I was out. No such luck. I reached for my old standby—an ankle-length sleeveless blue dress. It had a scoop neck and it was cut to cling in all the right places. Every girl had at least one dress like this. For special occasions. Like when the biggest flirt in the world came to stay with your boyfriend. I lifted the hanger and pulled the dress towards me. The bottom snagged on something and I bent down to release it before the material tore. I divided the clothes on either side and peered between. Two shiny green eyes peered back. It was Ping, curled up on the bottom of my dress. Hiding from Tina, no doubt. Poor cat. I stroked her back and gently eased my dress out from beneath her. She raised herself to sit on her haunches and blinked at me just as the bedroom door opened and Adam slipped in.

"I thought I heard you come home," he said and hugged me.

I stepped back because his shirt smelled of Tina. "Where is she?" I asked.

"She's in the backyard talking on her cell."

I started to change my clothes. "Good thinking. Keep her outside. You think she'd sleep in a tent? I'm pretty sure Laurent has one we could borrow. He may even have a port-a-potty."

Adam sat on the edge of the bed, pulled me down, and drew me to him. "I know she can be a pain, hon, but she's really hurting this time."

"You always think that. What makes this time any different from all the other times?"

"Because this time she really loves the guy."

I thought about that a minute. I tried to remember the times I'd seen Tina and her husband Jeffrey together. There was their wedding, of course. It had been smaller than Tina's previous weddings. Probably under ninety guests. And, she'd only had two bridesmaids instead of her standard six. The couple had seemed very taken by each other, but most couples do on their wedding day. Then there was the barbeque the summer after they married. We were never sure why we were invited because most of the guests were business acquaintances of Jeffrey's. Tina and Jeffrey had worked the room, mostly separately. When they were together, he had his arm around her waist a lot. At the time, it had seemed like part of the show. The happy successful couple show. Apart from those two occasions, Adam and I had dinner with them a handful of times. Nothing stood out in my mind about any of them.

"How do you know?" I asked him.

Adam laughed. "I just do."

"What about Jeffrey? Maybe he doesn't love her anymore. Or maybe he just can't stand to live with her. She did say it was Jeffrey who wanted the divorce."

He paused a moment. "That's true, she did say that." He looked at his hands. "But, isn't that all the more reason to give Tina some support here?"

I pulled away a little to get a look at Adam's face. "You're gonna meddle, aren't you?"

"I wouldn't say meddle."

"You already spoke to Jeffrey, didn't you? That's who you were talking to when I came in, isn't it?"

Adam's eyes met mine. "Yeah, I called him. He said it was good to talk to someone who understands. Someone who knows Tina. I'm going over there after dinner."

Hmmm. I was torn here. Normally I thought Adam was too quick to fix Tina's troubles. In the long run, I didn't think he was doing her any favors. I thought it would be better for her to learn how to take care of things herself. Not to mention that it would be better for us if she'd stop running to Adam every time she got a new wrinkle in her life. In this case, though, I wavered. If things were smoothed over between Tina and Jeffrey, she could go back home to the suburbs, and we wouldn't have to play nursemaids, accent on the maids part.

"Okay," I agreed. "Maybe it would help."

He leaned in and kissed me. "Doesn't everyone deserve to be as happy as we are?" he asked.

I kissed him back. "I guess." I steadied his face with my hands and we kissed a little longer. "Just how happy are we?"

There were footsteps on the stairs. Adam looked over at the door. "This is about it for now, but give me a few hours and I'll see what I can do." He gave me one last kiss before Tina knocked on our door.

"At least she knocks," I whispered.

The door opened before we had a chance to respond to the knock. "So, this is where you got to," Tina said as she approached the bed. "I was afraid you'd gone out."

Adam stood. "We were just talking about dinner," he said. "I thought you were on the phone."

Tina dropped herself onto the bed and assumed the fetal position. "I was. But your dog took a dump right beside the patio, so I came inside. My reception isn't very good in the house. So, I hung up and came looking for you."

I tried to muffle a sneeze and failed. I gave Adam my "get her out of here look."

"Bless you," he said to me and started to walk out to the hall. "I'm going down to start dinner."

Tina didn't make a move to get up.

Adam goaded her. "I guess Jeffrey will take the summer house too," he said.

Tina was up like a shot. "Over my dead body," she cried. She caught up with Adam. "Do you really think he's going to try that? I'll be left with nothing," she whined after him.

I whipped the blanket off the bed and checked the sheets below for Tina's perfume. I loosened the sheets from the mattress and pulled them off too. Damn that stuff's strong. On my way down to the basement to throw the bundle into the washer, I called over my shoulder into the kitchen. "It's four for dinner. Camille's coming."

"Okay," Adam said over Tina's droning voice.

I HAD JUST finished setting the table in the dining room when Camille arrived.

"What's that smell?" Camille asked as she passed through the entryway.

"Tina's perfume," I said.

Camille eyeballed the living room. "Where is she?"

"She's upstairs freshening up."

"You sure she's not embalming herself?"

I smiled. "You be good. She'll be down any minute."

Camille followed me into the kitchen and cheek-kissed Adam who was busy stirring pots on the stove. She put the tin she was carrying down on the counter. Adam and I both looked at it.

"It's a care package from my mother," she said. "Some little goodies for later."

Even though I was an adult, Camille's mom thought of me as an orphan and kind of adopted me as one of her own. Camille's family was like that—always taking care of people. It was one of the things I loved about them. My mom had been like that too. She was also Canadian, but her parents moved back to England when she moved to the States and married my dad, and I could only remember visiting Canada a handful of times when I was young. Now that I lived here, I really understood how much my mom's home country had formed the person she became and the person she taught me to be. I felt good here, like I belonged. And close to my mom. And when I found out that I could become a citizen because she was born here, I wanted that, too. I'd sent in my application months ago and couldn't wait for it to come through.

I lifted the lid off the tin to peek inside. Camille's mom made fabulous desserts. If we had been alone, Adam and I would have ignored the stuff in the pots and made a meal of the desserts.

"Any of them chocolate?" Adam asked Camille.

"*Ben oui*," she answered. "*Maman* would never send anything over without including something chocolate for you and something maple for Lora."

My eyes zeroed in on the maple tarts, and a flood of happy hormones surged into my bloodstream. I'd recently fallen in love with all things maple. It was a real delicacy in these parts. Beside the tarts, there were other pastries and several chocolate truffles set in the corner along with a few empty candy papers. No doubt the chocolates that hadn't survived the trip over with Camille.

"This is about done," Adam said, still chewing a strand of pasta he was testing.

He strained the pasta, and the three of us assembled the plates and set them on the table along with the salad before we took our seats.

"Isn't Tina coming?" I asked Adam.

"She should be. She knew we were eating at seven. I don't know what's keeping her."

"Should we wait?" Camille said.

I took a sip of water and straightened the cloth. "Let's give her a few minutes, but at least tell her it's on the table."

Adam got up, went to the bottom of the stairs, and called up to her.

No answer. He tried again. Still nothing. He went upstairs, and I picked up my fork and jabbed my salad. "I don't think it would matter if we started our salads."

Camille nodded, and we poked around at the bits of vegetables in our bowls.

"So, any luck yet tracing the Paul Bell name?" I asked her while we ate.

"*Oui.* As soon as Laurent punched it into the system a bunch of stuff came up. So far it all syncs with what Jim the Beardman told you, but there are still lots of gaps and nothing to show Puddles has been using the name since he left Francesca. It will take time to get more details," she said.

"How about the Spitfire? Any word on that?"

"Not yet. The police still have it listed as missing. But since we don't need it anymore to track Beardman Jim, it's more or less a police matter now. Especially considering the gun."

That was true, I guess. But the car's absence still gnawed at me. Probably mostly because it was taken on my watch. "What about the pictures we got from Miriam Tabor? We still need them or are there better ones online?"

"Nothing online. Nothing any newer anyway. But the ones we got are already scanned. We've got a bunch of copies now."

"I guess the originals could be returned tomorrow then. That's good. I get the impression that it was hard for Miriam to part with them," I said.

Camille swallowed before she spoke. "Either that or she didn't want us to see the album because of the note. When we go back to Guido's, I want another crack at Ingrid. If her leak about the Vladimir guy is any indication, the girl knows more about the goings on at Guido's than she does about the fashion."

I thought so, too. "Yeah, and about that note. When I was at Francesca's earlier I wasn't sure if I should've asked her about it. I never got the chance anyway, but you think I should ask her when I see her to talk about Sarah? And what about the falling out with her mom that Miriam mentioned?"

"The mom yes, the note no," Camille said. "I want to get a better sense of where it fits in before we let people know we have it."

That had been my inclination about the note too. Good to know I was right. Maybe I really was a natural at this PI stuff.

Camille went on. "Besides, now that we've got Puddles' name, more info should come rolling in soon. We'll know more tomorrow, but it's possible we won't need to figure out any of that. We may just luck out and find him happily living his life in a new city. Or even across town. Let's see how things look in the morning." She stretched and her eyes skipped over to the doorway before settling back on me. "How long you think you'll need to convince Francesca to tell Lucia about the bone marrow thing?"

With all the rush since I'd been home, I'd barely had time to think about what I planned to say to Francesca. The responsibility for handling it right weighed on me, though. A little girl's life could be at stake. "I don't know. I've never done anything like that before."

Camille shrugged. "You'll make it work. You always do. Then come by the office and we'll talk next steps." She pushed her empty salad bowl aside and centered her spaghetti in front of her. "How long do you think we should wait for the others?"

I was about to answer when a door creaked upstairs, and seconds later Adam and Tina came into the dining room. Adam's t-shirt was wet around the shoulder. Tina's eyes were a little puffy and her mascara was a little thick, otherwise her face was perfectly applied. Her blue silk blouse was tucked into ivory slacks. She waited for Adam to pull out a chair for her before she sat down and turned her attention to Camille. "It's so nice to see you again, Camille," she said, pronouncing the name Ka-mill instead of the French pronunciation of Ka-mee.

"You too," Camille said to her. "I was sorry to hear about your troubles."

Tina shook her head. "It's just unbelievable, isn't it?" She surveyed the table. "I see you've already started." She picked up her fork and twirled it in her pile of spaghetti. "It's just as well, I don't have much of an appetite."

We all nodded in understanding.

"Did I mention that Jeffrey will be made partner at his law firm? It's about fuckin' time, if you ask me. I told him just last month that if they didn't offer him partner soon he should take his legal sense and his client list elsewhere. Maybe even start his own firm." Tina paused to bring a mouthful of food to her mouth. "Then, not two weeks later, he tells me it's a done deal. They'll be making it official just before the Christmas holidays."

"That's great," I said, for lack of something better to say.

"Yeah, except I won't be around to see it. You know, a person doesn't make partner all by himself. I worked harder than any of the other wives. I even went out to lunch with his boss's hag of a wife. What a piece of work she is. All she could talk about was their latest house. Some little thing in Tuscany. Just a little getaway, she kept calling it. With just enough room for the grandkids to visit. She showed me pictures. It was out in the middle of a field or some such thing. Looked like the middle of nowhere to me. All grass, trees, and flowers."

Adam, Camille, and I exchanged looks of appreciation.

Tina ate as she continued. "Anyway, Jeffrey's nuts if he thinks I'm just going to let him get away with cutting me out. After all I did."

We had all finished eating and were just listening to Tina when Adam's eyes flicked to his watch. "I've got to step out for a bit," he said.

"Where are you going?" Tina demanded. "You can't just leave me all alone."

Adam worked to keep his voice even. "I'm just going out, Tina. And you won't be alone. Lora and Camille are here."

Tina let her fork drop onto her plate, and it rattled around some before the metal stopped colliding with the porcelain. Startled by the noise, Pong jumped up from her curled position at the end of the table and banged her head on the underside of a chair. She shook her head a few times until I reached out and massaged the sore spot.

"But, what am I supposed to do all night?" Tina said.

"What would you do if I stayed home?" Adam asked her.

Tina sat back in her chair and crossed her arms across her chest. "I don't know. Talk to you probably."

"Well you can talk to Camille and Lora."

"I know but..." Tina broke off.

Adam smiled. "Tina, you'll be fine for a few hours." He got up and started clearing the dishes.

Camille and I helped carry things into the kitchen and loaded the dishwasher. When the kitchen was more or less tidy, Adam gave me a kiss and headed out.

"I'll be back in a couple of hours," he said. "Dibs on all things chocolate." And he was gone.

I filled the sink with soapy water and started to wash the pots and pans. I tipped my head in the direction of the dining room, urging Camille to go in and talk to Tina. She made a face and pointed her finger at me. I returned the gesture, and we went a few more rounds before it broke into a rock, paper, scissors thing. In a rare moment of victory, I won and went back to my soapy suds while Camille headed into the dining room and sat down at the table across from Tina.

Tina glanced up, squished her eyes shut, and began bobbing her head up and down in small, fast motions. Tears ran down the sides of her nose.

Camille gave me a look then went around the table and tentatively patted Tina's back.

"I think he's having an affair," Tina blubbered.

Oh, no. The one call from a woman that other women couldn't ignore. Betrayal by a man. I dropped the pot I was washing back into the dishwater, grabbed a towel, and dried my hands on my way into the dining room. Tina was sobbing into her hands. I pulled up a chair, and Camille and I both waited. After nearly five minutes, Tina brought her hands down from her face. I handed her some Kleenex.

Tina dabbed her eyes and blew her nose. "This is just so full of shit. This has never happened to me before. I don't know what to do."

"Are you sure about the affair?" Camille asked her.

Tina nodded. "At first, I thought Jeffrey was just working a lot. You know, because of the partner stuff. But one night I needed to talk to him, and I called the office. One of the interns picked up and said Jeffrey had left hours ago. So I thought maybe we got our wires crossed, and he was at a dinner meeting or something. But then, when he got home I asked him how come he was so late and he said he was working at the office." She was crying quietly now. "It's happened several times since then. One time he didn't get home until almost three-thirty in the morning."

Camille and I looked at each other. Certainly sounded suspicious.

Tina was sobbing again. "I just don't know what to do."

I handed her another wad of Kleenex. "I'm going to get you some water. You're going to get dehydrated."

She reached for my arm. "Screw the water. I need a real drink."

Adam and I weren't big drinkers. The only alcohol we kept in the house on a regular basis was some cherry kirsch and a tiny bottle of rum, both of which I used for baking. Aside from that, we had a bottle of champagne in the basement and a bottle of vodka in the freezer.

I wasn't about to give up the champagne. "How about a screwdriver?" I asked her.

"If that's all you've got," Tina said.

Camille drummed her fingers on the table. "I could use one too," she said.

I went into the kitchen to make the drinks and decided to add in one for myself. When I got back, Camille and Tina had shifted into the adjoining living room and were both sitting on the loveseat. I placed the drinks on the coffee table, and they each reached out and took a glass. I sat down in the wicker rocking chair and adjusted the pillow behind my back. Ping appeared from out of nowhere, jumped into my lap, and curled into a ball that vibrated as she purred.

Tina drained her glass and set it down. "What really gets to me, is that I did everything for him. In bed, I mean. I did stuff I didn't even like."

Camille and I made faces at each other. Did we really have to hear about Tina's sex life? That had to be above and beyond our sisterly duties.

Tina went on. "I mean how much work is it supposed to be? I didn't mind buying the lingerie. I didn't even mind dressing up in the leather get-ups, but I drew the line at the maid outfits. Can you imagine *me* as a maid? I won't even tell you what he wanted me to vacuum."

Fabulous. Now I'd never get that image out of my brain.

"You are so lucky you have Adam," she said to me. "Adam's hot. Adam would never need to see you in crotchless panties to get off. Not that I would know what Adam's like in bed," she added quickly. "I just mean, he's a cool guy."

I forced a smile. I knew what she meant.

Camille finished the last of her screwdriver, got up, and headed for the kitchen. "*Ne t'inquiète pas*," she said to me when she saw the look on my face. Then she held up her glass and wiggled it back and forth. "*Deux secondes.*"

"What about that French guy you go with?" Tina called after her. "What's he like?"

Camille came to the doorway. "You mean Luc?"

"I don't remember his name. You brought him to that barbeque at my house. Remember, you came with Lora and Adam. He was real cute. Tall, thin, blond hair kinda long on top and short in the back. Really great cheekbones."

"Hang on a sec," Camille said. "Let me just finish this." A few minutes later, she came back in carrying a pitcher big enough for a Kool-aid party.

"That's a lot of screwdriver," I said.

She shrugged. "It's mostly juice and I put a lot of ice in it," she said. She refilled hers and Tina's glasses and topped up mine before she sat down. "Luc and I aren't a couple."

I raised my eyebrows, and she made a face.

Tina looked from me to Camille. "What? What am I missing?"

Camille scrunched her nose at me and laughed. "*Rien*. Nothing. Luc and I used to live together," she said, not bothering to mention their current understanding.

"So was he good in bed?" Tina asked.

Camille tucked her legs up under her and sipped her drink. "He's French," she said by way of an answer.

Tina took another swig of her drink. "Oh yeah, right," she said. "Well Jeffrey's not. But, I thought he was happy. I mean, why did he have to go out for something he got at home?"

"You don't know for sure that he's cheating," I reminded her.

Tina looked down at her hands. "I haven't told you everything. I haven't told you what I did."

Camille's eyes darted to mine.

"After the last time Jeffrey was late, I freaked out and ransacked his stuff. I went through everything. And I found a woman's name and number written on a napkin."

"There could be a simple explanation for it," Camille suggested. "A client maybe."

"I've tried calling it a bunch of times. It's a cell phone number, and I always get voice mail so I hang up."

"Have you asked Jeffrey about it?" I asked.

"I was going to, and then he threw this divorce at me. So I put two and two together. I mean, why else would he want a divorce?" Tina reached out to set her empty glass on the table and missed. The glass fell to the ground and rolled under the table.

Camille bent to retrieve it and passed it back to her.

"You know," Tina said. "I just realized we've been talking about me the whole night." She turned towards Camille. "How is your little business going?"

"The agency is going well. My brother and I make a good team."

True enough. When they weren't throwing the slinky around, they were fabulous.

"Isn't that nice," Tina yawned on the last word. "I don't have any brothers or sisters. I'm very close to Jeffrey's family, though. We have brunch at his parents' house every Sunday." Her lips started trembling. "I guess I'll lose them too," she said before the tears started again.

I wondered just what was going on between Tina and Jeffrey. It wasn't proven that he was having an affair, but clearly there were problems if he wanted a divorce. Yet, he was willing to talk to Adam about things. That showed some interest in a reconciliation, didn't it?

Tina's eyes grew wide. "I can't believe I didn't think of this before!" she said. "You run a detective agency, you could trail Jeffrey. Find out about this woman he's screwing around with."

Camille hesitated. "I'm not sure that's a good idea."

"Of course, it's a good idea. It's the perfect idea!" Tina was reenergized. "At least then I'd know who I was competing with."

I gave Camille a cautionary look.

"Look, I have a right, don't I?" Tina stood up. "I want to know who she is. I want to know what's so fucking special about her. And, if Jeffrey's going to leave me for her, then I shouldn't lose everything. I want to get the goods on him so I can fight him in court."

When we didn't respond right away, Tina went on. "If you guys won't help me, I'll just find someone else who will."

"All right. But under one condition. You sleep on it first," Camille told her, probably figuring Tina wouldn't remember this conversation in the morning. "If you still feel the same way tomorrow, come by the office in the afternoon and we'll talk about it."

Tina bent down and hugged her. "Oh, thank you. Thank you." Then she bent to hug me. "I feel so much better. I feel like I'm doing something about it, you know." She stood again. "And, I've got all the info too. The dates he was out fooling around and the napkin with the woman's name." She was waving her arms about and really getting into it. "Maybe I'll go by the house in the morning after Jeffrey leaves for work and search around for more evidence." She turned to Camille. "Do you have a business card or something with the agency's address?"

"Of course," Camille said, making her way out to the hall with Tina following behind her. Camille picked up her purse from the table, opened it, and sifted around. "*Une minute là.*" She pulled out her keys, her phone, a small change purse, an oversized envelope, and finally the card holder. She extracted a business card from the holder just as her keys and the envelope spilled to the floor. "*Merde.*"

Tina picked up the keys and started to push the contents of the envelope that had nudged out back in. "Hey, what's this? Pictures? Can I look at 'em?" she said while she was already pulling out the pictures of Puddles. "Hey this guy looks just like the guy from Jeffrey's firm. Oh, what's his name? I think he works in corporate. He was at the big wing ding last summer. Now, why can't I think of his name? Anyway, he looks just like him, only young. Like a son maybe." She handed the envelope back to Camille. "What are you doing with his picture?"

TEN

THE HOUSE WAS quiet. Camille had long since gone home, and Tina was finally tucked into bed in the pullout couch in Adam's office. Since sleep wasn't going to be happening for me anytime soon, I waited until I could hear her snoring before I went downstairs for a snack and a think.

I pulled out the bin of treats Camille had brought, sat at the kitchen table, and let the sweet goodness of maple fill my mouth, hoping it would squeeze out the thoughts buzzing around the rest of my head. Tina's lead about Puddles had me excited, but I knew it wouldn't necessarily help us find him any sooner. And even though we had a bit of leeway in the time department before Lucia's wedding, where Sarah was concerned, time was running out. If I wanted to help her, I needed to focus on the one relative already present and accounted for—Lucia. Which meant I had to convince Francesca to let Lucia know about the search for her father and her cousin's illness. And I needed to do it in the morning. Less than nine hours from now I'd be face to face with Francesca, and I still didn't have a clue what to say.

I fed my brain some more sugar and tried to focus.

"You're up?" Adam said, his voice startling me out of my thoughts and nearly making me drop the maple tart I was munching on.

"Yup." I pointed to the pastry container. "Hungry?"

He joined me at the little round pine table, glanced at the unwashed pots and pans still on the counter, and reached for a truffle. "Looks like you had some night."

"Oh, yeah. And from the looks of it, so did you." The crows feet around his eyes were deeper, his scruff seemed to have doubled, and his clothes were rumpled and dank smelling.

"I'd forgotten what a dweeb Jeffrey can be," Adam said and popped truffle number three into his mouth.

"So, is he having an affair?"

Adam's head snapped back a little. "Where did that come from?"

"Tina thinks he is. She thinks that's why he wants a divorce."

Adam chuckled. "Those two are some pair. That's what Jeffrey thinks about Tina, that she's having an affair with one of the partners in his firm. The Bennett guy."

"But, what about all his late nights?"

Adam got up to get a drink from the fridge. "He's been seeing a therapist about it. Some woman. She also recommended he relieve some stress through exercise so sometimes he goes to the gym."

"Hmmm."

Adam walked over and leaned against the counter. "He really is worked up over it, though. A couple of times, he followed Bennett around after work to see if he'd meet up with Tina."

"And did he?"

"Nope, not once. He even camped outside the guy's house one night and fell asleep until like two or three in the morning."

That all explained Jeffrey's late nights. "How come he thinks Tina's having an affair with Bennett?"

"Jeffrey claims that Tina has been hanging out with people from his office more and more over the last few months. One time when Jeffrey came back from an appointment, he found Tina in Bennett's office and they were being all touchy feely."

"Why didn't he just ask Tina about it?"

"He did. He said she just blew it off as ridiculous, said that she was just making the rounds and shmoozing to help his career."

I rubbed my hands together over the pastry box to get off some crumbs. "And, he didn't believe her?"

"Nope."

I munched on a bite of my third tart and swallowed. "That's why he wants a divorce? Because he *suspects* she's having an affair? Isn't that a bit drastic?"

Adam sat down again. "If it was anyone but Tina and Jeffrey, I'd say yeah. But, with those two," he shook his head.

"Do you think she is?" I asked.

"No. She would have told me. She's never held back from me before. Besides, she's too upset about this."

"So, did you tell Jeffrey that?"

"Sure, but he doesn't believe it. He's already convinced himself that it's true. He's hurt and angry."

"Sounds just like Tina."

Adam took a chocolate Danish out of the box. "I know."

Before I gave in to temptation again, I closed the pastry container and put it back in the fridge. "She wants to hire C&C to spy on Jeffrey and his lover."

"Really?"

"Yup."

"You know, that may not be such a bad idea," Adam said.

"Are you serious? It doesn't sound like there's anything to investigate. All they need to do is have one honest talk and all this could be settled."

"That's true," Adam agreed. "But it's not going to happen. Not with these two."

I sighed.

"Look, neither one of them is going to give in now. But, if they get objective proof that there's no evidence of any affairs, then they'll have to talk."

I didn't feel convinced. Plus, I couldn't rouse any enthusiasm for helping Tina with her fake problems when I had real ones of my own.

Adam moved closer and wrapped me in his arms. "It may also be the quickest way to get Tina back home," he said.

I liked the sound of that. "Okay, but it's ridiculous."

CAMILLE AND I had agreed to meet first thing the next morning to get on Tina's lead about Puddles. When I awoke bleary eyed and achy at seven, I decided first thing could be a subjective term, so I went back to sleep until eight. Turned out to be a good move because by eight Tina had already left, presumably to look for more goods on Jeffrey, and Adam had gone to a meeting.

I showered, dressed in jeans and a blue long-sleeved cotton jersey, and went downstairs to make a breakfast of the leftover tarts while I fed the pets and let out the dog. I checked the phone messages when I was done. Not a one. Ergo no more excuses to delay calling Francesca and asking if I could drop by on my way into the office. She agreed to see me, but said she was running errands and wanted to meet at Smithy's instead.

Smithy's was an upscale dry cleaners in Westmount—a predominantly English neighborhood valued for its hilly, tree-lined streets and posh properties. It made a convenient nearly midpoint meeting place between Francesca's neighborhood and the middle class Notre-Dame-de-Grâce area where I lived. Smithy's sat on a commercial block wedged between a hair salon and a shoe store. I lucked out and got a parking spot right in front of the cleaners with a full view of the glass front. No sign of Francesca yet, so I cracked my window and went into wait mode, still mulling over what I would say.

Five minutes later, a black sedan pulled in. Francesca stepped out and waved me over.

I locked up and headed towards her car. "Thanks for meeting me," I said to her.

Francesca adjusted the silk scarf that covered her hair. "Let's get out of the wind," she said and ducked back into the sedan.

I opened the passenger door and got in beside her. The interior was roomier than I expected. The seats were a smooth burgundy leather. The dash had a few more gizmos than mine and a sound system that I would wager cost more than our entire home entertainment center.

"I don't have a lot of time," Francesca said. "Lucia's soon to be in-laws are dropping by for brunch to discuss some wedding plans.

What did you need to see me about? Is it the attic? Because I haven't decided what to do about that yet."

I had hoped for a little small talk first. It wasn't easy to tell someone that her husband had invented an alias, let alone that his family was looking to borrow a little bone marrow. "No," I began, "It's not about your break-in. There's been some news about your husband."

Francesca rested her hands on the steering wheel, one gloved hand folded over the other.

I turned to her and eased into an explanation of Puddles' dual identity, checking her expression as I spoke to gauge if she could handle what I was telling her. Midway through, she looked unfazed, so I went on to give her his real name and fill her in on what I knew about his background. At that point, her face lost a little color.

"That's not possible," she said.

Okay. In her shoes, probably I'd be going the denial route too.

She blinked at me with blank eyes while she removed her gloves and reached up to unbutton her coat. The top button stuck. She worked it a few times then pulled it free, the button popping off and flying to the floor mat. She didn't seem to notice as she went to work on the next button and sent her fingers further down until her coat was open to the waist. Beneath her coat, she grabbed the top of her turtleneck and stretched out the fabric repeatedly as far as it would go.

I worried that she might pass out and was relieved when some pink returned to her cheeks. "I'm sorry," I said. "I know this must be hard to hear."

She nodded. "Are you sure? I mean you could be wrong, right?"

I thought about what Camille had said about Laurent's verification so far. "I don't think so."

"What was the name you said Puddles went by?" she asked me.

"Paul Bell."

"No, that doesn't sound right," she said, shaking her head. "It doesn't even sound Italian."

"I don't think it is," I said, taking note that her skin tone was better, her breathing normal. Still, my social worker side begged me to go slow with the next phase of things. "There's more. He has a brother who'd like to meet you."

"A brother?" she said, her voice rising.

If Jim hadn't told me about his attempts to contact her, I would have believed she had no idea Puddles had any family. But then again, she may not have believed the claim and since she never talked to Jim, she wouldn't have known about Puddles' other identity. "That's right," I told her.

"And he wants to meet me?"

"Yes. Puddles' brother is also trying to track him down for his own personal reasons. He has a sick little girl who Puddles may be able to help."

Francesca repositioned herself, turning her upper body towards me. "What does that have to do with me?"

I carefully explained a bit about Sarah's illness and how Lucia might be able to help.

She stared at me blankly again. "Lucia?"

"Yeah," I said, whatever confidence I had left ebbing the more I went on. "You know, because the girls are cousins."

Francesca's face faded to white again and she turned away. "No," she said. "This is too much. Forget it."

"Are you saying you don't want to meet Puddles' brother?"

"No. I don't. I don't believe it. He told me he was an orphan with no family left."

Her reaction was completely understandable. Most people would probably be touchy when it came to helping out unknown relatives of the lying husband who abandoned them. Francesca had every right to refuse. And, I had no grounds for approaching Lucia directly because that would violate the client confidentiality clause—especially when Francesca had explicitly requested that Lucia know nothing about the investigation. Not even *I* could bend that agency rule; at best it would ruin C&C's reputation, at worst, it would shut them down. If Francesca didn't want to help Jim and his family, my hands would be tied which would leave Jim back exactly where he started.

Problem was, even though I didn't know much about Sarah's illness, I knew enough to know that time was of the essence, and I wasn't quite ready to give up either. As much as I felt bad for what Francesca had to be going through, I couldn't let myself lose sight of the greater good. So I decided to bluff and hoped Francesca would think I was serious and cave. "Well, I suppose I could just talk to Lucia myself," I said.

"Talk to Lucia about what?"

"About the little girl. Surely, Lucia would want to know."

"No," Francesca said, her eyes narrowing.

"But, we're talking about a child's life, Mrs. Bellinni. I'm sure if Lucia was ill, you would move heaven and earth to help her. You must understand how her parents feel."

Francesca stared out the windshield and said nothing. When she finally turned her head back in my direction, I noticed an increased moistness in her eyes. "Look," she said. "I don't go around telling this to everybody, but I was pregnant with Lucia before I married Puddles." She paused to take a deep breath. "I was only seventeen, and I had an affair with an older man. A married man as it turned out. I was young and naïve and I thought he'd leave his wife for me. When he didn't, I got scared and told my mother. I begged her to help me and not tell my father because he was a devout Catholic. He had a standing in the community." She lowered her head. "And I knew he'd never forgive me.

"But, my mother did tell my father, and he was livid," she said. "I had never seen him like that. He wouldn't speak to me for a week. Then one day he brought Puddles home from work with him. Puddles was one of his favorite employees. He adored him. It wasn't exactly an arranged marriage, but it was close enough. We were married two weeks later."

A "wow" slipped from my mouth before I could stop it.

"Lucia doesn't know about it, and I want to keep it that way. She worshipped Puddles. And Puddles was a wonderful father. A good husband too, and I grew to love him." She looked up at me and held her gaze steady. "But now I'm not sure who he was anymore, and

Lucia can't help the little girl, so maybe we should just drop the whole thing."

WHEN I GOT to the office, Camille and Laurent were in the kitchen finishing off a breakfast of café au lait and croissants. Laurent was wearing black jeans and a white t-shirt and his hair was artfully unkept. Camille had on slacks and a black turtleneck. Her hair was slightly gelled and she had put on a dab of pink lipstick and some black mascara.

I stood in the kitchen doorway. "You two look like an old ad for one of those specialty coffees."

"I'd only do one for real coffee. None of that decaffeinated stuff," Camille said. "There's no point in drinking it. It's castrated."

Laurent winced, returned his mug to its saucer, and pushed the whole thing aside. "I hear we have a new case," he said. "That friend of yours. The woman with the squeaky voice."

I smiled. He meant whiney. "Yes, Tina. She wants us to investigate her cheating husband." I sat down on one of the wood chairs and put my purse on the table. After my chat with Francesca, I'd nearly forgotten about Tina. "Trouble is, he's not having an affair. Turns out he wants a divorce because he thinks *she's* having an affair."

Camille laughed. "Is that what he told Adam?"

"Yup. Adam met with Tina's husband Jeffrey last night," I explained and brought them up to speed on the situation.

Camille shook her head when I was done. "Sounds like an episode of *Three's Company*."

She was right. It did, but I was surprised at her reference. "How do you know about *Three's Company*?"

"*Mais voyons*, Lora. We're not barbarians. And we don't all live in igloos either. When I was a kid, the reruns were dubbed by French actors and ran on English channels too."

Naturally. I kept forgetting that Canadians knew so much about American culture and TV. Mostly because I didn't know much about theirs and was still learning. Especially when it came to old stuff. When Adam talked about TV shows from his childhood, he knew all about Sesame Street, Mister Rogers, and Reading Rainbow. But I had no clue about Mister Dressup, Magic Tom, or The Friendly Giant. Part of the fun of living in a new country is soaking up the culture—even pop culture—but sometimes it was comforting to be reminded of what we had in common. Even if it was just a goofy sitcom.

"Anyway, Adam thinks we should go ahead and investigate things for Tina," I said. "He thinks that's the only way she'll believe that nothing's going on."

"But, what about Jeffrey?" Laurent asked. "He sounds just as convinced about Tina's cheating."

"I guess Adam's hope is that if one of them would let go of the affair thing, then they'd talk. But, as long as they both feel scorned, neither is willing to show weakness by approaching the other."

Camille sat back in her chair and crossed her arms. "Ah, battle of the egos."

I shrugged. "I guess. The good part is that it gives us a chance to hang out around Jeffrey's company and look into the Puddles case." I assumed Camille had already filled Laurent in about the latest development.

"That's what we were just talking about," she said. "Laurent's going to check into Finestein, Bennett, and Fitch to see if Puddles is listed as an employee under any of his names. And I dropped Miriam's pictures by Guido's on my way in. Ingrid had classes today so she wasn't there, but I'm still keeping her on the to do list for later in the week."

Camille went on to say something about having picked up another nice sample while she was at Guido's. A blouse to go with the scarf. I figured if the case went on much longer, she might get herself a whole outfit.

"Sounds nice," I said but my heart wasn't in it. I was still thinking about losing Lucia as a possible donor for little Sarah.

Camille nodded towards me. "*Qu'est-ce que t'as, toi?*"

I told them about my conversation with Francesca.

"That's too bad," Laurent said when I was done. "But, remember, Lucia may not have agreed to get tested anyway."

That was true.

"Or, she may not have been a match," Camille added.

Also true.

Camille drummed her fingers on the table. "But are you also saying that Francesca wants to stop looking for Puddles?"

"Seems like it," I said.

Laurent and Camille exchanged a look. Not one of their snide sibling ones. The other kind. The all-business kind.

I felt something harden at the base of my stomach. "What?"

Another silent conversation passed between them before Camille said to me, "if Francesca called off the case, then there's nothing more to do."

"What do you mean nothing more to do? We still need to find Puddles."

"*Mais non.* Not if Francesca doesn't want to pursue things," Laurent said. "Then the case is closed, solved or not. We no longer have a client."

"What do you mean?" I said.

Camille leaned forward. "A client, Lora. You know, someone who pays us for our services."

I was getting it now. If Francesca dropped the case, we would be working for Jim and Jim had no money. My budding PI businesswoman side totally understood their position. But social worker Lora would have none of it. I was going to keep working this case one way or the other. I knew C&C took on low-income clients from time to time on a sliding scale, so I tried that tack first. "I'm sure Jim could pay something. You know, a reduced fee."

"How reduced?" Camille asked.

Probably very. "I'm sure we could work out something fair," I told her, smiling my best "really it's true" smile.

She shook her head, not buying it for a minute, got up, and headed towards her office. "Okay. We'll leave it open for now," she said over her shoulder. "But you'll be the one talking to Jim about billing."

ELEVEN

ABOUT AN HOUR and a half later, Laurent came over to Arielle's desk where I had decided to make myself useful by doing a bit of paperwork and organizing the piles of unattended mail. He waved at me to join him in Camille's office.

"Turns out Finestein, Bennett, and Fitch has three local offices," he said. "One main office downtown and two more in the boonies— one in suburban territory and the other near Dorion. None of the branches has an employee record under either of Puddles' names."

"Did you check the archives?" Camille asked.

"*Oui.*"

"Maybe he's going by another name. I guess when Tina gets here we should ask her which office the Puddles look-alike works in," I said, scanning the paper Laurent was holding with the company info.

"She did say he works in corporate," Camille said.

I nodded. "Yeah, but that could mean a few things. Like it could be corporate law or could be that he works in admin."

"What time is Tina coming by?" Laurent asked.

Camille headed to the kitchen. "I guess sometime soon. We should eat lunch before she gets here and I lose my appetite." She pulled open the second drawer down in the bank of drawers beside the sink and took out an order menu. "How about Chinese?"

AT NEARLY ONE-THIRTY Tina arrived. Without bothering to ring the bell, she came right on in. One of us must have left the door unlocked. Old habit. Since Arielle stopped coming in we usually locked it.

"Hellooo," Tina called out.

Laurent tipped his chair back and peered down the hall. "It's your friend," he told me.

We had been idling over green tea in the kitchen while Camille was in her office making more calls.

Tina walked straight through to the kitchen looking surprisingly fresh and alert. She had on her full face in warm fall colors. Her hair hung free and bouncy over her suede coat. Below, she had on an animal print mini-skirt, black sheer stockings, and suede shoes that matched her jacket. Laurent was already up and easing open the window to temper Tina's perfume.

"Hi," I said to her.

She shrugged out of her jacket, revealing a tight black nylon t-shirt beneath. She ran a hand over what I hoped was a fake fur collar before resting the jacket on the back of a chair. "Your receptionist was out," she said, sitting down. "So I just came right on in."

Laurent turned back and leaned against the counter. Tina's breath caught at the sight of him. It took her a full minute to pull her eyes away.

"How was your morning?" I asked her.

Her eyes flicked to Laurent again and then held mine with the same look mothers gave children when silently reminding them of their manners. Laurent and Tina had already met, but either she didn't remember or she just wanted an excuse to shake his hand.

"Laurent, you remember Tina," I said.

"Yes, of course," he said making no move to greet her formally.

Tina looked a little disappointed. Probably wanted the handshake, not the introduction. She recovered herself and threw him a big smile. "How kind of you to remember me," she said with a lilt to her voice. "What a charming accent you have. French people always have a way of making English sound so much nicer, don't you think?"

She'd never said that about Camille's accent. I looked at Laurent. I could tell he was trying to decide if he should play along or leave it be.

I tried to bring things back to focus. "Tina, did you bring the name of that woman you mentioned the other night? The one you found written on that napkin?"

She reached for her purse. "I've got the bitch's...," she paused and flicked her eyes in Laurent's direction before continuing, "er, the woman's name and number right here." She pulled out a small Ziplock bag containing a collection of items that clanked together. She unzipped the purple seal and took out a notepad. "I wrote everything down." She flipped a few pages. "Here it is. And, I've included the dates that Jeffrey was late too." She passed the pad to me.

I read the name. Hannah Bloomstone. Her name was familiar to me. Even though I couldn't officially belong to the local social workers' association, I still kept abreast of the community and recognized her from that. She was a psychotherapist now, but she used to be a social worker. She seemed to have a good reputation in both fields. She had worked for social services for nearly twenty years, then gone back to school and became a therapist. She'd been practicing for about a decade. Unless Jeffrey really was having an affair and he had a thing for older women, it was a good bet that she was his therapist.

I checked the other notes Tina had written. The next page had a list of dates and times. Presumably the late days. There was also a page of store names with money amounts written beside each name. Then there was a page that listed clothing and another page with an odd mix of things ranging from food items to cologne.

"What's this?" I asked Tina.

She glanced at the page. "That's a list of some of the new things Jeffrey's been buying. Everybody knows that when a man starts dressing up and caring more about his appearance, he's having an affair." She sat back. "He can't get things by me. I'm always thinking."

I caught Laurent smiling.

"And what about this list?" I held the pad out towards her and pointed to the page of store names.

"Those are credit card charges that he made. He never told me about any of the stuff he bought. One of them is even for a florist, and I never got any flowers."

I thought that if you matched the list of new items Jeffrey bought with the credit card records, you'd pretty much explain everything, but it was probably pointless to bring this to Tina's attention.

"This is a good start," I said for show. "Can we keep this pad?"

"I don't know," she said. "It's the only record I have of things."

Laurent walked over and took the notebook out of my hand. "I'll just run and make a copy."

I had to hand it to him. That was a smooth exit.

Tina leaned forward after he'd left the room and wrapped her fingers around my arm just above my wrist. "That man is gorgeous," she whispered. "And that accent. Yum. Is he married?"

"No."

She leaned back and let out a long breath. "If I wasn't married, I'd go for him myself," she said. It took all of five seconds before she added, "Of course, I might not be married for long."

I pointed to the Ziplock. "What's with the rest of that stuff?"

She reached for it. "Oh, that's my evidence bag." She picked out a crumpled paper and held it up. "See, this is the napkin I was telling you about." She put it back and resealed the bag. "I found a bunch of other stuff too. Some matchbooks from places we've never been together, some Altoids, a fancy lighter that certainly doesn't belong to me, even a pack of Virginia Slims and Jeffrey doesn't smoke."

A door opened, and bare heels pounded on the wood floor. Camille blew into the kitchen and headed for the cabinet beside the fridge. She yanked the door open, withdrew a box, and closed the door with a quick jab of her hip while her hands fiddled with the lid of the box. She got it open, fingered the contents, finally popping a round brown mound into her mouth. I tilted my head to read the side of the box. Ah, assorted. She must be desperate. Camille didn't like filled chocolates, she was a solid sort of girl. Preferably dark and imported.

I waited until the chocolate had time to melt a little before I ventured the obvious question. "Something wrong?"

Her glare softened a little when I came into view. "*C'est ridicule!*" she said. "She's not coming back. She says until my mother apologizes to her mother, she won't set foot in here."

By the "she" I figured she meant Arielle, her cousin and errant receptionist. "And, of course, your mother won't apologize," I said.

"*Ben non.*"

"Well, Arielle will have to come back sooner or later. It's her job. She needs the money," I reasoned.

"That's just it. She's taken another job. She's gone to work at the company where her boyfriend works."

"What's she doing there?"

Camille came over, set the chocolate box on the table, and sat down. "I don't know, something clerical I suppose, probably reception like she does here."

Tina eyed the chocolates. Camille noticed and pulled the box closer to her, encircling it with a protective arm.

"Doesn't sound like she's much of a loss," Tina said.

I cringed. Doesn't Tina know rule number one: never insult someone else's family no matter how much that person is complaining about the said family member. I gathered up the teacups on the table and took them over to the sink before Camille had a chance to throw one.

Camille drummed her fingers on the table. "Excuse me?" she said to Tina.

Tina looked straight at her. "Your cousin. She doesn't sound like much of a loss. You said she was only a clerk."

Camille was silent.

Tina continued, "I mean, how hard can it be to find another receptionist? It's not brain surgery."

I could have sworn I heard a door creak. Laurent *was* taking an awfully long time to make a few copies. Coward! At least I was braving the front lines, albeit from over by the sink.

"Are you saying my cousin isn't smart enough to be a brain surgeon?" Camille said.

Tina laughed. "It's an English expression. Maybe you don't know it. I just meant that being a receptionist isn't very hard. All you do is answer phones and greet people. I'm sure you'll find someone else." Tina pulled a compact from her purse and flipped it open. She used the mirror to check her makeup.

"So, you've been a receptionist then?" Camille asked her.

Tina snapped the compact closed. "No."

"Yet, you're so sure it's an easy job."

"Well, sure." Tina got out her hairbrush and brushed her hair. "Everybody knows it's easy. Really, you'll find someone else."

Camille gave me her "is she for real" look, probably deciding Tina wasn't worth the energy of a good argument. I shrugged and crossed back to sit at the table.

Tina dropped her brush back into her bag and closed it. "Anyway, if you really want her back, just tell your mother to apologize."

I marveled at Camille's restraint. She was as still as prey hiding from a predator in plain sight. I knew how hard that must be, especially with all the caffeine and sugar from the chocolates undoubtedly rushing through her veins. Her eyes squinted, though, and there was a definite crispness in the air.

Laurent came into the kitchen and passed Tina's notepad back to her. She held it to her cheek for a moment like a groupie with a rock star autograph.

"Thanks," she said. She stood up, tossed the pad into her purse, and started to gather her things. She pushed her Ziplock bag across the table to me. "I should leave this with you guys. See what you can make of it. I really need to get going. I've got a little date with a rather gossipy colleague over at Jeffrey's company. I'm meeting him for drinks."

I could see how Jeffrey might misinterpret that, but the thought seemed to have escaped Tina. What's more, she hadn't considered that a gossip who was perfectly willing to rat out his colleagues would be just as eager to grease the mill with news of her and Jeffrey's troubles.

She handed Laurent her coat and turned her back to him holding one arm out to her side and back a little, waiting for him to hold the coat open for her. Laurent held the coat up for her as far from his body as his arms would allow. She put her arms in the sleeves and paused to see if he would adjust the coat across her shoulders. When he didn't, she took hold of the fur on either side of the collar and shook it gently so the coat would settle.

I didn't want her to leave without finding out more about the Puddles look-alike. "Tina, the other day you said you'd seen a guy who looked a lot like the man in the picture Camille had in her purse. Remember?"

She nodded. "Sure, the guy from Jeffrey's office party."

"Do you remember which branch he was from?"

She tipped her chin up in thought. "Umm, I think it was the small one. The one outside the city."

Laurent was washing the perfume from his hands. "In the suburbs?" he asked over his shoulder.

"No. Not the suburbs. Some town. I don't remember the name. I'm really bad with names." She checked her watch. "I really have to run. Don't want to be late for my date." She winked. "Anyway, I'll see you at home later," she said to me. "We can talk some more then, okay? Oh, and do you think you could have supper ready by six-thirty? It really is better for my digestion if I eat at my normal dinner time." Before I could answer, she started for the hall then stopped in the doorframe and turned. "Oh, are you guys going to do a stakeout?"

"A stakeout?" I asked.

"Yeah," she said.

"Of who?" Laurent asked.

Tina giggled. "Of Jeffrey, of course. Isn't that what you professionals do? You know, track the suspect and catch him in the act. I really should get pictures. You know, just in case I have to go to court. I don't mind paying extra." She opened her bag and took out her checkbook. "Which reminds me, I forgot to ask what your fee is." She pressed the button on the top of her pen so the tip would poke out and held the pen aloft. She looked from Laurent to Camille and back again.

"It's hard to say what the exact fee will be. We don't know just what will be involved in the investigation," Camille explained. "Usually, we start out with a retainer and then bill the rest later."

"That sounds fine. Will one thousand be enough?"

Considering we wouldn't really be doing anything, that sounded like more than enough to me.

"Better make it two," Camille said.

TWELVE

A FEW HOURS later, I got home lugging a heavy heart and a bag of leftover Chinese food. I'd spent part of the afternoon procrastinating until I couldn't put off talking to Jim about Lucia any longer. Without going into details, I told him that she would have to be crossed off the list of suitable donors for Sarah. I knew my disappointment couldn't possibly rival his, but I felt crummy about it all the same. I especially felt bad for suggesting it and getting his and his wife's hopes up in the first place only to dash them less than a day later.

The state I found my house in did nothing to improve my mood either. I made my way past several dry cleaner bags and a plastic shoe bag that dangled from the hooks in my vestibule as I tried not to stumble on the various shoes that littered the floor. Then I squeezed by a stack of boxes piled against the wall at the base of the stairs before I could get to the kitchen.

I set the bag of food down on the counter, slipped my jacket onto the back of a chair, and felt a moment of gratitude that the kitchen remained free of Tina's possessions before I headed upstairs to see if Adam was home. At the top of the stairs I found his office door closed. The sound of music wafting out let me know he was deep in creative think mode, so I rapped softly on his door to let him know I was home and headed into the bathroom to wash off my day.

The bathroom was small and befitting a house nearing a hundred years old. A claw foot tub stood to one side with a free-standing shower curtain rod encircling it, and a toilet paired with a pedestal sink took up the main wall. All the fixtures were white. The floor had tiny hexagon tiles in a white mosaic pattern set off by the occasional black tile. The walls were painted, not tiled—the lower half a deep maroon red and the upper part cream to match the wood border that separated them. A large window above the toilet had crisp unbleached linen curtains that matched the shower curtain and were pulled back on either side. Hardware was silver and porcelain. Cream towels hung from fat, curved stainless steel rods. And, Adam had put up a narrow glass shelf that ran the length of the toilet and sink. The shelf was now cluttered with tiny travel bottles of shampoos, conditioners, beauty creams, and goodness knows what else. None of it belonged to me and none of it smelled good.

I washed up quickly and stepped back into the hall, nearly bumping into Adam who was just coming out of his office.

"Where's Tina?" I asked him, trying not to let my voice betray my sense of invasion.

"I don't know," he said. "She dumped off some stuff late this morning and then went out. I thought she was with you."

"She was for a while in the early afternoon, then she went off to meet someone from Jeffrey's office. She was on the trail of some dirt on Jeffrey."

"That's our Tina. The little girl scout. No bread crumb unturned," he said.

I went into the bedroom to put some moisturizer on my face, and I traded in my jeans and blue shirt for some sweatpants and an old flannel shirt of Adams's—needing comfort more than I needed to compete with Tina.

Adam leaned against the wall and crossed his arms, enjoying the show. "Maybe we should take advantage of our alone time?" he said to me.

The idea was tempting. I counted off days to the last time we had alone time. Had to be before Tina descended. Forever in couple time. Regular sex is one of the best perks of being in a live-in relationship. Probably the recent lull played a part in my current mood. A few more days of celibacy, and I'd be downright ornery.

I looked at the clock by the bed. Nearly six-thirty. Exactly when Tina said she wanted dinner ready. She'd probably be back any minute, and I did not want to live with the memory of coitus interruptus courtesy of Tina. "There's no time," I said. "She should be back any minute now. She made a big deal about having dinner at a decent hour. Did she call?"

"Not since I've been home, and there were no messages on the machine."

I started to head out to the hallway and Adam caught hold of me and drew me to him. "Are you sure you want to pass up this opportunity?" he said.

Up close, his clothes reeked of Tina again. Probably from sharing his office with her perfume vat. Nothing could have killed the moment faster. I shot him a look and went down to the kitchen to warm the Chinese food. When Tina still wasn't back fifteen minutes later, we ate in silence without her in front of the TV.

WE HAD LONG since finished eating. Prime time TV was done for the day. And there was still no sign of Tina.

"Do you think we should be worried?" I asked Adam.

He got up from the couch, stretched, and sat back down. "I'm not sure."

I got up, went to the front window, lifted the curtains back a little, and peered out. It was about the tenth time I'd done it that evening. I felt like a parent whose teenager had broken curfew. Odd, this ritual was. Looking out the window when someone was late, as though the very act of looking will bring them home faster.

It didn't seem to be working where Tina was concerned. I did learn a lot about my neighbors, though. For instance, the new lady across the street seemed to have had a mighty expensive shopping spree. She came home with huge bags from Holt Renfrew and Aldo shoes. Also, the teenage girl two doors over had a boyfriend who apparently had an affliction that required him to keep his hands moving at all times while they made out. And, Mr. Bolan from down the street, who never let his dog set foot on his own lawn, had no problem flinging the dog's business into Mrs. Feldman's bushes. This was true Reality TV and could probably be just as addictive, so when I found myself gaining sympathy for Mrs. Kravitz from *Bewitched*, I decided to stop checking outside for Tina.

I plopped myself down on the couch beside Adam and watched as he flicked through the channels on the TV. He stopped to listen to a local news update. Something about a possible teachers' strike looming, a convenience store robbery, and the discovery of an apparent suicide of some rich woman. Nothing about Tina. Not that I had expected there to be, but you never knew. I picked up the snack dishes from the coffee table and carried them into the kitchen.

"Do you think we should wait up?" I asked.

"One of us kind of has to," Adam said. "She doesn't have a key."

"Maybe she ran into Jeffrey at the office and they made up. She could be home tucked into her own bed by now," I said. It would be just like Tina too. Several times she had not shown up to dinner invitations in the past and not once did she ever call to cancel. We'd had to call her when she didn't show, and then she'd laugh and apologize without bothering to hide the fact that some better offer had just come up and we'd totally slipped her mind.

"I'll call," Adam said.

He picked up the phone and tapped in her cell number on the keypad. It went straight to voicemail, so he left a message and tried her home number.

"Oh, hi Jeffrey," Adam said into the phone. "I hope I didn't wake you."

Adam mimed bringing a glass up to his mouth as he tipped his head back a little. Evidently, Jeffrey had been drinking. Most of the rest of the call consisted of a lot of "Uh-huhs" on Adam's side but from what little was said, I gathered that Tina wasn't with Jeffrey.

When Adam hung up he asked, "What now?"

"I don't know. I guess we should call some of Tina's friends."

"We *are* Tina's friends," Adam said.

"Well she must have other people in her life. Goodness knows she's always talking about how busy her social calendar is."

"That's just hobnobbing. She's not really friends with the other social climbers."

"All the same, maybe she's out hobnobbing as we speak." I went upstairs and Adam followed. I went into Adam's office and started picking through Tina's things. "Maybe she's got an address book around here somewhere."

"She uses her cell to keep track of phone numbers," he said.

I wasn't about to lose a bona fide reason to snoop through Tina's stuff. "Maybe she has a book as a backup."

I had to hand it to Tina, she hadn't wasted any time settling in. The little closet that Adam had outfitted with shelves to hold his paper and computer supplies was now sans shelves and bursting with clothes hung from the clothes rail—the shelves having been removed and stacked in the bottom of the closet with his packages of paper piled high on top and shoved to the side. His desk had been pushed into the corner of the room, just under the window, to make way for a cardboard drawer unit that Tina seemed to use as a traveling dresser. It too was packed with clothes and the top had been made into a dressing table space complete with a three-panel lighted makeup mirror. I wondered if anything was left at her house. I also wondered just how long she planned to stay with us.

Adam pulled her suitcases out from under the pullout couch, which had forgotten it had a dual function and had simply become a bed. Her suitcases were empty. He shoved them back in and knocked something hard. He pulled the cases back out and peered underneath.

"There's something else back there," he said. "I can't make out what it is." He crawled around to the left side to get a closer look then reached under and pulled out a small, fire-safe lock box. "Hmmm. Wonder what's in here?" He tried the latch; it was locked. He looked around. "Must be a key around here someplace."

I thought the chances of her keeping an address book under lock and key were pretty slim. Chances were, Adam felt the same way. But, if he wasn't going to mention it, neither was I. Instead, I helped him look for the key. Adam set about riffling through her drawers and I checked her makeup bags. Nothing. I turned my attention to the bed. It was made up with Tina's own linens. Ours having been not-so-politely refused. The covers were pulled up, but the bed was not what you'd call neatly made. I pulled the covers down and felt under the pillows. Nothing under the first, but something grazed my fingertips below the second. I lifted the pillow. Under it was a personal-sized photo album. I flipped it open. Page after page, Jeffrey and Tina smiled out at me. As near as I could tell, the album was filled with pictures from their vacations. Adam had come over to see and stood looking over my shoulder.

"I guess she really misses him," I said.

"See," he said, more so to underline his rightness than to defend Tina.

I put the album back and recovered the pillows. "You know, the lock box is probably just jewelry. You know how Tina feels about her collection."

Adam shrugged. "You're probably right."

We both stood for a minute, unsure whether or not to continue our search. The doorbell rang and we looked at each other. "Oh no, she's here," I said. "You go down and let her in and I'll tidy up. We don't want her to know we've been snooping."

He went downstairs, and I tried to make the room look untouched.

"It's not Tina," Adam yelled up. "It's just a box."

"A what?"

"A box."

I was already downstairs by the time he brought the box into the hall. "Did you see who left it?"

"No."

We looked the box over. It was a plain, unmarked lidded box like the kind shoes come in only square, and it was tied shut with some twine. "Should we open it?" I said.

Adam jiggled it slightly. "I guess so."

He set it down on the hall table, untied the twine, and removed the lid slowly as if he expected some wild animal or disgusting insect to be inside. We both kept our heads back as far away as possible, allowing as much distance as our straining eyes could cope with while still being able to register the contents. Nothing jumped out. That was a good sign. We leaned in a little closer. No hissing or ticking noises. Another good sign. With the lid totally removed, we looked down on what looked like a bunch of white tissue paper. Adam gingerly sifted through the paper and pulled out a ring. Tina's ring. Tina's ten-carat diamond wedding ring. A flush of fear went through me. Adam started pulling out the paper and checking each piece carefully. For a minute, I thought he might be looking for her finger. We both knew Tina would never part with her ring. Not willingly.

Thankfully, there was no finger in the box. With all the paper taken out, a message written in thin black marker on the bottom became visible: "We've got the lady. Don't fuck with us or the trade is off."

THIRTEEN

FORTY-FIVE MINUTES later, Laurent and Camille arrived.

Camille took off her beige overcoat and set it on the back of a dining room chair. Underneath she wore a man's t-shirt with the police department logo on it and gray sweatpants. "Did you call Jeffrey?" she asked.

Adam set a pot of green tea down on the table. "I didn't think he'd be much use. I spoke with him earlier this evening, and he was barely coherent. About now, he's probably passed out and working his way towards a respectable hangover."

Laurent turned the box in his gloved hands then looked at Adam. "Any idea about the reference to a trade?"

Adam shook his head.

Laurent pulled a large plastic bag from his jacket pocket and put the box in it. "I'll pass the box over to Luc just in case it reveals anything other than your fingerprints."

My sheepish eyes flicked to Adam's. I had been working with C&C long enough for both of us to know better. A late-night delivery should have made us more careful, our earlier ignorance of the box contents not withstanding.

"What do you think about the ring?" Camille asked Laurent.

He picked up Tina's ring off the table and held it up between his thumb and index finger. "It's a quality stone," he said. "It's a good bet these guys aren't after money, or they would never have let this go." He set it back down on the table, pulled out a chair, and sat down.

Adam sat too. And when he wasn't swiping his fingertips over his mouth, he was repeatedly stirring his tea. Below the table, his right leg jumped up and down. Until Camille and Laurent had arrived, Adam had been calling Tina's cell every five minutes even though he got her voicemail every time. Now that he had nothing to busy his fingers, his excess energy was finding other outlets. "So, what do we do?" he said.

"We'll need to retrace Tina's steps this afternoon, and we'll need to talk to Jeffrey as soon as he's lucid," Laurent said.

"She was supposed to meet with somebody from Jeffrey's office after she left C&C," Camille said as she walked out to the hall where she'd left her purse. She returned carrying a jumbo bar of dark Swiss chocolate, sat down, peeled off the wrapper, and broke off a line of squares for each of us and dealt them out like cards. "First thing tomorrow, I'll go down and see what I can find out."

We were all quiet for a minute while we chewed on our chocolate.

Adam finally broke the silence. "I don't want to involve the police," he said. "At least, not until we hear from whoever has Tina."

My eyes skipped from Adam to Laurent. Laurent had trained as a cop and could be a stickler for following procedure. Naturally, he'd want to notify the police. Adam, on the other hand, watched too many movies, and even though he had no idea how things worked in real life kidnappings, would likely defend his position to the end.

Laurent started to speak, then caught the look in my eye and started again. "Look," he said in a voice clearly intended to mollify Adam. "The police are experienced with these situations. When I pass Luc the box, I'll fill him in. He'll know the best way to handle things. Don't worry. He won't do anything to jeopardize Tina's safety."

"But just talking to the police *could* put Tina in danger," Adam protested.

Laurent locked eyes with me. I knew he was having less than kind thoughts about my anglophone. Before the two men got into a big argument, I interjected myself into the conversation. "Adam, I don't think we have a choice here. We need access to the police records to trace any fingerprints we find on the box."

Adam wrestled with that logic a bit before relenting. "Okay. Just make sure to talk to Luc directly," Adam said. "I don't want just strangers on this."

"Not a problem," Laurent said. "I'm sure we can track Luc down."

We all looked over at Camille and eyed her t-shirt.

She shrugged. "I may have a vague idea of where you can find him," she said.

"Good. Now that that's settled, first thing tomorrow while Camille's at the law office, you and I will go over to Jeffrey's," Laurent said, swinging his index finger between himself and Adam.

"What about me?" I asked.

"You stay here in case they try to make contact again. We'll all meet back here when we're done."

AFTER ONLY A few hours sleep, Adam was off with Laurent to Jeffrey's while I sat on the edge of Tina's bed, clad in my robe and slippers and eating an apple, and thought about the mess she'd dumped into our lives. Part of me felt annoyed that we had to put our lives on hold to deal with yet another Tina crisis, but an even bigger part of me feared for her well-being.

I put down my apple core and retrieved Tina's ring from the cosmetic bag I had slipped it into the night before. I held the ring in my hand and wished for a psychic moment—some flash that would tell me where Tina was. Nothing came to me. Probably because I wasn't psychic. Or, maybe I wasn't connecting to her enough. Maybe what I needed was to wear the ring. I looped it onto my finger and bent my knuckle to keep the ring from sliding off. Still nothing. Nothing psychic, that is. But, I was picking up on something—how remarkably good the ring looked on me. Normally I found the idea of wearing a pointy wedge of stone on my finger unappealing—much too cumbersome and sharp—but maybe I had that all wrong. Maybe hefting it around all day could help prevent osteoporosis and the edges could come in handy as a weapon or emergency glass-cutter.

Like if my car plunged off a bridge into a river, and I needed to cut an air hole for oxygen. I splayed my fingers to admire the ring some more, and it slipped off and rolled onto the floor.

I got down on my hands and knees to fetch it out from where it landed near the lockbox under the bed, and then I put the ring back into the cosmetic case for safekeeping. After all, the chances of me having a psychic moment were about as good as me learning to speak French like a Québéqoise. The chances of me forming an attachment to Tina's ring, on the other hand, were much higher, so it was probably best put out of sight, out of mind.

I zipped up the case and turned to leave. Then it hit me. The lockbox. I had completely forgotten about it. I hadn't thought it was important. But, maybe it was. Maybe there was something in there. Something that could be worth a trade.

I got back down on the floor, hauled out the box, and tried the latch. Still locked of course. I had two choices: I could search some more for the key, something Tina may have even taken with her, or I could break it open. Ever the product of a democratic society, I looked over at Ping and Pong sitting in the doorway and took a vote. Counting both their upturned tails, the second choice won unanimously. Now, I just had to figure out how to bust the lock. I needed a little time to think. I placed the box on the bed and went to get dressed.

I threw on a beige sweater and some jeans and pulled my hair back and clipped it into a pony tail. A bobby pin. That's what I needed. People were always picking locks with bobby pins. Trouble was I didn't use bobby pins. I threw them all out because they had a nasty habit of stretching my hair while simultaneously pinching it and causing a piercing tug all the way to the root. I also threw out my old metal barrettes and plastic combs for similar reasons—torture devices all of them. All I had left were some stretchy headbands and spring-loaded hair clips. None of which were of any use for lock picking.

I searched the house and collected an artillery of other gadgets that might do the trick. I dumped the pile on Tina's bed, surveyed my options, and decided to try some of the mini keys first. I had a surprising amount of small keys. They came from everywhere—old diaries, file cabinets, suitcases, jewelry boxes, mailboxes—one even came from a "club" security bar we used to have for the steering wheel in the car. I tried them all. One of the mailbox keys came close but not close enough. So I started on the other stuff. The seam ripper didn't twist right. Ditto the tiny sewing machine screwdrivers. I tried a nail file, a safety pin, tweezers, a paper clip, and a corn-on-the cob holder. The whole lot proved useless. I picked the box up and shook it frantically, knowing full well that the shaking was not likely to cause it to open spontaneously. But it did wonders for stress relief.

I was about to start in on the keys again when my office phone rang. I ran to get it before the answering machine kicked in.

"Hello."

"*Merde.*" It was Camille. "*Merde, merde, merde,*" she said. "I forgot about the interviews."

"What interviews?"

"The temp ladies."

Oh, for the reception job. I'd forgotten about that too. "Was that today?"

"This morning. I was just checking my messages and there was a rather cool one from some woman at the agency saying her girls had waited for an hour outside the building."

"So she was pissed?" I said.

"She went on and on about it not being very professional of us." Camille's voice was dipping in and out. Must be on her cell. "I can't believe I forgot."

Seemed pretty easy to forget to me what with this Tina business keeping us all up half the night. But I knew Camille's pride was wounded. She hated being called on the carpet for anything. And this woman got her right in the tenders with that crack about professionalism. Camille was nothing if not professional. At least to the outside world.

I knew the best way to soothe her was to shift the blame. "Well, leave it to Tina to get herself wrapped up in some mess that kept the rest of us up half the night," I said to her. "It's not surprising the interviews slipped your mind." I knew it was wrong to use Tina like this, especially with her kidnapped and all, but it was for a good cause. It's not like I got any joy out of it or anything.

"Hmmm." Clearly Camille was deciding whether or not to allow this blatant attempt to sway her mood.

I eased her along. "So, speaking of Tina. Any luck at the firm?"

"Just a sec."

I heard some grinding, a slight whir, then a slam.

"Come down and let me in, will you," she said.

I placed the receiver on my desk and ran downstairs. Sure enough, Camille was standing on the porch holding her cell. She came in, took off her boots as she passed through the vestibule, and started up the stairs. "Nobody there claims to have seen Tina yesterday," she said, still talking into the headset of her phone.

"Claims?" I said, following behind her.

"What?"

"You said claims. Nobody *claims* to have seen her. Do you think someone was lying?"

Camille reached the top of the stairs and turned her head in the direction of my voice. "*Mais voyons*," she said as she pulled the earbud away from her ear and disconnected her phone. She dropped it into her bag, letting the bag slide from her hand to the floor and went into the bathroom. "It doesn't matter if someone is lying," she said through the door, "it still doesn't get us anywhere."

I went into my office and found the phone buzzing on my desk, so I replaced the receiver and returned to the lockbox.

I heard the toilet flush and Camille wandered in. "What's all this?"

I looked down at the pile of metal. "This was me trying to break into the lock on that box."

"Did you lose your key?"

"Not exactly. It's not exactly my box. It's Tina's."

Camille slipped out of the room a moment and came back carrying what looked like a travel-size manicure set. She clicked it open and withdrew something with a baby blue handle. She inserted it into the lock, turned it a few times, and the lock sprung open. She stepped back. "Do you want to tell me why we're breaking into Tina's private things?"

"It's the trade thing. I thought Tina may have hidden whatever these people want and this box is as good a place as any to look for it," I said.

I sat on the edge of the bed and took a deep breath. I don't know what I had to feel guilty about. I was doing this *for* Tina, after all. I opened the lid and looked inside. A large orchid stared back at me. Not a real one, a flat image of one. It was a greeting card. I picked it up and opened the cover. The card was from Jeffrey. I skimmed the writing. Seemed to be for an anniversary. Below it lay several other cards mixed in with some letters. All from Jeffrey. The box was filled with them. A personal history of their life together. Rather a lot too considering they'd only been together a short time. I passed the cards on to Camille, removing each piece from the box as I went, not wanting to overlook something else that may have gotten tossed into the pile. Nothing. A dead end. My disappointment overcame my sense of guilt at invading Tina's privacy.

"Look at this," Camille said holding up a card with a picture of three naked babies, all wrinkly and chubby, smiling into the camera. "Jeffrey's written something about not feeling bad because there are a whole bunch of babies in their future. Do you think Tina had a miscarriage?"

I'd never even known Tina to be pregnant. I took the card from Camille's hand. "You're not supposed to be reading those."

Camille raised her left eyebrow in an exaggerated arch. "There could be clues in here."

Yeah, right. Not likely. But one of the unspoken agreements Camille and I had was that we didn't call each other on occasional forays into partial truth territory. Not unless the partial truths were about something important like say, chocolate stockpiles or haircut disasters. I passed the card back to her. "Fine, have at it."

She put the card down and picked out a letter from the pile and started to open it. "Hey, careful," I said. "You'll get them all out of order."

Pong's tail started thumping in the hallway, the door creaked downstairs, and Adam called out, "Hey, hon."

Camille and I grabbed up Tina's love notes and threw them back in the box. I pushed the lid down, but it wouldn't close right.

"What did you do to this thing?" I whispered to Camille.

"Just shove the box under the bed as it is," she whispered back.

We were just straightening up when Adam's head popped into the doorway.

"Any luck with Jeffrey?" I asked, my voice thin and breathless.

"He's downstairs," Adam said as he looked from me to Camille then briefly scanned the room. "What are you doing in here?"

"Nothing," I said.

Adam surveyed the room again before heading back downstairs. Camille and I followed him down to the kitchen where Jeffrey sat wordlessly slumped in a kitchen chair, his brown and white checked shirt misbuttoned and only partially tucked into his beige pants. His scruff had escaped his razor at least twice and his hair was still damp, framing his face in an unfamiliar darkness. It was as unkept as I'd ever seen Jeffrey and, really, I'd never seen him look better. Hollywood bad boy suited him better than Wall Street stickler.

Adam leaned in to my ear, "He's been like this since we got him up. We persuaded him to take a shower, though. Believe me, big improvement."

"Can I get you something to eat, Jeffrey?" I asked.

His eyes remained fixed on his knees. He said nothing.

I looked at Adam who shrugged. I cocked my head twice in the direction of the hall and Adam trailed me into the living room.

"Does he know about Tina?" I asked.

"Well, we told him," Adam said. "That's when his hangover glaze was replaced by this. He hasn't said a word since."

"Did you tell him you had questions for him? Did you ask if he'd help find her?"

"Basically."

"And?"

"And nothing. He's not talking. We tried everything. Laurent even tried getting some coffee into him. Nothing. We didn't want to waste any more time waiting for Mr. Catatonic to come back to life. We decided to split up. I brought Jeffrey back here to see if you could get through to him, and Laurent is searching the house looking for anything that might shed some light on things."

We walked back to the kitchen. If Jeffrey had moved in our absence, he had done a good job returning his limbs to the slouched statue position. I thought briefly of how parents tell their children to be careful of making silly faces or their faces could freeze like that and suppressed the urge to make a similar comment to Jeffrey about the humped back he was courting.

What was the matter with him anyway? There wasn't any time for this. Jeffrey had to snap out of it. If this was a movie and I was someone like, say Cher, I would slap him. But, it wasn't and I wasn't, so I needed something else. I looked to Camille for inspiration. She was too busy foraging in the fridge. I took a mug out of the cupboard, filled it with water, put it in front of Jeffrey, and waited. When I was going through my social work training, I had learned a lot about silences. I knew enough to let him be for a while. Often, people break their own silences if you give them time.

Camille had found a bagel and some butter. She sat down at the table and was slathering up the bread. "So, Jeffrey," she said. "You want to help us find Tina or you want to pick out her coffin?" Camille had never been through social work training.

At that, Jeffrey covered his face with his hands and his shoulders shuddered as he began to sob. He went on for quite a while. Adam passed him a tissue, and Jeffrey took it and wiped the drips from his nose. Adam passed him a wad more and Jeffrey took the whole thing and blew his nose into it making a high-pitched whiney noise like a dog.

Camille moved her food farther down the table.

Finally Jeffrey said, "It's my fault."

"Excuse me?" I said.

"It's my fault," he repeated. "It's all my fault. Tina moving out. Tina missing. All of it." His cheek was clenching with a pulsating motion that was rapidly losing its grip on his lower jaw. The sobbing started again. He dropped his chin to his chest and pinched his eyes closed. Tears rode down the sides of his nose and curved around his mouth before slipping off his face.

I should have been sympathetic to his pain. And on one level I was. But on another level, I was running out of patience. Also, I wasn't sure how long I could look at him with his face all contorted. I'd heard it called the "ugly cry" before, but this was more pathetic than ugly.

"Look, Jeffrey, if you know something, you need to tell us," I said.

He used his sleeve to soak up the tears on his face. "Tina didn't really have an affair," he said.

Not exactly news. I waited for him to go on.

"I know that now, but a few weeks back I thought she did. And I was jealous. Really jealous." He paused to blow his nose.

The words "uh oh" were creeping into my brain.

He continued. "I thought Bennett was the one she was cheating with. I needed to know for sure, so I tried following him around trying to catch them together. But, it's not that easy. Not like in the movies. He'd go into buildings and the door would lock shut behind him. I couldn't get in. I had no way of knowing if he was meeting Tina or not. One night, I drove around for hours trying to figure out what to do and ended up at the firm, and I decided to search Bennett's office.

"I snooped around but wasn't finding anything—no letters or hotel receipts or phone messages. I was about to leave when I nearly bumped over a sculpture. I caught it before it fell to the floor and was putting it back when I noticed the back had come loose and opened. I looked inside and saw a mini camera. It was a surveillance camera, you know, like the kind people use to spy on babysitters. I figured it might show Tina and Bennett together, so I took out the tape and put the statue back.

"I was about to leave when I heard a noise so I ducked behind Bennett's aquarium. I watched through the glass as a guy came in, headed for the statue, and fiddled with the false door. He swore to himself when he found the film missing. He checked around the desk a bit then left. I waited a few minutes to make sure he was gone before I moved. Then I ducked out and slipped into my own office to give myself some time to calm down." He took a sip of water. "I've thought about it a lot and that must have been how they figured out it was me. That guy must have seen me when I left. He must have been waiting somewhere."

"You mean someone knows you took the film?" Adam said.

"Yeah, and they want it back."

"What was on the film?" I asked.

Jeffrey looked like he might break down again, but then composed himself and went on. "Well, I was right, Tina was on the film, but it was just like she said. She was talking me up to Bennett. She was charming and maybe flattering him a bit much, but nothing inappropriate."

Adam brought him back to the focus. "What *else* was on the film?"

"A lot of it was just Bennett working or talking on the phone. Near the end, though, some old guy came in and they got into an argument."

"What about?" I said.

Jeffrey looked at me as though I'd asked him to recite the national anthem backwards. "I don't know."

"Did you watch the whole tape?"

"Yeah, but I don't remember that part too well."

Adam pulled out a chair beside Jeffrey and sat down. "Where's the tape now?"

"It's gone."

I leaned against the counter and folded my arms across my chest. "What do you mean gone?"

"I can't find it. I've looked everywhere. It's gone." Jeffrey dragged a hand through his hair. "Until this thing happened with Tina, I thought they took it."

That begged a question. "If you knew Tina wasn't cheating, why didn't you try to get her back?"

Some attitude crept into Jeffrey's voice. "Don't you think that's what I wanted to do?"

Hey, it was a legitimate question. After all, this was Tina we were talking about. Maybe he saw an out and was going to take it.

Jeffrey toned it down a little. "At first, when I found the tape I was relieved. I started making some big plans to make it up to her. Flowers, perfume, jewelry—the works. I was still trying to work out how to apologize without having to tell her why I'd changed my mind. You know Tina, she's really smart, she wouldn't believe just anything."

Camille's eyes met mine and we both suppressed the urge to smile.

Jeffrey continued. "But, then, these guys started calling about the tape. They were nasty. And when I said I couldn't find the tape, they didn't believe me. They thought I was trying to get money for it or something. They got even more nasty. I started to panic. I thought Tina would be safer if she stayed away. So I really played up the divorce thing. I figured the more mad she was at me, the longer she'd be out of the picture."

I guess that made sense in a Jeffrey sort of way. I picked up the phone and dialed Laurent's cell. With any luck, he'd still be at the house.

FOURTEEN

THE GOOD THING about having an office in your home is that you can use it to escape now and then. It was selfish, cowardly, and maybe even a bit childish. But hiding sometimes helped me get through the day. Especially when Tina's goofy husband sat blubbering in my kitchen. Once again, we were drawn into another drama in Tina's life. And right when I was in the middle of an important case, too. I felt torn about where to focus my time. But, with Laurent searching for the missing tape and Camille off again to cover a few things at the office, there was little I could do for Tina but wait to see if we heard from the kidnappers again. So, I decided to go back to work.

Francesca had called ten minutes earlier and asked me to go by the house. She didn't tell me why, but I was hoping it meant she was keeping the case open. I had come upstairs to take the call, but now that I was done with that and dressed to go out, I found myself loitering. Eager as I was to get over to Francesca's, I still felt guilty leaving Adam when his friend had just been kidnapped. I hadn't seen him this upset since his mom died. I knew there was nothing I could do for him, but it didn't make it any easier.

I paced around my office weighing things in my mind and feeling a sudden kinship to mothers who had to leave their kids each day to go to work. The emotional tug-of-war had to be grueling. And to think, they faced it over and over again. All I had to do was get my butt out the door just this once. I told myself to suck it up and grabbed my bag, rushed down the stairs, yelled out to Adam that I was going to work, and left.

BY THE TIME I got to Francesca's, I felt much better. The mid-morning air was tinged with the smell of newly fallen leaves, the sun was shining, and my guilt wrangled. I parked in front of Francesca's garage and flipped down the visor mirror to check my hair. A blur of white glistened on the glass, and I blinked to protect my eyes from the glare. When I refocused, the blur of white had turned into a van idling behind me and blocking the driveway. A guy jumped out, dashed over to Francesca's door, set down a delivery of flowers, and hurried back to the van. As he pulled out, I read the writing on the back of the truck: *Fleurs de Fay* was inscribed in large red cursive letters with a phone number and web address written below in smaller black block lettering.

I locked up my car and headed over to the house. Just before I reached the porch, Francesca opened the front door and poked her head out. She took me in for a split second then shifted her focus to the flowers. "Did you see who left these?" she asked me.

I stepped onto the veranda. "Some guy from the florist just dropped them off."

"That's odd," she said. "Usually they wait for a tip."

"Maybe he was running late on his deliveries," I said. "He seemed to be in a hurry."

She bent to pick up the bouquet, and I noticed a small white envelope tucked into the top. Francesca noticed it too but made no move to open it. If the flowers had been left at my house, I would have been ripping into the card first thing.

She stepped back into the house, and I went in after her and followed her into the kitchen. It was a large rectangular room with a wall of windows facing the back. A long marble-topped table that seated eight stood in front of the windows. Centered on the wall at the head of the table, a massive painting of the Pope stood vigil. The rest of the room was done in black, white, and silver. The cabinetry was white, the appliances stainless steel, and the countertop black granite. The walls were covered in black wallpaper with white polka dots the size of bottle caps. An island took up the center of the work space and three long light fixtures hung down from the ceiling and lit the space. The rest of the ceiling had recessed lighting.

Francesca filled a tall crystal vase with water, cut off the tips of the flower stems, and placed the flowers in the vase. She set the mixed bunch in the center of the kitchen table and left them alone to settle. The envelope sat unopened on the counter by the sink.

I took a seat at the table. "You sounded quite urgent on the phone," I said.

"I wanted you to see something before Lucia got home," she said.

She opened a door off the side of the kitchen revealing a walk-in pantry. She went in and came out carrying a medium-sized square box. She put it on the table and lifted the lid back so I could see what was inside.

"This came today for Lucia," she said. "A wedding present."

I stood to get a better look. Inside was an old-fashioned wood clock. It had the shape of a hill. The wood was maple toned and the face was inset in a white with gold hands and a round gold surround. There were small gold claw feet on the bottom. It wasn't in primo shape, but still a decent antique.

"It's nice," I said.

"It belonged to Puddles," Francesca said.

I inspected the box. "Did it come with a card?"

"No. There was no card, and it was hand delivered."

"By a courier?"

"No. It was a private messenger," she said. "But the man insisted Lucia sign for it herself before he would leave it."

Sounded like Puddles wanted to be sure she got it. "What did she think of it?"

Francesca closed the top of the box. "She hasn't seen it yet. She was on her way out when it came. She just signed for it and placed it with the other gifts in the dining room."

"And you opened it?"

She sat down at the table, and I did the same. "We've been keeping a list of all the gifts as they come in," she said. "Who sent what and the date it arrived. Lucia wants to write her thank yous in batches so she won't have as much to do after the wedding. I was just adding this one to the list."

I thought about it a moment. This meant two things: that Puddles was alive and that he was probably reasonably close by. I didn't want to get away from myself with excitement, but this lead could be a big break in the case.

Francesca stood up and took the box back to the little room. When she came back, she paced in front of the table, her heels clacking on the ceramic tile and her fingers twitching on her right hand. Probably an ex-smoker longing for a cigarette. Was it just me or was Francesca not as thrilled with this lead as I was.

"Has the gift upset you?" I asked her.

"What upsets me," she said, "is that Lucia had this in her room when Puddles left. About a year later, she packed it up along with some of the other gifts he'd given her over the years, and it's been in storage ever since."

Let me guess. "In the attic?"

"That's right."

"So you think it was Puddles who was rummaging around in your attic?"

"Who else would know about the clock?" she said, walking over to the stove. She lit the burner below a shiny black kettle, opened a cupboard door, pulled a tin of coffee off the shelf, and measured coffee into two mugs. My taste buds cringed at the thought of drinking instant coffee.

When she continued, her voice was uneven. "I don't mind telling you, I'm a little scared."

She was confusing me now. She'd told me things were good between Puddles and her. Had she been holding out on me? "If there's something you haven't told me, maybe now would be a good time," I said. "Remember anything you tell me is confidential, and it might help us find Puddles."

The kettle whistled and Francesca turned to the stove to tend it. "I wasn't raised to air my dirty laundry in public," she said. "My mother was angry enough after Puddles left and I tried to find him. She said it would bring disgrace to the family for people to know he was gone." She turned back around to face me. "I didn't appreciate my parents' attitudes about family honor back then. But I do now. Nothing I tell you about our personal life is going to help you find Puddles. Just, please, find him before he breaks into my house again."

I'M NOT SURE what bothered me more. The fact that Francesca had been holding out on me, or that this was the second time someone had brought Puddles' character into question. Probably it was more the second. It just wasn't what I wanted to hear. I needed to get an accurate sense of the man to help me find him, but I wanted that sense to tell me he was the sort of man who would help a sick little girl. Not the kind of man who struck fear into his wife.

Really, I wanted to cling to his image of being a responsible husband and doting father. But that was getting harder and harder to do. On the surface, Puddles fit the profile of a rebellious teenager who eventually grew up, straightened himself out, and became an average member of society. If it wasn't for the pesky problems of a false identity, the abandonment of his family, and the mysterious alienation of his daughter, that is.

The good news was that Francesca was reopening the case, so I could keep working it with the full support of C&C. I thought about my next move and checked the time. Almost noon. I needed to get something to eat. The apple I'd eaten before everyone descended on my house earlier had long since burned off its calories, and I had been in such a rush to get to Francesca's that I'd skipped out without a proper breakfast. I was coming up on Starbucks and pulled in to refuel and plan my afternoon.

Rishi was just finishing up with another customer when he caught sight of me and elbowed his way past the server who had started to take my order. "Ah, *mademoiselle*, I have something for you," he said pulling a book from his back pocket. "It is about all the French irregular verbs."

I glanced at the cover. Oh my. So it was. A whole book on irregular verbs. Not a grammar book with a chapter on irregular verbs. A whole freakin' book. "Thanks," I said to him. "This will be a big help." No sense in admitting to Rishi that as far as I was concerned the whole language was irregular. He had no need to know how hopeless I was.

"You have to memorize them," he said. "It is tedious, but it is the only way to learn."

Rishi was a born educator. It was genetic. Both his parents were professors at Montreal's McGill University—one of the most renowned research centers in North America. His family took education seriously, and so did Rishi. He already had a degree in Philosophy and was now pursuing another one in Humanities. The only thing that matched his hunger for academic knowledge was his curiosity about people. He believed everybody had a story to tell. Which was why when things got slow around the coffee shop, he liked to point out people and ruminate about their lives. It was also why he found my job intriguing. He had a way of elevating PI work that made it sound like a sacred quest for truth. Unfortunately, somehow he also managed to transfer that admiration onto me and now he held great expectations about what I could accomplish. Like memorizing French verbs.

I told him I'd do my best and gave him my order.

When it was ready, he passed it over and waved goodbye.

"*Merci*," I said to him. "*À bientôt*."

He beamed. "Ah. Such an excellent student."

Back in my car, I munched on my food and pulled out my cell phone to call Adam to check in about Tina. No news yet. Then I called Camille and got her voice mail, so I left a message about Francesca keeping the case open and explained about the clock delivery. I also added in the bit about Francesca's mom being angry about the previous hunt for Puddles because I figured that explained the falling out between them that Miriam had mentioned. And by the time I was done eating, I knew what I wanted to do next. Since Francesca wasn't so willing to share personal details of her life, I decided to focus on someone less private. Ingrid. If I hurried, I could catch her over at Guido's before she went on lunch break. I had the feeling that although Miriam Tabor seemed quite adept at maintaining her friend's confidences, Ingrid was not so skilled.

THE PARKING LOT near Guido's was almost full when I pulled in, but with the street spots all taken, it was the nearest place left to park. I slipped my car into a slender gap of space near the wall at the far end. Not technically a bona-fide parking spot maybe, but big enough for my Mini. Then, before getting out, I reached over to my passenger seat and picked up the pile of magazines I'd bought on my way over to use as an excuse for dropping by. I opened the first one wide and pressed into the center to break the spine, switching pages now and then. With the second one, I bent back the top right corner until a triangle formed. Pouring a little water onto my fingertips from an old Evian bottle left behind in the cup holder, I dampened a few of the magazine's edges just enough to cause some unevenness in the fresh paper. With the third magazine, I bent the spine some then rolled it up like a newspaper before releasing it. Not bad, but it needed something more. I spilled a drip of water on the cover right over the "Sexy New Clothes He'll Love Too" headline. I watched the water soak in and form a modest bulge. Perfect. I popped the whole lot into my shoulder bag and headed over to Guido's.

Inside, Guido's reception was just as crowded as the parking lot. Clusters of women were everywhere chattering in low tones. A rather brassy voice rose above the others, and I honed in on the owner. She was standing with two other women to the left of the reception desk.

"Calm down," one of the other women said to her.

"It's not fair," she sniffled.

"I know, I know," the third woman said, patting her back.

I crossed the room to where Ingrid sat clutching a phone in her chin. As I got closer, I saw she was jotting down notes on a large pad. She finished the call, tore off the sheet of paper, and joined the three women.

"Here," she said holding out the paper to the oldest woman. "I hope this helps."

The woman took the paper and looked it over. "Thank you," she said.

"No problem," Ingrid smiled. Her face glinted and for a moment I thought she had pierced her eyebrow. On second look, it wasn't a piercing, just some glittery makeup. Which on someone else might have looked out of place, but somehow Ingrid pulled it off. Even with the black bell-bottom corduroy pants studded up the side and white ruffled blouse. Must be her youth. Suddenly the gap between my twenties and my thirties seemed huge. At thirty-one, I certainly wasn't old, but for the first time I felt older. I watched her expression change as she caught sight of me.

"Nice to see you again," she said.

The women started to gather themselves and file out.

"You too," I said.

Ingrid sat down in her chair and sighed as the door finally closed behind the last woman.

"Tough day?" I asked.

"It's the Pella wedding," she said as if that explained everything.

Pella. I knew that name. They were in the paper fairly frequently. And not always for nice reasons. Thinking back, though, I did remember hearing something about Rosa Pella getting engaged last summer. I remembered it because she was going to marry somewhat of a local celebrity. One of the VJs from Musique Plus, Québec's MTV.

"Wow, that must be a real coup for you guys. You doing the wedding dress?"

Ingrid nodded. "We're doing the whole deal. The wedding dress, the bridesmaids, the maid of honor, the mothers. We're even doing the groom, best man, and ushers."

"I thought tuxes were usually rented."

"Yeah, most people do rent, but these are special order. They have to match the dresses."

It was my turn to nod, pretending that didn't sound a tad neurotic.

She went on. "Even the little bride and groom on the cake are being made special. The cake people are having someone hand-paint them so they're wearing the same clothes as the real bride and groom. That's what the problem was today. Rosa's mother brought the cake-bride in to the fitting. She wanted to show it to the dressmaker, but when they compared it to the gown it wasn't quite right. I don't know, the colors were off or something and some detailing was missing. Rosa was very upset, so they're going to have the cake-bride redone by another artist."

Did I say a *tad* neurotic?

Ingrid shook her head. "It takes all kinds," she said. "So, how can I help you? I'm afraid my mom's not in right now."

"Oh, that's okay. I'm not here to see your mom. I just stopped by to drop these off for you." I set down the magazines on the desk. "A friend of mine passed them on to me, and I thought you might be interested in them."

She fingered the magazines. "That was really nice of you. Are you sure you don't want to keep them?"

I went into phase two: bonding. Phase one in my plan having been dropping by unannounced appearing casual and sans agenda. I often found I got more information if I kept things easygoing and conversational rather than interrogating. "No, I just like to look at the pictures for fun. I'm not that savvy about fashion. It must come easy to you, though, having grown up in the biz."

She smiled. "Yeah, I guess I learned a few things." The phone buzzed and Ingrid answered it and put the call through to the back offices. She made a pile of the magazines I had given her, held it upright, and tapped it on the desk, unifying the edges. "Anyway, thanks again for the magazines."

"No problem," I said stalling for time while I tried to think of something to say to keep the conversation going. "So, are you guys doing Lucia's wedding dress too?"

She shook her head. "We were going to, but the groom's mother decided she wants Lucia to wear *her* wedding dress. She doesn't have any daughters to pass it on to so she's trying to pawn it off on Lucia."

"What a drag."

"Yeah, Lucia's not thrilled about it. It's pretty frilly with big pouffy stuff happening around the shoulders and it just hangs like a cone."

"Yow. That doesn't sound like Lucia's style," I said. Not that I had a clue about Lucia's style. I still hadn't even met her.

"No way! She's all into form fitting stuff with classic lines."

"You'd think considering that fashion is Lucia's family business that her mother-in-law-to-be would understand if she wanted to have a new dress made."

Ingrid leaned back in her chair and folded her arms. "Not those people. I don't think they even think about stuff like that."

Those people. Hmmm. Why hadn't I investigated Lucia's fiancé? Maybe there was more of a link between Lucia getting married and Puddles' resurfacing than I'd given thought to. I figured Ingrid and I had bonded enough to risk a probe. "It's too bad Lucia's father isn't around. Maybe he'd stick up for her."

"Are you kidding? He would be useless. He's such a wimp."

"Really? The way Francesca talks about him I thought he was a great dad."

"Yeah, I used to think so too. When we were little I thought he was wonderful."

"So, what changed your mind?"

She eyed me before answering. "You're looking for him, right?"

I tried to give off an indifferent, offhand aura. "I'm trying to help the family locate him. It was supposed to be a surprise for Lucia."

"It would be a surprise, all right."

I went on, "I'm not sure it's going to work out, though. There's not a lot to go on. He could be anywhere." I put on a bit of a sad expression. "It looks like Lucia will probably be getting married without her dad."

Ingrid seemed relieved. "I don't know what Francesca was thinking, to tell you the truth. You'd think she, of all people, would know that Lucia wasn't interested in her father, let alone want him at her wedding." She leaned forward and lowered her voice, "I don't know how much you know about the family background, but Lucia's parents aren't divorced or anything, her dad just took off."

I hoped there was more to Ingrid's distaste for Puddles than that. That was old news. Maybe this was a waste of time. "I know. That must have been tough."

"Yeah, well, that's not the half of it. Before he left, he told Lucia he was planning on leaving but not to tell her mother. She begged him to take her with him. He was her whole world practically. She was never close with her mother. He said he couldn't take her just yet, but he promised to come back for her as soon as he could. Poor Lucia waited for him every day. She only went out to go to school and then hurried home to wait. She kept a packed suitcase hidden in her closet. She did that for a whole year."

"How sad."

"Yeah, then one day she just stopped. In fact, she did the exact opposite. She avoided being at home, only showing up in time for dinner and bed. That's when our friendship changed too. She joined a bunch of clubs and stuff and got involved with all new kids. I didn't understand it at the time. I was pretty hurt, I kinda felt snubbed. Later, I got it though. I think it was just too hard for her. I think she needed to create a whole new world for herself and that meant letting go of whatever she could from her old life." She sat back. "At least, that's what I've always thought."

Her phone buzzed again. She answered it, spoke briefly, hung up, and stood. "I gotta go," she said. "I'm meeting my mom for lunch."

The door behind her opened and a frail, petite, older woman approached the desk carrying a small paper bag. As she got closer, I placed her as being from the Philippines. "Thanks for filling in," Ingrid said to the woman, whose lips barely widened to form a shy smile. The woman applied the same minimalist movement to the nod she offered me.

Ingrid removed her jacket from the back of her chair and put it on. She grabbed her purse from a drawer, picked up the magazines, and walked out with me to the parking lot.

I hurried along to match her pace. My mind was brewing with questions, only at this speed we'd reach the parking lot before I had the chance to utter anything besides goodbye. To buy time I said, "maybe Lucia will be happier in her new family."

Ingrid's heels grated along the pavement as she struggled to keep her feet in what were obviously shoes too large for her. "I'm surprised she's marrying into that lot," she said. "You'd think she'd have more sense than that."

I couldn't think of her fiancé's name so I just said, "You think they're really that bad?"

She stopped walking and faced me. "The Como family is worse than the Pella family. They're politicians."

AT C&C, I went directly into Camille's office and tossed a Green & Black's chocolate bar on her desk. Dark, unflavored.

She looked up from the fax sheets she was studying. "Ah, lunch," she said as she tore open the wrapper. "You got something?"

"Yeah, but first, any news on Tina?"

"Not a word."

I sat down in the window seat and pulled my legs up, hugging them to my body. "I was just talking to Ingrid over at Guido's. Turns out there's more to the old disappearing daddy story."

Camille reclined in her chair and took a drag on her chocolate. After I filled her in, all she said was, "hmmm, interesting."

"Is that all you have to say? This is some good stuff." Okay, so maybe I hadn't learned anything earth shattering, but I'd found out a bit more about Lucia and picked up some possible leads. Camille could show a little enthusiasm.

She detached the ends of the paper wrapper, unfolded it, and ironed it with her hands. "I also had some news today on the Puddles case." She came around the desk and passed me the fax pages she had been looking at when I came in. "It seems Piedro Bellinni has turned up dead."

FIFTEEN

"**DEAD!**" **I TOOK** the papers. The documents bore official letterhead from a town not far from here. Sure enough, they said Piedro Bellinni had been found dead. Apparently, from cancer. The last page of the fax contained a photo of a man's face. It was nearly impossible to identify that the face was of a man let alone that it belonged to Puddles. The picture was so blurred and pixilated. "How do we know it's really him? Couldn't we get a better picture?"

"Their internet is down, so this is the best they could do. And we don't know for sure yet. Someone has to identify the body in person."

"What makes the authorities think it's Piedro Bellinni?"

"That's what his identification said. The body was found by a UPS guy when he arrived for a delivery."

"No one there identified him?"

"Nobody knew him well. He lived alone out in the country and kept to himself. His body is being held in a neighboring town."

I tried to think what this could mean. No father-of-the-bride for Lucia. No real answers for Francesca. And worse yet, no possible donor for Sarah.

The doorbell rang and Camille stepped out to get it. I heard some mumbled greetings and then she reappeared with Jim.

Jim's head nearly grazed the doorframe when he stepped in, and the scraggly hair on the top of his head slid off to the side from the small breeze that was created. He reached up to readjust it, and the safety pin that was holding the broken zipper closed on his windbreaker popped open. "Good to see you again, Lora," he said to me. From the eager expression on his face, I was sure Camille hadn't told him anything about this yet. He glanced from me to her then back again. "I came as soon as I got your message," he said.

Message? What message? Surely Camille hadn't called him? I tried to catch her eye, but she wouldn't allow it. The corners of her mouth were set though, and I knew what that meant. Sometimes business had rules that I didn't like but she had to follow.

"Thank you for coming so quickly, Jim," she said. She pointed to the kitchen chair that had been set kitty corner to her desk. "Would you like to sit down?"

I hadn't noticed the chair before. Damn. I wished I'd been paying more attention to that. I knew she only brought kitchen chairs in when she was expecting extra people. Now I'd missed my opportunity to run interference.

She sat down at her desk and fingered her slinky. When she spoke, it was slow and deliberate. "We've received some information, Jim, which may or may not be about your brother."

I was glad she got that "may not" in. She was good.

She went on. "A man has been found with the identification of Piedro Bellinni."

Jim sprang up, "Oh, thank God!"

Camille put her hand out as if to calm him. "Wait, there's more. We have no way of knowing if this man is your brother. No positive I.D. has been done. You see, unfortunately the man is deceased."

Jim deflated and sank back onto the chair. He brought his hands up to his face, rubbing his fingertips along his eyebrows, and went quiet.

I wasn't sure what to do. How to comfort him.

Finally, he said, "When will we know for sure?"

"Well, that's the tough part," Camille said. "We need someone to identify him."

"What about his wife?"

"I've left a message for her, but she hasn't returned my call yet." She paused. "If you'd like, we could wait to hear from her. Or, you could go yourself."

"And I could go with you," I added in quickly, trying to be supportive.

It was obvious he was mentally gathering strength to once again roll the rock life had dealt him up the hill. "I'd appreciate that," he said to me. "Where do I go?"

Camille jotted down the name and address of where the body was being held. I reached across and took it from her before she could pass it to Jim. "Come on," I said to him. "We can take my car." I didn't think he should be driving. Plus, this way I could save him the gas money.

I FIGURED THE drive would take about an hour. Turned out to be a tad longer with traffic, and it felt like forever because Jim was quiet for most of the ride, only speaking to give me directions. The only real conversation I had was with a gas station attendant when I stopped to refuel the Mini.

When we finally got to the building, the man at the front desk directed us down a long hallway to a bank of elevators. We had been told to go up to the fourth floor. I was relieved. I had visions of frigid basements with cement floors and stainless steel furnishings. Worse yet, no windows and dim fickle lighting fading in and out. Maybe even making sharp zzzizzing sounds as the bulbs went out. The fourth floor I could handle.

We stepped out of the elevator and checked the directional signs. Rooms 400-415 were to the left and rooms 416-430 were to the right. We both turned to the right. Room 421 was the first door after the bend in the corridor, right across from the emergency exit. Good to know just in case a quick getaway was in order. We stood in front of the door and looked at each other for what seemed like maybe the second time since we'd left C&C. Neither one of us seemed ready to reach out for the doorknob. I could feel my stomach fluttering. I could only imagine what Jim was feeling.

The door swung open and a young woman in a white smock nearly walked into us. She stepped back, startled, her hand automatically springing to her chest. "*Mon Dieu*," she said. Her dark hair was pulled back in a short ponytail rather tightly which seemed to tug at her forehead, raising her eyebrows up a bit and heightening her look of surprise.

"So sorry," I said. "We were just going in."

"No, no, is fine," she said in somewhat broken English with a thick French accent, her breath still returning to normal. "*Je m'excuse.*" She held the door open for us and we had no choice but to go in. She let go of the door, and it closed slowly on its own.

The room wasn't what I had expected. More sitting room than sterile lab. It was dimly lit by three floor lamps placed around the room, and the effect was cozy. A large round table surrounded by six office chairs sat off to the side across from what looked like an entertainment center with a large monitor, some other gizmos, and a computer. The far wall behind the desk had a sofa buffered by an end table full of magazines on one side and a water cooler on the other. Two doors separated by a gigantic painting of a meadow took up the remaining wall. One door had a red buzzer beside it and a tiny sign taped above it that said: "Please ring for service." The "e" at the end of the last word was a fill-in on my part, the edge of the sign having been ripped away along with the strand of tape that was supposed to hold it. Above the tiny English sign, a much bigger French one said pretty much the same thing. That sign was laminated and fastened securely.

Despite the décor, there was no hiding the smell. I couldn't name the chemical blend, but I would never forget it.

I rang the bell and a second later the door opened and a large squared man with a thick, full moustache and a shock of graying red hair looked out at us. No smock, just an outdated navy pin-striped suit. "*Est-ce que je peux vous aider*?" he asked.

"We're here concerning Piedro Bellinni," I said in English, hoping he'd switch languages.

Luckily, he did, although his English was somewhat broken too. "Ah, yes," he said. "Miss Weaver and Mr. Bell. A minute, please." And he disappeared behind the door.

I smiled over at Jim who only increased his attention on the loose sweater button his fingers massaged.

The door opened again, and the same man entered and led the way over to the table. "Given the circumstances and the condition of the deceased, I thought we should start with the pictures." He took a moment to settle himself. "*Bien,*" he said. "Let's see what we have." He pushed a button on the computer and the screen lit up. The same picture appeared that we'd received by fax.

Is this how it was going to work? I could handle this. As I sat down in the chair next to the one Jim had taken, I wondered if this was typical or if Camille had arranged it. I fixed on the screen, but the photo still wasn't very clear. I leaned in for a better look. The face was all bone with poky skin. "He looks old," I said, unintentionally aloud.

The two men looked at me.

I felt a flush in my cheeks. "I meant, he looks too old to be Puddles, er, Piedro."

The moustache man's joules jiggled as he spoke. "Probably his poor health. Maybe another photograph will help." He punched a few keys on the computer and another photo came up. This time it was a profile. When we didn't respond he went on through what was quickly becoming a series.

Jim pointed at one picture on the screen. "Stop!"

The shock of hearing his voice after so long jolted me.

A large close-up of a birthmark filled the monitor. "What's that?" Jim asked the man.

"It's an enlargement of a birthmark on the deceased's upper arm." The dark brown skin in the photo was shaped like an oversized raisin.

"Puddles never had a birthmark on either of his arms."

"Could it be something else?" I asked. "A scar? A burn mark? A tattoo removal?"

The man shook his head. "No, it's a birthmark, definitely. It's in the report. But, if you want to see for yourselves, I could take you to see the body."

I shuddered.

Luckily, Jim refused. "No. I didn't think it was him anyway. The hairline is all wrong and Puddles had a dimple. Not to mention a scar on his chin from when he was a kid."

Moustache needed to be sure for his records. "Are you saying this isn't Piedro Bellinni?"

"I don't know who that is," Jim said, the tension in his face visibly lessened. He stood to leave.

"What a shame," Moustache said as he changed the name in the computer, quite likely to the French equivalent of John Doe. "A dead man deserves to have a family."

Good thing Moustache was so sensitive about the feelings of the dead. He wasn't so careful about the feelings of the living. I pulled out a business card from my pocket and offered it to Moustache. "Can I get a copy of all the photographs," I said. "I'd like to run them by another client who's looking for a missing person." I was thinking of Francesca on the off chance that her Piedro wasn't the same Puddles as Jim's after all.

Moustache read my card and immediately took it upon himself to pass me his as though this was some modern form of exchanging greetings or shaking hands. I had noticed he hadn't bothered to introduce himself when we'd arrived. I'd taken it as a lack of manners. Maybe it was simply passé to him. He turned back to the computer and keyed in the appropriate instructions. A whirring came from behind a door in the "entertainment center" and seconds later, he reached in for the printouts, passing them directly to me. "For you," he said. He saw us to the door, calling out as we left, "come again."

I DROPPED JIM back at C&C to pick up his car, and we said our goodbyes before I ran into the office to check on things with Tina. No news yet. This was getting nerve-racking. I wasn't sure the "no news is good news" theory applied here.

I reminded myself that we were doing all we could while I watched Laurent slam drawers in reception. "What's up?" I asked him.

"Just looking for something," he said.

"Can I help?"

He stopped and turned to me. "Not unless you know where my iPod went."

I slipped past him into the kitchen to see Camille. "Nope. Sorry."

"How did it go?" she asked me.

"Jim was sure it wasn't Puddles." I tossed the pile of printouts on the table. "I brought back some copies of the dead guy's photo shoot. Just in case."

"In case what?"

"In case it still is Piedro Bellinni. Always possible that Puddles a.k.a Paul Bell and Puddles a.k.a Piedro Bellinni aren't one and the same. Maybe they just look alike."

Camille crooked her left eyebrow at me but said nothing.

I stepped back into the hall. "I think I'll head home for a while then try Francesca later. Maybe run the pictures over to her."

"You may want to hide out here for a while," Camille suggested. "Your house is being investigated by the police."

"My house is being investigated? For what?"

"The police are there looking for evidence, fingerprints, that sort of thing."

I didn't like the sound of that. "In my house?" I stood in the short hallway between the reception and the kitchen. "Why?"

"Not so much in it," Laurent said. "Mostly outside around your porch, the path, your door. They're talking to neighbors, checking to see if anyone saw who dropped off the package last night."

Fabulous. I picked up the reception extension and speed dialed myself. Adam answered after two rings.

"Hey," I said as I sat down in Arielle's chair. "How's it going over there?"

"I'm glad you called, hon. The police have been here for a few hours and Jeffrey's a mess."

"Have the police gotten any leads?"

"Nothing they're telling me about." He lowered his voice. "They've been really giving Jeffrey the third degree. He's not holding up well. He keeps running to the bathroom."

Eww. Mental note to get disinfectant on the way home. "Okay," I said to Adam. "I'll just finish up with a couple things here and leave."

We said our goodbyes and hung up. I knew if I headed home straight away, I'd get stuck in a round of police questioning. On the other hand, if I lingered here a tad longer, there was a good chance the police would finish up with Jeffrey and be on their way. I surveyed the pile of stuff Laurent had dumped on the desk earlier in the search for his iPod and decided he could really use my help cleaning up.

"Where does all this stuff go?" I asked him.

"Drawers," he said, head deep in the cabinet behind the desk, still in the throes of his iPod search.

I opened the large bottom drawer, scooped a bunch of stuff from the top of the mound, and dumped it in. I continued until the mound was reduced to a bump. Excellent progress only now the drawer wouldn't close. I shuffled things around a bit hoping to smooth out the top. A particularly lumpy Ziplock bag wasn't cooperating, so I pulled it out. Hmmm. Tina's bag of evidence against Jeffrey. Figures. I debated the sense in even holding on to the stuff and eyeballed the leftover pile on the desk. Probably it would all fit in the drawer if I left out Tina's bag so I set it aside, scooped in everything else, and closed the drawer. Perfect.

I tossed the Ziplock into the trash bin under Arielle's desk and gathered my things, but something stopped me from leaving before I made it through the door. It was that pesky do-gooder inside me. She wasn't happy. She didn't like me throwing out Tina's things because even if it was just a pile of useless junk, it was Tina's useless junk, and it meant something to her. Damn. Sometimes I wished that do-gooder Lora would keep her opinions to herself.

I retrieved the Ziplock from the garbage and was about to slip it into my shoulder bag when I noticed the match books. They weren't from hotels or clubs like Tina said. They had generic images on them like the kind that come from a grocery store. I unzipped the bag, took out the matches and checked the flaps, expecting to find something scribbled inside, but they were all clean. It figured. It was just like Tina to be suspicious of nothing. I checked the Altoids pack too, and it only had mints. I moved on to the Virginia Slims, opened the pack, and peered inside. There, nestled between a bunch of dented cigarettes, was a mini tape cassette. I smiled, and the hair prickled on the back of my neck. So, it wasn't just a bag of useless junk after all.

SIXTEEN

MINUTES LATER, CAMILLE, Laurent, and I were huddled on the couch in Laurent's office watching nannycam footage of Jeffrey's boss Henry Bennett of Finestein, Bennett, and Fitch Incorporated.

The onscreen office was a tribute to traditional masculine conservatism. Floor-to-ceiling bookshelves in dark wood were on the left of the screen and to the right, a massive wooden desk with intricate carvings stood with a tall, plush, weathered leather chair behind it. In the chair sat a man equally weathered to comfortable softness yet clearly not weak in the springs. His silver-gray hair, rather long for a man in his sixties, was tastefully slicked back. I couldn't make out the color of his eyes, but they had the same healthy glow as his skin. As he moved about the room, I began to suspect he was an athlete. Perhaps less so now, yet still active. Jeffrey's suspicions of an affair didn't seem as absurd as they once had. If this man was a bit of an impresario with the ladies, it wasn't merely for his wealth.

In the interest of time, Laurent fast-forwarded over the parts with Bennett working solo. Any time someone came in or the phone rang, he played it out. We got to the bit where Tina arrived and listened. Pretty boring, just some campaigning on her part and some ogling on his. We got to the section Jeffrey had mentioned about an argument with an older man. We watched it twice. Camille took down some notes of names and such they talked about. Nothing of obvious importance jumped out. Certainly nothing we could see that would be worth taping. Aside from a few interactions with a woman we figured was his assistant, he had no other visitors.

"Hang on," I said to Laurent as he played a phone conversation. "Go back."

He stopped, rewound, and started the conversation from the beginning.

I wasn't sure if I was hearing right. "Can we go back again and up the volume?"

He went back again.

"There," I said. "Did you guys hear that?"

Camille and Laurent both shook their heads. "What?" Camille asked.

"That bit about 'Don't worry, Franny,'" I said.

We listened again. It was definitely there. Bennett's end of the conversation went like this: "It'll be fine," pause. "You know everything is set," pause. "But it *will* work," pause. "That won't happen," pause. "Because there's nothing *to* find," pause. "Don't worry, Franny. It's all going to work out. It will be over before you know it."

"What's the big deal?" Laurent asked. "He's probably talking to his wife about redecorating or something. Or, maybe one of their kids."

"His wife's name is Barbara," I said remembering the company profile info Laurent had added to the file after his employee search of Finestein, Bennett, and Fitch Inc. "And, anyway, what about that reference to there being nothing to find?"

"What do you think it's about?" Camille asked me.

"I'm not sure what it's about, but isn't Franny a nickname for Francesca?"

ON THE WAY home, I thought about how grateful I was for Laurent's love of gadgets. He had been able to copy the tape onto a couple of discs before I left, leaving him free to pass on the original to the police, keep a copy at C&C, and let me have one.

As I turned onto my street, Joshua, a neighbor who lived three houses down from Adam and I, waved me over. Joshua was a nice kid who planned to study horticulture when he started university next year, and since neither Adam nor I had any interest in gardening, we hired Joshua to take care of our yard. He had a real gift for working with plants and an entrepreneurial spirit, and for the past couple of years, he'd made pretty good pocket money servicing the neighborhood. I pulled over next to him and rolled my window down partway.

"Hey there, Miss America," he said to me. "Quite a bit of action goin' on at your place today."

I smiled at the Miss America reference. He'd been calling me that since we met. I had mixed feelings about the whole pageant bit, but somehow the term made me feel patriotic—like an ambassador abroad of sorts. Any implied association to beauty was totally lost on me. Really. "So I hear," I said back to him.

"Just wanted to warn ya, old Mrs. Millar has cooked up a cherry pie with your name on it."

Mrs. Millar was the self-proclaimed neighborhood watch committee. She saw no reason for other members. She used her I.D. card like a press pass, wielding it to gain access to what she termed "the neighborhood's right to know." In other words, she took advantage of any visible occurrence to wrench as much personal information from her neighbors as she could over a piece of home-baked cherry pie.

"Thanks for the warning. Can I give you a lift home?"

"Nah, I'm just heading out."

"Okay, see you around."

Joshua waved and sauntered off down the street.

I pulled up as far as I could in my driveway, wanting to keep the car out of easy view of Mrs. Millar. Closing the door quietly was no easy task. Car doors don't generally catch well without a good slam. I gently pushed it until it was nearly shut then shoved against it with my hip, forcing it closed. Not exactly noiseless, but definitely missing the attention-getting smack of a slam.

Key in hand, I made a dash for the front door. I let myself into the vestibule and was nearly knocked over by Pong before I even had the door closed. Lack of height and heft didn't stop her from using her assets to full advantage. A good, swift body-check behind the knees and she could bring anyone down to her level where she could freely lick them to death. "Enough, enough," I said trying to sound authoritative through my laughs.

Adam hung back, watching. "You missed everything," he said.

"Yeah, too bad for me, eh?" I stroked Pong's back as I made my way into the house.

"Well, everyone's gone," Adam said.

"Even Jeffrey?"

"His lawyer took him home after the police were through questioning him. They suggested he stay there in case the kidnappers tried to reach him."

"Do the police think it's bad that we haven't been contacted by the kidnappers again yet?" I was in the kitchen now, getting some water from the cooler. It gurgled at the exchange of air.

Adam straddled a chair backwards, folded his arms over the back, and rested his chin on top. "They don't know."

I sat down beside him. His stubble was long enough to see the bits of blond scattered in the brown, and the tiny lines around his eyes didn't look so tiny. What he needed was a shower and a long nap. Completely understandable considering the day he'd had. Still, a part of me didn't quite like that it was Tina who elicited all this exhaustion and strain. I wasn't proud of it, but there it was. I reached out, stroked Adam's hair, and reminded myself that it was his warm heart that had attracted me to him in the first place. It was a good thing that he cared so much for a friend. Even if that friend was Tina.

And I was worried about her, too. But finding the Bennett tape had helped with that. I told Adam about it, and he perked up considerably at the prospect of being able to make the "trade" if and when the goons got back in touch.

"The weird thing is, the tape didn't seem that important," I said.

"You watched it?"

"Yeah, we all watched it. Want to see it? I've got a copy."

"Absolutely," he said and we both headed for the living room. While we got things set up for viewing on his laptop, I told him about my afternoon.

"You look tired," he said.

"I feel it." I left him to start watching while I went to make myself a sandwich. When I came back into the living room, the footage wasn't that far along. Clearly he wasn't fast-forwarding as we had. I sat beside him on the couch and took a bite of my avocado on spelt. "This thing goes on for hours. You might want to fast-forward some."

"It's okay," he said and went on watching in real time. "Makes me feel like I'm doing something. I hate all this waiting around."

The doorbell rang and we both started. Adam went to the door while I peered out from behind the living room curtains. Someone was standing very close to the door. I couldn't make out much more than that. I ran to the door before Adam opened it. "Wait," I whispered. "It could be Mrs. Millar. Joshua told me she was on the hunt."

Adam paused. We huddled together in the corner of the vestibule to keep clear of the window. The ringer went again. Pong barked and scratched at the inner door, trying to pry it open. "We have to answer it," Adam whispered back. "It could be important."

He was right. "Okay, but we need a plan if it's her. We can't let her in."

"Fine, I'll say I've got the flu."

That was good. Mrs. Millar had a germ phobia. "Okay."

The mail flap flipped up. Chipped fingernails partially coated in purple polish poked in. Automatically, we both flattened ourselves to the wall and waited until the flap knocked shut then Adam scrambled for the door and I hid behind it.

Mrs. Millar was on the second stair down when the door opened, and she turned to face Adam. "Oh, you *are* home," she said. The expression on her face said she suspected as much. She came back onto the porch. Sure enough, she had a large circular Tupperware container clutched to her body. She was wearing the same wool coat she wore every fall, mid-length navy blue, over dark poly-cotton sweatpants pilling from numerous washings. Her gray roots had been recently touched up to match the bronzy shade her hair had once been naturally. The short layered cut was flat on the sides accentuating the poof of the top, leaving the impression of her head being topped with meringue. It was hard to tell for sure looking through the crack in the door, but I'd bet her curling iron was still cooling down at home.

"Mrs. Millar," Adam said. "So nice to see you." He paused to add a small cough.

She came closer. "Hello."

Adam smiled and coughed again. "I'm sorry, I'm afraid I've got a fairly nasty flu."

She stepped back a bit. "Oh, I'm sorry to hear that." She held out the Tupperware. "I was just bringing over a pie. I noticed the police at your house for quite some time. I hope nothing's wrong."

I jabbed Adam in the back. He hacked as though about to bring up some phlegm. "No, nothing really," he said. "You know the police, you call them for a little thing and they go all out."

"A little thing?"

He evaded her probe. "Yes. I'm sure you know how it is. But, it was so nice of you to think of us." He reached out for the pie, and she passed it to him. "I'll let Lora know you stopped by."

"Yes, well," she stammered, clearly unsure of her next move.

Adam let out a longer cough, making a big production out of trying to cover his mouth with his forearm.

That seemed to do. Mrs. Millar turned to leave. "Bye, now," she said.

"Thanks again," Adam croaked out.

As soon as the door was closed, he held the container with his left arm and we high-fived each other.

"Just in time for dessert," he said, carrying the pie through to the kitchen. He put it down on the counter and reached into the cupboard for some plates. The doorbell rang again. We looked at each other.

"You don't suppose she came back, do you?" I said.

Adam strode off for the door. "She's not getting the pie back."

It wasn't Mrs. Millar. It was Camille. Dressed in black jeans, a black sweater, a black ball cap, and black Doc Martens. A mini black knapsack was strapped on papoose-style. Damn. That could only mean one thing. What she liked to call "sitting guard." In other words, a stakeout. Only with peeping, prowling, and anything else the situation called for thrown in.

"You're just in time," Adam said. "We were just about to have some pie."

"Chocolate cream?" she asked.

"Cherry."

"That'll work."

I cut generous slices for each of us. "So, what's up?"

She took her plate and started in on the pie. "Guess which law firm used to represent Guido and Antonia Mauri?"

"Finestein, Bennett, and Fitch?" I ventured.

"*Exactement*. I did some checking after you left the office this afternoon. You may be right about Bennett talking to Francesca. His firm represented the family until Antonia passed away. They handled all their legal affairs, personal and professional. They even helped Antonia transfer ownership of Guido's Garments to the employees."

I swished some water around my teeth to pick up some errant cherry bits and swallowed. "So Francesca probably knows Bennett."

Camille pushed her empty plate towards the center of the table. "She not only knows Bennett, she spent quite a bit of time with him while she was contesting her mother's will."

"Why'd she contest the will?"

"Not sure yet. What we need to do now is establish a current relationship." She patted her stomach. "That's not bad pie. When did you have time to make pie?"

"We didn't make it," Adam said, already on his second piece. "It's from our neighbor Mrs. Millar."

"My neighbors never give me pie," Camille said.

"Mrs. Millar isn't an ordinary neighbor, she's more of a spy," I said. "The pie wasn't exactly a gift, it's more like the bait in an ambush. Only in this case the ambush was thwarted."

"Well, whatever you did to warrant her ambush, you should do it more often."

I could see Adam giving the suggestion serious consideration. *I* was seriously considering locking myself in the bathroom upstairs. It was late and I was tired. I didn't want to put on my "Catwoman" garb and play sitting guard with Camille.

Camille checked her watch. "Okay, time to go." She turned to me. "You better get dressed. And for goodness sakes, don't wear that red hat like the last time."

The last time she was referring to was on a previous case, and I had a good reason for wearing that hat. It was cold and it has extra insulation over the ears. When my ears get cold my head hurts. When my head hurts I get distracted. I needed that hat to do my job. It wasn't my fault the little logo in the front had a reflector. Who knew I'd be hiding in bushes trying to dodge flashlights.

I went upstairs to change. I got undressed and put my hair into a fresh ponytail. There weren't a lot of Catwoman clothes to choose from. I squeezed into a white turtleneck covering it with a plain black hooded sweat top. I checked over the matching pants for decals and such. All clear, so I pulled them on. The tiny inner pocket was just large enough for my keys and a couple of twenties folded three times into a square. I threw an old black headband of Adam's in the jacket pocket in case the night grew frosty. That left me one jacket pocket. I pulled a few Kleenexes from the box on my nightstand and put them in. A quick stop by the bathroom and I'd be ready to go.

Camille was already on the porch when I got downstairs. Adam drew me to him before I went out. His scruff prickled and his kiss tasted like cherry.

CAMILLE GUIDED HER Jetta through the streets with the finesse of the native she was—including generous lane hopping and not so generous signaling.

"I assume we're going over to Francesca's?"

She slowed for a red light. "*Oui.* I haven't heard back from her since I left the message about Puddles. Curious, no?"

"You didn't tell her the guy was dead did you?"

"Of course not. When I left the message I didn't know anything for sure. I left her the same message I left for Jim. I said something urgent had come up concerning Puddles, and I needed to speak with her as soon as possible. I've tried calling her several times since. I just keep getting the machine."

"So, she went out for the day. People do that, you know."

Camille gave me a look before she got the car moving again. "What's with you?"

"Nothing. Sorry. It's been a long day. I'm just tired." And cranky and cold and really not into this. And, if I wanted to be totally honest, I was feeling anxious about Tina. We still didn't know who had her, where she was, or how she was being treated. She may not be my favorite person in the world, but I didn't want her to suffer. Well, not in any serious way.

Camille pulled the car over in front of a house down a few and across the street from Francesca's. There were a few lights on inside Francesca's. No car in the driveway. Closed garage doors not offering any insights.

"Damn those blinds," Camille said. "Why can't people just use curtains? I can't even make out any shadows with those things." She put down her mini binoculars.

Given the Catwoman garb, I thought it was unlikely that we were just going to go up and ring the bell. "So, what's the plan?"

She got out her phone. "First, I call over again." She punched in the speed dial number and held the phone to her ear. Camille always put the main phone numbers related to a case on her speed dial. It was all about efficiency, she once explained to me. I suspected it was originally another way of playing with one of her favorite toys. After a moment she disconnected. "Machine again."

"That doesn't mean she's not home," I said. "She could be screening."

Camille started the car. "That's the problem. We're going to have to get a better look." She drove around to the street behind the house. No street parking, permit holders only. She tapped her fingertips on the steering wheel, clearly in think mode.

I pointed to the end of the street. "Look. There's a dog walk. Maybe we can pull into there."

She edged the car up. There weren't any bona fide parking spots, but there was a wide path with two parallel rows of worn grass, bearing the unmistakable look of tire marks, leading into a cove of trees. We turned in and parked.

Camille flicked open the glove compartment and took out two pairs of black gloves. She passed one to me.

"You're not expecting to get into the house, are you?" I asked.

"It could happen."

"She's got an alarm," I reminded her.

"What kind is it?"

"I don't know. The kind that makes noise and notifies the police."

She squinted at me briefly. "Let's go," she said.

We got out of the car and made our way back to Francesca's. Still no car in the driveway. We stood under an ancient maple tree nearby to shield us some from the streetlight. I noticed the lights in other houses going out downstairs and new ones popping on upstairs. Bedtime. On my street, there were still quite a few people out and about at this hour. Here, there weren't a lot of pedestrians. Occasionally, a car went by, but no one walked a dog or ambled home.

Camille was eyeing Francesca's. Nothing had changed. No new lights on, no old lights out. This wasn't good. To Camille, this was encouragement. I could feel a knot forming in my belly.

"I think we should go back to the car," I said.

She looked at me. "What's wrong? You don't look right."

I didn't have a chance to answer before headlights flashed in my eyes and Camille pulled me back behind the tree. A car neared and turned into Francesca's driveway.

Francesca got out of the passenger side, slammed the door, and stomped up the pathway, her ankles wobbling with each strike of her foot. A man got out of the driver's side and went after her. He caught her by the arm, and she pivoted toward him.

"Leave me alone," Francesca said.

"We need to talk this through," the man said. Even in the dark, I recognized the man as Bennett.

She wrestled to free her elbow from his grasp. "Talk what through? How stupid you are?"

"I know you're angry, baby, but it's not that bad. We can make this work for us."

"Us? What us? The you and me us or the you and your wife us?"

He sighed. "You know there's only one us."

Francesca turned away from him and headed for her front door.

"Wait," Bennett said, reaching for her arm again.

"Stop grabbing me," she said as she whirled around and smacked him on the chest.

I jumped, startled by their interaction, and my feet crunched a pile of dry leaves that had pooled at the base of the tree Camille and I were hiding behind. Camille put an arm out to steady me, and I held my breath, bracing myself, feeling sure we'd be spotted.

But Francesca smacked Bennett again, seemingly oblivious to us. "There's nothing to talk about, Henry," she said. "It's over."

"It can still work, baby," he assured her. "You'll see. I'll make it work."

Her struggle weakened, and he hugged her to his chest. "Let's go inside," he said. "We don't want to give your neighbors a show."

"No. You shouldn't be here," Francesca told him. "You should go."

"I already am here," he said. "A little longer won't make any difference."

"Yes, it could. And Lucia may come home." She started to push him towards his car. "You have to go. We'll talk later."

Bennett hesitated. "All right. I'll call you as soon as I get back."

Francesca watched him drive off then hurried for the door and went inside.

I WAS EXHAUSTED when I got home. It was nearly midnight. Adam was flaked out on the couch with Ping nestled in his warmth. A late night talk show was on low on TV. Pong, yawning, had come to the door to greet me. There was little gusto in the tail wag, but I appreciated the effort.

My stomach was feeling a little empty now with the earlier anxiety dying down. I went to the kitchen for some pie to take upstairs with me. I found the pie plate in the fridge. A pathetic sliver lay on its side, structurally unsound to stand, amid a torrent of crumbs. I smiled. Quite a testament to Adam's willpower really. I decided to skip the pie and mixed up a glass of chocolate soy milk instead.

Adam came in just as I was finishing up. "Hey," he said. His hair stuck out on the left and he was scratching his nether regions. Put a teddy bear in the crook of his arm and he could have been five years old. I think there was even some dried drool crusted on his cheek.

"I didn't mean to wake you," I said.

"I was waiting up for you," he said. "Only late night TV isn't what it used to be."

"That's all right. You didn't have to. You should have just gone to bed." I swallowed the last of my milk. "Let's go up, I'm exhausted."

"It went all right, then?"

"Yeah. We were at Francesca's and luckily she showed up before Camille got us into any trouble."

"Learn anything worthwhile?"

"Maybe."

Adam closed up and let the dog out while I took a quick shower. When I slipped under the covers he was already dozing off. It occurred to me that I hadn't asked if there was any news about Tina. If there had been, I'm sure he would have told me. For about a minute and a half I luxuriated in the warm softness of the bed then fell into a deep sleep that didn't last nearly as long as it should have.

But then, no one likes to be awoken by a strange man in their bedroom.

SEVENTEEN

AT FIRST, I thought I was imagining it. Surely, the man standing at the end of the bed was Adam. Yet common sense told me he couldn't have shrunk a few inches and grown a beard overnight. I instinctively reached over to Adam's side of the bed. It was barely warm. Pong wasn't in her dog bed either. I heard a woman shriek and realized it was me.

"Don't freak out," the man said. "I just want to talk to you."

His words probably would have been more effective if they hadn't come from a man who had just broken into my house. Better still if the man wasn't decked out in Hell's Angel gear complete with motorcycle duds, earrings, and a serpent tattoo running across his hand.

I sat up, holding the covers up to my neck, my initial fear quickly being replaced by irritation. I wasn't used to having my home encroached upon. First Tina and now this. "What? My doorbell not working?" I said to him.

"I just want to talk to you," he said again.

Hmmm. I wasn't sure what to make of this guy. Break-in aside, he wasn't acting like a rapist or anything. And being a New Yorker, not to mention a trained social worker, had taught me a few things. One of them being to trust my instincts in situations like this. And right now my instincts were telling me to stay calm. Of course, I would have felt a tad more confident on this point if I wasn't wearing my b-list nightie that had thinned to the sheerness of onion skin.

He spoke again. "Look, we don't have much time. Your husband will be back soon." He looked at his watch. "How long does it usually take to walk your dog?"

So that's where Adam was. Good to know he wasn't locked in the basement or something. "He's not my husband," I said. "We just live together." Why I felt the need to correct that point was beyond me. Must be nerves. I pointed to the back of the bedroom door. "Would you pass me my robe? It's the white one on the right."

The biker lifted my robe off the hook and handed it over. I wrapped it around me, letting the covers droop only when I had the sash in place. I pivoted and got up. And now that I was a bit closer to him, the biker looked faintly familiar. "Whatever you have to say, better make it quick," I said to him in answer to his question about Adam's walk with Pong.

He put his arm out, leaning against the footboard. "I know you're looking for me," he said. "I'm Paul Bell."

Paul Bell. That was Puddles' real name. "You're Puddles?" I said.

He smiled. "This isn't how I normally look. It's a disguise."

I went over to him to get a better look at his face. And that's when it hit me. This guy was the other member of the bearded posse. So he *was* following me. And now that I was looking for it, his face did have some similarities to the pictures I'd seen of Puddles. Hard to tell for sure, though, having never seen him in person. "Let's say for the moment that you are Paul Bell, why do you need a disguise?"

He looked me in the eye. "I can't really explain that now," he said. "I have my reasons."

Reasons. Hmmmph.

He went on. "Look, I know my wife hired your agency to find me, but I hear my brother is looking for me too. I need to know why."

I was about to answer when I hit my pause button. So, he wanted information from me. That gave me some clout. Maybe I could use it to get a few answers of my own first. "Look here," I said. "You can't just break into my house and expect me to answer a bunch of questions." Although, clearly he could and he did. "Just who do you think you are? And what's with the following me around? Since I've been on your case I've been run off the road, forced to steal a car, and uncomfortably close to a dead guy. Not to mention that my friend's gone missing."

"I know. I'm sorry about that."

"You're sorry. You're sorry about what?"

"I'm sorry about your friend."

"What do you know about it?" I asked.

"I'm sure she's being well cared for," he said.

"How do you know? Do you know who has her? Do you know where she is?"

He opened his mouth to speak then froze. I heard the front door open. Puddles lunged for the hallway. I tried to grab hold of him, but he was too fast. He ran for the bathroom and out the open window. I peered out as he rolled down the roof of the downstairs outcrop over the sunroom. I heard him land and run. A minute later, a bike's motor started up.

"What are you doin'?" Adam reached around me to close the window. "It's freezing in here."

I turned to face him. His cheeks were rosy from his walk, his eyes bright. "Puddles was just here," I said.

"You found him?"

"He found me," I said.

"**LET'S GO OVER** this again," Laurent said. "You want me to go to Stanley's and ask around about a guy with a serpent tattoo on his hand?"

I had thought that up on the way over to the office. Stanley's was just the kind of place Puddles might go. It was probably a long shot that he made a habit of the place, but it was as good a place as any to start nosing around. I would have gone myself except I knew that with Laurent's connections, he stood a better chance at getting a lead. "That's about it," I said.

Camille sat across from us at the café table in the kitchen. She had one hand on her mug handle while the other squeezed her slinky. The office phone rang, and she sprang out to reception to answer it.

Laurent watched her go then got back to our conversation. "Why?"

It was out of my mouth before I could stop it. "I have my reasons," I said.

Laurent gave me a long look. We were both standing by the counter near the sink in shootout position. Which suited him better than me. In another life, he could have pulled off the holster and hat easy. "Your anglophone is not taking care of you properly, eh Lora? Or you would not be so short with me."

I glowered at him, not sure if I was more annoyed at him for making the comment or at myself for wondering if it was true.

"Look," he said. "Lots of people have snake tattoos. Anything else you can tell me about the guy?"

I gave him a physical description but held back on telling him the snake belonged to Puddles.

Laurent watched my face as I spoke. "Is that it?"

I tried to look him in the eye but failed. "Pretty much."

He went quiet a minute then said, "Montreal is a big city. Chances are low I'll get any information on your man at Stanley's."

He was right, but low chances were better than none. I shifted my feet and toyed with the keys in my pocket, trying to think of something persuasive to say. My finger got tangled in my key ring and my knuckle jammed. I pulled the ring out to release my finger and the keys dropped to the floor.

Laurent shook his head and picked up the keys. "It is important to you, eh?"

I nodded.

He held the keys out to me. "Okay," he said. "I'll see what I can do. But I don't promise anything."

I thanked him, reached for the keys, and smiled. He kept his eyes on mine and slowly placed the keys in my hand, then we both turned as Camille came in waving a piece of paper.

"Got it," she said. "Diane, *ma cousine*, sent over an email with the dates and times of calls between Francesca and Bennett. She was able to check their land lines and their cell accounts. There were a lot of calls, so she only went back six weeks."

I knew better than to ask how *cousine* Diane got her hands on the information. I knew she worked for a phone company. I also knew phone companies weren't in the habit of disclosing details of client accounts.

"Not only do they speak quite regularly, the calls often go on a long time," Camille added. "Between this and what we saw last night, there's no doubt Francesca and Bennett have a connection that goes deeper than lawyer and client."

The phone rang again before she could continue. She stepped back into the other room to pick it up. "*C'est* Jim for you," she called out to me.

I took the phone. "Hi, Jim."

"I'm calling from the hospital," he said. "Sarah's been admitted."

I sat down on the edge of the reception desk. "Oh, Jim, I'm sorry. How is she?"

"We're not sure yet. The doctors are running tests." His voice stopped. I could make out whispering amid the background speaker static. On the other end of the line, Jim's voice was replaced by Joanne's. "My baby is dying," she said. "Please, do something. Please."

I LEFT C&C right after the call. I was determined to do something. Anything. I sat in my car and went over my options. Pretty quickly, I realized I didn't have any. I had no idea what to do next. I felt frustrated and a little sheepish for not telling Camille or Laurent about my encounter with Puddles. I wasn't sure why I hadn't. I guess I hoped Puddles would still be looking to finish our conversation, and I wanted to gain his confidence, let him see that I wouldn't give him away. Also, given that he had singled me out for some reason, I figured I'd be more approachable solo, and I didn't want anyone hanging around to babysit me.

With nowhere to go, I went home. Adam had left a note on the fridge letting me know he'd be out for the morning. He didn't say where. I perused the fridge and pantry for something to eat. Having no desire to actually prepare something, I settled on some vanilla ice cream with lots of maple syrup drizzled on top. I was halfway through the bowl when it occurred to me that Francesca still hadn't returned Camille's message about Puddles. At least, not that Camille had mentioned. That was odd. We knew she had gotten home. Presumably she checked her messages. I went up to the office to see if she'd called my machine. No messages. I called Camille. She hadn't heard from her either.

Another thirty seconds and I knew what to do. I got my fanny pack, loaded it up with the basic necessities, and then I switched my outfit for some jeans, a cream turtleneck, and a sweater long enough to cover the fanny pack, which although practical, was about as flattering as a migrating lump of cellulite. I made a pit-stop at the bathroom, fastened my hair back with a clip, and headed downstairs to let the dog out. While I was waiting for Pong to finish her business, I flipped Adam's note over and wrote him a note of my own letting him know where I was going to be and secured it to the fridge with an x/o magnet at each corner. I gave Pong a Milk-Bone from the box in the sunroom and grabbed my dog-walking jacket, the red corduroy with a cotton fleece lining. A bottle of water in one pocket, my cell phone and sunglasses in the other, and I was off.

I HAD DECIDED it was best to march up and ring the doorbell. I pressed it three times before the intercom crackled.

"Yes?"

"It's Lora Weaver, Mrs. Bellinni."

There was a slight pause before she answered. "This isn't a good time."

"It's rather important," I said. I wasn't sure yet what reason I would give for my visit, but I knew now it had to sound pressing.

"I'll call you later. I'm busy now with my daughter. I hope you understand."

I did understand. I understood that I was getting the brush off. I doubted Lucia was even home. "I don't mind waiting," I said. "I'll just be in my car here in the driveway whenever you're free."

A loud buzz like feedback from an amplifier screeched at me before the intercom went silent. I paced a bit before strolling over to my car. Even with my layers of clothes, the cold infiltrated enough to kick-start my nervous system into shivering. Clearly, Wonder Woman never worked the north. Not in that outfit.

I was off by maybe five minutes. I was out there ten before the front door opened and Francesca stepped out. She wore a knee-length, long-sleeve dress. Black and white color block pattern, maybe rayon. It stretched some with her pigeon steps over to my car. I rolled my window down a nudge.

"Hi there," I said. "Would you like to get in a minute?"

She shook her head. She leaned in to me, her arms crossed over her breasts, forcing a cleavage that threatened to bury her crucifix. "You should go," she said. "Lucia's in-laws will be here any minute."

"I need to talk to you about the case."

"I'm dropping it," she said. "I need to focus on Lucia's wedding."

Dropping it? Again? First it was on, then off, then on, now off again. With her constant mind changes it was a wonder she managed to dress each morning.

She must have felt my skepticism because she went on. "I'm sorry." Her teeth were starting to rattle with the early signs of chattering. "But I've decided it would be healthier to let it all go. It's time I got on with my life."

"But what about the break-in? I thought you were worried about that."

"I was overreacting," she told me.

That may have made sense at an earlier time. I may even have believed her now if I didn't know she was lying. I motioned to get out of the car and she stepped back. "Okay. That's your choice, but there's something I need to show you before I can close your file."

"Show me? Oh no. I'll sign whatever you need to end the investigation." Her eyes flicked away from me for a second. She urged me back into my car. "Now, really, you should go."

I wasn't about to let her get rid of me so easily. I leaned into the car to get the envelope of photos that supposedly belonged to the deceased Piedro Bellinni. My hand was just about to close in on the envelope when a harsh shove to my backside propelled me clear across the passenger seat. My head rammed the door causing sudden pain and then nothing.

I AWOKE ON a hard, wood lounge chair. My back ached. And so did my head. I reached up to find loosely wrapped gauze strung around my head like an '80s sweatband. My fingers traveled a little south to find some crusting of dried liquid between my eyebrows. I scratched at it and smelled my fingertips. Blood.

I had no idea where I was, but it was dark, dank, and cool so I was guessing basement. I eased myself into a sit, watching for dizziness, and checked my waist for my fanny pack. Still there. Luckily, I had weaved it through my belt loops to keep the bulge from sliding back and forth which seemed to have had the added benefit of keeping it securely fastened to my body. I opened the zipper enough to get my hand in and rooted around for my penlight. It was dim, but it was working. I skimmed the room. Without getting up, I couldn't make much out except that the room was small and didn't seem to have any windows. The only source of lighting was what filtered in from between the slats of the door. I switched off the light to save it and checked my pockets. The phone, sunglasses, and water were all still there. Either nobody bothered to frisk me, or my fanny pack and pocket contents were left with me on purpose. I preferred to think it was the former. The thought of some stranger's hands groping my unconscious body unnerved me.

I pulled out my cell phone to call Camille. It wasn't giving off any light, so I tried powering it up. Nothing happened. Dead battery. Damn. I slipped the phone back into my pocket and took out the water bottle, broke the seal, and took a swig while I got my bearings. First, I needed to check my head injury, then I could figure out where I was and how to get out. I pulled out a compact from my fanny pack and slipped off the bandage. Feeling my head, it seemed that the only soreness was in the front. I pointed the light at my forehead and held the mirror up. A thick wavy line of dried blood stretched from just inside my hairline to the top of my nose. I poured some water onto the bandage and gingerly cleaned the area. Once the blood was cleared away, I was left with a gash no longer than a chocolate chip. An antibiotic Band-Aid would cover it. I stuck one on then checked my watch. It was a European digital one with a twenty-four hour reading. Camille had given it to me. Fourteen thirty-eight was lit up. Just after two-thirty in the afternoon. A few hours had passed, and I was sure I wasn't out that long just from the bang on my head. The realization did nothing to ease my nerves. I dug into my fanny pack again, grabbed a protein bar, and took a bite, hoping the energy would do me good.

A couple small bites later, penlight in hand, I walked the perimeter of the room. It was solid brick. Old, even moist in places. Efflorescence had formed here and there creating a nearly stucco effect. There were a few rows of warped wood shelving that probably stored preserves at one time. They were empty now except for dust. The door was planked wood with a rickety metal doorknob. I pulled on it. Locked. The lock wasn't a deadbolt or connected to the doorknob. It was some kind of slide bolt on the outside. There must have been one near the top and another on the bottom judging by the movement of the door when I pulled. I shined my penlight into the crack between the door and the doorframe. The locks were clearly visible. One large metal one about two-thirds up the door and a thinner one just a foot up from the bottom. I tested the doorframe. Wood. It would probably give if kicked just right.

Problem was, even if I was a kick-ass door-kicker, which I wasn't, I didn't know who might be on the other side. Even a small noise might bring some steroid-popping thug with a gun running in. I definitely didn't need that. I sat back down on the lounger. What I did need was to think some more. Figure out how this happened and what to do next. Only I was having trouble concentrating. Basements kind of creeped me out. Nothing good ever happened in basements. Especially dark locked cellars. Also, I saw a report on some news show a few weeks back about toxic mold. This place could definitely have some of that. Not to mention spiders. I didn't do well with bugs either. And then there were all the strange noises like pipes creaking and little scratchy sounds. I tried real hard not to think about what was making those scratchy noises. Which wasn't easy because the noises were getting louder. More like someone scraping ice off a car windshield.

Then it occurred to me. Maybe Tina was locked down here too. Maybe in another room just like this one. I imagined her on the other side of the wall carving her initials or marking off days with the tip of a rusty nail she had found on the floor. I got up and tracked the noise back to the last row of shelves. Closer up, it took on more of a tapping sound. Seemed to be coming from the center of the top shelf. I leaned in to pinpoint it and a sudden cracking sent me back a step, knocking me into the shelves behind me. In an effort to regain my balance, I reached out, automatically clutching at the air then closing in on something solid, something warm. I looked down to see a snake. I tried to let go but it held me fast. I looked up into a heavily bearded face. Puddles.

EIGHTEEN

"HOW DID YOU find me?" I asked him.

"Let's go," he said, ignoring my question. "Fast." He motioned at me with his hand.

I felt my midsection for my pouch and checked my pockets to make sure I hadn't left anything back on the lounger and considered the situation. "And, just how do you expect me to leave? In case you hadn't noticed, you're talking to me through an opening barely large enough for your head. Not to mention the fact that it's about four feet off the ground and surrounded by rotted, rickety shelves."

He glanced at the wood. "It's fine. You're small, and the shelves will hold your weight. What are you, maybe five feet and a hundred pounds? A hundred and ten? Just climb up, I'll pull you through from this side."

"I'm almost five two," I said like it mattered, not bothering to comment on my weight. I stepped onto the lowest shelf with half my foot, pressing into it, testing its strength. It didn't crack. That was encouraging.

"Hurry up," he said.

"Okay, okay." I hoisted myself onto the middle shelf and pivoted into a crouched position. The wood gave a little moan. I turned to Puddles who was now on the other side allowing me to fill what space there was of the opening. I bent my arms and tucked them into my chest, my fingers faced forward like small claws, and I started through the hole. Puddles grabbed hold of my shoulders and yanked. There was a faint burn as my skin grated along the sides before he held me up and set me down upright. I could only imagine what this guy would do with forceps! I looked around, my eyes squinting, still adjusting to the light. I didn't recognize anything.

Puddles clasped my wrist. "C'mon."

He walked quickly while I stumbled along trying to keep up. He pulled me into some tall, thick cedars making his way to a fence. He released me and slid aside a wide plank. I went through. He followed and replaced the plank, not bothering to secure it. He directed us across a path and into a cluster of trees where he'd left his bike. He held the helmet out to me.

"Oh no," I shook my head. "Motorcycles aren't very safe."

"You're kidding me, right? You're not seriously giving me grief about my bike."

Was I? "No, of course not. It's just I'm a little scared of them. I've never been on a motorcycle before."

"You didn't get that little ding on your noggin from a bike," he said.

I touched my Band-Aid. "That's not fair. My car wasn't even moving when this happened."

"Well look, you can stand here and debate safety statistics if you want, but I'm leaving." He got on the bike, adjusted his goggles, and released the stand.

Really, I didn't have a choice. I had to get away from here. Besides, I wasn't about to lose Puddles now. I took a few deep breaths, fastened the helmet, and got on. I placed my hands on his shoulders to steady myself. He pulled them off and wrapped them around his waist. My face pressed into his back, my nose filling with leather. As much as I hated to admit it, there was something comforting about the smell. Before I got to liking it too much, I forced myself to think about cute baby cows frolicking in a meadow.

It wasn't until we had gone a few miles that I remembered about Tina.

WE'D BEEN DRIVING a while, maybe half an hour, heading west. Beyond that, I had no idea where we were going. In the time I'd lived in Montreal, I rarely ventured outside the city core. And when I did, it was usually as a passenger. And, as Adam liked to frequently remind me, I had a poor sense of direction. My navigation skills relied more on landmarks and buildings, especially commercial ones like stores and restaurants. I hardly ever used street names. My idea of giving directions was something like "drive three blocks till you hit The Gap, make a left, then a right at the Tim Horton's." It drove Adam crazy. Luckily, Camille and I spoke the same language on that front, so I'd never had to change my ways for work.

Finally, Puddles pulled off the main highway and after a few more road changes, we pulled into a laneway winding up to a barn. He parked directly in front of the door, and I got off the bike. My legs found the firm ground new, having grown accustom to the vibrations of the bike.

Puddles took off his goggles and dangled them off the handlebars. "So, how'd you like it?"

"What?"

"Your first motorcycle ride?"

Truth was, it was thrilling. Exhilarating, seriously addictive. "It was fine," I said.

He grinned at me. "I'm no shrink but even I know that's a load of crap."

"I'm *not* a shrink," I told him.

He got off the bike, opened the barn door, and wheeled in the bike. I followed him in and watched as he took off his jacket and hung it from an iron hook on the side of a support beam. "So, what are you then?" he asked me.

"I'm a social worker."

"What's the difference?"

"For one thing, social workers don't get rich. And for another, we don't dole out drugs."

From the outside, the building had looked like a barn. Inside, it wasn't so much like a barn as a fairground outbuilding. It looked to be about sixty feet wide and twenty-five deep. The far end had a loft accessed by a ladder. The main level was cement floor. The walls, worn wood shingles on the outside, were finished on the inside with drywall. Given the relative warmth of such a large space, probably insulated too. A wood stove set on a ceramic tiled platform sat dead center along the back wall. No wood stock, though. The warmth seemed to come from electric baseboard heaters fastened to the wall several feet apart around the edges of the room. Behind us, a wall with double doors to the left opened into a storage area. I peered in. Shovels, rakes, and other tools.

"Nice place," I said.

"It does the job," he said. "You want something to eat?"

Given that those couple bites of protein bar were all I'd had to eat in the past few hours, I was definitely hungry. I was also a little skeptical of any food he may have hanging around a place like this. I tried to think of something safe. "Have you got any fruit?" I ventured. "Maybe an apple?"

He stepped into the storage room. That's what I was afraid of. Some dingy barrel stuffed in the corner with a few root vegetables, maybe some autumn fruit, kept from rotting too quickly by the seasonal northern temperatures. My eyes followed his movements, trying to locate the source of his rations, my mind searching for a polite way to decline his offer if the source proved too questionable. He fiddled with something that hung from a pegboard panel that housed his smaller tools. The panel slid off to the side revealing another doorway.

He waved at me to follow him. "Let's see if I've got any."

I went in. It was a full-sized galley kitchen with an eating area up front. The kitchen was equipped with the major appliances, including a microwave in stainless steel. There was even a double sink and plenty of cupboards. The only thing missing was a dishwasher. And maybe windows. The room reminded me of many I had seen in condos designed in the late '90s.

"Wow. I'm impressed."

He checked the fridge. "You're in luck. I have two. You want a yellow or a red?"

"The yellow, please."

He took it out and rinsed it before wiping it on a paper towel and tossing it to me. He took a pear for himself and joined me at the table.

A lot of questions were racing through my mind. How did Puddles know where I was? Why did he help me? Where were we? Would he help little Sarah? I had to quiet them all for a while. "Do you have a phone?" I asked him. "I need to call home."

"Can't do that," he said.

"What do you mean?"

"You can't call home."

"Why not?"

"One, you'd be in more danger if you did. And two, calling from here would risk blowing my cover."

I could understand about blowing his cover. Clearly this wasn't a residence he would want listed in the White Pages. Not a place out in the middle of nowhere with false exteriors and secret passageways to kitchens. "How would I be in more danger?"

"You don't get it, do you," he said. He waited to swallow the last of his pear before going on. "You've gotten yourself in the way."

"In the way of what?"

He went over to a standing garbage can, stepped on the lever to open the lid, and threw out his core. He grabbed two bottles of water from the fridge and came back. He placed one of the bottles in front of me. "I can't tell you," he said.

"What do you mean, you can't tell me?"

"I mean I can't tell you."

I don't know if it was the weight of the day sinking in or the head injury, but annoyance started rising up inside me. I opened my water bottle and drank down nearly a third of it hoping it would calm me down. No such luck. "Look," I said. "Don't give me that. You owe me."

"I owe you?"

"Yeah, you do. I've done nothing but try to help your family. Which isn't easy, by the way, and you keep blocking me."

"Blocking you. How am I blocking you? I just saved your ass."

"Yeah, about that," I said. "Why did you do that? And how did you know where I was?"

He didn't answer fast enough for me so I added. "And don't say you can't tell me."

He was quiet. I hoped he was formulating an answer and not giving me the silent treatment. I hated when guys did that.

Finally he said, "I saw what happened at Francesca's. That's how I knew where you were."

"Which was where exactly?"

"That was one of Henry Bennett's properties."

"Bennett? What would Bennett want with me? I don't even know the guy."

"Like I said. You got in the way."

That brought us back pretty much where we had started. "What about my friend Tina. Is she there too?"

"Not sure," he said.

"Well, couldn't we have checked around before we left?"

"There wasn't enough time. Bennett could have seen us."

"You mean he was there?"

"He was upstairs eating lunch," he said.

I didn't know if I should be impressed by Puddles' nerve, flattered by his willingness to risk exposure to help me, or suspicious of his motives. "So why'd you do it? Why'd you get me out?"

"Let's just say I like you."

"That's very kind, but I know there's more to it than that. And how did you know where I was? That was a big place."

He linked his fingers together and pressed them into his chest, cracking his knuckles. "I spent time there myself once," he said.

This was getting more interesting. "When were you there?"

"It doesn't matter. It was a long time ago."

I thought it best not to pick at that scab for the moment. I didn't want to get on his bad side. Instead, I focused on the present. "So now that I'm out, what's the plan? I get the impression you don't think I can just go home."

"For now, no," he agreed. "But I can get word to your husband that you're all right."

"He's not my husband. He's my boyfriend." Why did I feel the need to keep correcting that?

"Boyfriend then," he said.

"Thanks. That would be good." Then I turned my attention to much more pressing matters. As much as I tried to ignore it, my bladder was becoming impatient. It had the holding capacity of a peach pit. "Is there a washroom around here?"

He pointed to a door at the end of the kitchen. I headed over, tossing my apple core in the garbage can on my way. Inside, the bathroom door closed with a latch. It was pretty flimsy hardware only meant to keep the door from falling open. I flipped it up, glided it into place, and flicked on the light to find a tiny pedestal sink, narrow toilet, and the smallest shower stall I'd ever seen. Everything was white. Not warm white, more blue white. And the lone naked bulb in the center of the ceiling cast a shadowy glow. My image in the mirror was not flattering. I blamed the lighting. I washed my face with what smelled like Ivory soap and readjusted my hair. Not much better. Definitely the lighting.

When I came out, Puddles wasn't in the kitchen. I stepped through the storage passageway into the main area. He had his jacket on and was strapping on his helmet.

"I'll be gone an hour or two," he said. "You can make yourself at home. There's a little TV in the cupboard beside the sink if you get bored."

Bored? I wasn't bored, I was frustrated. I didn't want to sit around out here in the middle of nowhere. I had stuff to do. And I hadn't even had a chance to talk about Sarah yet. "I don't want to stay here," I said. "I've got things to do. And we've got to talk some more."

"Trust me, it's best this way." When I didn't look convinced he added. "I'll explain everything when I get back."

That promise to explain everything had me intrigued. That and it occurred to me I could do some pretty good snooping while he was away. If I changed my mind, I could always leave. I'd noticed a bunch of other farmhouses on the way here. It would be a few miles to the nearest one, but I could walk over to it if I wanted. "Okay."

He started up the bike and told me to close and lock the big door when he'd gone.

I watched till he turned out of the lane then struggled with the door. It was heavier than I thought. I had to thrust my whole body weight on it to draw it closed. Then I slid each hefty metal bolt into place and raised up the iron doorjamb I found recessed into the floor for added security. I figured Puddles must have had all this stuff installed to keep out the scaries, and I wasn't about to be responsible for letting them in.

That done, I turned my attention to the task at hand. Snooping. I didn't even have to think about where I should start. I headed straight for the loft.

NINETEEN

UNFORNTUNATELY, ACCESS TO the loft involved a ladder, and I was not keen on ladders. Even short ones. Anything other than a step ladder had me seriously questioning the laws of physics. This ladder was the metal extendable kind. It hooked over a bar at the top. The increased stability should have inspired confidence. Instead, I wondered about the strength of the bar and how securely it was attached to the loft. I held both sides of the ladder and shook it. Seemed stable enough. I calculated the height of the loft to be about nine feet. I told myself that wasn't too nasty a fall if it came to that, gathered my courage, and climbed up. At the top, I looked around for something solid to pull myself up with. Nothing. I started to panic. I couldn't pull myself up without letting go of the sides of the ladder. I pictured myself falling backwards. Not exactly a confidence-building image. Unbelievable. I made it all the way up, and I was going to have to just climb back down.

Of course, maybe I didn't have to actually walk the room to snoop. I could probably do some pretty good snooping from here. After all, I had a pretty good view and the loft was sparsely furnished. A futon on the floor covered with a thick marshmallowy quilt and two pillows took up most of the left wall. An old wood nightstand with two drawers and one open shelf stood beside the bed. A lamp and a book on top. And, along the far wall ran a wide double bureau with eight drawers. The surface wood looked like it had water damage, maybe from being left out in the rain. In the corner, a lone chair was stacked with several small boxes. One of the boxes looked suspiciously similar to the one dropped off at our house with Tina's wedding ring inside. Damn. I had to go and find something interesting.

I moved up a step so I was waist level with the loft floor and bent over until my torso hugged the ground. Assuring myself that I was anchored by the heaviest part of my body, I started to shimmy myself forward. When I cleared a few feet, I drew myself onto my knees before standing up and going over to check out the boxes. They were stacked four high. I removed the first two, placing them on the bed, to get to the third. The one that looked like Tina's ring box. Even up close, it looked the same. Carefully opening it, I saw that it held sheets of paper divided into piles by elastics. I took out the first bundle. Seemed to be files. Names, notes, payment amounts. Nothing too interesting. The next bundle was the same. I didn't recognize the names and the other notations meant nothing to me. Then I did notice something. There was something different about the last bundle I pulled out. Took me a moment, but I caught it. The papers had the letterhead from Finestein, Bennett, & Fitch. Okay, so the files were a little interesting. More interesting was what Puddles was doing with them.

I checked the other boxes. One of them had more files. The other two held a hodgepodge of things. Kind of what you'd imagine would be in those grab boxes auctioned off by the government as seized property. The kind you just bid on without knowing the contents and hope you get lucky and find some valuable relic the *Antiques Roadshow* guy appraises at thousands of dollars. These boxes would have been a disappointment.

I replaced the boxes, still wondering if there was any significance to the similarity between Puddles' box and the one left at our place. Could just as easily be a coincidence. They were pretty basic boxes. Probably sold in bulk at office supply stores. Still. What did I really know about Puddles? So far, I had trusted him. Recently because of need, but mostly based on instinct. But how did I know he wasn't the one who took Tina? How did I know whether he had been helping me by releasing me from Bennett's basement or taking me away for his own purposes. Maybe he and Bennett were playing a game of cat and mouse and I was just a piece of cheese.

Thinking about cheese made me hungry. Apples don't exactly pack in the calories. I took out my protein bar and ate the remainder while I examined the contents of Puddles' drawers. The bureau was, not surprisingly, filled with clothes. Mostly jeans, t-shirts, and sweaters along with the expected amount of socks and underwear. A smear of chocolate from my fingers got onto one of Puddles' boxers as I was shuffling them around checking for hidden objects. I tried to rub it off but the smear just got bigger. Not good. A big brown stain was not going to go unnoticed. Particularly on underwear. I bunched it up, shoved it behind the bureau, and stepped back a pace. I could still see a hint of white cotton. I tried pushing it farther down, but it got stuck. Just what I needed. I pulled the chest forward slightly, hoping the underwear would fall to the bottom on its own. Sure enough, the boxers disappeared. I shoved it back into place and moved on to check out the nightstand.

No luck there either. Just regular stuff. Reading glasses, more books, a watch, spare change, condoms. Hmmm condoms. That answered a few questions about Puddles. Clearly he was not living a life of abstinence pining for his estranged wife. I wondered if he brought his sexual partners here or just kept his safety stock handy to his dressing area. It was hard to imagine him bringing dates here. Harder still to imagine him trusting anyone enough to keep this place a secret. Of course, he was trusting me by bringing me here. Unless he figured I'd never have the opportunity to expose his little hideaway. Now that wasn't a nice thought.

I wished I knew more about Puddles. I was still struggling to merge a profile out of the man his family and friends described with the man I had met. I sat on the bed and picked up the book on the nightstand. It was *The Catcher in the Rye*. They say you can tell a lot about a person by the books he reads. I wasn't sure what significance *The Catcher in the Rye* had. Almost everyone I knew had read it. I think it had even been required reading in high school. I looked through Puddles' other books. Older fiction mostly, several classics. A couple of non-fiction about business stuff. No self-help or exercise books. No crime novels or manuals on how to build a bomb or the latest in poisoning techniques. It was the kind of library any guy might have. So, based on the book theory, Puddles was just an average guy.

I got up and rolled the futon up a bit. Nothing under there that I could see. I lay on the floor and stuck my arm underneath the mattress as far as it would go, moving along to cover as much area as possible. Nothing. Aside from the boxes of files, the significance of which I had yet to figure out, my snooping had earned me a big zero.

Relying on memory, I set about putting things back together, stood back, and surveyed the room. Something wasn't right with the chest of drawers. The underwear forced it out at an awkward angle. Maybe pulling the right side out a bit would match it to the left. I nudged it forward and something scraped behind. Oh, oh. I took a breath and pulled the whole thing about a foot away from the wall then went around to have a look. A picture frame was dangling on one side from a piece of duct tape connected to the back of the bureau. More duct tape, still attached to the picture frame, hung loose in the air. I eased the remaining tape free from the bureau and lifted the frame out. I wasn't sure what to make of the photo I saw. It was a picture of Puddles with Lucia at a park. Lucia was sitting on a swing. Puddles was standing behind her holding onto the chain above where her hands were clasped. They were both laughing. Not smiling, laughing. It was a snapshot of sheer happiness. Lucia must have been about nine. I reattached the frame to the chest, pocketed the stained underwear, and put the bureau back to its original position.

Getting down from the loft was easy. I discovered two finger-sized iron rings embedded in the floor that I hadn't noticed on the way up. The rings were painted light brown to match the stain of the wood. At quick glance, they looked like notches. Holding on to those made backing down the ladder feel a lot safer. I released each ring one at a time, shifting my hands to the sides of the ladder as each ring fell back into place. Then with both hands firmly holding the sides of the ladder, I stepped down. At the bottom, I bumped into Puddles.

"Having a nap?" he asked.

I smiled. We both knew what I was doing. "Yeah, sure. Really comfy bed you got there."

He still had his coat on and radiated cool outdoor air. He held a paper bag out to me. "Here," he said. "You'll need these."

I peered into the bag. A toothbrush, some toothpaste. A few pharmacy-quality cotton panties. Moving them aside, I saw a package of dental floss, some soap, and a plastic comb. Hmmm. I wasn't liking the message he was delivering. "What, no tampons?"

His cheeks upgraded from pink to red. His eyes fixed on my kneecaps. "I didn't know you needed those."

"I don't. I was kidding."

His shoulders relaxed. He unzipped his coat, crossing back towards the kitchen.

"How'd you get in?" I asked following behind him. "I had the place all locked up."

"You didn't answer when I knocked. I came in the back way."

I didn't know there was a back way. I looked around for a door. Didn't see one.

He started to undo all the locks I'd secured, opened the big door, and a second later he was back with the bike. He rolled it over to the side, put the stand on, replaced the locks, and went into the kitchen.

A grocery bag sat on the counter. He must have brought that back too. I watched as Puddles unpacked more fruit, some frozen veggies, a box of cereal, a package of cookies, and a carton of soy milk. As he moved about putting everything away, I couldn't help noticing that for a compact space, it was certainly well used. Not an inch wasted. I regretted having lost my snoop time before I got a crack at all those cupboards. The better stuff was probably hidden in here. After all, the room was like a secret vault.

He set the table with two large bowls, a soup spoon set in each. He took out two other boxes of cereal, placed them on the table along with the one he had just bought, and finished off with the soy milk and a carton of 2%. When everything was out he said, "dinner."

The new cereal was an organic health kind from the supermarket. Some kind of whole grain flakes. It was that,

Honeycomb, or Fruit Loops. I opted for the flakes. Puddles was already bathing his Honeycombs in milk.

"Thanks," I said to him as I poured the cereal into my bowl. "I really appreciate the food." I gestured to the organic cereal and soy milk carton. "I get the feeling this kind of stuff isn't usually on your grocery list."

"No problem," he said, shoveling in the last of his cereal and pouring out another bowl.

"How'd you know?" I asked him.

"Know what?"

My eyes held his for a beat.

He broke the gaze and shrugged. "I just thought you vegetarians liked soy and stuff."

"But how'd you know I was vegetarian?"

He looked back at me again, this time keeping his gaze steady. "Just did."

Hmmm. I crunched on my flakes while I studied Puddles with what I hoped was discretion. He had taken off his jacket and was wearing a long-sleeve jersey in a medium blue just a nudge darker than his eyes. The shirt was not tight, but it held to the contours of his body. He was still as lean as he had been in the wedding photos I'd seen. Not simply slim, lean with muscles that are normally seen on younger men. I did a quick mental calculation and placed him at about forty-five or forty-six. Jim would be about two years younger yet wouldn't pass for under fifty. Puddles retained his thick hair too, having only a few strands of gray, mostly skirting his ears. He wasn't wearing it gelled back anymore, though, it had long layers, the back nearly reaching the bottom of his neck, the front cut in a side part with long bangs hanging over his right eye. Even his beard, left to grow thicker than scruff, added only a raw grittiness rather than an unkept air.

All in all, he was in pretty good shape for a runaway. For the first time, I wondered if there was a new Mrs. Puddles. "So tell me," I said, "what have you been doing with yourself for the past fifteen years or so?"

He set his spoon down in his empty bowl and placed it aside. I did the same, only a gummy lump remained in my bowl.

"Look," he began, "when I said I'd explain everything, that didn't include my personal life. And I don't appreciate people going through my stuff either."

Okay, that was fair.

He continued. "What I will explain is what you're caught up in. Got it?"

I nodded my acceptance of his terms.

"Let's start with your little vacation at Bennett's. First off, you were in the wrong place at the wrong time. Also, my guess is he thinks you know more about him than I'm willing to bet you do. That probably got him scared."

"Scared of what?" I asked.

"Scared you'd turn him in for his, let's say, dirty dealings."

"I don't know anything about any dirty dealings," I said.

"I didn't think so," he said. "Otherwise you would have done something about it."

I thought about the box of files up in the loft. "You do, though, don't you?"

"That doesn't affect you," he said.

"Oh, come on," I said. "I'm here aren't I? I'm not at home tucked into my own cozy little bed. Of course it affects me. Whatever he's done, it must be pretty bad to not mind adding kidnapping to the list."

There was a brief silence before Puddles said, "I don't think he was too worried about a kidnapping charge."

It took me a moment to register what he was saying. "You think he was going to kill me?"

"He would've questioned you first. To see what you knew. What other people might know. Then, yeah, I think he was planning to get rid of you."

I was starting to really dislike Bennett. I was also starting to really worry about Tina. "If he would have killed me, what about Tina?"

This time there was a long pause before Puddles said anything. Finally, he got up and gestured at me to follow him. He opened a cabinet door above the kitchen counter. A small TV was inside. He switched it on and fiddled with some buttons on another gizmo on the shelf above the TV. He still hadn't answered my question.

Something came on the screen. "There," he said.

The screen was a lot smaller than I was used to. I leaned in to get a better look. It looked like a studio apartment. A fairly nice one too. I didn't see what it had to do with Tina, though. Then someone came into the room. I fixed on the face. It was Tina. She was wearing overalls with an open sweatshirt on top. No shoes, just some gym socks. Her hair hung flat. I couldn't make out any makeup. But, that was her. "That's Tina," I said, surprised.

Puddles nodded.

I looked back at the screen. Tina was eating ice cream out of a Ben & Jerry's tub and watching TV. I made out an empty bag of Cheetos on the couch beside her. "What is this? Some kind of hidden video? And why do you get it?"

He sighed. "It's my set-up. Unfortunately, your friend has become my houseguest."

Slowly, it was starting to make sense. At least partly. For some reason, Puddles was gathering information on Bennett. He had the files and it must have been him who set up the statuecam in Bennett's office. He must have been the one looking for the tape the night Jeffrey took it. He probably also knew about Francesca and Bennett.

He switched off the TV and closed the cupboard.

"So you're the one who wants the tape?" I said. "I had the impression from Jeffrey that it was a group of vicious henchmen."

Puddles smiled. "No offence, but your friend Jeffrey is a bit of a dweeb."

This was true. "Yes," I agreed, "but he's a nice dweeb."

We went back to sit at the table. The wood chairs were starting to hurt. I wished he had something more comfortable. I fidgeted trying to find a bearable position.

"Back hurting?" he asked me.

Yeah that and parts south. "A little," I said.

He went to a low cupboard, pulled out a cushion, and handed it to me. "Here, try this."

I centered it on the chair and sat back down. Much better. "Thanks."

He got some water for us from the fridge and opened a bag of oatmeal cookies before he sat back down. Looking at him, I had a hard time thinking of him as being a careless deadbeat dad, let alone a young offender type.

He caught me watching him. "What?" he said.

"I'm just trying to get a fix on you. Despite much public opinion to the contrary, I get the distinct sense that you're a good guy. And I don't get it. Why let people think those things about you? Why let Lucia believe them?"

He shrugged. "Sometimes that's best."

It felt like he was shutting me out again. I decided it was time to give him the information he wanted. Although, considering his obvious resourcefulness it was hard to imagine him not already knowing. "About your brother. You asked me why he was trying to find you. I'm afraid it's not very good news."

His expression told me he did already know.

"You know, don't you?" I said.

He nodded. "I do now. I didn't when I came to see you."

"Did you see him?"

"No. I just know."

"Are you going to help?" I asked.

He looked down at the table. "I can't do anything for anybody until this mess is over with," he said.

I was about to ask him why when his cell phone chimed. He hadn't had the phone with him earlier, and I wondered where he'd picked it up when he was out. He reached into his jean pocket for his phone and checked the caller I.D. I recognized the expression his face took on. I had seen it many times, mostly on myself. I had no doubt the caller was Tina.

TWENTY

PUDDLES LET ME watch the TV monitor as he spoke to Tina. I had to be quiet, though. He didn't want her to hear me. It was harder than I thought it would be. Having no more fears for Tina's safety, I was completely free to delight in her dissatisfaction with her newfound accommodations.

She contended that her call was urgent. Apparently, her cable had gone out. Worse yet, she had run out of the Chocolate Chip Cookie Dough ice cream and was left with only Cherry Garcia. Having already read her *People* magazine cover to cover, she couldn't possibly be expected to get through the evening under these conditions. Puddles told her to sit tight for the moment. Help was on the way. Then he pressed end. On the monitor, Tina went back to the bathroom.

"What are you going to do?" I asked him.

"Nothing."

"But you told her you'd help. She's expecting something."

He shrugged. "She's always expecting something. Yesterday she complained that her French fries weren't thin enough."

"So how does this work exactly? Tina must know who you are if she calls you. Not to mention your apparent concierge services. Aren't you afraid she'll give you away after the trade?"

"She hasn't ever seen me. We have a system for dropping things off. And I took her cell phone away. She calls this number from one of those kiddie cell phones that can only call a few pre-programmed numbers. She has no idea where she's calling."

I looked back at the monitor. Tina was now on the couch. She pulled a comforter up over her legs and held a book on her lap. I figured she got it from one of the shelves flanking the sofa. She opened the book and started reading. I didn't think I'd ever seen Tina with a book before. There was something else off. She was wearing glasses. I had never seen Tina with glasses before. Without the overdone makeup, the prissy clothes, and the super pert hair she almost looked like a real person.

To Puddles I said, "despite her Tinaism requests, she seems like a cooperative hostage. I'm a little surprised."

"I was too. I thought she'd go ballistic when she realized her ring had been taken. She was still let's say, sedated, when it was removed from her finger. But when I told her about the trade, she was flipping excited. Acted like she just won the lottery. Said it would do her husband good."

I would have been shocked if that wasn't a classic Tina move. Back onscreen her glasses were slipping off her nose, the book lay open on her chest. So much for reading anything thicker than a magazine. "Looks like she's nodded off," I said. "I guess that gets you off the hook for tonight."

"I figured she would. She sleeps a lot. That and she makes a lot of trips to the bathroom." He turned off the set. "Speaking of which," he added and headed for the bathroom himself.

I went back to sit at the table and got to thinking about the Ben & Jerry's, which got me thinking that I was still hungry. I wondered about the etiquette of going through Puddles' rations. There probably weren't a lot of manner books that covered this one. Not even Emily Post. After all, I wasn't exactly a guest, but not exactly a captive either. This situation was new even for me. I was feeling fidgety, so while I waited for Puddles to come back I decided to busy myself by making a list. So much new information was coming up, I didn't know how it all fit together. A list would help me see the big picture. I checked the counter for some paper and a pen. I found a phone message pad tucked behind the microwave. A couple of pens had slipped underneath. Using my fingers like a pincer, I tried to pry one out.

Puddles came out of the bathroom. "Geez. You can't keep your hands off my stuff even for a minute, can you."

"I was just trying to fish out a pen," I defended myself. "I wasn't going through anything."

He lifted up an end of the microwave with one hand and took out the pens with his other. He passed a pen to me and tossed two more on the counter.

I thanked him and crossed back to the table. Probably not the best time to ask for more food just yet.

With Puddles watching me, I felt a little self-conscious about my list habit. I had to write something, though, now that we had the whole pen incident. The pen poised over the pad, I tried to look thoughtful while I searched for something to put down. My fingers started writing. I tore off the top page and passed the notes to Puddles.

He skimmed them. "So, you've seen the tape?"

"Yeah. And I don't know what all the fuss was about. It was pretty boring."

"You don't happen to have it on you, do you?"

"No, sorry. But I do have a copy at my house."

"Great. Let's go," he said.

BEFORE I GOT back on the motorcycle I wanted to clear up a few things. "I thought you said it was dangerous for me to go home."

Puddles zipped his jacket. "I did."

"So, what's changed?"

"Nothing. Don't worry, I've got a plan."

Oh, yeah, great. He had a plan. "Care to let me in on it?"

"You'll see," he said putting on his goggles.

I folded my arms across my chest and stood firm. "I think I'm going to need a little more than that."

He sighed. He was big on the sigh thing. "Look, there's a time issue here. Bennett's gotta know you're gone. And you being gone is going to make him nervous. When people are nervous they do risky things."

I followed him so far. "Okay. So?"

"So I'd like to prevent that."

"Prevent what exactly?"

He shook his hands out, expelling some not so happy energy. No doubt, some of it frustration with me. "Bennett's not the kind of man who plays by the rules. I don't want anyone to get hurt."

I got the distinct feeling all this concern wasn't over me. I flashed on the picture of him and Lucia at the park. "You mean Lucia," I said.

Another sigh. "Okay, yes, Lucia."

"Why would Bennett hurt her?"

"Look, I don't want to stand around here and play twenty questions." He held out an extra helmet and goggles towards me. "You coming or not?" He took off the stand and started to wheel the bike towards the big door.

Something told me to just go. I knew he wasn't bluffing. I knew he'd go without me, and I didn't want to get stuck here alone again. That and the nervous people do risky things comment. I didn't want Puddles to be one of those nervous people.

WE WERE A few blocks from my house. It was already dark. Puddles had pulled into a gas station, presumably to refuel. Probably to buy time to come up with his supposed plan. I waited with the bike while he went in to pay. He came back with a bag of corn chips and two bottles of water. So far, good plan.

He passed me my water and tore open the bag, holding it out between us. "Okay, here's the deal. See the phone booth over there?" He pointed to a glass booth on the corner. "Go call your boyfriend and ask him to come here for gas. Tell him to bring the copy of the video. Tell him to slip it into the first *Time* magazine on the rack when he goes in to pay. I'll be inside watching. When he's done, tell him to leave and go home. I'll pick up the magazine and we're done."

Sounded simple except for one small thing. "What about me?"

"What about you?" he said.

Where to begin. "First of all, he's going to expect me to go home since he doesn't know squat about the danger I may be in. Second, if someone is watching my house, which you seem to think is likely, and that someone follows Adam here, that someone will see me."

"Hmmm," he said, sucking the salt off a corn chip.

I was glad to see he was giving the matter serious consideration.

"You'll just have to hide then." He looked around. The station was on a corner. One street had a few shops, closed now. The other street was residential. "You've got two choices. You can walk up the street a bit, maybe dip into someone's driveway. Or, you can stay here with the bike. Keep the helmet on, put on the goggles, and I'll give you my jacket. You could put some air in the tires or something to look busy."

A disguise. I liked that idea. I'd rather stay here in public than be on my own in some dark driveway. He gave me his coat. It fit right on top of mine. A tad bulky, maybe. But it held his warmth like a slab of marble placed near a fire. I went to make the call.

Ten minutes later, Adam pulled up to a pump. I had a good view of him from the air machine. His neck barely moved, but his eyes were scoping the area. Our call had been brief. He understood I wouldn't be going home with him. I knew by his tone he didn't like it. He went in to pay, and I lost sight of him.

I fiddled with the air doohickey. It made high-pitched whooshing noises while I pretended to screw on the little black cap that kept the air from escaping the tires. Some leaves crunched behind me, and I froze. A hand, scented with chocolate, tapped me on the shoulder, and I turned to face Camille dressed in her Catwoman garb.

She took a quick inventory of my condition. No doubt checking for broken bones and such. Good thing the helmet hid my Band-Aid. I must have passed her scanner because she only said, "What's going on?"

I was a little disappointed that she'd recognized me so easily. "I'm here with Puddles," I said.

"You found him?" she said, surprise in her voice. "Where is he?"

As much as I would have loved to take credit for finding Puddles, I couldn't. I told her about his visit to my house, then I briefed her on my stop by Francesca's and the layover in Bennett's basement. "There's more going on here than we thought," I said by way of summation.

Even in the dim light I could see Camille's squint. She was not happy.

I went on. "He wants to see the tape from Bennett's office. That's why we're here."

Her eyes picked up something over my head. Adam had come out and was headed back to his car. "Adam's done. Let's go," she said.

"I can't go. I have to stay with Puddles."

She raised an eyebrow at me.

"It's safer for me," I explained. "Bennett's looking for me. It's better if I don't go home."

She wasn't buying it.

Adam started up the car and left.

"Isn't he going to wait for you?" I asked.

"He doesn't know I'm here," she said. "And don't change the subject. Yesterday we didn't have any firm leads on Puddles, today all of a sudden he's your safety buddy. Explain that one."

I told her how he had freed me from Bennett's basement. How he was really a good guy. How he was trying to help Lucia.

"Where does Lucia fit in?" she asked me.

"I'm not sure yet. That's part of why I want to stay with Puddles. It's the only way I'm going to figure any of this out."

Her eyes were still squinted. Not a good sign. I didn't have a lot of time. Puddles would be out any minute. I wasn't sure what he would do if he spotted me talking to Camille. "Look," I said. "Somehow I'm involved in this now. I have to figure it out for my own sake, too."

"Fine," she said. "Go. But keep in touch, eh? That's what the bloody phone is for."

"Yeah. About that," I said, feeling sheepish again. "My cell phone's kind of broken."

"Broken?"

"Yeah."

"What's wrong with it?" she asked.

"No battery," I mumbled to the ground.

"*Mais voyons*, Lora." She shook her head, reached into her pocket, pulled out a phone, and handed it to me. Then she backed into the trees and disappeared.

A moment later, Puddles came out. A paper bag was crooked under his arm, projecting a casualness I knew was false. I had his jacket off before he reached me. He put his bag in one of the saddle packs at the back of the bike and got into his jacket. We both got on the bike and were gone in less than sixty seconds.

THERE'S A LOT of time to think on the back of a bike. Mostly I thought of how easy it would be for some car to send me spiraling through the air with barely more than a bump. Sometimes trucks would pass, filling me with visions of the bike somehow lodging underneath and being dragged to a stop. My mangled body grafted onto Puddles. These were not happy thoughts. I needed happy thoughts. I certainly needed something because this case was still fuzzy and it was depressing me.

I did the list thing, only mental. On the pro side, I had connected with Puddles. On the con side, I was in hiding, one of my clients was connected to a goon, my other client had an ill child, and things were turning out to be more complicated than the run of the mill missing person's case. I wasn't sure where to put Tina on the list. I decided to count her as a pro, partly because I knew she was safe and sound, and partly because she wasn't residing in my house for the time being. Imagining myself looking at the list, one thing stood out. Sarah's illness was getting worse. And as long as everything else was all muddled, there wasn't a chance that Puddles could even try to help her. That meant I'd have to resolve the Bennett situation. So job one would be prying every detail about Bennett out of Puddles that I could.

We pulled into the lane that ran up to the barn. Puddles stopped and cut the engine.

"What are you doing?" I asked.

He put a hand out. "Shush."

He took off his helmet and cocked his head.

I crossed my arms and held my face tight, annoyed at being shushed. I was also way cold and wanted to get inside where it was warm. One of the drawbacks of a motor bike is no heating. Natural central air, but no heat beyond the output of the engine. That and the output of the guy in front of you.

He motioned for me to get off the bike. I did. He did too. He waited another minute then started walking the bike towards the barn door. I had to hurry to keep up with him. I lost my footing, stumbling, my shoe grating against the gravel. Several stones jumped into the grass on the side of the path. Puddles scowled at me. I scowled back. I was beginning to understand why he lived alone out here in the middle of nowhere.

Once inside, I turned to him. "What was all that about?"

"Something's not right," he said. "Stay here. I'm going to have a look around."

Either this guy was the real deal or he'd watched too many action movies. Probably the second. I was getting the impression lately that guys put way too much stock in movies. But, I was getting tired of Puddles' protection. I appreciated his coming along and pointing out the emergency exit at Bennett's place and all, but this macho stuff was above and beyond. Anyway, I would have found the window at Bennett's on my own, give or take an hour or two. Okay, maybe a day or two. But I would have.

"Look," I said, taking off my helmet and easing the goggles down to hang from my neck. "Why don't you take the loft and I'll take the kitchen."

His smile was amused. "Excuse me?"

"I don't know what year you're living in," I began, "but women aren't wallflowers anymore." I started towards the kitchen. "Just tell me which gizmo opens the secret door and I'll take it from there." He came up behind me, reached out for a screwdriver and froze. That time, I heard something too.

In a flash, he opened the door and we both slipped into the kitchen. He slid the door closed without a sound. We each pressed an ear to the backside. This time there was no mistaking it. Someone, or something, was poking around outside. Hard to tell if they'd made their way in yet. Puddles' breath still smelled faintly of corn chips. His hair smelled like coffee. If he got any closer, I could probably make out his brand of laundry detergent. I felt his fingers on my waist. He was nudging me aside. Again with the macho stuff! I tried to catch his eye to let him know I wasn't moving. Instead I caught sight of a gun muzzle. Whoa. Nobody said anything about guns. This was Canada for pity sake. It wasn't supposed to have so many guns!

I let myself be edged over and stood behind him. I took a quick gander at the kitchen counter. No knife block. A small iron fry pan was on the stove. I picked it up. It felt solid and heavy in my hands. Perfect. I wasn't about to be the only one without a weapon. Apparently this party was BYOW.

I went back to stand near Puddles and caught the smile return to his face when he took in the fry pan.

The sounds were closer now. As if someone was on the other side of the door. We both stood completely still. After a while, we heard receding footsteps. The large barn door closed with a clank. Then nothing. We continued to hold our positions for a good five minutes. I broke first, desperately needing a bathroom break. When I came out, fry pan still in hand, Puddles was leaning against the table staring straight at me.

"Didn't your mother ever teach you it isn't polite to stare?" I said.

He put his finger up to his lips.

I wondered if I'd missed something while I was in the washroom. I gave him the international shrug for "what's up?" leaving my arms up a little longer than necessary to wave the pan at him.

He pointed at the door. I went over to look at it. He had opened it. I could see into the main room. Looked clear. He signaled for me to check it out. Must be teasing me about my earlier macho comments. I shot him a pupil hit to the eyes and headed out. He was right behind me. I took about three steps forward before I was pushed to the ground, fry pan clanking as I dropped it. All I could see was the gun in Puddles' hand. Then my mind turned what must have been instantaneous into a slow motion replay of the gun being kicked out of Puddles' hand followed by a crunch to his chest that bent him over.

"Wait," I called out. "Wait, don't hurt him."

Camille's arm stopped just short of clubbing the back of Puddles' head.

TWENTY-ONE

"**WHAT ARE YOU** doing here?" I asked Camille. We were all in the kitchen. Puddles sat at the table with an icepack pressed to his knuckles where they had collided with Camille's Doc Martens. I was starting to think boots were to Camille what bracelets were to Wonder Woman. Except Camille did more with her boots than defend herself. First chance I got, I was going to have to get some boots of my own. Black, shiny ones.

"*Mais voyons.* Did you think I'd just let you go off again?"

This was one of those times that Camille's overprotective streak didn't seem so welcome. What with that and Puddles' protectiveness, I was feeling like I was all of two years old.

"I was doing fine," I snapped.

"Well, how was I supposed to know that?" she yelled.

"You were supposed to trust me," I yelled back.

"This isn't about trust," she shouted over Puddles' head. "This is about caring. This is about watching each other's back. That's what we do, remember?"

She was right, of course. I would have done exactly the same thing if the situation were reversed. Minus the kick-ass bit, since I didn't have her skills. When I didn't reply right away she sat down and started tapping her nails on the table. I was grateful her outfit didn't leave room for the slinky.

There were only two chairs, so I leaned against the wall. "Did you bring any supplies?" I said by way of a peace offering.

She reached in her pocket and tossed a shiny package across the table. I had to move quickly to keep it from tumbling off the side. I unwrapped a corner. A hint of bitter cocoa hit the air. It was the good stuff. Dark and strong. I broke off a row and passed it back. She broke off a row and offered it to Puddles before taking some for herself. Some people broke bread together, Camille and I broke chocolate. The finger tapping didn't resume.

"What's with the Band-Aid?" she asked in a remarkably even voice.

My hand automatically reached up to dab at my cut as though checking to see if it was still there. "Just a tiny cut," I said. "Nothing really."

She raised one eyebrow ever so slightly. Probably not even noticeable to the untrained eye.

"It doesn't even need a Band-Aid," I added. "I'm just wearing it for the sympathy factor."

Puddles, oblivious to our conversation, pulled out his cell phone and checked his messages. When he was done, he clicked it shut and returned it to his pocket. "I hadn't expected another house guest," he said looking from Camille to me. "But we'll have to make the best of it. It's late, we should get some sleep. We can clear things up in the morning."

It was late. Nearly eleven. And it had been a long, exhausting day. Sleep would be real nice. I could tell by Camille's expression, though, that it wasn't going to be happening any time soon.

She brushed at some crumbs on the table. "Perhaps you have some coffee, *monsieur*," she said. "There is still much to talk about before bed."

I could have sworn I saw Puddles squint at Camille. Probably just tired, heavy eyelids. He did look at her for a while before he spoke. No doubt appreciating her sleek figure the black catsuit did nothing to hide. She was possibly the only woman on the planet who could live off chocolate and coffee, not to mention an abundance of croissants, bagels, and cheese, rarely sleep, and still have the body of an athlete. Not to mention translucent skin with no dark bags under her eyes. She could even pack away oodles of poutine without getting so much as one zit. If she wasn't my best friend, I would probably dislike her immensely. At the very least, I wouldn't want to stand next to her at a party.

"I'm sorry," Puddles finally said. "I didn't catch your name."

"Camille Caron," she said extending her hand.

"Paul Bell."

"Yes. The infamous Mr. Puddles," Camille said.

"Just Puddles. No Mister. And that was a long time ago. You can just call me Paul."

"That would be confusing. I have a cousin Paul," she said.

I wasn't sure what to make of this banter. It was like watching an old game of pong on fast forward.

"Well, then," Puddles began.

Camille cut him off. "I think Bell suits you."

Puddles picked up the ice pack he had put on the table and reapplied it to his hand. "Then I'll have to think of a name that suits you. Like the Crusher."

If he was waiting for Camille to apologize for her earlier assault, he would be disappointed. She considered martial arts an indispensable skill, and she never apologized for exercising it.

She was willing to concede him that round, though. She got up and went into the prep area of the kitchen. "About that coffee," she said. "Where would I find it?"

Puddles joined her in the kitchen. He flipped open a lower cupboard and lifted out an espresso maker. It was all stainless steel. "That's all I've got," he said.

Camille did not look disappointed. He set it up and let it work its magic.

By the time the coffee was ready, I had also scrounged some toast and a plate of biscotti had appeared on the table. Meanwhile, Puddles squeezed a folding chair in between the two wood ones, and we all took our places at the table.

I started the conversation by telling Camille about Tina and Tinavision, which we tuned in briefly only to see she was still sleeping. I went on to recap the events of the day, excluding for the moment my search of Puddles' loft, and ended by pointing out the need to know more about Bennett's involvement with Puddles.

The natural flow of the conversation then fell to Puddles. A simple point of etiquette that seemed to elude him.

Camille's fingertips found their way to the table again, but she said nothing.

Puddles too was quiet. I noticed his hands fingering something inside his pocket. Then I remembered the copy of the tape. "Look, I know you want to watch the tape," I said. "But, before you do, you should fill us in on what you know. You're not alone anymore. We're a team now and it's possible that if we pool our bits of information, we may just have a complete picture. You said yourself we were running out of time. We can work faster if we work together on this."

Puddles looked at me. "I'm used to working alone," he said. "I never talk about this with anyone. It wouldn't be a good idea for me, and it wouldn't be good for them."

I guess I could understand that. And considering the elaborate lengths he had gone to with this place, he had some need for his own protection. Unless he was a nut job. Either way, he couldn't protect us. We were already on Bennett's radar. "I get that," I said to him, picking up on his last point. "But we're already involved. We need to clear this up as much as you do."

He let out a long breath before answering. "Okay. Here's the deal. This mess goes back a long way so some of it may be hard to follow. I don't like to repeat myself so listen closely." He bit off a piece of biscotti and waited until he had finished chewing to go on. "Bennett was the lawyer for Francesca's family. He also took care of the business. Not always him directly, but his firm. For reasons that aren't important here, he started skimming money from Guido's Garments when Francesca's dad, Guido, became ill a couple of years before he passed away. Bennett was very good. Nobody knew at first. But I spotted some irregularities a few months before Guido died. I didn't want to tell Guido about it until I figured out what was happening. With his heart condition, it wasn't right to upset him, so I thought I should take care of things myself. By the time I made sense of it, Guido died.

"Bennett knew I was on to him. Somehow, he doctored everything up to make it look like I had been stealing from the company and took this information to Francesca's mother when the company passed to her ownership. She didn't believe him. Francesca did. They argued about it. Francesca wanted charges filed against me. Her mother refused.

"That's when I decided to leave. I couldn't stay with Francesca after that. I also wanted to clear my name. Not just for me, but for Lucia. So I went to stay with a friend. Vladimir. A guy I knew at Guido's. He was one of the only people I knew I could trust. I worked on putting together evidence against Bennett. Then one day I came back to the apartment to find my files missing and Vladimir dead. Not long after, Bennett got me too." Puddles gestured at me. "That's when I did time in his basement."

I nodded understanding.

"What about Vladimir?" Camille asked.

"Bennett killed him. He denied it, of course, and claimed he only questioned him. But Vlad was dead when I got there. Bennett covered it up by making it look like a suicide. Something Vlad would never do. As soon as I saw him, I knew what happened. That's when I grabbed my stuff and took off. I wasn't fast enough, though. Bennett caught me."

I asked the obvious question. "Why didn't Bennett just kill you?"

"He probably would have except that he knew I still had some evidence against him. He had no idea where it was or who knew about it. He may have even suspected I had something to link him to Vladimir's death. He tried to get me to tell him, but I held back."

Camille and I exchanged a look of respect.

"Don't bother to be impressed," he said. "I probably would have caved if I hadn't gotten away first."

"So you've been hiding ever since? For fifteen years?" Camille said.

"Not exactly hiding. More like staying clear. Unless I could clear my name, it was best for everyone."

"And after fifteen years you still haven't nailed him?" I said.

"It's not easy. And I needed to support myself, too. I couldn't spend all my time on him."

"So what's different now?" Camille asked him.

He fiddled with the ice pack. "Here's where it gets tricky. After a while, I figured out that if Bennett was skimming from Guido, he was probably ripping off some of his other legal clients too. Turns out I was right. Problem is, it's hard to prove. Bennett covers his ass very well. And without real proof I can take to the authorities, I'm nowhere. So I've been trying to collect evidence. That's where the video recorder from Bennett's office comes in. I planted it there."

"Pretty risky," I said.

"Yeah," he admitted. "But necessary. This is the thing, Bennett would have no qualms about killing me now if he had the chance. It would be pretty obvious even to him that I didn't have much on him, or I would have done something with the information a long time ago. Also, there's Francesca. Bennett and Francesca go back a long way."

Hmmm. A long way. Was it possible Bennett was the man Francesca told me about? The married man she had the affair with that produced Lucia?

Puddles went on. "Francesca's in a bit of a financial bind now," he said. "She lost a lot of money in the markets a few years back. She depends on her investment income to support herself. She's never held a job, so it's all she's got. See, Francesca's father had a provision put in his and his wife's wills. It stipulated that upon their passing, their assets would only go to Francesca if she was still married to me. Otherwise, the entire inheritance would go to Lucia, either upon marriage or when she turned thirty. There was a trustee appointed to make sure Francesca had an allowance for herself and to run the household while Lucia grew up. But after that, she'd be on her own."

So that was it. That's what was different now. Lucia was getting married.

Puddles continued. "The only extenuating circumstance would be if Francesca was widowed."

"But with you gone so long," Camille commented, "isn't there some technicality there like abandonment or something?"

"Not the way the will is worded. She had to remain married with us living together as husband and wife. Legally, after a long absence, she may be entitled to have a divorce decreed even without my involvement, but that wouldn't be of any help to her."

That seemed odd. That meant Guido was practically disinheriting his own daughter unless she lived the life he wanted her to. Francesca's dad wasn't looking like the nice, caring man I'd been given to think he was. He was sounding more like a tyrannical parent. I was sure there was more to it. "Why would Guido care if she stayed with you?" I asked Puddles.

Puddles shrugged. "He never said. I only found out about the wills when he died."

Camille cleared the dishes from the table. "But what about the house, the furnishings, the art? Couldn't Francesca just sell it if she needed the money?"

"It's not hers. It's all Lucia's. And probably when she gets married, she'll want Francesca to move out."

It was all starting to make sense now. This wasn't about clearing his name anymore. This was about saving his daughter. But would Francesca really hurt her own child just for money? Then again, what if it wasn't up to Francesca? I thought about how she tried to get me to leave her house before Bennett knocked me out. What if Bennett was the real threat here? "There is another extenuating circumstance," I said, voicing what I knew was Puddles real concern. They both looked at me. "If Lucia was dead."

PUDDLES WAS IN the kitchen watching the copy of the video. Camille and I had gone up to the loft to get some rest. She had just gotten off the phone with Laurent after filling him in. We lay side by side on the bed. She had her eyes closed, arms at her sides. My eyes were wide open, arms crossed behind my head, elbows pointing at the wood beamed ceiling above. My mind connecting the dots.

The mental image I had went something like this: The first dot was Guido which connected to the Antonia dot. Combined they connected to two other dots—Guido's Garments and Francesca. The

Guido's dot also linked to Bennett, Finestein, & Fitch. The Francesca dot connected to Puddles. Together they connected to Lucia who connected to her fiancé what's his face Como. Another line from Francesca went to Bennett. Puddles also linked to Jim and his family.

Imagining the image, I had only one conclusion. There were a lot of dots. None of which did anything to explain the clause in Guido's will. Why would it matter to him if Francesca and Puddles remained married? And why would he bypass his own daughter to leave everything to his granddaughter? I thought back to my conversations with Francesca. She claimed her father was a proud, moralistic man. That he had been upset by her unplanned pregnancy. That he had essentially arranged her marriage to Puddles because of the pregnancy. If any of this were true, and given that he was a strict Catholic some of it may very well be, it would make sense that he would want his grandchild born to married parents. I guess if I carried that one step further, Catholics frowned on divorce too. But that didn't seem like a good enough reason to cut his daughter out.

"The whole will thing could explain the dead guy with Piedro Bellinni's I.D.," Camille startled me by saying.

"I thought you were asleep," I said.

"*Pas encore*," she said.

"What do you mean about the dead guy?"

"If Francesca needed to be a widow before Lucia got married, maybe she tried to produce a dead husband."

"Hmmm." That could be. "But, if she was going to do that, why would she hire us to find Puddles?"

"Simple. That's *why* she may have hired us. She wanted us to find him. The dead Puddles I mean."

Okay. That could work. "That would explain why she didn't give us a picture of Puddles. If she had been the only one called to identify the body, she could have identified anyone as Puddles." I thought a bit deeper. "That might also explain her on again off again commitment to the investigation. Jim showing up had to put a wrinkle in her plan because he would know the dead guy wasn't his brother."

Camille adjusted the pillow behind her head. "And the clock delivery. How would that figure in?"

"Maybe she staged the attic break-in and the clock delivery." A not so pleasant idea popped into my head. "Maybe that was her backup plan in case the fake dead Puddles idea didn't work. Maybe she was trying to set up a case for self-defense. That way, she could kill the real Puddles and get away with it."

"Poor, stalked woman accidentally kills estranged husband," Camille said like it was a headline.

"Something like that."

Camille turned towards me and propped herself up on one arm. "Okay, assuming that Francesca and Bennett are connected and that together they were trying to secure her parents' inheritance for her rather than let it go to Lucia, what about you? Why would they take you?"

I thought back to my visit to Francesca's this morning. Was that really just this morning? It seemed like days ago. "I don't think that was Francesca's doing. She was definitely trying to get me to leave. I think that was Bennett. And I don't know why he would take me. It would seem that I would be of more use to them working the case. Better cover for the story that Puddles was somehow stalking her or something." As an afterthought I added, "If that's what they were trying to set up. Maybe we're wrong about that."

Camille pulled out her cell and dialed Laurent again. The receiver was so close to my ear, his voice was as clear to me as it would be if I had made the call myself. It didn't sound like he had been sleeping yet either. Camille asked him to get more info on Bennett and his law partners. When she disconnected, she pressed speed dial and reached Francesca who did sound as if she'd been asleep. Which probably explained why she picked up. "I'm sorry to call so late," Camille said in her best agitated voice. "It's Camille Caron calling from C&C Investigations."

There was a hesitation before Francesca offered a tentative, "Yes?"

"It's about Lora Weaver. We haven't heard from her since this morning. I'm looking at her day-planner here," she rustled the bed sheets over the phone. Not too convincing a replica of paper shuffling. "The last anyone heard from her was just before her appointment with you." She waited to see if Francesca would respond. When she didn't, Camille went on. "Do you remember what time she left your house?"

There was no answer right away. This time Camille waited the silence out.

At last, Francesca said, "Maybe around one. We didn't actually have a meeting, she just dropped by briefly to give me an update."

"Oh yes," Camille said. "How *did* you feel about that?" She said it gravely as if I had given Francesca some very serious and important news.

There was another long pause. "About what exactly?" Francesca asked.

"The news about your husband. I was very sorry about that."

This time Francesca was quick to respond, curiosity clearly at attention. "What news?"

"I'm sorry, didn't Lora tell you? I'm afraid your husband has passed on. We were notified by the authorities."

I got my ear as close to the receiver as I could, eager to hear any reactions. The line went dead.

We looked at each other. "That will buy Lucia some time," Camille said.

TWENTY-TWO

WE MUST HAVE dozed off after the call because when I opened my eyes, there was mild light sprinkling in through a small window in the rafters. Camille was breathing evenly beside me. Puddles had taken a pillow and blanket and was curled up on the floor. The blanket was tucked in tightly around his chin, his beard grazing the cotton. I didn't want to move, afraid to wake someone. Problem was I really had to go to the washroom.

I slipped out as quietly as I could and made my way down from the loft. I was getting pretty good at navigating the ladder. I didn't even notice the height anymore. My bare feet made little noise as I crossed over to the bathroom, but the cold floor didn't make the trek any easier. Clearly, the barn conversion was done by a man. No woman would ever design a living space with the bathroom so far away from the bedroom.

In the bathroom, I came across the bag of toiletries Puddles had bought for me. I decided to brush my teeth and hop in for a fast shower. Afterward, I dressed in the same clothes and combed out my hair, trying to drape a little onto my forehead to cover the booboo because I didn't want to put on a new Band-Aid over the newly formed scab. I searched for a hair dryer. Nothing. Probably Puddles didn't use one. And apparently, he didn't need one around for guests either. Which also likely meant those condoms didn't see a lot of action around here. I dried my hair as best I could with a towel and left it to dry on its own. In a couple of hours, it would be frizzy in all the wrong places and flat in even worse ones. Next time I left the house for work, I'd have to remember to pocket a hat.

When I came out, I flipped on Tinavision to amuse myself while I got something to eat. Tina was watching TV again. Guess her cable came back. She was still huddled under a blanket on the couch, but there was no hint of overalls. Instead, a pink hooded sweatshirt was zipped up partway. No telling if she had on matching bottoms. The room looked pretty much the same as it had yesterday. Maybe a few more empty glasses on the coffee table. She adjusted a pillow behind her, reached down beside the couch to a small blue cooler I hadn't noticed before, and took out a single-serving yogurt. She peeled back the top and started eating. Seemed like she had some new supplies. Puddles must have taken care of that while Camille and I were sleeping.

I switched off the TV, tossed my apple core, and got some cereal. I ate sitting at the table alone and listening to the birds outside. Some people find the country quite relaxing, but to a city girl accustomed to the background rhythm of street noise, it was a tad disconcerting. Adjusting to the relative quiet of my neighborhood in Montreal had been enough of a change from the constant buzz of New York. This stillness was too much. It would drive me batty if I had to live here all the time.

I dug in my pocket for the cell phone Camille had given me and dialed Adam. He picked up on the first ring. His voice had the edge of sleep shaken by sudden alertness. "What's going on?" he said when he knew it was me. "I've been worried."

Just hearing his voice loosened the tightness in my gut. "It's good to hear you," I said. "And I'm fine, really. Camille is here with me too, and she's keeping in touch with Laurent. How are things there? How are the animals?"

"We're all good. We miss you, though. Pong slept with her head on your slippers."

I could imagine her little head resting on the puffy white combed cotton. I was such a sap that it made me want to cry. "That's so cute."

"So, when are you coming home?" he asked.

"Not sure yet," I said. I explained briefly about Bennett and Francesca. I also assured him that Tina was alive and well, probably returning soon but not to mention that to anyone for the time being.

I heard some noise through the phone and Adam's voice dipped out then came back. "Sorry, I dropped the phone. But, I'm so glad you called. It's been hell not knowing anything."

"I know," I said. "I'll call again when I get the chance. I should go now, though, I don't want to run down the phone. I just really needed to talk to you."

"Me too you," he said. "Be careful."

After I disconnected I held onto the warmth of the phone for a moment before stowing it back in my pocket.

BY EIGHT-THIRTY we were ready to roll. The plan for today was simple. Get the goods on Bennett. How exactly to go about that was a bit more fuzzy. I leaned back against the wall outside the kitchen to stay clear of round three between Camille and Puddles, which, not surprisingly, round-for-round matched exactly the number of espressos Camille had already packed away.

"There was nothing on the first video," Camille was saying to Puddles. "Why do you want to record again?"

Puddles was determined to meet Camille's raised voice with his own even one. Nothing would have infuriated her more. "For the hundredth time," he said, "that wasn't the first tape. I've been recording Bennett for quite a while. I needed that tape as part of the series. If you match up bits of his conversations," he paused to look her in the eye, "and you know what you're looking for, it makes sense."

Camille's cheeks were starting to pinch. I could almost see the energy surging off her skin. That third espresso probably wasn't helping. This time when she spoke it was with control. "How long have you been collecting these tapes, this evidence?"

"Long enough to know what I'm doing."

"That must be a long time," she shot back.

Frankly, I was on Camille's side. I didn't see why Puddles couldn't just go to the police with the whole story. Seemed to me he already had enough on Bennett to at least warrant a police investigation. And once he came forward, Bennett would be crazy to touch him or Lucia. Or me for that matter. "Look," I said. "Let's not lose focus."

Somehow I must have pierced their orbit because they both stopped talking long enough for me to suggest a compromise. "Camille can drop by Bennett's to see if she can plant another tape for you," I said to Puddles, then turning to Camille I went on, "and then you can meet us back at the office to go over whatever stuff Laurent has turned up. Maybe we'll get lucky, and he'll have something solid we can take to the police."

Puddles looked satisfied with that. Camille didn't. "Why would I go to Bennett's?" she said to me. "He must know by now that I work with you, so I don't have any chance at an anonymous cover. And, there's no logical reason I would be looking for information on your supposed disappearance at Finestein, Bennett, & Fitch."

Those were some good points. Puddles might need an espresso of his own to respond to those.

"You don't need a cover," he said. "You can go there to follow up on Tina. After all, Jeffrey is a friend of a friend."

Oh yeah, I nearly forgot that Tina was supposed to be missing too.

"Fine," Camille said in a tone that meant that it wasn't but that she would go along with it. "*Encore* Tina," she muttered to herself. "*Espèce d'idiot*." And she picked up the new tape Puddles had given her earlier from where she'd placed it on the seat of his bike. "What about her?" she said gesticulating at me.

What about me?

They were both looking at me now. "I'll stick with her," Puddles said.

"You better. No telling how many people Bennett has looking for her. And you," she pointed at me. "Stay out of sight."

CAMILLE LEFT FIRST so Puddles could lock up before we left. On the way to the office, I asked Puddles to stop at a health food store so I could restock my fanny pack with my favorite protein bar.

I got three bars this time just to be on the safe side, all chocolate. Puddles picked up a couple of different flavors for himself claiming he just wanted to know what all the fuss about protein bars was about. More likely, he probably wanted to keep his energy up for the next round with Camille.

At the office, we left the bike in the alley, hopped the fence, and made our way over to the back entrance that opened into the basement of C&C. Laurent had suggested it would be better to use that rather than the back door off the kitchen just in case any clients happened to be in the office when we arrived. He had left it unlocked for us which was a good thing because I had long ago lost the key they had given me. I turned the rusted knob, gave a small kick to the bottom of the door to release it from its frame, warped from years of alternating bouts of humidity and cold, and pushed the door open.

Once we were in, I led Puddles down the hallway of the unfinished basement into an open area that served mainly as storage. The floor was gray cement and the brick walls were painted white. The space was heated only by the boiler housed in its own room and separated by a steel door. Half the area held unwanted furniture; the other half had two tall file cabinets, a long metal table, and an old photocopier. A small steel supply cabinet sat tucked at the base of the stairs leading up to the reception area above.

Halfway up the stairs, I heard familiar voices. One was Laurent. The other belonged to Francesca. I instinctively put my arm out to signal Puddles to stop. We both listened. We could only make out the odd word or two, so we tiptoed up the rest of the stairs. I turned sideways and put my ear to the door, allowing Puddles enough space behind me to do the same.

Francesca's voice sounded agitated. "Well, when will she be back? I need to talk to her."

"I understand," Laurent was saying. "I can't say exactly. Most likely this afternoon." There was a tense pause before he spoke again. "Are you sure there's nothing I can help you with?"

The steady stroke of high heels drew closer. A wave of irrational paranoia sent my hand to clench the doorknob. My neck felt a wisp of warm air letting me know Puddles found my action amusing. The footsteps passed, lessening as Francesca headed for the front door, and the voices became barely audible.

I heard the door close and listened to make sure Laurent was alone before stepping out. I found him in his office tapping away at the keys on his laptop. His hair was damp and he had on a long-sleeve black shirt open at the collar. He looked up at me then scanned over to Puddles. If he was surprised by the Hell's Angel get-up, he didn't show it. "You just missed Mrs. Bellinni," he said as he rose and crossed the room to shake Puddles' hand. "This is Mr. Bellinni, I take it."

"What did she want?" I asked him.

"To see Camille concerning her dear departed husband." He waved his arm in Puddles' direction. "Good thing she didn't see you. It would have been quite a shock."

The puzzled look Puddles wore reminded me I hadn't told him about the dead guy with his I.D. Nor had he been briefed about Camille's late night call to Francesca. I quickly filled him in on both.

"What did he look like?" Puddles asked.

"Who?"

"The dead man."

"We have some pictures if you're interested," I told him and went into Camille's office to check her desk for the envelope of photos. When I didn't find it, I remembered I'd had them in my car with me when Bennett had knocked me out. I fished out the fax Camille had originally received with the pixilated photo and passed it to Puddles. He took it over to the window to study in the light while I followed up with Laurent about my missing Mini.

"Any sign of my car?" I asked him.

"Not yet. Bennett probably moved it away from Francesca's to throw off suspicions about your disappearance. Luc has it reported as stolen for now."

"Which means?"

He leaned against the doorframe and folded his arms together across his chest. "Which means that if someone comes across it and notifies the police, you may get it back. Or, the police could find it themselves."

I sat in Camille's desk chair. "And the chances of that?"

His shoulders went up and his arms went out in the international mime for "who knows?" which I noticed was very similar to the sign for "who cares?" Then he left the room for a moment. I heard the front door bolt turn and the chain slide into place. He came back into the room and pulled the curtains in the bay window closed. "Anyway, you won't be needing your car for a while," he said to me. "You'll be riding with me or Camille until Bennett gets you off his radar."

Puddles, having lost the light from the window, set the fax sheet aside and anted in. "Or she can ride with me."

Laurent and I both looked over at Puddles. I didn't know what Laurent was thinking, but I was thinking I'd had enough of being babysat. "Nuh uh," I said. "I'm perfectly capable of fending for myself. I'll just rent a car or something."

"No," Laurent said.

No? Where did he get off telling me no? He wasn't the boss of me. Well, okay, maybe technically he was, but there were limits to the employer/employee thing. I eyed Camille's slinky sitting on the corner of her desk.

Laurent followed my eyes and lunged for the slinky, but proximity was on my side, and I reached it first.

He took a few steps back from the desk and held up his hands. "Okay," he said. "I can see you're not in the mood to discuss it now."

"That's right," I said. "I'm not." What I was in the mood for was a change of clothes. Despite my shower, I didn't feel fresh and clean. My day-old clothes were permeated with the grime from Bennett's basement. And, I won't even go into the separation anxiety I was feeling for my hair dryer. I knew Camille kept some extra clothes in her office, so I shooed the men out while I checked her cupboard for something I could borrow. For pants, I had a choice of jeans or gray sweatpants, and for tops a black tank, a white T-shirt, or a lime green cotton sweater. I picked the jeans, tank top, and sweater and got changed. Then I twisted up my hair and stuffed it into a green cap I'd found at the back of the shelf. When I came out, the guys were in the kitchen. Laurent was over by the counter filling mugs with coffee and Puddles sat at the table.

Both men turned to look at me.

Laurent grinned. "I hope you brought enough Lucky Charms for all of us."

Was he saying I looked like a leprechaun? I looked down at my body swimming in green sweater on top and cut short by rolled jeans at the bottom. Then I scrolled my eyes upwards towards the hat. Hmmm. Maybe he wasn't far off. I sat down at the table to minimize the effect and changed the subject. "Any news on Bennett yet?" I asked him.

He set the coffee out and sat down beside me. "Yeah. It seems like skimming money here and there didn't cut it for him. He's also been into blackmail. It seems client/lawyer privilege is an optional thing for him. He uses old cases that were handled by other attorneys in the firm as his source material. It's been a while since his last big payout, though. Not sure why. Maybe he ran out of patsies. At any rate, the other partners don't seem to be involved. They also don't seem to have noticed. The firm has gone through some transitions over time, and the partners don't seem that close on a personal level anymore. Both Finestein and Fitch have offspring on staff now and they're more focused on grooming them to take over."

A quick glance in Puddles' direction told me none of this was news to him. "Do we have enough evidence to turn Bennett over to the police?" I asked Laurent.

"Not yet, but we will. Puddles has filled me in on what he has, and if we add that to the stuff coming in, it's just a matter of time before my contacts gather enough proof. The toughest part is trying to secure records on the Guido dealings. Bennett has covered his tracks on that one pretty well. And without that, Puddles could still be accused. Especially if Bennett has kept whatever documents he had to frame Puddles in the first place. If we act too soon, Bennett could be charged and released on bail until his court date, and Puddles will just add a police warrant to his list of problems."

That didn't sound good. Puddles would have to go even deeper into hiding with no chance of helping Sarah at all. "The thing that keeps nagging at me," I said to Laurent, "is that if Bennett was willing to kill Vladimir Dobervitch and Puddles," not to mention possibly me, "just to cover his neck in the Guido's case, who knows what else he's done to cover his other dealings."

Laurent nodded. "I've thought about that too. That's part of what we're still hoping to find out."

I took a sip of my coffee and realized it needed something. Food. I went to the fridge, found a blueberry muffin, and squeezed it gently with my fingers. Not too hard. Probably not too old to do me any harm. I peeled off the paper, dipped the muffin in my coffee, ate the whole thing in about four bites, then washed it down with the last bit of java. I got up to put my dishes in the sink and found walking in the oversized jeans tough. Flared bottoms didn't roll up well. Plus they felt bulky and heavy. Better to switch them for the sweats. I went back to Camille's office to make another change. The phone rang as I passed her desk, and I picked up automatically. It was the temp agency about the receptionist job. I scheduled a round of interviews for the beginning of the next week, assuring them that there would be someone here to meet the candidates, then hung up and started to undo the jeans.

"Not too smart."

I turned to see Laurent staring at me from the hallway.

"What?" I said, holding the jeans together by the fly.

He came over to me, slipped the baseball cap off my head, and dropped it on the desk. "Answering the phone. Someone who's not here shouldn't be answering the phone."

Oh yeah. I wasn't thinking. "It was just a reflex," I said, rearranging my grip on the front of my pants so I could hold them up with one hand as I reached for the cap with the other. "And give me back the hat."

Laurent moved it farther from my reach. "It looks ridiculous."

"So what? I need it to cover my hair. It's a mess." I tried to stretch around him to get the hat, but he stood firm.

"It's not a mess. It's fine." He slipped his hand into my hair and adjusted some errant waves, his eyes locked on mine. "And from now on leave the phone to me."

For a moment my defiance dipped away and was replaced by something else. Something I didn't want to think about.

Puddles poked his head in then quickly retreated. "Oh. Sorry," he said.

Laurent let his hand drop, and I called after Puddles, "Wait. It's fine. What's up?"

"I gotta run a quick errand. You coming with me or staying here?"

I felt the defiance rising up again. I so did not like the way this was going.

"Better wait for Camille to get back first," Laurent told him. "She wants to talk to you."

Puddles checked his watch. "I don't know."

Before Laurent could respond, I called attention to my current state of partial dress. "Guys, a little privacy please. Why don't you debate this somewhere else."

Both men left, not bothering to close the door. I closed it myself before putting on the sweatpants. I folded the jeans up nicely and put them back where Camille kept them. A piece of jean pinched in the cabinet door as I closed it. I opened it again and folded the material back some so the door would close. A jab of sympathy went through me. It was awfully cramped in the cupboard. I opened the door again and pulled the material back out, resting the door on it.

"It's okay," I said to the jeans. "I understand. It's a little claustrophobic out here too."

TWENTY-THREE

LAURENT WAS ON the phone in his office. Puddles was in the washroom. This was as good a time as any if I was going to do it. I made sure my fanny pack was on good and tight and put on my jacket. I had decided it would be better to risk the front door. It was easier to hightail it to the corner from there. No tricky fence climbing necessary. A few minutes head start should be enough to flag down a taxi. Taxis weren't quite the fixture on the streets of central Montreal as they were in Manhattan, but they were still aplenty.

I quietly undid the chain lock first then turned the bolt. Without looking back, I slipped out and dashed down the street. A few minutes later, I was safely tucked into the back seat of a cab, my lungs still contracting at a rapid clip. When this case was over, I so had to work on my cardio.

The cab driver dropped me off downtown at Centre Eaton. An amalgamation of what used to be three shopping centers, it was now a mix of chain stores and boutiques and connected to the "underground city" accessed by the Montreal Metro. I wasn't sure why I'd picked the mall to come to except that it was central, public, and had a decent food court. I stepped through the double doors and my recently recovered lungs were immediately accosted by mall air—that ever so distinct brew of perfume, sweat, and fast food. And, if you stood in just the right place, this mall air had the extra ingredient of hot Metro air.

I found my way to a vacant bench to think about my next move. From where I sat, I had a view of a music store and a fresh juice kiosk. Six people were in line at the kiosk. An older couple, a teenage girl, a man in a suit, and a mom with a preschooler in tow that reminded me of Sarah. I wondered how Sarah was doing, and if she was still in the hospital. Not wanting to run down the cell phone Camille had given me, I bought a phone card from a local store, headed over to a bank of public phones, and started to look up the hospital in the Yellow Pages, stopping when I realized I didn't know which hospital Sarah was in. Figuring it was probably one of the children's hospitals, I looked them up and tried St. Justine's first. No luck, so I tried the Montreal Children's Hospital. This time, my call got put through and a woman picked up, answering in a hushed voice that was difficult to hear over the mall noise.

"Hello," I said. "I'm not sure I have the right room. I was looking for Jim Bell. His daughter is in the hospital there."

"Who is this?" the woman asked.

"Just a friend of the family," I said.

"Oh really," the voice said. "Well, this is Mrs. Bell, and I don't know you."

I had the distinct feeling she was going to hang up on me. "Wait, Mrs. Bell, er Joanne, this is Lora. Lora Weaver."

"Oh, Lora. I'm sorry. We've been getting some strange calls. I thought this was another one."

I had to cup my other ear so I could hear her better. "Calls from who?"

"A woman. Well, there were two calls with different voices, but I could tell it was the same woman. And a man called, too."

"What did they want?"

"I'm not really sure. One of the calls from the woman asked after Sarah. And I didn't take the call from the man. He spoke to Jim. I know he asked about you, though. He wanted to know if you'd been by to visit."

Bennett, I thought. Well, no, if it was recent it could be Laurent. "How long ago did he call?" I asked her.

"I think it was early this morning."

Had to be Bennett. "Please, Joanne, if anyone calls again, anyone, don't let them know you've spoken with me. It's very important. It's better for Sarah."

She said she understood. She wouldn't say anything.

"So, how is Sarah?"

"She's doing all right. They're thinking of letting us take her home."

"That's wonderful," I said. "Look, we're making some progress here, too. Don't give up hope."

"Progress? Really?" Her voice rose a little with each word.

I wanted to give her some encouragement. And, after all, we did have Puddles now. That was progress. Still, I hoped I wasn't misleading her. "Yes," I said. "There's been some developments I find very encouraging. Let's keep our fingers crossed."

"If I cross mine anymore, I'll break the bones," she said.

A man had come over to use the phone beside me. "I'd better go now. I'll be in touch."

THE GOOD NEWS was that Sarah was not only holding her own, but doing it well enough to go home. That meant there was still time. The bad news was Bennett was actively looking for me. I had to work fast. There was only one sure way I knew of to get the straight goods on a man—his wife. That meant I was going to have to figure out a way to meet with Mrs. Bennett. Alone. It probably wouldn't be too hard to track her down. Most women of her social standing had fairly regular schedules. A few calls to the right people and I could probably find out what time of day she recharged the batteries for her vibrator. Problem was, I didn't know the right people. But, I knew someone who did.

And thanks to Ingrid over at Guido's, about ten minutes later, I had what I needed.

Barbara Bennett's afternoon was booked solid. Barbara, or as I had repeatedly been reminded, Babs, sat on just about every volunteer committee in town. Today, she had a four o'clock board meeting for the French branch of the Designers on a Dime foundation—an organization that recycled rich women's designer clothes to low-income women looking for work—and before that, she had some do at one o'clock at the museum that was supposed to run about an hour. Both of those would be hard to crash. My best bet was her two-thirty at a place called Bernard's which I was guessing was either a restaurant or a hairdresser's. It was nearly eleven-thirty now, so I had plenty of time to make it. I hauled the Yellow Pages up again and flipped to the restaurants. No luck. I couldn't find it in the hair salons either. Hmmm. Could be a problem. I eased the Yellow Pages back down and tried the White Pages. Bingo.

I dialed the number and got picked up after two rings. A women's voice answered. "*Bonjour.* Dr. Bernard's office, please hold."

Doctor? A doctor's office. I looked back at the listing. It was just under Bernard's. No Dr. Bernard. That threw me. What kind of doctor was this? It was really hard to crash a doctor's office.

The voice came back. "Thank you for holding. How may I help you?"

Clearly this doctor catered more to an English clientele because the receptionist had already dropped the French bit. Lucky for me. "I'd like to make an appointment, please."

"Have you seen the doctor before?"

I wasn't sure what to say. Part of me wanted to just hang up. Was this a real doctor? What if it was a specialist? I didn't have a chance of getting in without a referral. Worse yet, what if it's a gyno?

"No," I admitted.

"Well then," she said. "The first appointment I have for new patients is just after the new year."

"Oh," I said. "I was hoping to get in today. It's, umm, kind of an emergency." A little pop-up window appeared in my brain. Large capital red letters flashed 'GOOD ONE. WHAT KIND OF EMERGENCY?'

I heard another voice in the background. "Just a sec," the receptionist said to me. I could hear sniffling and a slight thud as the phone was put down. A little fainter the voice said, "Don't worry, Dora, skin can sometimes be a little red after a chemical peel, you just go home and have yourself a good rest. Before you know it, you'll be good as new. Better!"

A dermatologist. Great. Now all I needed was a skin emergency. A glint caught my attention as the same teenage girl from the juice stand went by, this time carrying a bag from The Gap. From this angle I could see the source of the glint. She had several facial piercings. She also had the image of a tiny star high up on the cheekbone, almost at her temple. I took a chance and let the phone dangle while I sprinted over to the girl.

"Excuse me," I said, tapping her on the shoulder.

She turned. The shine off her blue eyes nearly made me squint. They were the brightest, happiest eyes I'd ever seen. "Yes," she said, immediately welcoming me with a smile.

"I couldn't help noticing the star on your cheek," I said to her. "It's really nice. Could you tell me where I could get something like that? Is it a transfer or something?"

Her fingers automatically stroked the star. "No, it's a tattoo. I got it down on St. Laurent at a place called Pièces des Arts. They're really great there. Really clean. It's the only place I'd go." She raised her shirt up some to reveal a red flower that used her belly button as a center. "I've got quite a few," she said and grinned. "I'd have to know you a lot better to show you the others, though."

"They're great," I said. "Do they take a long time?"

"Not the small ones."

I glanced over to make sure the phone was still dangling. "Thanks," I said. "I've gotta run, but you've been a big help." I started off for the phone.

"No problem," she shouted after me. "Hey, if you go, tell them Lily says hello."

"Sure thing," I called back.

I picked up the phone to hear, "hello, hello."

"Yes, I'm still here. Sorry, I couldn't hear you."

The receptionist didn't sound quite as pleasant as before. "I was about to hang up."

"Sorry," I said again.

"You said you had an emergency?"

"Yes, I'm having a reaction to a tattoo I got." The pop-up window in my head sent me an inspiration. "I'm only in town on a shoot for a few days, and Jen (Jen who?—Jennifer Aniston, Jennifer Garner, Jennifer Lopez—that was for her to figure out) told me if I had any problems I just had to see Dr. Bernard. She said he was the only one she'd ever trust to work on her." I held my breath while I waited for the receptionist to respond. Luckily she didn't take long.

"Come on in a little later this afternoon, and I'll try to squeeze you in."

"Thanks a million." I gave her a name and hung up. Okay. Now all I needed was a tattoo.

TWENTY-FOUR

ST. LAURENT WAS a long street. A pretty important one too. A divider of sorts between the predominantly French neighborhoods to the east and the predominantly English neighborhoods to the west. At least it used to be. More recently, those lines had become blurred as more and more anglophones left the city allowing the balance of immigrants and francophones to weigh more heavily on the scales.

The taxi dropped me across the street from Pièces des Arts where it was easier to pull over. Traffic was pretty bad in this neck of the urban woods no matter what time of day, so I jay-walked my way through the weave of cars to cross the street. Once there, I paced back and forth on the sidewalk. I told myself it was to take time to size up the place—clear glass windows, awning in good repair, neighboring a frozen yogurt place and a clothing store specializing in yoga wear—because surely I couldn't be having second thoughts. Nope. No second thoughts for me. After all, professional PIs don't have second thoughts.

I pushed open the door and went in. See, nothing to be afraid of. Tile floor, stainless steel counter, walls papered with images available for tattoo. A few plastic chairs with metal legs forming a line in front of the window, a tall, thin tree-type plant with long, wide, droopy leaves at the far end in a large earthenware pot. Three closed doors behind the counter. That was it. Nothing scary.

The middle door opened and a tiny woman, maybe thirty-five, stepped out amid a breeze of Vivaldi. The door closed, and the room went quiet again. Her pink smock crinkled as she took her place behind the counter. A nametag near her lapel had Peggy printed on it. She removed her glasses and began wiping at them with a white cloth. "*Est-ce-que je peux vous aider?* Can I help you?" she asked, the words strewn together like one sentence. A common custom among people dealing with the public. Those wanting to maintain a bilingual image that is, others just stuck with the French.

I leaned against the counter, trying to look casual. "I'm interested in a tattoo," I said, hoping she'd pick up on my cue and serve me in English.

She did. She put her glasses back on and said, "People in here generally are." She looked at me waiting for me to continue. When I didn't she said, "Any idea which one you want?"

I looked over at the wall. "I'm not sure. They all look so, so big."

"That's so people can make them out. You can get them any size you want." She pulled out a large book that looked like a photo album and plunked it on the counter, spinning it around to face my side. "There are a lot more in here," she said.

I leafed through the pages desperately trying to figure out how to get out of this gracefully. What was I thinking? I had a million second thoughts. I didn't want a tattoo. This was crazy. How did I get this lame idea anyway. There had to be a better way to get to Babs Bennett.

Okay, so that wasn't completely true. There was a little part of me that had always secretly wanted a tattoo. Not some gaudy thing like a heart with a boy's name in the middle or anything. Something tasteful, something small, something discreet. Something other people didn't even have to see but I would know was there. I'd just never had the guts to do it before. I'm not sure I really believed I needed one now. I may have been using the situation as an excuse to finally get one. But it was an excellent excuse. It might even be a business deduction.

I stopped and pointed to an image.

Peggy flipped the book around and nodded. "Is that about the size you want?"

I checked out the size. "Maybe a bit smaller."

"Okay, and where do you want it?"

Where? Hmmm. I'd heard people say it was more painful to get them on parts that were close to bone, the fleshier parts were better. The fleshiest part would naturally be the derrière. I didn't think I knew Peggy well enough for that. I took a quick inventory and decided on the upper thigh. No that was no good. People would think it was a varicose vein. "The upper arm," I heard myself tell her.

"Color?"

"Umm. Blue, I guess."

"Okay, let's head on back," she said. She stepped to the front door and turned the lock before leading me back through the middle door.

What was that whole bit about? "Umm..."

"You're wondering about the door, eh? Everybody does. That's just so the little dinger that goes off when people come in won't be triggered while I'm working. Happened a couple of times, not a good scene."

That was good. She was conscientious *and* careful.

She led the way back to the room Vivaldi was still filling. She pressed a button on a computer and Vivaldi dropped away, leaving the room to a sterility that would have given an ice cube the shivers. I slipped my jacket onto a hook on the back of the door and pulled my sweater off over my head then draped it around my shoulders. She motioned for me to sit down and started talking as she flitted about the room readying her equipment. "So, here's how it works. First off, it hurts. More so at first then less so after a few minutes in. Most people find it feels more tingly at that point." She must have caught the look of retreat in my eyes because she followed that up with, "I'm not telling you that to scare you, I'm telling you to prepare you. That way, you won't be surprised and jerk away. If you do, it could ruin the tattoo image."

I nodded. "Got it."

"The whole thing shouldn't take more than twenty minutes because it's pretty small."

That was good. It was after twelve, and I needed to get to Bernard's with enough time before Mrs. Bennett's appointment to do the bonding thing without leaving so much time that I could get called into the doctor's office first.

"When I'm done, I'll bandage it. You'll get this kit," she held up a small transparent plastic bag with a few tubes of ointment inside along with a folded piece of paper. "It has some cream and a list of instructions on how to take care of your tattoo over the next few weeks along with some regular maintenance tips. Things like keeping it out of the sun or using really intense sun block on it." She sat down on a rolling chair and wheeled over a cart with the tools she'd just removed with tongs from the sterilizer. It may have been my imagination, but I could have sworn steam was still rising off them. "Not every tattoo artist gives out a kit. I do. People need to understand the importance of aftercare."

I didn't fully take in everything she said because I was stuck at the bandage part. "What did you mean about the bandage?" I asked her.

"The skin needs to be protected after it gets a tattoo. I bandage you up when I'm done and usually recommend you keep it on overnight. Some people get excited and want to show off the tattoo too soon, so they don't keep it covered." She looked me in the eye. "I don't recommend that."

At that moment, I couldn't imagine anyone not keeping the bandage on for less than a week.

Peggy rose, went over to a sink in the corner and washed her hands, pumping the container of antibacterial soap twice and rinsing repeatedly before finally drying her hands on a fresh paper towel she pulled from the silver holder above the sink. After dropping the used towel into a garbage can she opened with her foot, she turned and slipped two vinyl gloves from a box on the counter and put them on.

This could be a serious problem. I couldn't show up at the dermatologist with a tattoo freshly swathed in sterility. I needed something that could be seen and could pass for at least a little older than two hours. Of course, I never really had to go into the doctor's office. I could just hightail it out of the waiting room after I'd talked to Mrs. Bennett. But then, why do this at all? Did I think the receptionist was going to ask me to show her the tattoo to verify that I had a bona fide reason for crashing the doctor's day?

A feeling of wetness on my arm broke into my conversation with myself. I looked over and saw that Peggy was swiping a cotton ball soaked in alcohol over my skin. A second later she was pulling a thin coating off a small piece of what looked like cardboard. "What's that?" I asked.

"This is a transfer." She turned it so I could see the outline of the image I'd chosen from the big book of tattoos out front. "It's kind of a guide. I just press it against your skin like so," she said as she pressed it onto me then pulled it away with one quick movement. "That way we can be sure it's placed just right before I fill it in with the ink."

A second later I was looking into a hand mirror she was holding for me to see the image on my arm. There was a faint outline on my skin. It reminded me of a page out of a coloring book. A page that hadn't printed very well and lacked the bold lines coloring books typically had. Instead, the line was thin and pale, nearly dotted.

"Well?" she prompted, making no attempt to disguise the impatience in her voice.

"Well what?"

"Does it look right? Can we start?"

Hmmm. What to say? "Actually, I'm kind of having second thoughts," I said.

She sat back in her chair and waited. Clearly she was used to people chickening out. I was sure her silence was a form of intimidation. After all, time was money and she'd already spent time with me, not to mention the money and time it would take to re-sterilize her equipment.

I too, was running out of time. Hmmm. What to do? To tell the truth, the whole truth, and nothing but the truth? Or, to opt for a reasonable knockoff of the afore-to.

"Look, it's not that I don't want a tattoo. It's that I kind of need it right now. I mean, I need to be able to show it right away, and for it to look like it's not brand new."

"Not going to happen," Peggy said, giving me the once-over. "Who has to see it?"

"A dermatologist."

She wheeled her chair back a bit and slid open the third drawer down in her drawer trolley. She shuffled around and pulled out another square of cardboard. Back by my side, she swabbed my arm again with rubbing alcohol, this time wiping harder to dissolve the outline she'd put on earlier. "Here's the best we can do," she said, pulling out another contraption before returning her attention to the new piece of cardboard. "I'm going to do a hand painted tattoo using an air blowing technique. If no one looks real close, it'll pass. I wouldn't risk giving you a real tattoo that won't stay bandaged."

I nodded agreement, totally unsure whether this was a good idea or not.

She looked at me briefly. "Don't worry it doesn't hurt."

I didn't much appreciate her tone with that last part, but I wasn't about to make an issue of it now given my current need of her expertise. I didn't want to have to resort to the press on tattoo from a pack of kid's bubble gum. I sat quietly and watched as she worked. It looked like she was stenciling on my arm. I couldn't make out how it was coming along from this angle, so I was surprised when she said she was done already. It was super fast. She held up the little hand mirror again. It wasn't until I saw the wee image of the Tasmanian devil that I realized we hadn't discussed what she would have to use instead of the tattoo I had chosen from the big book. And now that I really looked at it, it wasn't all that wee either. I bet it could be seen half a block away.

Peggy's smile was slight. "Sorry, there wasn't a lot left to choose from. I get a new shipment next week, though, in case you're interested in something else."

"I just thought it would be, umm, a little smaller."

Peggy shrugged and began cleaning up. "It'll only last a week or less. You can get it wet once it's dry. To get it off, just use soap or rubbing alcohol."

I stood and looked at it in the full-length standing mirror tucked in the corner. I hadn't noticed the mirror before. It looked a little out of place amid all the white tile and stainless steel. It probably came in handy for those clients who got tattoos in hard to see places. Mine was easy to see. I was no tattoo expert, but it did look pretty good. At least it was something in case it came to show and tell at Bernard's.

I dressed and followed Peggy out front to pay. While she got the bill together, I perused the wall of tattoos. My eye caught on a rather intricate snake. I knew that snake. That was Puddles' snake. "Wow, that's some really amazing work," I said sounding as impressed as I felt. "You're a real artist."

Peggy stopped fiddling with the computer and came to stand beside me. "Which piece?"

I pointed to the serpent. "That one. I can't believe the detail. It's amazing. That must have taken hours."

For a moment, I thought Peggy might even show a real smile. Then she looked down rather quickly, using her glasses to shield an emotion that was brewing. "Yes. That did take a long time. That was an original piece. I made it for a friend."

A friend. Wow. Puddles had a friend.

"I don't mean to pry," I began, although I most certainly did, "but this friend of yours, was this a man?"

She stepped back behind the counter and kept her eyes on her computer screen. "Yes, it was."

Wow. I couldn't believe my luck. What were the chances of running into someone who actually knew Puddles? I couldn't let the opportunity pass without finding out more. "You guys must have been really close," I said. "That kind of work takes a lot of care."

She turned her attention to the printer that was spitting out my bill. "Yes, it does."

This wasn't working. She still keeping her comments confined to the professional realm. I tried a different track. "You know, I think I saw a tattoo like that," I said. "Come to think of it."

She stayed focused on the printer, but there was a change in her posture. She turned back to the counter to hand me the bill. "Really?" she said. "Around here?"

Now I had her attention. No woman can resist an update on an ex. Even if at the end of the relationship we thought the guy was a jerk, we still wanted to know what happened to him. Not that I could really offer her an update on Puddles, but I could fake it. I tried to sound casual. "Yeah, it was maybe a month ago at a club or something." I pretended to be searching my memory. "I think it was that place down by the arena. Stanley's. You know it?"

A look of excitement flashed in her eyes. "I've been there a couple of times," she said.

"I remember because the guy was sitting near me at the bar, and I noticed his hand when he reached for a napkin. With it flexed like that, it was like the snake was moving." Having never been to Stanley's, I steered clear of too many details of the place. It was a safe bet that it had a bar and napkins, though. And there was another kind of detail I did know for sure that I could add in. "Pretty good looking guy. Had a real quality about him. You've got good taste."

She laid her forearm across the counter. "He was a good man."

"Those are hard to come by," I said.

"They sure are," she agreed. "But, sometimes you just have to let them go."

So she was the one who broke it off. Now I wondered why. "True. But a guy like that wouldn't get kicked out of bed for having an extra toe. Must have been really something awful."

"Let's just say he had a lot of baggage. That and he didn't want any kids. Well, any more kids, I should say."

What was that about Puddles not wanting any more kids? Peggy was a minefield. I had to keep this conversation going. "Oh, yeah. A divorced dad," I said like that had some specific characteristics. "I know what that's like. I knew a guy once like that who was just looking for a new mommy for his twins." I shook my head, partially for effect and partially because I was amazed at how fast I was coming up with my lie. "Not what I was looking for. I like kids and all but I felt like I was interviewing for a babysitting job."

"He wasn't divorced, either," she said. "That was another problem." She had both forearms on the counter now, hunkered into talk mode.

"Really?"

"But he had this kid he was madly in love with. The mother wouldn't let him see her. He had to sneak into her recitals and stuff. He even disguised himself so the mother wouldn't notice him and make a scene. He didn't want to embarrass his daughter."

Puddles must have been keeping an eye on Lucia all along. "Sounds like a really great dad. Sounds like the kind of guy who'd want oodles of kids."

"You'd think," Peggy said. "But no. He'd already made sure that wouldn't happen long before I'd met him."

Made sure. What? A vasectomy? I thought about all those condoms in Puddles' loft. Must be to ward off STDs. Either he was vigilant about his health, or he didn't have a steady in his life.

"He just didn't tell me right away," she continued. "He didn't think it was important. Not until I started talking about having a family anyway."

"Must have been pretty important to you. It's too bad things didn't work out."

"Oh I got my kids," she said pulling out a framed photo from behind the counter. Two preschoolers, sitting in a kiddie pool. "Ariana and Malcolm," she said. "They're the loves of my life." She pulled out another photo; this one had a nice looking dark-haired, dark-skinned man sitting on a stoop with the kids beside him. They were all smiling and one of the kids was waving. "Christopher, the guy I'm with now, comes from a big family. He'd have a baseball team if I wanted." She glanced over in the direction of the snake tattoo on the wall. "But, I still wonder sometimes."

Yeah, I got it. Puddles was probably her first love. Maybe the love of her life, if you believed in that sort of thing. The Christopher guy was probably nice, safe, predictable but no electrifying sparks. No matter how great the guy was, it must be hard always feeling like something was missing. Especially if you had had it with someone else.

A rap on the glass door diverted our attention. I turned to see a pinched face pressed against the glass with two hands shielding the eyes. I couldn't make out if the head belonged to a male or female.

Peggy looked at her watch. "I'll just let this customer in," she said crossing the room to unlock the door. A short squat man came in followed by a tall thin one. "*C'est ouvert*?" the little man said.

"*Oui*," Peggy answered, switching to French. Then she went on to tell him she was just finishing up with me, and, plunking the big book down on the counter, she invited him to have a look through it while he waited.

I pulled out my money to pay, and she handed me a receipt. I turned to go. "Thanks again. Was nice talking to you."

Peggy barely nodded, already having turned her attention to the two men.

Out on the sidewalk, I knew I needed sustenance for the task ahead, so I decided to grab something to have en route before I hailed a cab. I dropped into the yogurt place and perused the takeout menu looking for something a girl with a tattoo would order. Okay, so maybe it wasn't a real tattoo, but it was still hot. Maybe a tad too hot. Feeling this hot could be dangerous in my condition. After all, I didn't know how long it would be before I got back to Adam and our bed. I settled on something called "chocolate chiller." I figured the chocolate part would pacify my brain while the chiller part pacified the rest of me. At least for the time being.

DR. BERNARD'S OFFICE was in an upscale building on the edge of downtown on the west side of Sherbrooke Street. The awning out front had the address inscribed on it in fancy white italics. My cab driver pulled over at the nearest intersection, hurrying me to pay before the light changed to green. I stepped out and took a moment to finish my drink and go over my plan before going into the office. When I'd sucked out the last drops of my chocolate chiller, I forced my empty cup into the garbage can near the curb, carefully avoiding contact with the annoyingly tight flap guarding the garbage opening. Darn things usually spring closed so quickly my trash gets clamped before it has a chance to make its way into the depths below. I lucked out this time, and my cup made it in. Well, the straw didn't quite make it, but who was going to mind a thin strip of white and red plastic poking out. It was kind of decorative. Cheery almost, like a candy cane.

A car honked behind me and somebody yelled out, "Hey."

Immediate guilt set in with a touch of irritation. I couldn't believe someone was really going to call me on it. I did the only dignified thing and started to walk away, pretending I hadn't heard a thing. A large dark shadow followed me as a moved. I sped up a bit.

"Hey," I heard again. "Get in."

I tilted my head enough to get a glimpse of the street, not wanting to do a full head turn in case the caller wasn't talking to me. The nose of the car looked familiar. On closer look, so did its driver.

A car honked from behind. "Move it, sweetheart," a male voice boomed.

"Piss off," Camille yelled back. Then to me, "hurry up, will you. I'm holding up traffic."

Not wanting to be responsible for a road rage incident, I darted over and got in the passenger side of the Jetta. Camille pulled ahead, turned into the next block, and found a side street with an available meter. I checked the dash clock. If I ran back, I would still have enough time to catch Barbara Bennett if I was lucky.

"Look," I said to Camille, "you're probably really annoyed with me right now but could you be annoyed later because I've got to get back to get a crack at Mrs. Bennett."

Camille flipped down her visor to check her face in the mirror. She wiped away a stray eyelash from her cheek and reapplied some lipstick. "I figured that's what you were doing. I've been following her around all afternoon. She wasn't there yet when I picked you up." She replaced her visor, pushed some silver foil into the mound protruding from the pocket in the car door, and got out of the car. I joined her on the sidewalk and we started off, doing the best imitation of speed-walkers we could muster.

Unlike me, Camille had had time to go home and change at some point. She had on cranberry corduroy jeans, a long-sleeved vintage Tee, and an open knee-length cream sweater with a hood and two outer pockets. Her hair was freshly spiked, her makeup in the pink tones. She looked very casual-chic, even with her boots. I knew she'd noticed my wearing her clothes and was most likely cringing inside at my mismatched ensemble.

It also occurred to me that I may not be dressed well enough for Barbara Bennett. Or, for the waiting room at Dr. Bernard's, for that matter. If it was a room full of the economically endowed, I would stand out as a poor relation. And, nobody wants to be seen talking to the poor relation at the family reunion. Plus I was starting to worry about my fake tattoo passing muster.

Just before we got to the entrance, I pulled Camille aside. "Here's the thing," I said. "Mrs. Bennett has an appointment at her dermatologist here."

"I know," Camille said.

"Well, I made an appointment too, so I'd have an excuse to be in the office. Only now I don't think I'm really dressed for this place. I think you should do it instead."

Her forehead gained a few temporary wrinkles. Camille hated doctors. She never went unless threatened with certain death. She scheduled her annual physical the way some people celebrate birthdays: once every three years or so. Even the idea of a pretend appointment was draining her cheeks of some of their color. "I don't think that's a good idea," she said.

"It's not like you'll have to go in," I reassured her. "We'll duck out before it's your turn. It's just for the waiting room. Mrs. Bennett is more likely to spill her guts to someone who looks like someone." I gestured down at myself. "Look at me, I look like a major nobody."

She couldn't disagree with that. "Okay. Who am I?"

"Marie Lavoie." I told her. I figured Lavoie was a good name to use. There were always a lot of Lavoies in the phone book.

"Then who are you?"

"I can be your assistant."

"Why would I bring my assistant to a doctor's appointment?"

"Because you're a very busy, very important gal in the film biz."

"Why don't you just be my friend or my sister?" she asked.

"I could, I guess, but it wouldn't be as much fun. Anyway, I bet big shots have their assistants take the pain if there are any unpleasant procedures."

She thought about that one a sec. "What am I in for? Is it something unpleasant?"

"You're having a problem with a tattoo you got recently."

"I don't have a tattoo."

I did. Now. Sort of. "That's okay. We're ducking out, remember?" I checked the time. "We better go up or we won't get there in time for our 'chance encounter.'"

We went through the door a man was holding open for us. He pointed over to a counter that could have been the check-in desk of a ritzy hotel and directed us to sign in.

I reminded Camille what name to use and wrote one down for myself. I chose Ann Mead. I got the surname off a notebook a boy beside us was carrying. The attendant in charge of the sign-in book turned it around to read our entries then put it back before returning his attention to his computer screen, no doubt concerned he'd missed some move in the game he was playing.

We got into the elevator and Camille punched the eleven. On the way up, a slight problem occurred to me; how was I supposed to know Barbara Bennett? I'd never seen her. I didn't think Tina's description of a hag with a vacation house in Tuscany would cut it. I tapped Camille and whispered, "do you know what Barbara Bennett looks like?"

"Babs," she corrected me, clearly having been filled in on the nickname. "She's about five-ten, pear-shaped, short red hair, with the facial tone of someone fifteen years her junior."

Impressive. "Lucky guess?"

"She goes to *Ciseaux*."

So that was Camille's source. *Ciseaux* was her cousin Albert's hair salon. That was another bonus in having a large family—it was virtually a built-in network of informants. Even better than that, it was like having an in with every gossip columnist in town. Which, on the surface may seem trivial, maybe even a little shallow, but in this line of work, could be considered keeping yourself well-informed. Some professions had workshops to upgrade their skills or journals to keep abreast of new developments in their field. We had the Caron family.

The elevator hit our floor and we got out. The quality of the downstairs décor was obviously carried through to the upstairs hallways. We were greeted with unstained black marble floors and dim yet flattering lighting from wall sconces. Quite a stretch from the usual medical building construction-grade flooring and fluorescents. Bernard's office was at the end of the hall. We went in and the first person we saw was Babs Bennett. It was easy picking her out from the other women in the waiting room. There was no mistaking her. She had a rather distinctive accessory—Henry Bennett.

TWENTY-FIVE

JUDGING BY HIS change of expression, Bennett had no difficulty placing me either. He shifted in his seat. No doubt containing an urge to leap across the room and ring my neck. I didn't imagine that too many of his previous cellar guests had left on their own accord. He wasn't the sort of man that would sit well with. He was the sort that was accustomed to calling the shots. He stopped shifting and jumped up, and I wasted no time edging closer to Camille.

Babs put her hand out trying to catch hold of her husband's arm. "What's the matter with you?" she scolded. Then, taking in the glances around her, she warmed her tone. "I don't think they called us yet, dear," she said as though the receptionist had just called a name. "Why don't you sit down." She tugged his arm firmly. He sat down slowly, probably not so much to go along with her as to give himself a chance to think.

The other patients went back to their magazines, what with the show being over. I wasn't quite as ready to look away. I didn't much like the small grin he was putting on. It reminded me of a chess player who'd just realized he was one turn away from checkmate. Not only was this annoying, but it was a tad unnerving because I didn't play chess.

Camille leaned into me. "In about a minute, pretend to faint," she whispered before she rushed forward. "Babs," she called to a bewildered Barbara Bennett. "So good to see you again." She lowered her voice a little. "Isn't it a shame about Marcia Grossman? What some kids do to their parents."

I didn't have a clue who Marcia Grossman was but clearly Babs did. Her eyes twinkled. It didn't seem to matter to her that she had no clue who Camille was. The lure of talking about poor Marcia Grossman took precedence. "Yes, that was a shame," she said. "Some of us did try to warn her, but she just wasn't ready to hear it from us. It really did come as quite a shock to her."

I'd bet that no one else in the room knew who Marcia Grossman was either, but their ears became tiny satellites, ready to pick up on any details about poor Marcia's life.

The receptionist started to slide open the glass window that separated her from the patients. Not wanting to have to answer any hard questions like who we were or why we were here, I took that as my cue and went into faint mode. I was pretty good at it having done it before. Camille was a little off her game though. I hit the floor before she attempted to catch me.

"Oh my," I heard Babs say as she moved her feet aside, probably afraid I might go into convulsions and throw up on her shoes.

The other patients looked on, but no one made a move to help me.

The receptionist got to her feet. I heard a long buzzer sound before she opened the door of her cubicle and stepped out. "What's going on?" she asked Camille who was crouched beside me.

"She's fainted," Camille told her.

I wasn't sure if the receptionist had any medical training, so I started to stir before she had a chance to check my vitals. I opened my eyes slowly, as though the lids were heavy, and blinked a few times. A new face appeared between Camille and the receptionist. Another woman. This one was wearing a smock. The nurse, I figured. "What's her name?" I heard her ask.

Given that at the moment I had two names on the go, I wondered which one Camille would give.

"She's coming around," Camille said, totally sidestepping the question. Then, she started to help me to my feet.

"Not too quickly," the new woman said. "We don't want to lose her again." She waved at the patient sitting in the chair nearest to me until the lady finally got the message and got up. I allowed myself to be maneuvered into the seat.

The nurse bent down beside me, checked my pulse, and inspected my eyes. "She'll be all right," she concluded.

"I think she needs to lay down for a bit," Camille said. "Is there somewhere she could go?"

The receptionist sighed through her nose. The other woman gave her a stern look. "Why don't you get back to the phones, Susan. I'll take care of this." She turned to me. "Do you think you can walk?"

I nodded, careful to stand up gingerly as though still unsteady. I wasn't sure what Camille was trying to accomplish yet, but I knew enough to play along. I was guided to the sacred hallway that held the doctor's private office and the examining rooms. The first room was empty. The nurse guided me in and helped me onto the examining table. She checked my pulse again and clipped something onto the end of my finger before she excused herself, saying she'd be back in a few minutes to check on me.

I was adjusting the pillow when I saw Babs Bennett come in. "Oh, hello dear," she said. She pointed towards the door, "your friend, umm," she stumbled for Camille's name finally giving up, "your friend out there asked me to sit with you while she made a few calls."

I mentally high-fived Camille. Her plan worked. I now had a guaranteed audience with Barbara Bennett. Problem was, now *I* didn't have a plan. I had no idea what to say to Babs to get her to talk. I decided to buy time with pleasantries. "That's very kind of you," I said in a low voice, not wanting to appear too strong. "I hate to be a bother."

She moved closer. "Oh no, dear. Don't concern yourself with that. You just rest." She looked me over quickly. "If you don't mind me asking, dear, are you pregnant?"

I debated, briefly, telling her I was. Seemed like a good explanation for my fainting, but I decided to take a page out of Camille's book and prey on Bab's interest in gossip. "I wish it was that easy," I said, trying to look overwrought. "Actually, I'm having some marital problems."

"Oh dear," she said. "You poor thing." She pulled up the doctor's stool next to the examining table, sat down, and arranged the skirt of her perfectly tailored navy Chanel suit to act as a buffer between her panty hose and the coolness of the stainless steel stool.

Clearly, her curiosity was piqued. I moved into the next phase and went for the misery loves company approach. "I'm sure you wouldn't understand," I said to her. "I saw you and your husband in the waiting room. You look like a very happy couple."

She reached up and smoothed the back of her hair, which, no offence to Camille's cousin Albert, closely resembled the color of mashed sweet potatoes. "Oh, we all have our troubles from time to time," she said.

"Really?" I said, playing the innocent young wife. "You're probably just saying that to make me feel better."

"No, really," she said, reaching out to pat my hand. "All marriages go through ups and downs. The trick is to hang on during the downs and wait for the ups to come around again."

Actually that sounded like very sensible advice. I could imagine her saying that to her own daughter. She was obviously experienced at the mothering thing. Perhaps not quite so astute as a wife, though. I needed to know if she knew about Bennett and Francesca. I couldn't just come out and ask her, so I decided to imply that my husband was having an affair and see how she reacted to that. "I've been trying to do that," I told her, "but I'm not sure my husband is doing the same. I think he's lost interest in me."

"Oh they all act like that now and then," she said. "That's why we have to be one step ahead." She lowered her voice to a whisper as though someone may be listening. "That's why I'm here. I'm getting some Botox." She blushed. "I've never done anything like this before. I know everybody thinks I've had the works. Truth is, I've never had any cosmetic procedure. Don't get me wrong, I worry about aging like everybody else. I take care of myself, I stay out of the sun, I have facials regularly, and I've spent a fortune on skin creams. But never anything like this. You see, the truth is I'm afraid of needles. I didn't even have electrolysis when that was all the rage."

Was electrolysis a rage? Must have missed that one. I nodded encouragement, hoping she'd go on.

She did. "Normally, I don't discuss my personal life, but I tell you, it never hurts to keep up the looks. You know how it is, men look even better with a few years behind them." She paused. "We women need to make sure they don't wander to greener pastures. That's what I do with my Henry."

I had the picture now. She was just an insecure wife grasping at the only straw she thought she had, her looks. It was surprising really that a woman of her social standing and accomplishment had such low self-esteem. The right suit, the right shoes, the right committees. Inside she was just a little girl dressed up like a powerful woman.

I felt bad for her. She was just a nice older woman struggling with the same issues we all did. She just did it with more money. I also felt bad for me. I had hit a dead end. Barbara Bennett was a woman still in love with her husband. She wouldn't do anything behind his back that could hurt him. I also doubted she knew anything about Francesca or whatever dirty dealings he had afoot. She probably didn't even know about his no-frills guest room in her very own basement.

A head poked in the room. It was a woman I hadn't seen before. "Mrs. Bennett, the doctor is ready for you now," the head said.

Babs stood up and smoothed her skirt. "Wish me luck," she said to me with a wink. "And don't worry about your marriage, dear, everything will work out fine."

I had a split second to decide what to do. She might be inclined to help me if I told her about Francesca. Problem was, I was pretty sure she didn't know anything that could help. If that were the case, telling her about the affair would just hurt her. And as much as she deserved to know, it shouldn't be me doing the telling.

"I'll cross my fingers for you," I said to her. "You're lucky your husband came with you for moral support. Not all husbands would do that."

"Oh, he's not here for moral support," she corrected me. "He's been seeing the doctor on his own for some time. This is just my first time tagging along."

CAMILLE AND I hightailed it out of there while the Bennetts were otherwise occupied. Babs Bennett had been in with Dr. Bernard, and Henry Bennett had been accidentally locked in the women's washroom. Camille swears she had nothing to do with it. She also claimed to be very surprised at the discovery of his cell phone in her sweater pocket. I believed her on both counts.

We drove a few blocks and pulled into an empty space in front of a café. A few smokers sat on the patio sipping their drinks between puffs. One young couple sat with their heads close together, connected at the lips. I eyed the woman's pink tuque while Camille took out Bennett's Blackberry and started working the controls.

"Wonder how long he's had this," she said. "Not much on it. And he doesn't seem to use all the features." She played with the buttons for a while then placed the phone on the dash and turned to me. "So, tell me," she said.

I filled her in on my day, ending with my conversation with Barbara Bennett.

"Interesting," she said.

I opened the glove compartment and sorted through the stash until I found a square of dark chocolate. Gotta love the cold northern climate for keeping chocolate from melting. I dug out another square and offered it to Camille, and we ate them while she filled me in on her day—or at least what there was of it before we met up. Apparently, after a brief pit stop by her place to clean up and change, her morning over at Finestein, Bennett, & Fitch had been cut short by a call from Laurent reporting my AWOL status. What a tattler. She'd left without placing the fresh video tape in the statue and started tailing Babs shortly thereafter.

"So," I said when she stopped talking. "I guess it's okay for me to go home now. Bennett doesn't seem too concerned about me."

Camille started rooting through the compartment at the bottom of the dash where she kept loose change for parking money. She fished out a few dollars while she talked. "What makes you say that?"

"Well, the guy clearly has bigger things on his mind."

"Like?"

"C'mon, no guy, even a very vain one, would be off getting beauty treatments if he was so hyped up over me or any other urgent business dealings."

She palmed the change. "How many men do you think keep their dermatologists on speed dial?" she asked me.

"I don't know. Ones with really bad skin? Or maybe ones with a chronic condition. Or in the middle of some sort of treatment."

"Or maybe ones who have a relationship with the dermatologist that's about more than epidermis," she added.

"You think Bennett and Bernard are in cahoots of some sort?"

She pivoted towards me, tucking one leg under the other, her knee grazing the parking brake. "You remember the dead guy with Puddles' I.D.?"

"Yeah."

"Well, it turns out, he didn't die from such natural causes after all. Laurent checked on the report that came in after all the tests were done. The man did have cancer, but that's not what killed him. He died from an overdose of painkillers." She paused a sec to let me take that in. "You want to guess what kind of cancer he had?"

I put all of ten seconds of thought into it. "Skin cancer?"

"*Exactement*. And, the painkillers he died from were the heavy duty kind. The kind that only come by prescription."

I figured I knew the answer, but I asked Camille anyway. "Do we know who prescribed them?"

"One Dr. Bill Bernard."

I WAITED PATIENTLY while Camille ran into the café for a coffee. I thought I'd had enough caffeine for a while, so I asked her to pick me up some herbal tea. What I really wanted was to go home, take a shower, and crawl into bed for a day or two. Somehow, I didn't think that was likely to happen anytime soon. So I needed something else. Something that would break this case open. I was about to think of something brilliant when Camille opened the car door and got in. The aroma of coffee that got in with her immediately rushed to my hard drive and deleted all traces of brilliance.

She opened one of the bags she was carrying, pulled out two cardboard mugs, and plopped them into the car's cup holders. Then she opened the other bag and extended it towards me. "You've got a choice between chocolate chip cookies or brownies."

I peered into the bag. Sure enough there were half a dozen large cookies and what looked like four brownies. "You got all that with the parking change?"

She dug into her pocket. "*Mais non.*" She poured the money back into its compartment, probably having used her debit card. "That was only enough for a coffee. A coffee would have gone straight to my head on an empty stomach. I need food. And these are baked fresh every day the guy said. All pure ingredients too. I thought you'd appreciate that."

That was probably true. After two bites of one of the cookies, I could personally attest to the fact that it was pure. Pure sugar. I took a few swigs of my tea to soothe the sugar burn in my throat.

"You know," I said, getting back to our earlier conversation. "It could be a coincidence."

Camille crooked an eyebrow at me.

"Bernard being the dead guy's doctor, I mean. And, the overdose could have been accidental. It does happen. Or maybe it was a suicide. It's not unusual for someone who's dying to speed up the process."

"Except this guy wasn't dying. His cancer was caught early and totally treatable."

Hmmm. So much for that theory. "Could still have been accidental."

"It's kind of hard to accidentally take two bottles worth of medication."

"Okay then, let's think. What have we got. We know Bennett is into some illegal stuff. Anything from pilfering from his clients to blackmail to murder."

"Maybe more than one murder," Camille interjected.

"Right," I said.

She took a swig of her coffee. "Maybe even more we know nothing about."

"True. And we may also have a connection to Dr. Bernard." Which, for the life of me I couldn't figure out. "Then we have the Bennett/Francesca connection. But, the thing that stumps me is why Bennett would care about Puddles anymore. It must be pretty obvious to him that Puddles doesn't have anything on him. At least not enough to hurt him. And, assuming that Bennett was involved with the cancer guy's death, why would he want to make it look like Puddles was dead?"

"So Francesca could inherit her parents' money before it goes to Lucia," Camille reasoned.

"Okay. But, why would Bennett care if Francesca gets her inheritance? By the looks of things, Bennett's got enough money for the both of them."

Camille finished munching on her third cookie. "Greed?"

"Yeah, but enough to kill for it? Something's got to be missing here."

We were both quiet a while, finishing up our snacks and thinking. I was just scrunching up the empty food bag when a ring came from the dashboard. We looked at each other. It was Bennett's phone. Camille snatched it on the second ring and checked the caller I.D. Unknown caller. She opened the phone and cradled it between us so I could hear. The scent of a faintly familiar cologne tickled my nose. Neither of us said anything. We just listened, hoping the caller would identify him or herself first.

"I know you're there," a voice said. The voice belonged to Bennett. When we didn't say anything he went on. "I also know Puddles isn't dead, and I bet you know where he is. Girls like you really get to me. Why don't you just mind your own business before your asses are so far in you'll need a colonoscopy to get out." And he disconnected.

I looked at Camille. "That doesn't even make sense," I said.

BACK AT C&C, Puddles, Laurent, Camille, and I sat around the table in Laurent's office. Technically, we were having a meeting. In reality we were having a staring contest. My bet was on Puddles to break first. After say fifteen years or so of hiding out and dealing with Bennett, he had to be fed up.

Frankly, I thought this whole meeting was a waste of time. All this cerebral business was getting to me. I wanted to get out and do something. I didn't want to brainstorm theories or possible strategies. As far as I saw it, this all boiled down to one thing. Puddles needed to be free to come out from hiding. That meant we needed to make sure Bennett wouldn't kill him and that there wouldn't be any old criminal charges laid against him for the supposed swindling of Guido's all those years ago. In the meantime, we also needed to keep Lucia safe in case Puddles was right and she was a target because of her impending inheritance.

So far, we had gone along with Puddles' approach. We'd made efforts to add to his evidence against Bennett in the hopes that Bennett would get arrested and Puddles would be cleared. If all went well, Puddles would finally be free to live a regular life and Bennett would no longer be a threat to Puddles, Lucia, or even me. In principle this sounded fine. My problem with the approach was that it was taking too long. I didn't have the patience for it. I wanted Puddles to see if he could help little Sarah pronto.

Plus, it seemed to me there had to be a better way to resolve things. Puddles had already been working the same angle for ages with no results. Granted, he was compromised by having limited mobility considering his need for a low profile, and probably limited resources too. And then there was the trust factor. Puddles didn't seem to have any. Most likely, if he'd trusted other people to help him early on, this would all have been dealt with long ago.

I shifted in my seat. The excess sugar in my system wasn't helping my feeling of impatience. I had convinced Camille to drop by my house on the way back to the office so I could take a quick shower and throw on some jeans and a warm sweatshirt. Adam hadn't been home, but I'd had a minute with the pets and left him a note. Now, I was wishing I had grabbed a sandwich while I was there to balance out my blood sugar.

Camille avoided the sugar fluctuation by keeping up a steady stream of chocolate. When she stopped drumming her fingers on the desk, she began tapping one of Laurent's pencils instead. Her pace quickened every time the phone rang, which seemed to be incessantly. We missed Arielle more with each ring. Each call rang three times before it went to voice mail. Not wanting to lose focus on our meeting, we had agreed not to answer any calls until we were done. Finally, Camille gave in and answered one.

When she hung up, she turned back to us. "That was Luc," she said. "There's been an accident. A hit and run. Jonas Como is in critical condition at the hospital."

THAT WAS ONE loophole we hadn't thought of. In all our concern for Lucia, nobody had bothered to realize that Lucia couldn't get married without a groom. The hit and run was major headline news on all the local channels. Normally, the story wouldn't have gotten this much coverage. It was the Como connection. Ingrid had been right. They were a big-time political family. Jonas was being groomed to be the third generation MP and there were rumors he had the looks and the savvy to reverse those initials.

The good news was that he wasn't dead. Yet. The bad news was that whoever tried to knock him off would most likely have the access to try again. And this time it wouldn't take much. The tinkling of a knob on a machine, an adjustment to his IV. People died in the hospital all the time. Human error, electronic malfunction, maybe even infectious disease. All would be ruled accidental just like most hit and runs are assumed to be. Only in this case, it would be murder.

The police were asking witnesses to come forward the news anchor said. They were looking for more details. So far, all they had was the color of the car. They weren't releasing it to the public yet so as not to influence other possible eyewitness accounts.

"One of us better get over to the hospital," I said.

The others looked at me. "What good would that do?" Puddles asked.

"You don't think this was an accident do you? Someone's got to watch over Jonas Como," I explained. "Whoever went after him presumably still wants him out of the way. Probably more so now because he may have recognized the car that hit him or seen the driver."

"She's right," Laurent agreed. "I'll go over and check things out. It makes the most sense. No one involved knows me. Only Francesca has ever seen me, and I doubt she'll remember me even if she's there."

That was debatable. While Francesca was so self-involved she probably couldn't pick out her own neighbor from a line-up, this was Laurent we were talking about.

Laurent stood and started gathering a few things. One of the things he took was a gun. He was the only one of us who carried a gun. Generally, PIs here didn't have guns. And those who did had to prove necessity before getting one. That let Camille out, but Laurent, being an ex cop, had made a few enemies and sometimes had to deal with some risky situations, so he qualified to not only own but carry. Not all the time, but when circumstances called for it. He saw it as an unfortunate necessity. He'd never killed anyone, even while he was on the force, but he'd needed it plenty of times to keep assailants in line, and he didn't rule out the possibility of having to shoot someone someday. He put his holster on over his black shirt. The holster fit easily over the form-fitting shirt and left plenty of room to zip up his dark jacket without calling attention to the bulge of the gun.

Puddles rolled his chair back from the table. "That works for me. I need to run an errand."

Camille raised an eyebrow. "What errand?" she asked him.

He looked at her. I could tell by the tightness in his face, he didn't exactly welcome the question. The tiny hairs on his balls were probably at attention, ready to protect the kingdom of male ego housed in his scrotum. "Just an errand," he said to her.

"I'm not sure that's a good idea," she said back.

He stood up and looked down at her. "I don't remember asking for your opinion."

Camille stood too, her voice rising with her. "I didn't realize I needed your permission to speak. Like it or not, Bell, we're a team now. You're not some vigilante. What you do affects the rest of us."

Laurent eased around my chair on his way to leave the room. His glance suggested I do the same. I took him up on his suggestion and followed him out to the kitchen. We could still hear the voices from the other room, but we pretended not to notice.

"You still think I need to be concerned about Bennett?" I asked him. I knew I could gauge how much I needed to protect myself on Laurent's opinion. He had the most thorough knowledge of Bennett out of all of us, and I knew his cop instincts were still alive and kicking.

"Not sure," he said.

Fabulous. Big help there.

He went on. "He exposed himself by taking you to his house. And, he knows we're on to him. That means he can't just make his problems go away by getting you out of the picture."

That was good news.

"On the other hand," Laurent continued, "he's got to be feeling pressured. He's got no idea how long it will be before we have him up on some sort of charges. He's going to have to work overtime making sure his ass is covered. That will mean eliminating paper trails and the like connecting him to any illegal activities, and possibly ridding himself of anyone who can incriminate him. All you really have on him is the abduction accusation. My guess is that's pretty low on his list of offences, so you're probably not his top priority right now."

Okay. That I could work with. That meant I'd have some more mobility.

Laurent cast me a warning look before heading for the door. "That doesn't mean you don't have to be careful. But it's Puddles Bennett will be after now," he said as he left. "And Camille knows it."

TWENTY-SIX

I OPENED THE door to Laurent's office to dead quiet. It was evening now and the only light source in the room came from a halogen lamp on the desk. When my eyes adjusted to the dim light, they focused in on Puddles. He was tied to one of Laurent's chairs. And he didn't look happy.

Camille was stretched out on the couch, recliner style, going through the buttons on Bennett's phone again. I looked at Puddles, but he wouldn't meet my eyes so I tried Camille. "What's up?" I asked.

"Your mister Puddles is being a pain in the ass," she said. "He's refusing to tell me about his errand, so we're stuck here doing nothing. NOTHING," she said again stretching it out, her accent making it sound like "nut ting." "Laurent will be checking in soon and we'll have *nothing* new to report because of this sorry ass." She got up and dropped the phone onto the couch. "Watch him a minute will you, I've got to go to the bathroom."

"Sure," I said and took her place on the couch. It was warm. She must have been there a while. I'd hid out in the kitchen for a bit eating a toasted bagel and having tea, and now I felt much better. I'd hoped by the time I checked back in, Camille and Puddles would have settled their disagreement. But clearly not. Camille left, and I picked up Bennett's abandoned Blackberry and tried the buttons. I didn't know much about Blackberries, so I was trying things at random. I'd only recently learned my way around the menu on my own phone and still found most of the features too complicated to bother using. As far as I was concerned, as long as my cell made and received calls, I was good. This phone, with all its fancy extras was beyond me.

Puddles laughed. "You don't have a clue what you're doing, do you?" he said to me.

I looked over at him, my pride not wounded in the slightest. "Nope."

"Why don't you pass it to me?"

I gestured at the bungee cords Camille had secured him with. "It's not really the best time for you," I said pointing specifically at his arms which were pinned at his sides. "There's not a lot you could do with a phone."

"You could untie me," he said.

"Not if I want to continue breathing," I said. "You must know by now not to tangle with Camille. This is the second time she's taken you out."

"I could get loose if I wanted," he said. "I'm just playing along."

"Yeah. Sure," I said.

"It's true. And she only got me because she caught me by surprise. I thought she was a fox, not a wolf."

"So you think she's a fox?" I said.

"I'm tied up," he answered. "I'm not blindfolded."

I was beginning to think maybe he *had* let Camille corral him. "Why don't you just tell us about the errand. We could all go. Then we could get back to normal and get on with things."

"It's just something I have to do on my own."

My guess was the errand probably wasn't even that important. What I was hearing was more stubborn male pride. He just wanted to do what he wanted the way he wanted to do it. So far, Puddles had proven himself fairly reasonable, though, so I didn't think it would take much convincing to change his mind. "I think you can forget about the being on your own thing for a while. I was talking to Laurent before and he said you're the one Bennett wants. With things coming to a head now, he's got nothing to lose going after you. There's no way Camille's going to leave you alone. Camille and Laurent take their jobs very seriously, and neither one of them is going to let anything happen to you if they can help it. You're lucky

Laurent didn't have you taken in to the police station and held there."

He was quiet a minute then sighed. "What time is it?" he asked.

I checked the clock on the cell. "It's nearly six."

Puddles shook his head. "Fine," he said. "You can come on my errand."

"Where do you have to go?"

"Judging by the nearly constant vibrations in my pocket, Tina's run out of food again."

I CONVINCED PUDDLES and Camille to swing by Le Pois Chic to get some food for Tina. That way, I could get something too. The bagel had helped, but it would break down to more sugar pretty quickly. I needed some protein and vegetables. I'd been operating solely on pretty slim pickins of late, and I was beginning to feel the effects.

Puddles looked into the container filled with three-bean salad that I had put together for Tina. "You sure Tina eats this stuff?" he asked.

"Sure, she loves it," I lied.

"With all the ice cream and KFC I had to get her, I never would have guessed," he said as we stood in line to pay.

"Okay, so she doesn't exactly love it," I admitted on the way out, "but she'll eat it if she's hungry enough."

We got back into Camille's car and quickly ate the food we'd gotten for ourselves—spinach quiche for me, lasagna for Camille, and a bunch of samosas for Puddles. When we were done, Camille followed Puddles' instructions to an apartment building in the west end. An old school that had been converted to residential living a few years back. It didn't have tenant parking, so Camille pulled into a spot on the street.

"Okay," Puddles said. "You wait here and I'll run in."

I shook my head at his vain attempt. He just didn't get it. "I'll stay with the car," I told Camille.

They both got out. I could see them exchanging a few animated words before heading up to the front door. The street was pretty dark. There were only streetlights on one side, and a few of the old trees still had some tenacious leaves clinging to their branches and blocking much light from reaching the sidewalk. It was also a tad on the cool side. I had on the jacket I'd been wearing earlier, but I still felt a chill. I went to zip it up, my hand knocked something hard, and I realized I had put Bennett's Blackberry in my sweatshirt pocket. I pulled out the phone before zipping up the coat. I figured the likelihood of Bennett getting his phone back was close to nil. I also figured he could afford another call, so I dialed home and settled into my seat.

Adam picked up on the second ring.

"Hey. It's me," I said.

"Where are you calling from?" he asked. "I don't recognize the number."

"It's just someone's cell phone. Did you get my note?"

"Yeah. I take it everything's cool now. You know, since you came home."

"It's getting there," I said. I didn't think he needed to know the whole story right now. "It'll be nice to sleep in my own bed again."

"Yeah. I think the bed misses you too."

"Glad to hear it," I said. "Listen, did I get any calls? Any messages?"

"Not that I know of. Want me to check your office machine?"

"That'd be great," I said.

He put me down while he went to check. When he came back to the phone his voice didn't sound so breezy anymore. "There's a message from Jim," he said. "He says you need to bring Puddles to some place in the boonies. That you have to hurry or some guy is going to take away Sarah's meds."

I got the address, and we hung up. I checked to make sure Camille had taken her car keys, got out of the car, locked up, and ran over to the building. A young couple had the door propped open while they unloaded groceries, and I scooted through and started for the stairs. I stopped when I realized I had no idea which apartment Puddles was using. I went over to check the names out front. Nothing matched his. A few were even unmarked. I spotted the mail room and tried in there thinking sometimes people put more information on their mailbox to make sure they got the right mail. There were seventeen boxes in all. The building had four floors. That meant about four apartments on each with one left over. Maybe something in the basement. No box had Puddles' name, but a couple of names sounded like ones he might use. One was on the second floor, the other on the third. I'd start with those.

The main staircase was walled off from the lobby by glass. Quite likely it was the original school stairs. I took them two at a time like I often did as a child in my own school. I pulled open the large glass door, stepped into the hallway and listened. Average homey noises drifted to my ears—televisions, music, quiet conversation. I stepped back into the staircase and went on up to the third level. I stood quietly in the hallway again and listened. There it was. I'd know that nasal whine anywhere. I turned right and followed the voice to the end of the hall. The door of Tina's apartment wasn't closed completely. I pushed it open and peered in, hoping I could get Camille's attention before Tina spotted me. The place looked just like it did on Tinavision.

"But it comes like that," Puddles was saying.

"You can't expect me to eat that," Tina said. "It's got oil in it. Oil will make me fat."

"It's olive oil," Puddles told her. "It's good for you."

"You should have got it on the side."

"I told you, it doesn't come on the side. It comes mixed in."

Tina was sitting on the couch with a quilt over her lap. She had the container of food on top and was poking the food with a fork. "Did you ask? You have to ask." She placed the lid back on and started to seal it up. "Take this back and ask for a new one."

"I'm not taking that back," Puddles said.

"Well, I'm not eating it," Tina said. "I'm not going to get fat just to save you another trip."

"Then don't eat it." That was Camille's voice. I couldn't see her from this angle. She must have been near the bathroom door. I heard her footsteps as she crossed the room. "We have to go. Oh, and if you're worried about getting fat, I'd lay off the ice cream if I were you."

Tina jumped off the couch and followed Puddles and Camille as they headed for the door. I ducked back into the hallway.

"Where are you going?" Tina called after them. "I want to go, too. I'm tired of staying here."

Tina's whine was like nails on a blackboard. I silently prayed for Camille to give Tina a good going over. As a perfume cloud approached, I knew I wasn't going to get my wish. My eyes darted back and forth looking for cover. Nothing. I'd never make it back to the stairs in time. I'd have to feign my arrival. I jumped back a few feet and made out like I was walking up to the door. Camille stepped out followed by Puddles followed by a giant pink marshmallow topped off with Tina's head.

I had to stop myself from jumping back a few feet again. "Tina," I greeted her. "So glad to see you're all right."

She turned her attention to me. I noticed the pink marshmallow effect was coming from a rather roomy version of a celebrity-cum-clothes-designer sweat suit ensemble. "Lora! Thank goodness you're here." She reached out to touch my hand, and I resisted the urge to pull it away. "You've got to get me out of here. I need to go home. Jeffrey has suffered enough. I'm sure he's come to his senses by now. Could you help me pack up my things?"

I looked to the others for help. Camille couldn't hide a look of disgust. Puddles couldn't hide a look of relief. He would be more than happy to pass the baton on to me. "Actually, Tina," I began, "now's not a good time. I could help you tomorrow, though. Why don't you just give yourself one more day of rest before you have to deal with Jeffrey." I could see she wasn't going for it so I added, "I think one more day would really teach Jeffrey a lesson. He would never take you for granted again."

"Well," she said, wavering.

I was worried about the time we were losing. I wasn't sure what to think about the threat to little Sarah. I started to edge Tina back into the apartment. Camille took the key from Puddles' hand and was ready to lock Tina in as soon as the door closed.

Tina stopped in the threshold. "If I don't go home, then I want to go with you. I'm really bored, and I think I might be claustrophobic. I need to get out of this place."

While the apartment was on the small side, I didn't think it qualified as a cause of claustrophobia. "You don't want to go with us," I told her. "You'd be even more bored." I searched my brain for something Tina would really hate to do. "We're going to a dog show," I said.

The others looked at me.

"I don't care where you're going," Tina said. "It's got to be better than this. And I can get something to eat on the way. You should see what this one," and she pointed to Puddles as she spoke, "brought me. Even you wouldn't eat it."

Camille was clearly running out of patience. "Look, Tina, you can't come with us."

"Oh, yes I can," Tina said putting on her best two-year-old-about-to-pull-a-tantrum face. "And if you leave me here, I'll scream."

That would be a shame for the neighbors, but it was a tempting option. Somehow I had to get Camille and Puddles alone to tell them about the new development with Jim and Sarah. "Okay," I said to Tina. "You can come, but you have to change first. You can't go to a dog show dressed like that." I had no idea what people wore to dog shows, but I thought she might buy it.

"But you guys aren't dressed up," she protested.

"We've got a change of clothes in the car," I said. I was getting really good at lying to Tina. I was going to have to remember this new skill for the future.

She went back into the apartment, and Camille moved to close the door.

"What are you doing?" Puddles asked.

"I'm locking her back in."

"You heard what she said. She's going to scream if we leave her here."

"Yeah?"

"I can't have her screaming in here. This place belongs to a friend of mine. I don't want to get anybody into trouble."

Camille's eyes narrowed. "Friend? What friend? I thought you were all alone in the world."

"I never said that," Puddles said.

Oh no. Here we go again. What was it with these two? "Look, guys," I interjected. "We've got a problem." I told them about my call with Adam.

Camille immediately pulled out her cell and called Laurent to fill him in and get his input. "Okay," she said when she was done. "Let's go. He'll meet us there with backup. He's getting a guy in place to watch over Como in the meantime."

"What about Tina?" I said.

"We leave her here," Camille said. "Let her scream all she wants. I think she's bluffing anyway. She wouldn't want anyone to find her like this. She must have gained ten pounds the last couple of days."

"It's just the clothes," I said. "They're all baggy. They make her look dumpy."

"She's not wearing clothes on her face. How do you explain those cheeks?"

Tina's cheeks had seemed a little puffier than usual.

There was a noise from inside the apartment and Tina called out, "I'll just be another minute."

"I say we take her," Puddles said. "We can always dump her somewhere along the way. At least then she's not here causing any trouble."

That sounded reasonable. I looked at Camille. She made a face but agreed.

"Okay then. If she's coming, she's got to get a move on," I said. "I'm worried about Sarah."

"Do either of you have a scarf or something?" Puddles asked us.

"For what?" Camille asked.

"For Tina. I need to cover her eyes so she doesn't see the outside of the building. I don't want her to know where it is."

Camille laughed. "You don't have to worry about that. She'll never remember this place. She couldn't find this place again if it was the location for the launch of a new perfume created by Chanel and Louis Vuitton as their first ever collaboration."

Here I had to disagree with Camille. Tina would not only find that party, she would buy the new concoction by the vat.

Puddles went back into the apartment and came back with Tina dressed in gray slacks, a purple sweater, and a pink headband stretched around her head to cover her eyes. "We're ready," he said.

TWENTY-SEVEN

CAMILLE HAD TAKEN an iPod out of the trunk. It was one of the many gifts she had stuffed there from the early Christmas shopping she did every year. She'd filled the iPod with Arcade Fire and a few other bands, and it was intended for a cousin's kid. Now it had a much higher purpose. It was helping keep Tina tuned out. Puddles sat beside her in the backseat. He made sure she kept the headband on and the volume up.

Laurent told us he'd checked out the address Jim had left in his message. It was one of the offices for Finestein, Bennett, & Fitch. The one near Dorion. Recently, it had been closed down for renovation. We could be there in under an hour, but first we needed a plan. And we needed a place to drop Tina that wouldn't take us out of our way.

The plan part was hard. It would be easier if we knew what we were walking into. At this point we could only guess that Bennett had Jim and Sarah with him because he couldn't just be holding her meds, or they'd get some more. Where Joanne figured in was unknown. If Bennett was working solo was another question mark. And, we had no idea if Jim and Sarah were at the same place Bennett wanted us to deliver Puddles or being detained somewhere else.

"*Qu'est-ce-qu'on va faire avec l'autre?*" Camille asked.

"What's with the French?" I said.

"*Plus privé,*" Camille answered.

It was private all right. I could follow some of it, but given my lack of skills, she may as well be talking to herself.

"Tina can't hear a thing with those headphones on. Trust me," Puddles said from the back.

"You understand French?" Camille asked him.

"Some."

Camille nodded ever so slightly, not enough that most people would notice the movement, but I could tell she was pleased.

"Why don't we drop Tina off at a restaurant along the way?" I suggested. "She did say she was hungry. Then I can give Adam a call, and he can come pick her up."

"That'll work," Camille said. "Then we can talk strategy."

A few blocks later, Camille pulled over in front of an upscale Italian place that only served dinner and was known for changing its menu daily.

Puddles turned down the volume on the iPod. "Okay. You can take off the blindfold now," he said to Tina.

She lifted off the headband and blinked a couple times. "Where are we? Is this where they're having the dog show?"

"We thought you should get something to eat here first. The food at the dog show is pretty much popcorn and hot dog stuff," I said like I knew.

"Oh. All right. Are you sure we have time?"

"Sure," I assured her.

She undid her seat belt, picked up her purse, unlocked the door, and started to step out. "Aren't you guys coming in?"

"We're just going to find parking," Camille said. "You go in and get us a table."

Tina sat back down and pulled the door in a bit. "I'm not going in alone. I've never gone into a restaurant alone in my life."

I thought about that. She had arrived alone at Le Pois Chic that time she was meeting Adam for lunch, but I guess that was acceptable to her because she was meeting someone. I wondered what she did if she was meeting someone and arrived first. Come to think of it, that probably never happened. That would ruin her ability to make an entrance. Maybe that's why she had such a habit of being late.

Tina went on. "Anyway, it doesn't take three people to park a car."

I sighed. "I'll go in with you."

"If it's going to be just two of us, I think it should be the man."

The man. What was up with that? Sometimes Tina wasn't the best poster child for feminism. Calling him "the man" did make Puddles sound sort of like a big shot, though. Come to think of it, Tina probably didn't know Puddles' name.

I noticed Puddles checking his watch. "That's fine," he said. "I'll do it."

I figured there was little to no risk that Puddles would take off. He seemed just as concerned about Jim and Sarah as we were. In case Camille thought otherwise, I undid my seatbelt so I could get out too. Camille rested her hand on my forearm letting me know she didn't think it was necessary.

When Tina was out of the car, Puddles leaned into me before he closed his door. "Just pull out and go to the end of the block. I'll meet you there in a couple of minutes."

"Okay," I said.

He shut the door and went into the restaurant with Tina. Camille pulled back into traffic and pulled over again farther up the street.

I wondered how Puddles was going to ditch Tina. I knew from past experience that the Carons wouldn't endanger innocent people if they could help it. In this case, Tina was an innocent person, and we didn't know what we were walking into. Every effort had to be made to leave Tina out of it.

Camille put on the parking brake, pulled out her cell phone, and made some speed-dial calls. When she was done, she turned to me. "No one is answering at Jim's or Francesca's. You have any thoughts on this?"

I didn't. I had been so busy thinking about ditching Tina, I hadn't put much thought into a plan yet. "Not really," I told her.

"The way I see it," she said, "if we let Bennett get his hands on Puddles, Puddles is as good as dead."

That was probably true. If I was going to be honest about it, I wasn't so keen on giving him another chance at me either. But I didn't think this was about me. "I agree," I said. "I think his feud with Puddles goes a lot deeper than self-preservation. Puddles mere existence seems to be a thorn in Bennett's side."

"You mean like a rivalry thing because of Francesca?"

"Could be," I said. "What we need is a way to help Jim and Sarah without putting Puddles in any danger."

Camille tried Jim's number again on the cell. Still no answer. Not great. We still had no confirmation on the situation. We had to be careful how we proceeded. We couldn't just call in the police because we didn't know what we were dealing with, and we couldn't just show up and rush Bennett because if he was holding Sarah, he could hurt her. One more murder wouldn't matter to him at this point.

The phone in Camille's hand rang. She answered it, and after a few seconds of listening she said into the phone, "*Non. Attends. Ne t'inquiète pas. C'est temporaire.*" There was another pause while she listened some more. When she spoke next it wasn't with the same patience. "*C'est toi qui es partie. Qu'est-ce que...*" she broke off and held the phone away from her head. "She hung up!" she said to me.

I ventured a guess, "Arielle?"

"She heard we were interviewing receptionists. She's pissed off."

"Hmmm," I said, not wanting to say anything that could be held against me later.

Camille reached into her bag for a single dose of chocolate. It was wrapped in a fancy gold paper with the makers name printed across the top. She unwrapped it without looking and pushed it into her mouth, holding it against her cheek as she spoke. "What did she expect us to do?"

I stayed quiet. This was a rhetorical question.

"She's the one who screwed us, and it's her crazy mother who started the fight!"

I figured the chocolate would kick in in another minute or so. She wasn't biting it like she usually did in emergencies. She was letting it melt. That meant a small delay before it took effect. I could wait it out.

A thump came from my window, and Camille and I both jumped. I turned my head to see what it was and came face to face with Tina. I moved to roll down my window and took in the unmistakable sounds of the door locks being clicked into place and the emergency brake being released.

I tried to sound casual. "What's up," I asked Tina.

"I lost the man," Tina said.

I felt my heart drop. I couldn't believe Puddles would take off like this. I really thought this new development with Sarah had changed things. If he had managed to get away from Tina, where was he?

Camille leaned across me. "What do you mean lost him?"

"I lost him," Tina said. "He said he was just going to run to the bathroom, and he never came back."

"Maybe there was a lineup," Camille suggested. "He's probably in the restaurant right now looking for you. You better get back in there."

Tina hugged herself. "I'm too cold," she said. "It's a long walk back. I don't know why you couldn't find parking any closer. I had a bitch of a time finding you." She stepped back to the rear door and pulled the handle. "I think it's locked. Open it, will you."

I looked at Camille. She had her finger on the master lock button, but she hadn't triggered it yet.

"There you are!"

It was Puddles. He had come up behind Tina. "I've been looking all over for you," he said to her. So he hadn't gone off after all. She just beat him to the car.

Tina turned to him. "You've been looking for me? I was looking for you. Where did you go?"

"The washroom, remember?"

"But you never came back."

"You were supposed to wait at the table," he reminded her.

Tina hugged herself tighter. "I don't like to sit alone," she said.

"Fine. Let's go back together then."

She looked in at me. "Well, okay. We can all go now that we have a parking spot. I just need to jump in the car for a few minutes and warm up." She tried the door handle again and found it still locked. She bent down and looked in at Camille. "Hurry up, will you. It's freezing out here."

I heard the lock release and the engine turn over. Tina got in and slid over to make room for Puddles behind me. Within seconds we were back into traffic.

"What are you doing?" Tina called up from the back.

Camille said nothing. Her driving, on the other hand, said a lot. She was weaving between the two lanes and gunning it when approaching intersections had yellow lights. Her turns were only slightly less dramatic. The tires never actually left the pavement, it only felt that way.

I fiddled with my seat belt, trying to snap it into place. I didn't know what Camille had in mind, but I was guessing her new strategy had something to do with flinging Tina out of the car.

We turned again and came to a full stop, which at the speed we were going practically had Puddles sitting in my lap. My body was pitched forward giving me a good view of my shoes. I righted myself and looked out the windshield at the golden arches.

"Out!" Camille ordered.

We all went for our door handles.

"Not you two," Camille said. "Just her."

By her she meant Tina.

"Excuse me," Tina said. "I am *not* getting out into a dark parking lot alone."

Camille reached into her purse and pulled out another chocolate. This time she popped it in her mouth and crunched it so hard I thought she'd crack a tooth. "You've got exactly two choices," she said to Tina. "You can either get out on your own, or I can drag you out. Either way, you *are* getting out. Whether or not you stay in the parking lot after that is your decision."

I didn't dare turn around. I didn't want to risk Tina catching my eye. As much as I was anxious about Sarah, I was feeling a little bad for Tina. I knew she'd be fine here—the food was fast, the place was well heated, and if I called Adam to pick her up, he could be here in twenty minutes. But still, there was a part of me that knew even Tina had real feelings, as misguided as they usually were.

As we pulled away, Tina grew smaller and smaller in the rearview mirror until she looked like a lost child. Then we turned the corner, and I lost sight of her.

THE PLAN WE settled on was simple. We were going to show up at Bennett's building with Puddles, do whatever we had to do to make sure Jim and Sarah were safe, and then we'd all leave. Technically, we would be doing our bit by showing up with Puddles. The message said nothing about turning him over or anything. We'd worry about collecting Bennett later when we could do it with the proper authority. We thought it was a pretty good plan. The details were still a little fuzzy, but they'd come to us. First, we had to meet up with Laurent.

He told us he'd wait for us at the Wal-Mart just off the main highway near Bennett's building. As we headed west, I was feeling pretty good until we hit a bridge. I didn't realize we'd be leaving the island. I closed my eyes as Camille drove and pretended I hadn't noticed the bridge. Probably unnecessary. Surely, my fears about going off-island were silly superstition, but it couldn't hurt to be careful. I opened my eyes again when I felt the car cross over onto regular pavement, and it wasn't much longer until we got to the turnoff and the big white Wal-Mart letters came into view. Camille pulled into the parking lot and cruised the lanes until we spotted Laurent's Beamer. She pulled in beside him, and we got out.

Laurent's passenger door opened, and a hockey stick poked out followed by a man fully decked out in hockey gear, minus the skates. I recognized the guy. He was Laurent's oldest friend, Jean-Pierre. Laurent came around from the other side of the car. He too was in his gear. Then the doors opened on an SUV parked two spaces over. More men got out. Within a few minutes, we were surrounded by seven men in full gear. Apparently, the minivan in the next parking space bred hockey players.

Camille grinned and hugged Jean-Pierre. "Ah, the Canadian Cavalry," she said.

Laurent opened the trunk and took out some shoulder pads. "These should fit," he said as he held them up to Puddles.

And in no time, Puddles was fully kitted out complete with helmet, face guard, and a flak vest under his jersey for extra protection. Standing next to the other guys from Laurent's team, it was impossible to pick him out. Eight hockey players all in a row. Three ex-pros, four amateurs, and Puddles. It was the perfect team for these playoffs.

TWENTY-EIGHT

CAMILLE AND I drove the rest of the way solo while Puddles joined his teammates in the minivan. Laurent and Jean-Pierre followed in the Beamer. Nearly all of us had cell phones, Laurent had a gun, and all the players had their sticks.

The new revised plan was pretty much the same as the old plan except now we had the team for backup and to provide camouflage of sorts for Puddles. It had been decided that Camille and I should arrive first to scope things out. Whatever confrontation with Bennett lay ahead, we wanted to make sure we knew what was going on with Jim and his family first. That was priority number one. We did not want to rush the place and end up with a hostage situation. As soon as we knew Jim and Sarah were all right, Camille and I would hightail it out of there and let the Cavalry do their thing.

We were keeping the line open between Bennett's phone, which I still had, and Jean-Pierre's so Laurent could track us when we went in. As we approached the Finestein, Bennett, & Fitch office we couldn't make much out. It was a narrow, two-storey building with lots of tinted glass. Very modern. The place was dark. Not even the outside lights were on. It looked like what it was; a building temporarily deserted.

The parking lot was empty except for a few skips with construction debris poking out of the top. We parked near the main entrance, got out the Mag-Lites Camille kept under the seats, stepped out, and locked the car. I tried the front door of the building, and it was unlocked. We went in, flashlights shining. Camille found the light switch and flicked it on. Nothing happened.

Could have been because of work being done to the building or because Bennett wanted it that way. We moved through reception down the hallway to the right of the elevator. A door on the left went to the stairs. The rest of the doors seemed to be offices or meeting rooms. Each had drop cloths on the floor and vats of paint. One had a step ladder. None appeared occupied. We went back out to reception. A lock clicked into place and the lights came on.

"Good evening, ladies." It was Bennett. He stood with his back to the security desk and had a gun pointed at us. "Please forgive my manners. I'm usually very cordial with women."

We switched off our flashlights and stood to face him. I'd never had a gun pointed at me before. It was oddly surreal. I barely registered it. I was so focused on finding out what was happening with Sarah that I'd slipped into social worker mode. Must have temporarily distracted me from my own sense of safety.

I glanced down at the cell phone I'd tucked into my fanny pack belt to make sure it was still on, and I edged toward Bennett, unsure about the range the phone needed to pick up his voice. Camille moved with me to avoid a gap between us.

"I'm familiar with your hospitality," I said to Bennett.

He smiled. "I do admire your chutzpah."

"Thank you. That's a nice gun you're packing. You got a license for that?"

"Of course. I wouldn't dream of breaking any laws."

"Naturally," I said back. "Being a lawyer and all." I hoped Laurent was getting all this. I wanted him to know as much about what was happening in here as possible. "Nice place you have here. Pretty fancy lobby."

Camille probably figured Laurent had a clear enough picture by now. "Where's the little girl?" she said.

Bennett smiled again. "Ah, a woman who cuts to the chase. I like that." He paused as he slowly ran his eyes up and down Camille. "Quite a treat for the eyes too."

The elevator pinged and Bennett shifted his eyes to the doors. The elevator opened and out walked Francesca wearing a short black and white dress in a hounds-tooth pattern. Dark opaque stockings and a solid black blazer broke up some of the dizzying lines. Her black pumps clicked on the tile floor as she crossed over to Bennett. She looked from me to Camille, then scanned the rest of the room. "Where's Puddles?"

"I was just getting to that," Bennett said to her.

"Well, hurry up. We haven't got all day. That kid is getting on my nerves. Her father told her we were related. She keeps asking me questions, calling me aunty."

"Where is Sarah?" Camille tried again.

Francesca turned to her as if she'd just realized we were there. "She's downstairs. Don't worry. You'll be joining her soon enough." She stepped behind the desk, leaned down, and pushed a few buttons before coming back out. "Did you come alone?"

I figured she'd been checking some kind of security monitor. I hoped it hadn't picked up Laurent's Beamer or the minivan. "We came to see about Sarah and her parents," I said by way of an answer.

Francesca looked at Bennett. "You told me Puddles would be here, Henry. What is she talking about?"

Bennett lowered his voice some. "That's what I told them, baby. They were supposed to bring him."

"Well," Francesca glowered. "Where is he then?"

Camille shifted beside me but didn't speak. I took her cue and stayed quiet too.

Bennett tried to turn Francesca back towards the elevator. She resisted. "Where is he, Henry?" she repeated. "He has to be here. You know I need him to..."

Bennett pressed one hand to her back and kept the one holding the gun trained on us, his eyes darting back and forth between Francesca and us. "Shush, " he said to her.

"Don't shush me," Francesca shouted. "How dare you! Nobody shushes me!" She brushed his hand away from her back. "That's enough. You're botching things up again. You always botch things up!"

The expression on Bennett's face softened. He tried again to get hold of her, this time reaching for her arm. "It's all right. Everything will work out," he began.

She cut him off, pulling her arm away and gesticulating wildly as she spoke. "It's not all right, you idiot. It hasn't been all right for a long time. I don't know why I listened to you. It's your fault I'm in this mess in the first place!"

It was like watching a soap opera. I was eagerly waiting for the moment where she slaps him. In a soap opera, the lady always slaps the man eventually. Camille tugged at my sleeve and motioned towards the elevator. She was right, of course. This was the perfect time to slip away. But, slipping away would mean missing the best part. We slowly backed up and pushed the elevator button. Francesca was swatting at Bennett now with both hands, her arms flailing. Bennett was desperately trying to stop her. One of her hands caught him in the face, but it did nothing to slow her down. She just kept pummeling him and shouting about his inadequacies. The elevator doors opened. Bennett and Francesca were so focused on each other, they didn't even seem to hear the elevator ting. We stepped in, pressed down, and held the "close doors" button until the doors slid together.

The basement level was clearly not used space. The walls were a drab concrete and the lighting source dingy. The hallways were narrow and seemed to go off in numerous directions. Like a maze. Searching it would not be easy or quick. Camille held the elevator door open with her arm. She pointed to a large box just down the hall a bit. "Bring that over, will you?" she said to me.

I dragged it over and helped her lodge it in the elevator doors to keep them from closing completely. At least Bennett wouldn't have use of the elevator. When I turned back, I noticed Camille rigging a ladder and some paint in front of the stairwell door to slow down access there too. "Okay," I said. "I'll take the right."

Camille started off in the other direction. "Yell if you see anything."

That wouldn't be hard given my aversion to cellars. Probably I had watched way too many scary movies as a child and never quite shaken off the residual willies.

As I walked, I opened doors and scanned the rooms. So far, I'd only come across storage areas and a utility room. All empty of people. But something was off in the utility room. There was a dolly stacked with paint and a box of matches on the top. I took in the gas furnace and gas water heater. Most people knew enough not to store flammables near gas sources. The matches weren't a good sign either. It looked like Bennett was planning a little "accidental" fire sometime in the near future. Possibly one that could be blamed on the renovation. That would be one way to get rid of any evidence or pesky witnesses. I closed the door and resisted the sudden need to locate the nearest exit. Instead, I pulled the cell up to check in with Jean-Pierre. "You there?" I said.

Jean-Pierre's voice came back. "Check."

"We're in the basement looking for Jim and his family," I explained. "We left Bennett and Francesca in the lobby. We don't have much time before they realize we're gone. I found something in the furnace room. It looks like someone may be planning a fire later. We've got to hurry if we're going to get these people out."

I brought the phone back down from my ear, paused a second to ponder an intersection in the hallway, and went left. A chill went through me as I got to the first door. I took a deep breath, put my hand on the knob, and opened the door. I felt for a light switch. Not finding one, I clicked on the flashlight again.

The room didn't look scary. It seemed to be a storeroom for old case files. It was dusty and there were probably some pretty big spiders calling it home, but nothing more. I scanned the boxes in the rows of shelves. They were organized alphabetically and by date. I walked between the shelves trying to get a beat on the source for my chills. I didn't see a thing. Most likely just the whole scary basement thing. I panned the light as I made my way back to the door. The light caught on something orange in the corner. I got closer to check it out, and my foot stepped in something wet and sticky. I darted the light to my shoes. My heart started pounding harder. Blood. I shifted the light up to the orangey glint and my breath caught. It wasn't so much orange as the color of mashed sweet potato. It was hair. Barbara Bennett's hair. She was covered in blood and slumped in a chair with her head bent over her chest. I heard the cell phone and the flashlight crash to the ground, and I was out of there.

If I had been thinking clearly, I might have remained calm. If I had stayed in social worker mode and remembered I was trained to handle crises, I might have remained calm. If I had retained any of the skills Laurent and Camille had drilled into my head, I might have remained calm. As it turned out, I didn't recall any of those things. I was wrong about the screaming thing too. It wasn't so easy to scream. I opened my mouth but nothing came out. My feet still worked, though. In fact, they worked double time. I'd heard that in times of great stress the body can perform miracles. I was sure my body's miracle was to temporarily grow two more legs. I felt like a horse galloping in the wild. I galloped all the way back through the door, down through the corridor, back into the main hallway, and straight into Henry Bennett's chest.

TWENTY-NINE

BENNETT PULLED ME through a doorway, slammed the door closed, and threw me down on the ground. I landed on my back, winded. He held his gun over me.

"Where is he?" he demanded.

By "he" I could only guess he meant Puddles. I didn't know what to say. Just as well because I was still freaked out about Babs Bennett and too winded to speak.

He came closer and started poking me with the gun. "Look. I've just about run out of patience with you. Where the hell is Puddles?"

Where the hell was the Cavalry was what I wanted to know. And where was Camille? Hopefully, she'd found Jim and his family and was spiriting them away as we spoke.

I tried to say something, but my body wasn't ready to cooperate yet.

Bennett saw my incapacity and pulled his hands up to his face. "Oh God, when will this nightmare end?" he said. He sat down on a box and leaned back against the wall. "How did I get myself into this? This is too much. Francesca is too much. I should just give it up. I should just retire and take Babs to live in Tuscany like she wants. I'm too old for this. I'm going to be a grandfather in less than four months for Christ's sake."

Take Babs. Omigod. He didn't know. He didn't know his wife was filed away down the hall under D for dead.

It was all starting to make sense now. This was all Francesca's doing. Bennett wasn't some powerful, hardened criminal. He was just a puppet. Francesca was the one behind the curtain pulling the strings. And right now she was out in the building somewhere doing who knows what. I had to get out of here.

I needed to take advantage of Bennett's weakened state. Only I wasn't exactly in a position of strength either. Bennett was still holding onto his gun. And while he was down, he definitely wasn't out. I needed some kind of weapon. I glanced around the room. Nothing but boxes. The Mag-Lite would have been great if it wasn't sitting back in the file room along with the cell. Not that I would have been adept with it anyway. I was no fighter, and I would never have Camille's skills, boots or no boots. I was just going to have to rely on my own special skills—my psych training. Lucky for me, that only required the use of a quick mind, a little manipulation, and a fast tongue. And use of the latter was slowly coming back to me.

"You're right," I said. "You should just move on. She's setting you up."

He seemed startled by my voice. "So you can talk now," he said.

"You don't have to go along with Francesca, you know. The way things are going, you're going to take the fall for everything, and she'll get away with the money."

My mention of the money clearly surprised him. "What money?"

"The inheritance," I said. "She's only using you to get the inheritance. You watch, after she gets what she wants, she'll turn you in."

He smiled. "She wouldn't do that. You don't understand. You don't know everything."

"I know she's strung you along for years. I know she could have divorced Puddles a long time ago and married you. It's not like she needed the inheritance. You make a fine living."

"It's more complicated than that. I thought you were supposed to be some hot shot shrink or something. You don't know much for a shrink."

I gritted my teeth at the shrink comment. And then I did know something. Something I hadn't realized until just then. "I know she told you Lucia was your daughter and she's not."

This got his interest. "What?"

"Lucia's not yours," I said. "Francesca only told you that to make sure you'd help her."

"You don't know what you're talking about."

"She holds onto you like a well-trained dog. She knows whenever she calls, you'll come running. Whenever she gives a command, you'll obey. Haven't you ever noticed that you're the only one who gets dirty hands? Francesca never does her own dirty work. She's got you for that."

He was getting angry now. I was getting to him. Normally, this is where I might back off a little, let him stew for a while. I didn't have the luxury of that kind of time, so I went on. "She's had you on her leash ever since the Vladimir incident."

"That was an accident," he said. "I don't even know how that happened. I could have sworn he was only passed out when I left."

"Why do you think she wants to get Puddles out of the way so much? She could never control him the way she can control you." And once I said it, I knew it was true.

"That's where you're wrong. We're in love. We were before she married Puddles. She would have married me then only her father threatened to disown her. She couldn't bear that. She adored her father."

Yeah. More like she adored her father's money.

He went on. "Guido was a devout Catholic. I was a married man. You don't know how many times I wished I'd met Francesca before I'd married Babs."

I was thinking that Babs was probably wishing that too about now.

"Guido made Francesca marry Puddles when he found out she was pregnant," he said.

I interrupted his story. "What makes you so sure she was pregnant with your baby? Or, *before* she met Puddles? Maybe she was two-timing you. Think about it. What about the clause in her parents' wills about her only getting her inheritance if she stayed married to Puddles? Maybe that was for a reason."

"That was just Guido. He was very traditional. Family appearances mattered to him. He wanted to make sure Francesca would never dishonor the family by getting a divorce after he died."

"It sounds like Guido knew his daughter pretty well. He knew her well enough to know that he could control her with money."

Bennett was weighing what I was saying. This was good. I was gaining the advantage. Like a lawyer, all I needed to do was establish reasonable doubt and I'd win. I went in for the kill. "Didn't it ever bother you that the love of your life wasn't willing to give up her family money to be with you? It wasn't like she would have been living the life of a pauper with you either. Makes you wonder how much faith she had in your ability to earn a decent living." And the clincher. "Faith in you as a man."

Bennett went quiet.

I took advantage of his silence to get in another jibe. "On the other hand, Barbara, your devoted wife, married you when you were just a struggling lawyer, and I'm guessing never pushed you to break the law to keep her in fine linens." I stopped talking when I heard a commotion outside in the hall.

Bennett went to see what was happening, and I was right behind him. It was Francesca. She was standing with her back to us. Over her shoulder, I made out what looked like the tip of a gun. In front of her Camille was on the floor. I gasped and Francesca spun around. I bolted over to Camille. She was still breathing.

Francesca pointed her gun at me. "What are you doing with her, Henry?"

"Don't shoot her!" Bennett said, trying to wedge his way in between me and Francesca's gun. "I was just questioning her," he said.

"Forget about that," she told him. "Help me with this one."

"What did you have to shoot her for?" Bennett asked, clearly agitated.

"Don't be such a wuss. I just zapped her with a stun gun."

A flood of relief went through me.

Bennett seemed thrown off. "What are you doing with a stun gun? That wasn't part of the plan."

"Never mind that, Henry," Francesca snapped. "C'mon, pick her up! We'll put these two in with the others."

"But what about Puddles?" Bennett asked her. "We don't have him."

Okay. That was good. That meant Puddles and the Canadian Cavalry were still out there.

"He'll be here," Francesca assured Bennett. "He's close by. I know it." She turned to me with a condescending smile. "You're not the only one who can analyze things."

Bennett helped me to my feet. He had his gun front and center lest I forget who was in charge after his little meltdown earlier. He needn't have bothered. Annie Oakley over there already had my full attention. She may be using a stun gun now, but it was no stun gun that took out Barbara Bennett. I knew she had to be packing another gun. I also knew she wasn't afraid to use it.

Once I was off to the side, Bennett pocketed his gun, picked up Camille, and led the way down the hall. I marched behind him with Francesca's stun gun pointed at my side. We stopped just outside a door at the end of the hall. Bennett stepped aside so Francesca could unlock it.

Inside, was a large, partly renovated room with an assortment of office furniture clustered here and there. The walls had new board up, but the seams were still showing. There were fluorescent fixtures dangling from above but no ceiling tiles. In one corner Jim and his family were tied to chairs. They looked more mellow than I would have expected. Sarah seemed to be asleep. The others were fighting it.

Bennett put Camille down on the floor and tied her hands behind her back with what looked like a computer cable. Francesca pushed me towards one of the chairs near Jim and held the stun gun on me while Bennett bound me to the chair.

When they backed off, Jim muttered to me. "We've been drugged." His eyes traveled over to some mugs on a table pushed to the side. "Don't drink anything."

So that was it. They were going to sedate us all, set a fire, and leave us here to die. By the time Jim finished speaking, Francesca was already heading for the table. She brought a mug back for me and shoved the drink toward me. "Drink," she ordered.

I turned my mouth away.

"Drink it you little bitch," she said.

I looked at her. "Or what?" I said. "You going to shoot me like you did Barbara Bennett?"

At the mention of his wife's name, Bennett's eyes widened. "What's she talking about?" he said to Francesca.

"Nothing," Francesca said, fixing me with an icy stare.

My heart was beating fast. I knew I was taking a big risk. I knew Francesca was capable of cold-blooded murder. But I needed to stall for time until the Cavalry found us, and this was my only chance. "Didn't you know?" I said to Bennett. "She killed Babs. If you don't believe me, check down the hall. Her body is in a storeroom."

Bennett crossed the room to confront Francesca. "What's she talking about?"

Out of the corner of my eye I saw Camille stir on the floor. She was quietly working her hands free. "I'm talking about your wife," I said, shifting my eyes away from Camille so I wouldn't draw attention to her.

Francesca moved toward me. "Shut up!" she said. She jabbed her stun gun towards me and pointed it at my thigh. I braced myself for the pain about to come just as the door burst open. Francesca whirled around, and a bunch of hockey players spilled into the room.

Bennett turned, holding his gun on the players.

"It's Puddles," I heard Francesca yell. "Get him."

"Which one is he?" Bennett yelled back, panning his gun between the players. Then the gun went off and one of the hockey players staggered back. Two other players rushed forward and body checked Bennett into the wall. Bennett wrangled them for control of the gun.

Francesca dropped her stun gun into her pocket, pulled out a handgun, and pointed it at little Sarah. "Idiot!" Francesca screamed at Bennett. "You're not supposed to shoot him. He can't die here."

Now I understood the stun gun. She wanted Puddles incapacitated so they could move him somewhere else to kill him. Of course. She would need an intact body if she wanted to assure his identification this time. She wasn't leaving anything to chance anymore if she could help it.

Then to the others she said, "Let him go, or I'll shoot the kid."

For a minute, everyone froze and looked at Sarah. Jim and Joanne's faces both went ashen. Then, in one swift motion, Camille sprang from the floor and knocked Francesca from behind, forcing them both to the ground. A shot went off followed by a groan. Camille and Francesca struggled for control of the gun until Camille's foot made contact with Francesca's wrist, and the gun fell to the floor. Francesca planted her teeth into Camille's leg. Camille kicked her off and got off another kick to Francesca's head. This time Francesca went down and there was silence.

THIRTY

IT FELT WICKEDLY good to be back in my own bed. Adam's arms were around me, and I was nestled into his warmth. Pong was on the floor beside the bed and Ping was curled up at my feet.

"So tell me again why Francesca was so obsessed with finding her husband," Adam said.

I sighed. I just wanted to forget everything for a while and bask in the glory of my clean cotton sheets and puffy white quilt. "She didn't want to find her husband. She wanted her husband found. There's a difference."

"How so?"

"Francesca wanted us to find a fake Puddles. One that was dead. It was the only way she could inherit, and she wanted her family's money. Over the years, the investments had grown into a not so small fortune. She had already gone through her own money and the money she had extorted. She liked to live a lavish lifestyle but had absolutely no financial sense, so she spent everything faster than it could be replaced. She and Lucia weren't close, and Lucia wanted her to move out of the house after the wedding. That would have left Francesca homeless not to mention practically penniless."

"Why didn't she just go off with Bennett? He had money."

"He had some. Not nearly enough for Francesca once his wife got her half, but it was her backup plan in case the Puddles thing didn't work out."

Adam stretched and repositioned his arm a little higher up on my body. "So, it's all over now."

"Yup."

"And Tina and Jeffrey have patched things up."

"Yeah. I saw." It was one of the first things I'd noticed when I got home. All Tina's stuff was gone, and I was able to hang up my coat in my own vestibule. The place still smelled, though. A few hours of scrubbing the walls and laundering everything that wasn't screwed down would go a long way towards ridding the house of its presence. If that didn't do the job, there was always a full scale exorcism and new paint job.

I snuggled down into the quilt some more and felt my body relax.

Adam's hands were moving again, and I felt lips on my neck. "So, you *very* tired?"

A COUPLE DAYS later, it was home. Standing proud in the driveway. So cute I wanted to pinch its fender. My Mini. It had been found a few blocks from Francesca's in a mall parking lot. It hadn't been towed, and there wasn't a ticket on it. The police officer who found it said it was a miracle. The cops found the Spitfire, too. Or what was left of it. It wasn't so lucky. Turned out some kids had stolen it, used it for drag racing, and banged it up pretty badly. The guy Jim had borrowed it from was understandably upset. But, he did get his gun back once he was able to prove he owned it legally.

After I gave my Mini a good cleaning inside and out, I went down to C&C to add my notes to the Puddles file before it was closed. Laurent was at reception putting in a new phone system when I walked in.

"What's that?" I asked him.

"Our temporary receptionist," he said. "It's got multiple lines with multiple voice mail. Arielle didn't like the idea of someone else sitting in her chair." He dipped under the desk, presumably fidgeting with some wire doodad.

"How very modern sounding." Camille had been trying to get one of these systems for years, but Laurent thought they were obnoxious and impersonal. Camille thought that was true but would add practical to the list, too.

"There's even an extension for you," he said, coming up from under the desk and making his way over to me. The muscles in his arm were still flexed and his brow a little sweaty. Maybe not his brow exactly, but something was adding a nip to the air.

"Does that mean what I think it means?" I said.

He put his screwdriver on the desk and wiped his hand on a cloth. "*Ça dépend.* What do you think it means?"

Laurent and I had never talked about how I went looking for Beardman Jim at Beaver Lake. Or any of my other rule bending. But that didn't mean he hadn't talked to Camille about it. Or about my career plans. I figured I was about to find out. "I'm hoping it means I'm moving up to full time," I said.

He smiled and stepped closer to me. "You're impulsive. You think with your heart first and your head second. You harbor delusions that justice always wins and probably still believe in fairy tales. And, you don't listen well. You ducked out on me when I told you to stay with one of us and keep a low profile. On top of that, you're hiding assets for a client."

With everything going on, I had completely forgotten about Marie Roy's jewelry. But how did Laurent know about it? My stomach tightened, and I tried to think of a good defense for all my behavior.

He reached out to tuck some hair behind my ear. "You're also determined, clients like you, and you have a cute American accent. *Puis,* you're Camille's friend, and she's looking into getting you registered in PI school. The next session starts in a few months. If that goes well, then when your citizenship comes through, the job is yours."

My anxiety quickly turned to excitement, and I threw my arms around him and hugged him. "Oh, thank you. It'll be good. Really."

Camille's office door opened and she poked her head out. "What's going on?"

"I just told *mademoiselle* Lora here about the job," Laurent said.

I shifted my hug from Laurent to Camille. "Thanks for going to bat for me," I said to her.

Camille's eyebrow shot up and down, she looked at Laurent, and one of their silent sibling conversations passed between them.

"Am I missing something?" I asked.

"*Non, rien*," Camille said as she steered me into her office. She closed the door and went to sit at her desk.

I sat in the window seat and pulled a cushion onto my lap. "So, how are you feeling?"

Camille had been taken to the hospital for treatment of her leg bite, along with Jim's family who had all been checked to make sure the sedatives they were given hadn't hurt them. They were all fine. Even the member of the Canadian Cavalry who got shot. All the players had flak vests under their jerseys, so the bullet never touched him. Babs Bennett had been taken to the hospital, too. Turned out she wasn't dead. She had lost a lot of blood, but the gunshot wound didn't affect any major organs. After surgery and a blood transfusion, she was holding her own in ICU and things looked hopeful.

Camille's bite turned out to be pretty minor, so she had been in and out but still needed to rest her leg. "I'm good. It's nothing," she said, tipping her slinky back and forth a few times. "*Mais*, some case your mister Puddles turned out to be. Lucia was at the hospital visiting her fiancé when I was there. She met Puddles. She also met Jim, Sarah, and Joanne. And she agreed to get tested along with Puddles as possible bone marrow donors. The Comos pulled a few strings and had them tested right away. Looks like she's a match."

That really was great. "I'm so glad," I said. "I just knew she was Puddles' real daughter."

"So I heard. You must have had some talk with Henry Bennett. Whatever you said persuaded him to give evidence against Francesca. That and the fact that she tried to murder his wife and shot him in the ass. He told the police everything. How she was the one behind the stolen funds at Guido's, how she was responsible for the Jonas Como hit and run, how she masterminded the blackmailing scam, how she was the one who arranged the death of the poor man with skin cancer..."

I broke in. "That was her?"

"*Oui.* It turns out she was a patient of Dr. Bernard too. She met the guy in the waiting room, befriended him, and set the whole thing up. Dr. Bernard had nothing to do with it."

"So Bennett was also just a patient?"

"He did everything he could to hold on to Francesca."

"Poor sap," I said.

"At least he's finally rid of her. They'll have enough evidence against her to convict for sure. Of course, he'll be spending a fair bit of time in prison too, but it will be far away from her."

I thought about Barbara Bennett. I wished we'd been able to nab Francesca before she had a chance to go after Babs. Guess that was part of Francesca's backup plan in case she did end up losing everything and had to go off with Bennett. With no wife to split his assets with, Bennett would have been pretty well off. "If they include the attempt on Barbara Bennett's life along with the cancer guy's murder, I doubt Francesca will ever get out of prison."

"Two murders, two attempts, and one assault," Camille corrected me.

"Two murders?"

"Yeah. The skin cancer guy and Vladimir the old guy from Guido's. Turns out Bennett was right. He left Vladimir alive. But the man wasn't so lucky after Francesca finished up with him. She just let Bennett think he'd killed him. She'd been holding that murder over his head for years."

"Nice," I said. "And what's going to happen to Puddles? Will he be charged with anything?"

"*Non.* He's a free man. Everyone knows he never stole from Guido's, and Tina told the police the kidnapping was a misunderstanding. As far as they know, he was never involved."

"At least now he can get a proper divorce from Francesca," I said. "I don't know why he agreed to marry her in the first place."

"That story about the arranged marriage Francesca told you wasn't exactly true," Camille said. "Guido did insist they marry, but only after he knew Francesca had committed adultery, gotten pregnant, and had also been sleeping her way through the company roster. Puddles was just unlucky enough to be her latest conquest.

He probably went for the idea half out of fear and half out of financial gain. Don't forget he hadn't spent his young years as a boy scout. But Puddles didn't seem to know about Francesca's relationship with Bennett, or that may have changed things."

I thought about the note in the mini wedding album. "It was probably Guido who wrote the note about making everything good then. Maybe to his wife. They must have been frantic over Francesca's out-of-wedlock pregnancy. I bet the albums got switched when Francesca's mom gave the identical one to Miriam at Guido's."

Camille nodded. "Makes sense."

The front door opened and closed and there was a knock at Camille's door. I went to open it.

"*Attends*," Camille said. "Just a sec." She put the slinky down and smoothed her hair. "Okay."

I gave her a confused look and opened the door. It was Luc. He looked well rested after the escapades of the other night. He had shown up with the other police when Laurent called for backup. Apparently, there was a bit of a panic when our Canadian Cavalry couldn't get to us. Bennett had locked up the building tight once Camille and I were inside. And even after the Cavalry gained access, they had to deal with a locked stairwell and the sabotaged elevator. That's what took them so long to get to us.

Luc was out of uniform now and wearing a stylish mocha brown trench coat with a cream colored scarf. His short blond hair was messy from the wind and his light scruff just long enough to accent his cheekbones. It was hard to look at him and not think movie star. His eyes darted right by me and into Camille's.

I had the sudden urge for a cup of coffee. "I'll just be in the kitchen," I told them and left. As I closed the door, I heard them speaking in French. From what I could make out, Luc wanted to know why a Hell's Angel guy carried Camille out to the car the other night. I had been kind of curious about that myself. Not as curious as I was about the motorcycle I'd seen parked outside Camille's place when I'd passed by on my way to the office earlier. But curious.

I decided to forgo the coffee and go home. I'd had enough adrenaline hits to my system lately. Anyway, I was eager to show Adam the little item I picked up on the way over to the office. I got it at Pièces des Arts. I hoped he'd like it because it was non-returnable, and it *wasn't* the Tasmanian Devil. From what I had been able to tell in Peggy's mirror, it had turned out just right too. I couldn't wait to see Adam's reaction.

Acknowledgments

Countless hours go into writing a book: the ones where words are filling the writer's page and the ones where words are filling the writer's heart. The first isn't possible without the second.

I have deep gratitude for everyone who has shared their words with me.

To my early readers for giving of their time and for having such awesome insights: Emily A., Dana B., Terry C., and Susan H.

To all the industry professionals for generously offering their kind thoughts.

To Private Investigator Dave R. for sharing his expertise.

To Richard S. for reading multiple drafts, answering my many questions, allowing me to use his fab car for inspiration, and all the laughter and support.

To Fran J. for teaching me the meaning of friendship, for all the boundless encouragement, and for reserving my spot on the park bench.

To Tyler P. for helping with the cover and possessing great patience.

To Caroline V. and Maud L. for polishing the French bits.

To my family, and especially my mom, for passing on her love of books and for letting us read at the dinner table.

To my son for his unwavering certainty.

To my husband for loving this series as much as I do and for the longest and best conversation of my life.

And to Montreal and its people for imprinting a passion for life on my heart. Je me souviens.

About the Author

Katy Leen is a native Montrealer who grew up on baguette and chocolate milk in a house full of pets and books. She writes the Lora Weaver mysteries and is currently working on the next book in the series.

Visit katyleen.com to learn more about Katy or to drop her a note.

Books in the Lora Weaver Mystery Series

The First Faux Pas
The Pas de Deux

Short Stories in the Lora Weaver Mystery Series

The Nearly Nixed Noël

Made in the USA
Monee, IL
24 July 2021